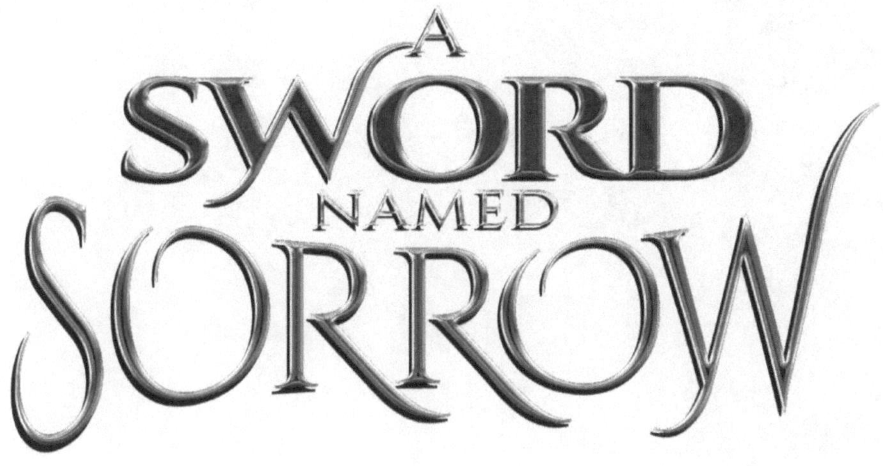

A SWORD NAMED SORROW

KARA DALKEY

A SWORD NAMED SORROW

KARA DALKEY

EERIE RIVER PUBLISHING

www.EerieRiverPublishing.com

ALSO BY KARA DALKEY

THE NIGHTINGALE
EURYALE
ASCENSION
REUNION
TRANSFORMATION
GENPEI
CRYSTAL SAGE
BHAGAVATI
THE HEAVENWARD PATH
STEEL ROSE
BIJAPUR
LITTLE SISTER
GOA
THE SWORD OF SAGAMORE
EURYALE
THE NIGHTINGALE
THE CURSE OF SAGAMORE

WWW.EERIERIVERPUBLISHING.COM/SWORDNAMESORROW

To my fellow authors in Sound on Paper, Amy, Edd, Manny, Laura and Karen. For the good company. For the laughs. For all your kind, patient encouragement. And for putting up with my manuscripts as I submit them over...and over...

Prologue

The small silver bell chimed as the inn door creaked shut behind the young man. Campesinos and cart drivers glanced up from the rough-hewn tables in the dim and dusty public room beside the Camino de Royale, sparing him scarcely a nod before returning to their worries and wine. The young man, Filipo del Utherio, went to the stool closest to the darkest corner and pulled his last rial from a flaccid leather coin purse, spinning it upon the polished manzanita bar. The innkeeper, a stout man in his forties wearing a spotless white apron, approached as he usually did at the sound of money.

"Anything?" Filipo asked.

"Not what you want," the innkeeper muttered. "How old are you now, *joven*? Sixteen?"

"Seventeen," Filipo grumbled.

"Old enough to be making your own way in the world. Not to be chasing ghosts."

Filipo reached to retrieve his coin, but the innkeeper's meaty paw slammed down on it.

"But perhaps the Madre smiles upon you after all, joven," the innkeeper went on, leaning his elbows on the bar. His breath was rich with garlic. "For I have heard a thing. From the groundskeeper for the orphanage Nuestra Señora de la Pacifica...have you heard of it?"

"No."

"I am surprised, given the rumors. Anyway, this groundskeeper comes here sometimes to drink, which I am sure the holy sisters of the orphanage would prefer he does not do."

Filipo reined in his impatience. "What has this to do with my concerns?"

"Well, this groundskeeper had seen a thing. Not long ago, a messenger arrived, a boy on a mule, nothing to make a great matter of except that he was carrying a narrow, wooden box. It was about the length of a man's arm. I am sure you know the sort of box I mean. This messenger boy demands to see the Mater at once for he has an important delivery to make. Being a helpful but curious man, the groundskeeper shows the boy to the servants' entrance where, once the boy shows the box to the holy sister who comes to the door, the boy is whisked inside with no further question."

Filipo, opened his hands. "I expect there is a reason for this uninspiring tale, señor?"

"Well," the innkeeper said with a half-shrug, "I only thought it might interest you because the groundskeeper noticed a name carved into a corner of the box...Salamago. Ah, the widening of your eyes shows that catches your fancy, I see."

Filipo tried to mute his attention with a shrug. "It may be nothing."

"It may be all you have left, joven." The innkeeper stood, taking Filipo's last rial with him. "Or you could go to the harbor, sign onto a ship, see more of the world, as do many fellows even younger than you. Might bring you better fortune than to stay."

"What am I supposed to do with your information?" asked Filipo, his patience nearing an end. "Sneak into the chapel treasure room like a thief?"

"I expect you will do what you must. That or keep chasing a mystery that perhaps does not wish to be solved."

Filipo stood, kicking the stool forward under the bar with a grumble. "Muchas gracias."

"Buena suerte," replied the innkeeper.

Filipo went out the front door and blinked in the dusty sunlight. In the far distance, he heard what might have been cannon fire. Or perhaps it was just the waves of the nearby sea, pounding against the shore like a blacksmith's hammer.

Chapter One

Thunder rolled across a cloudless sky. Coraza Salamago glanced up at the chaparral-dotted ridgeline as hot, dry wind blew strands of her long, black hair across her face. The scruffy mustang she sat on stamped one hoof, its ears twitching back with unease. A strange burnt-orange light flickered atop the nearby coastal hills.

"Tzinn wind," Coraza murmured with a shiver of both fear and excitement.

"Stop trying to scare us," said Rosalita riding beside her in the corral. "We are not so foolish." The two other girls taking the horse lesson that afternoon nodded in agreement. "Tzinn are desert demons. They never come so near the sea."

"No talking, señoritas, please!" said the hawk-nosed, middle-aged riding instructor, Maestra Olympia, clapping her hands for their attention. "Do not distract each other! Bring your horses heads up. Sit up straight, chin forward, arms in a graceful arc. Remember, be like the Great Ladies of Old España, ride as though you are the most elegant creation of the Madre."

"Now *that* is foolishness," muttered Coraza.

They were, after all, not in Old España, but Alta Califia, a struggling, rustic colony on the far western edge of the New World, America del Norte. And it was not the age of Great Lords and Ladies, but the year of the Madre 1843. Coraza and the other girls were just orphans at the Our

Lady of The Pacific Girls School and Orphanage. And as far as the *sacer-dotas*, the holy teachers at the orphanage, were concerned, sixteen-year-old Coraza was anything but an elegant creation of the Madre.

"Then why do the holy sisters warn us about the tzinn, if the demons never come here?" Coraza persisted as she tried to keep her mustang walking in a circle.

There was no point in mentioning the unnatural light in the hills. Coraza knew only she could see it. She wished she could be certain of what her eyes and the strange thrumming in her blood were telling her. But all afternoon she had been dazzled by the sun and blue sky, the cries of the sea gulls and the smell of the sage, juniper, and mesquite. She couldn't be sure it wasn't just her imagination.

I have been kept inside so long, she thought sadly. *Nearly a year.*

Coraza had been raised at the orphanage, the only home she knew. Aware of having a famous father and an unknown mother, she dreamed that someday a relative would come to claim her and take her into her true family. But no one had come, and the holy sisters avoided speaking to her about any future she should hope for. Someone had named her Coraza, meaning "shield." Was that meant as a protection for her, or was she meant to protect others?

Sometimes, she imagined she might someday become a *Protectadora*, one of the wise cabals of *brujas*, or witches, formed during the Great Revolt of 1798, who watched over Alta Califia, guarding the citizens from tzinn and other enemies. It was said they could feel danger through the land itself. Coraza wished she could become something that good and useful and...appreciated. She was sure it was a foolish dream—she had no idea how Protectadoras were chosen—but it gave her a hope to cling to.

"They warn us about many things we don't have at the orphanage," said Rosalita. "Like money. And men. Really, Coraza, they should never have let you out of the cellar. You haven't changed a bit. Still talking nonsense. Besides, the Protectadoras have wards everywhere, even the orphanage."

"The witches of the *Presidio* are getting old and feeble," said Coraza, repeating something she had overheard. The Presidio was the largest, strongest fort in Alta Califia, the main defense of the city of Los Mensajeros and the surrounding land. If the keepers of the fort were to become weakened, who knew what it could mean for the colony as a whole?

Coraza's cellar room had a small window high in the wall, and it was amazing what visitors in the orphanage courtyard would say, thinking no one listened. Rumors claimed the Protectadoras had grown so old, they needed all their magic power just to keep themselves alive. "Perhaps they can no longer protect us."

"I said stop it!" insisted Rosalita.

"No, it's true," said Lupe, riding behind them. "My uncle has said so in his letters. He fears the brujas of the Protectadora can't do their magic anymore." She leaned forward over her horse's neck and whispered, "He says this could mean trouble, as there is probably war coming. The Nuevo Aztecas have been seen heading north toward our border."

"Yes! I have felt this very thing," said Coraza, remembering her recent dreams of a great snake, covered in black feathers, coiling and uncoiling. She sensed it meant something bad was approaching, though she was not certain what.

"Shut up! That's treasonous talk!" cried Rosalita. "I should tell Mater Urania what you two are saying."

"Señoritas, please! Pay attention. How can you ever hope to guide a husband if you cannot control a simple animal?" asked Maestra Olympia.

Coraza could see faint purple light rippling over the hands of the horse instructor. Clearly, the Maestra herself was cheating, using sorcery to control her own fine black stallion.

However, Coraza kept her ability to see the glow of magic use secret, having been slapped often by the holy sisters for saying or knowing the wrong things. Since her confinement, Coraza had learned a small bit of caution.

But if they so mistrust me, why was I allowed outside today, for a horse lesson of all things?

Another gust of wind blew through the corral, kicking up dust and dry leaves. It sang through the branches of the nearby manzanita bushes with a low moan, similar to that made by a grieving woman.

"La Llorona," whispered Coraza, her skin prickling and stomach turning cold. La Llorona was among the most feared of the tzinn.

"Stop it!" cried Rosalita, slapping Coraza's arm with the ends of her leather reins.

Coraza ignored Rosalita and looked down the hillside. The safety of the brick orphanage was many yards from the corral, the ruins of the Mariano mission many yards farther to the south. The adobe chapel stood a quarter mile to the north, on a low ridge, with the blue of the Pacific Ocean beyond the orphanage. Tzinn despised water, but the beach was at least a mile away.

Too far, too far, thought Coraza. She gently nudged the mustang's flanks with her heels, but the horse stood as if transfixed, staring at the hills.

The wind blew harder, throwing sage-scented dust through the corral. Coraza blinked and rubbed her face as dust got in her eyes. Rosalita and Lupe sneezed. The Maestra's horse raised its fine black head and stared as the mustang did, ears flicked forward in acute attention.

The blast increased in force, and the moaning became louder. The bare, red-barked branches of the manzanita bushes outside the corral waved toward them like a myriad skeletal hands.

"Ai mi, no!" cried Rosalita, pointing toward the hills.

Coraza looked back at the mountain ridge. A cloud of brown dust was billowing over the crest. It flowed down the slopes toward them, fast as water, behaving as no natural cloud would.

"Dust storm!" cried the Maestra. "Everyone dismount and lead your horse back to the stable barn, quickly! Follow my voice!"

But dust storms never came to that part of Alta Califia, and Coraza could see the glowing burnt-orange light of Sere sorcery at the heart of the approaching cloud.

Within seconds, the dust cloud hit the corral. Coraza was knocked halfway out of the saddle by the force of the wind. She flung her arm across her face as the dust stung her cheeks and eyes. The girls' shrieking and the horses' screaming blended with the roaring, shuddering moans of the wind.

"To me, to me!" Maestra Olympia cried. "Hurry!"

Coraza slid off the saddle and felt for the reins on the mustang's bridle. When she found them, she tugged. "Come on!"

But the horse wouldn't budge. It stood whickering, eyes rolling, legs trembling.

"Please, move!" Coraza yelled at it, getting a mouthful of dust for her trouble. Suddenly, the mustang tossed its head, yanking the reins out of her hands, the leather burning her palms. Coraza reached toward the horse to grab the bridle, but the horse dashed away. A blast of wind pushed her back, and she stumbled. She spun around but could no longer see the mustang or even the corral fence.

"Maestra Olympia?" Coraza shouted, but her voice was faint in the roaring of the wind. Coraza could no longer hear the horse instructor's calls or the cries of the other girls.

Downhill, she told herself. *The orphanage is downhill.* Trying to sense the slight slope to the hillside corral, Coraza staggered forward, fighting to get through the swirling dust. At last, her shoulder struck a wooden post.

The fence! If she followed it around, she might find the gate, and the stable door was directly downhill from the gate.

Coraza tried to walk north along the fence, but the wind blew against her like a wall of stinging darts. She could make no headway against it. With a groan of frustration, Coraza turned and squeezed between the horizontal beams, yanking her long skirt through, hearing it tear on the rough wood.

As soon as she stood again, the wind eased. Her face no longer stung from the onslaught of dust, and she could breathe without getting a mouthful. Coraza coughed and wiped her face.

"Merciful Madre," Coraza sighed. As she blinked dirt out of her eyes, Coraza's heart froze again. She was standing in an area clear of wind, but the dust cloud roared around her, as though she stood in a circular chamber whose walls were made of blowing dirt and leaves. The air within the circle was unaccountably silent.

In the middle of the clear space stood a female figure draped in black, her face invisible behind a black veil. The air around her was suffused in a dark orange glow. The figure turned to Coraza and raised its arms. "Oh, beautiful child," the creature intoned in a low, honeyed voice so sorrowful that Coraza felt compelled to listen. "Beautiful child, come to me. I am so alone. I have lost so many little ones. Will you not ease my pain?"

For a confusing moment, Coraza wondered if a madwoman had wandered onto the orphanage grounds and she should, in pity, warn her away. Then a breeze momentarily lifted the visitor's black veil, revealing a face of dried skin stretched taut over a skull, a lipless mouth showing brown, jagged teeth.

It is La Llorona herself! Coraza stared, unable to tear her gaze away from the shadowy tzinn, unmoving, the only sounds her ragged gasps and the pounding of her heart. *Am I about to die?*

"Oh, come to me, child!"

Despite the fearsome aspect of the creature, Coraza sensed a true loneliness in that sightless face, those imploring skeletal arms. She felt *simpatico*, a connection somehow with the terrifying spirit. Loneliness was something Coraza understood, every waking day of her life. *Could I truly ease her pain and ease my own as well?*

The tzinn tilted her head and stepped toward her, imploring. "Oh, beautiful child, do not turn away. Are you not as alone as I? Do you not seek a mother's love? Will you not take mine?"

Coraza's heart squeezed in her chest, and a dusty tear ran down her cheek. *Does La Llorona know?* Coraza wondered. *Can she see into my soul? Might she have secret knowledge about me?* Strangely, Coraza found herself longing to embrace the demon, to bury herself within the bosom of her shadowy black garment. To lose herself to oblivion. Perhaps she might, in some way, give the sad creature comfort. Perhaps Coraza might receive a comfort she herself had never known in return. She took a step forward, her throat choked with fear and pity. "I...I...

Suddenly, from beneath La Llorona's flowing black skirts, two skeletal children with gaping eye-sockets emerged and stared at Coraza. One of them, ever so slightly, shook its head in warning. If she gave in, it seemed to say, she would become as they were, a mere dried husk, only hungering for a liveliness they can never have.

"Coraza! Are you there?" cried another voice to her right, from beyond the dust wall.

The familiar shout shook her out of her strange reverie. It was Sister Phoebe, a young novice, one of the few holy sisters who had showed kindness and helpfulness to her.

Coraza stepped back, bumping up against the corral fence. With a badly shaking hand, she drew the sign of the Sacred Trisect Circle in the air. "Sister Phoebe, I'm here! It's La Llorona! Please help me!"

Steadily, the tzinn approached her.

"No!" Coraza cried, finally finding her voice. "In the name of the Holy Madre, stop!"

"Oh, beautiful child, why do you resist? Are we not meant to be together?"

Coraza's fear turned to anger at her own helplessness. How could she think of protecting others when she could not even protect herself? Her face grew hot with shame and anger, and her arms trembled with her rage. "You cannot have me! Do you hear me? Begone! Go away!" she screamed.

"Oh, beautiful child—"

"Don't listen to the tzinn!" A glimmering object arced through the wall of swirling dust to Coraza's right. It burst upon La Llorona's head, scattering glass and a bright spray of water.

Holy water, thought Coraza. *Thank the Madre.*

The tzinn stopped, lowered its arms, and stared down at itself in astonishment.

Sister Phoebe, in her sky blue habit and white wimple, dashed out of the swirling dust and grabbed Coraza's arm. "Come! Run! Don't look back!"

Coraza ran beside her into the wall of howling dust. She closed her eyes tight against the scouring wind.

"Madre, save us. Madre, save us," Sister Phoebe prayed as they ran. Behind them, an unholy scream rose into the air.

Coraza ran into a wall of wood. "Ai, what—"

"Servant's entry door to the orphanage," gasped Sister Phoebe. "Help me open it. Hurry."

Coraza grasped the iron latch, her hands atop Sister Phoebe's, and yanked with all her might. The door creaked open, and she stumbled through into a dim storage room. Sister Phoebe shut the door and shoved the wood bolt home. A blow of tremendous force slammed into the opposite side, knocking Sister Phoebe and Coraza back. The boards bent and splintered, and the iron bands groaned, but they held. Burnt-orange light glowed and flickered around the edges of the door like fire.

"In the name of the Blessed Madre, hold!" cried Sister Phoebe. A blaze of blue sorcerous energy poured from her outstretched arm to the door. The light flowed over the portal, sealing out the Sere sorcery. An eerie howl came from just outside the door, and then it faded, drifting away on the wind.

Gasping heavily, Sister Phoebe sank toward the storeroom floor.

"Thank you! Thank you for saving me. Are you all right?" Coraza crouched beside Sister Phoebe and put her arms around the novice's shoulders.

Sister Phoebe slowly sat up, nodding. But there was still fear in her pretty dark eyes.

"Thank you so much for coming for me!" Coraza said. "I didn't know what to do!"

Sister Phoebe smiled sadly and brushed dust out of Coraza's hair. "It's not your fault, chica. Few can withstand the call of a Great Tzinn. They are like serpents, trapping their prey in their gaze. Thank the Madre for sparing us this day. We were very lucky." She pulled Coraza close and hugged her.

Trembling, Coraza asked, "Why did the wards fail? How could a tzinn get so close?"

"I don't know," said Sister Phoebe, her face turned away. "I don't know."

The inner door, opposite the one they had entered, slammed open and Coraza shrieked.

The figure standing in the doorway in a charcoal-grey habit was nearly as frightening as the tzinn. Mater Urania, head of the orphanage, her eyes narrowed in her dour, wrinkled face, glared back and forth between them. Finally, her disapproving gaze came to rest on Sister Phoebe. "You disobeyed." Her voice rumbled like a waking volcano.

"Forgive me, Holy Mother!" said Sister Phoebe. "But Coraza was still outside."

"No one was to leave the orphanage. You disobeyed my express command."

"Don't punish her, Mater!" said Coraza. "Sister Phoebe saved my life!"

The hateful stare her comment earned adequately conveyed her assumption—Mater Urania felt that Coraza's life was hardly worth saving. Sister's Phoebe's expression changed to dismay.

"Mater, is it possible the tzinn's arrival...might it have to do with the death of Coraza's father?"

"That is enough!" snapped Mater Urania.

"My...my father?" asked Coraza, confused. "What has this to do with my father? He's dead?" All Coraza had known of any father was the rumor that he was a famous swordsmith. And of her mother, she knew nothing at all.

Sister Phoebe placed her hands on Coraza's shoulders. "We received word from the Cathedral in Los Mensajeros this morning. Your father, Erculeo Salamago, died sometime last night."

"Died...died how?"

"Silence!" growled Mater Urania. "It should matter little to you, Coraza. Your sire abandoned you to us as an infant. You may as well have had no father."

"But he paid for her care!" protested Sister Phoebe. "Who will support her now?"

"Enough!" roared Mater Urania.

Coraza saw sorcerous energy gathering in the sacerdota's forearms and knew she was preparing a punishment spell. Having suffered enough painful enchantments at her hands, Coraza shut her mouth.

"You," Mater Urania said to Sister Phoebe, "go to the kitchens for the preparation of supper. Then you will report to my office. You"—she turned to Coraza—"will go to your cellar chamber where you will pray to the Madre in thanks for your deliverance and spend your time contemplating our teachings concerning sorcery."

"But...but my fa—"

Mater Urania held up one finger that, in Coraza's sight, was glowing a potent dark purple. "Go."

With a last concerned and thankful glance at Sister Phoebe, Coraza hurried through the doorway, along the hall, and down a short flight of steps into the cellar room. Closing the door, Coraza let out a long sigh, still trembling. Narrowly escaping a tzinn, a real tzinn, the legendary La Llorona no less, was a terror she was certain she would never forget. But worse, far worse, was Mater Urania's anger at Coraza's survival. The hatred on Mater Urania's face had blazed bright as the summer sun. Coraza could not stop the thoughts circling in her mind like hungry sea gulls.

Mater Urania wants me dead.

Chapter Two

*H*er back pressed against the cellar room door, Coraza clenched her fists, her heart torn between fear and fury. *How could she? How dare she?* thought Coraza. *What kind of person is Mater Urania that she'd wish harm on an orphan in her care?*

As Coraza pushed away from the door and stepped into the room, however, her thoughts echoed back in darker form: *What have I done wrong, that a high holy priestess should wish soul-killing death on me?*

All her life in the orphanage, Coraza had suffered the dislike of the holy sisters, as if they barely tolerated her presence. She always seemed to know too much, see too much, be too much. The only one who had cared was Sister Phoebe, and now Coraza had gotten her in trouble.

Merciful Madre, at least soften Mother Urania's heart to Sister Phoebe, so she won't be punished. She only tried to help. Sister Phoebe often stood between the harsher holy sisters and the orphans, protecting them. Coraza admired this deeply and hoped to be like her, often rescuing spiders and ladybugs and once even a bat that had taken shelter from the rain. But it only enhanced her reputation at the orphanage that she was just too strange.

Coraza's gaze fell on the almost life-sized plaster statue of the Madre standing in the far corner of the cellar room. Sometime long before, it had been placed there for storage and eventual repair. The statue had become a source of solace for Coraza for the months she had lived in the cellar. The Madre was damaged, as Coraza felt herself to be, yet the statue remained ever patient and smiling, as Coraza wished she could.

As her anger drained from her, Coraza crossed the room to kneel before the broken image. "Mother of all creation, what have I done to deserve Mater Urania's hatred? Am I misjudging her? Why hasn't she ever told me about my parents? Is my family cursed?"

The statue gazed down at her with loving, humble, forgiving eyes, but Coraza could read no answers in them. The Madre's plaster face was smudged and dusty. The paint on Her blue robe and white wimple was chipped and scratched. Her dainty, slippered right foot that peeked out from beneath Her robe, treading lightly on clouds and a crescent moon, was dark with soot and grime. The left arm of the Blessed Madre was held out to the side, broken fingertips extended in a gesture either giving or beckoning, or both. The right hand of the Blessed Madre held the neck of her robe demurely open to expose the Sacred Trisigil on Her chest.

Everyone in Alta Califa or perhaps the world, as far as Coraza knew, was given a trisigil in early infancy. It was a magical tattoo drawn above the heart of the individual, always in the shape of a circle divided into three parts with a symbol in each section. The combination of symbols was supposed to be unique to every person, an indication of their heritage and destiny. Therefore, by custom, one's trisigil was kept private and hidden. The magic used by the holy sisters of the Great Cathedral that allowed one's trisigil to grow and stay with one throughout life was a secret never revealed by the church.

The plaster Madre's painted trisigil held a sun disc in the upper right section, the upper left a silvery flame. The lower, third symbol, however, was hidden behind the Madre's hand, forever Her mystery.

Coraza unbuttoned her plain cotton shirt and lifted up the edge of the under-vest that hid her own trisigil. Peering down, she saw the hand-bearing-a-flame in the upper right, on the bottom third a cross-hatch, and on the upper left a big, black spot as if the curandera who had put the magical tattoo on the baby Coraza had thought better of her first attempt and tried to correct it.

A mistake, is that what I am? wondered Coraza. *Do they think I am tainted by the evil of Sere sorcery? Still, is it not a sin to wish death on me?*

Death has a worthy place in the cycle of life, the holy sisters taught, like the servant who drives your coach and waits respectfully at the back door. Santa Muerte, the blessed death. But Sere sorcerers sought to bring death, or rather that which had never been alive, into the house of life, where it did not belong. They honored the strengths of drought over moisture, of cold over warmth, of stone over flesh. Sere sorcerers haunted the deserts of the world, seeking the power of the tzinn. Their dark arts arose in the ancient kingdom of Cartago, where Molochistas would sacrifice their children to the tzinn of the sands to learn the demons' secrets. The holy sisters taught that soldiers of the Church of the Madre had wiped out all the Molochista priests long before. But Sere sorcerers still existed, passing down the Molochistas' secrets.

"Why did Mater Urania ask me to think on such things?" Coraza whispered to the mute Madre. *How could the Protectadoras have let the tzinn through? Is the gossip about their weakness true, then?*

Coraza tried for several minutes to calm her mind with prayer and meditation. It was no use. Her thoughts kept spinning, spinning with the memories of La Llorona and Mater Urania. And thoughts of a now-deceased father. Coraza wondered if she should pray for him. She stared at the Madre, hoping for some sign or answer.

But no miraculous tears appeared on the Madre's placid face. No droplets of blood appeared on Her foot, no whispered prophecies flowed from Her gently smiling mouth. No help was forthcoming from Heaven for the moment.

Coraza re-buttoned her shirt, stood, and paced the little room, running her hands through her wind-blasted hair. *What should I do?*

A knock at the door made her jump. "Who is there?"

"It is Gracia from the kitchens. Sister Phoebe sent me to bring you supper."

"Oh. Momentito." Coraza opened the door.

Gracia, one of the kitchen servants, an elderly Chumash Indian woman, held a ceramic bowl with a folded cotton dishrag beneath it. Coraza could tell from the smell that the bowl held mutton stew, an unfortunate staple at the orphanage.

"Stand aside, chica. Sister Phoebe directed me to place this on your table myself. The bowl is hot, and you know how clumsy you are." Gracia seemed to enjoy passing along the secondhand scold.

"Thank you, but I am not clumsy," Coraza said, frowning in confusion. She stepped back to let the old woman pass. Sister Phoebe had never called Coraza clumsy, at least not to her face.

"Hmpf," said Gracia dubiously. "Shut the door behind me."

With a sigh, Coraza closed the door. "Why? Does Mater Urania think I'm going to run away?"

"Perhaps you should," said the old woman, setting the bowl down on the trestle table.

"Pardon me?" Coraza wondered if Gracia was being cruel.

The kitchen maid turned and faced Coraza, brown hands folded in front of her. "I must speak quickly, for I have little time. I bring word from Sister Phoebe. She says you should flee at once."

"What?" asked Coraza, staring with shock.

Gracia raised a finger of warning. "Do not interrupt. She believes Mater Urania intends to do you ill and deny you your inheritance. The holy sisters of the chapel are saying a Remembrance for your father this evening. Between the Remembrance and evening prayers, your inheritance will be placed in the storeroom nearest the back door of the chapel. If you can, take it without being seen, and go to the hacienda of Don Malaguez, two miles to the north. Tell him you are Salamago's daughter. The box you bring will be your proof. The Don is an admirer of your father's work, so he will be inclined to help you, perhaps even take you in as a ward and offer you patronage. That is your best chance for survival."

Coraza stared at the old Chumash woman, mouth open, unable to speak for a few moments. "Survival?"

"If you intend to have hope of a free life, or any life at all, you should take her advice, child, and go. You have a chance to be more fortunate than I."

"But why does Mater Urania hate me so?"

Gracia shrugged. "She is a strange, brittle, bitter woman. Who can say?"

"Um, thank you, I think. But won't you get in trouble for bringing me this message?"

A dark smile played at the edges of Gracia's mouth. "Mater Urania treats the kitchen help no more kindly than her orphans. Now go, if you know what is good for you." She turned to leave.

"Wait! This inheritance—what is it?"

"Your father was renowned as a swordsmith, so I presume it is a sword. Now I must go, and so should you."

"But...but what if La Llorona is still out there?"

The old woman sighed with tried patience. "Tzinn are like lightning. They appear and are gone, and they rarely strike twice in the same place. I would fear Mater Urania more, if I were you." She walked out the door, shutting it behind her.

Coraza listened as Gracia's footsteps went up the stairs and down the hallway.

Do I trust her? Coraza could not think of a reason the old woman would create an elaborate lie. And remembering the hate on Mater Urania's face, the warning was all too likely to be true.

Coraza glanced quickly around the room, wondering what to take with her. The basket of talisman beads and yarn? A holy book? A rolled-up blanket? She had no idea what would be needed or useful, and anything heavy or bulky might slow her down.

"Enough," she murmured to herself. "The Madre, or Don Malaguez, will provide."

As quietly as possible, Coraza opened the door. She padded up the short flight of steps to the main hallway and looked to her left. The long terracotta-tiled hallway ran the length of the building. Doors on either side led to the dining hall, the holy sisters' dormitory, Mother Urania's office, the library, and the stairs to the girls' dormitories. Though no one stood in the hall and the orphans and students would all be in the dining room, there was far too great a risk of meeting someone or being seen. Coraza's only other choice was to turn right, to go back to the servants' vestibule and out the door the tzinn had chased her through.

Coraza swallowed hard and tiptoed to the servants' vestibule. Mater Urania had left that door open, so Coraza slipped in, seeing nothing different from when she and Sister Phoebe had taken refuge there not even an hour before.

Coraza walked up to the outer door, amazed again at the damage the tzinn had done. The iron bands bowed inward, and the wood boards splintered and bent. Coraza unlatched the door and tugged it open. The hinges squealed like piglets, and Coraza glanced fearfully behind her, hoping no one heard. She stopped when there was just enough room to squeeze through. But first she peered around the door, glancing left and right.

The outside of the door had great, gaping gashes across the outer boards, as if an enormous lion had raked its claws across it. *What must the tzinn have looked like when it made this?* She'd heard stories of the strange and terrifying shapes tzinn could appear in, usually some form of wild animal. Coraza felt another surge of gratitude toward Sister Phoebe.

The late afternoon sky was clear, and only a gentle, warm breeze was blowing. Save for the evidence of the door, it was as though La Llorona had never been there. Keeping close beside the orphanage, Coraza looked around the corner, finding the hillsides and corral behind the building empty. Coraza lifted her gaze up the hill to the north where the chapel stood but saw no one.

The path to the chapel won't be safe, Coraza thought. It's too visible from the main road. Travelers and traders rode the Camino Del Real between Los Mensajeros and La Escarpa all the time and might wonder at seeing a girl by herself. Coraza knew of a deer path on the hillside above the corral that she had explored as a child, when she'd had more freedom.

She raised the hems of her skirt and began to run as fast as she could, her feet pounding the ground.

On the far side of the corral, she found the deer path, but it was more overgrown than she remembered. Sagebrush and manzanita twigs scraped her arms and caught at her skirt and hair. Her pulse pounded loudly in her ears, and her feet slid on the sandstone scree of the path. At last, Coraza had to stop and crouch beneath a juniper tree to catch her breath. Her forearms itched with fresh scratches, bright lines dotted with blood like strands of tiny cinnabar beads. But she did not know any healing spells to close the wounds. She wiped her arms on her skirt, trying to ignore the sting.

Coraza peered through the juniper branches at the hundred-year-old Chapel of Our Lady of Califia, still yards away up the hillside, atop a ridge that pointed like a finger at the sea, poised to bless the setting sun each day. The bright vermilion ball of the sun was already sinking toward the horizon.

I must be quick or not do this at all. Evening prayers will begin soon. Coraza felt like a grubby thief. Would stealing her own inheritance be a sin? Just in case, Coraza prayed softly, "Madre of Messengers, Lady of Sigils, forgive me."

Coraza sprang from the cover of the bushes and scrambled up the last few yards of scree to the top of the ridge. Gasping for breath again, she crouched beside the adobe wall of the chapel. The singing voices of the holy sisters within chanted the Remembrance.

Coraza sighed. Usually, holy music was a blissful experience for her, one of the few joys of her life. But her momentary enjoyment curdled to anger and confusion as she recognized the chant as the Sorrowful Remembrance. That chant was particularly sad—used for those whose sinful acts in life doomed them to be banned from Heaven. Coraza could not understand the words of the chant, as they were in the Holy Language, said to be the same as that spoken by the Madre long ago. But she heard a name she clearly understood...Erculeo Salamago.

They chant the Sorrowful Remembrance for my father? What did he do? Is that why Mater Urania hates me? Coraza wished she could storm into the services and demand an answer, but she knew that would be suicidal. Perhaps when I am established at the hacienda of Don Malaguez, I can ask the Don to help me find out. Perhaps he already knows. Her anger sharpened her resolve.

Coraza crouched, ran past the tall windows along the wall, and rounded the corner to the back of the chapel. Summoning her courage, she turned the latch, opened the door, and crept inside.

She stood looking down a side hallway that flanked the main chamber of the chapel. A large marble basin, inscribed with the name of Doña Galvez, one of the wealthy patrons of the order, stood on a pedestal just inside the door. Coraza gazed at it guiltily; she didn't have the time to ritually wash her hands and feet as all entrants to the chapel should. At the far end of the corridor, on the left, an archway opened into the nave. On the right were three doors. The closest one led into a storeroom.

The voices of the holy sisters resounded in the last stanzas of the Sorrowful Remembrance, the tones echoing between the high walls and vaulted ceiling of the chapel. The sound washed over Coraza like a wave, conjuring a memory of a day at the beach shore when the gray-green waves rolled toward her and over her, her skin burning from sun and salt-brine, the voices of the other orphans daring her to keep wading deeper and deeper into the sea. Coraza shook her head to stay focused on what she had to do.

The chanting ended, and the voices softened to whispered murmurs as the holy sisters changed their stations for the evening prayers. A tall, thin nun named Sister Mercuria stepped through the archway, carrying a narrow box about as long as Coraza's arm. Coraza ducked down behind the marble basin. The holy sister walked to the storeroom door, went inside, and emerged again quickly without the box.

That must be it! thought Coraza. *My inheritance. They prayed over it during the Remembrance.* Coraza took two slow breaths, then she padded down the short hallway. Through the archway, Coraza could glimpse the round stained glass window over the chapel entry doors. The cut-glass pieces shimmered with the gold of the late afternoon sun. At just the right moment, when the sunlight struck certain prisms in the window, the glass would be ablaze with light, illuminating golden-winged messengers cleverly hidden in the window's design.

But Coraza dared not let her attention be captured now. As soon as she was sure no one was looking her way, she crossed the corridor to the storage room door, opened it silently, and stepped in.

Coraza glanced quickly around. The room had once been an office and was still cluttered with bookshelves, a desk, and a table. Items needing repair, such as a broken broom, a cracked washbasin, and a bent set of iron fire tongs, were set here and there. The air smelled of lemon oil, cedar wood, old leather, and mouse nests. An open window to Coraza's right let in a warm breeze, stirring up golden dust motes. On the table she saw the long box. The name

"SALAMAGO" had been burned into the wood, and a red ribbon encircled its width.

Coraza placed her hand on the box with a sigh and smiled. "Here you are," she whispered. She tugged on the ribbon and pulled it away from the box, then lifted the lid.

Within, on a cushion of royal-blue velvet, lay a butter-hued leather bag that, from the shape, clearly contained a sword. The bag was tied at the top, the leather sealed together with a black wax depicting the ancient hero Hercules. A piece of paper peeking from beneath the sword bag caught Coraza's gaze, and she snatched it up.

It was a note in a rough, sprawling hand.

This is the last of my works. It is my wish that a certain individual may hold it to learn what she truly is.

ES

Mixed emotions flowed through Coraza. The words were so cold, and yet...*Is this truly meant for me? If so, he knew I existed. But he never came to see me. Never wrote to me. Still, he gave me this, his last sword. Did he come to care, at the last? Did he regret that he never knew me?* Coraza put back the note and closed up the box again, murmuring, "Let us hope you will save my life, good sword, when Don Malaguez sees you."

A shadow emerged from behind a bookcase, and a leather-gloved hand slipped over hers. With the ring of steel against steel, the tip of a rapier slipped just beneath her chin. "Forgive me, señorita," said the young man in the black domino mask in front of her, "but I cannot let you take what is rightfully mine."

Chapter Three

Unable to believe her bad luck, Coraza stared at the young man before her. There was a certain handsomeness in his square jaw and golden brown hair. But his nose appeared to have been broken once, and the hazel eyes behind the domino mask were quite serious.

"No!" protested Coraza, as loudly as she dared, hoping that the chanting of the holy sisters drowned her out to anyone but him. She tried to pull the box toward her despite the sword point at her throat. "I will not be cheated by some common thief!"

"Odd words, coming from another thief," said the young man in the mask. "It would seem we are on a similar errand. I have no wish to harm you, señorita, so kindly let go of the box."

"No, it is mine," Coraza said fiercely.

"I regret to inform you, senorita, that that is a matter of dispute."

"You don't understand—"

"I understand very well, señorita. Did I not hear you just say you were taking this to Don Malaguez? How much is he paying you?"

"He isn't paying me anything," Coraza growled. "I just...need to show it to him."

"Ah. You've some more complicated scheme in mind. Forgive me for interfering in what I am sure are brilliant plans, señorita, but I need this sword."

"So do I," insisted Coraza. "It's the only proof I have."

"Proof?" The young man's brows raised above the mask. "Proof of what?"

"That I am Salamago's daughter!"

"His da…" then the young man chuckled and grinned. "An excellent try, señorita, but I know for a fact that Salamago had no children."

"And I regret to tell you that you have been misinformed, señor. He did. My name is Coraza Salamago."

"Hmm." The sword point wavered but quickly returned to a position beside her neck. "Coincidence. Or a lie."

"I am not lying to you, señor!" said Coraza, stamping her foot with frustration. "Besides, how would you know if he had children or not?"

"Because he…because I…" The young man paused in thought for a moment. "Never mind. Just give me the sword, señorita, and let us be done with our little dance."

"Never." Coraza flipped the box up, knocking his rapier blade aside. She stepped backwards, shifting the box behind her back, until her heels were against the door. "It is all I have of him, señor. I beg you to leave it with me. If all you want is money, go rob a bank or some wealthy person. But this sword will save my life. If you must have it, then you might as well kill me to get it." Coraza raised her chin defiantly, hoping he did not take her at her word.

The young man paused again, the point of his rapier wavering. "Well. You have Salamago's spirit, at least. Still, I am not convinced. My reasons for wanting the sword are vital, and I am in a hurry. Therefore…" He raised the point of his sword once more.

Coraza swallowed hard, wondering if he truly intended to kill her. She thought about trying to open the door behind her to flee, but that would mean dropping the box.

"If you hold very still," the young swordsman went on, "this will not hurt."

"Ai…"

Should I kick him? Coraza wondered. *Should I spit in his eye?*

The rapier point slashed down, cutting across the front of her shirt and through her undervest, just above her breasts. With a flick of the sword point, the young man lifted back the cut undervest and stared hard at her trisigil.

"You monster!" cried Coraza, feeling violated. "How dare you! You are no gentleman!"

"No, I assuredly am not," said the young man, pulling the blade away, allowing the flap of cloth to fall across her chest again. His face seemed a shade paler. "You have the hand with a flame in your sigil. As did your fa... as did Salamago. Forgive me."

"Is that proof enough for you?" growled Coraza, wrapping one arm across her chest, her face growing hot.

"It is not certain proof," said the young man. "But it is possible. The symbol is that of a magical artisan. Mierda. Could he truly have had a child and not told me? But then...it appears there is much he did not tell me." The young man rubbed his chin and regarded her with a wry smile. "Maybe he just did not want me to know he had a pretty daughter, yes?"

Coraza sighed heavily, starting to tremble as her fear caught up with her anger. She heard the evening prayers enter their midpoint cadences, and she eyed the open window across the room. "If you will excuse me, señor, I must be going." She tried to rush past him as she headed toward the window, but he caught her arm.

"No. Forgive me, señorita, but I will not let you take this sword to Don Malaguez."

Coraza struggled to free herself from his grip. "Why not? What is it to you?"

"Your father, if indeed he was, would not have wished it."

"My father is dead. And I will be, too, if I stay here."

"Surely you exaggerate. Who would want to kill you?"

"Mater Urania, the headmistress."

The young man chuckled. "I've heard school punishments may be harsh, but death—"

"She tried to give me to La Llorona this afternoon!"

"What? To the...tzinn?" His eyes widened, and his mouth twitched in an incredulous smirk.

"Certainly, the tzinn! You must have heard it moaning."

"I've been hiding in this chapel all day, waiting to get a chance at that sword. I heard some wind and saw dust blowing outside the windows. Really, señorita, to be an accomplished thief, you will have to invent more believable lies."

Coraza found it hard to breathe, and her jaw worked in outrage. But the singing of the holy sisters was entering the last set of verses, and she mastered her anger. "I don't have time for this. Let me go."

"Wait!" he said, releasing her and sheathing his rapier. "I have a horse. Let me help you."

"Why?"

"Because…if you are my master's daughter, then I am honor-bound to protect you."

"Your master?" Coraza frowned. "Were you my father's servant?"

"His apprentice. I served as a blacksmith in his forge for five years. Filipo del Utherio, at your service, señorita." He bowed a little from the waist.

Coraza paused. "You knew my father."

Doubt crept into the young man's eyes. "I thought I did. He was much like a father to me."

Anger welled up in her again. "How fortunate," Coraza spat, "while I, who bear his blood, have no memories of him. Only the holy sisters' word that he is my father and his name. Why weren't you attending the Remembrance for him, if he meant so much to you? Instead, here are you are, hiding and wearing a mask."

Chagrin was plain on Filipo's face, even with the mask. "Yes, well, it seems the association with your father makes me a wanted man."

"Wanted? Wanted for what?"

"I should very much like to know that myself, señorita," Filipo said hastily. "Now, I have a suggestion. We should take the sword but leave the box behind. That may delay the discovery that it's missing."

Coraza stared at Filipo, torn by curiosity, distrust, and anxiety to get away. "As you say, then. But I will take it from the box."

Filipo sighed heavily. "Very well."

"And I will be the only one to carry it."

"I…Oh, all right."

"And you will tell me about my father."

"What do you want to know?"

"Everything."

"I will tell you all I can, I promise. But let us hurry."

Coraza turned away from him and opened the box between herself and the wall. She pulled out the sheathed sword with one hand and handed him the box with the other. The sword rustled inside the sheath like a baby bird inside its egg.

The note that had been inside the box drifted out, and the young man snatched it up and stared at it as if mesmerized.

As he read it, Coraza slipped the leather strap of the sheath over her head and across her chest, arranging the strap to hold the cut portion of her shirt and undervest firmly closed.

"You believe you are this person in my master's note?"

"Yes."

He shook his head. "So many mysteries." Filipo handed the note back to Coraza. "Keep this."

Coraza rolled up the paper, reached back, and tucked it into the opening at the top of the sword sheath.

Filipo rummaged through the discarded items in the room, finally selecting the bent set of iron fire tongs. He put them in the box, closed it, and tied the red ribbon again around it.

Coraza and Filipo both froze as footsteps approached the door. Voices murmured just on the other side.

Coraza pushed the window casement open a little further and jumped out. The window was not high off the ground, but her ankle turned under her as she landed. She fell on her side, and the air was knocked out of her.

What am I to do now? she thought as she fought to catch her breath. *What if the holy sisters come out?*

Filipo jumped down nimbly beside her. He grasped her shoulders and pulled her up to her feet. "Are you all right?" he whispered in her ear.

Coraza nodded, unable to speak. Through the window, they heard the latch in the office turn and the door open.

"Come on!" Filipo pulled Coraza into a run.

She willed her legs to move but found it hard to do more than let the young man half pull, half drag her away. Coraza noted his arms certainly had the strength of a former blacksmith. "Stop!' she wheezed.

"Not until we're safe," he whispered.

They ran into the partial cover of the Garden of Contemplation on the north side of the chapel. A high hedge of holly fenced the garden, over which Coraza could see the tops of poplar, rowan, and oak trees glowing golden in the light of the setting sun. They dashed and stumbled down a path of white stones until Coraza saw a sorrel stallion ahead, tethered to an oak tree. The horse raised its head in attention as Filipo and Coraza ran up to it. Coraza fell gasping against the side of the horse, grabbing the stirrup strap for balance.

Again, Filipo asked, "Are you all right, señorita? Can you ride?"

"Just...catching...my...breath. Of course, I can ride," said Coraza, grateful to be able to take full lungfuls of air again.

She looked around at all the exotic plants that had been brought to Alta Califia as seeds or saplings from sacred shrines of the Madre throughout Europa. Only the holy sisters were permitted in the garden.

"Ai, we could get in so much trouble for being here." And then Coraza laughed, considering all the trouble she had already earned by stealing from the holy sisters and running away. *Can I truly go through with this? Leaving the only home I have known, however cruel? But I must. I must learn why my father, and therefore I, and apparently this boy I just met, are so disparaged.*

"Then let us be gone. This is my horse, Tulio. Tulio, we have a new friend."

The horse planted his nose in Coraza's hair and whuffed. Coraza smelled sour grass on his breath as she patted his neck.

Filipo untied the reins from the tree, put his foot in the stirrup, and vaulted into the saddle. He leaned over and held out his arm to Coraza. She hesitated, full of misgivings.

"I swear, I will not harm you, señorita. Now, please, before the holy sisters come out and see us."

Coraza took his arm and pulled herself into the saddle behind him. Reluctantly, she placed her arms on his waist. She had never been so close to a boy before. And now the rise of the back of the saddle pressed her against his back, her legs against his thighs. All the warnings with which the holy sisters had filled her ears concerning the beastliness of the male sex flooded into her mind. As well as all the whispers the orphan girls would share at night, when no holy sister was listening, about how enticing certain men seemed to be.

Filipo clicked at his horse, and they cantered down one of the garden paths. They passed the elaborate beds of roses and poppies and the central stone fountain carved in the shape of a giant water lily, but fortunately, they encountered no holy sisters. At the far end of the garden, Filipo pulled his horse to a stop at a gap in the holly hedge. Before them, Coraza could see a steep hillside that sloped sharply down to the road winding through the arroyo below.

"We aren't going down that way?" protested Coraza.

"Would you rather go back to the chapel and use the Camino Del Real?"

"Ai, no…"

"Well, then. Hold on." Filipo urged his horse forward, and the steed cautiously stepped down on the slope. Half walking, half sliding, the horse carefully but surely picked its way down as if it did this sort of thing all the time. When the horse stepped at last onto the road, Coraza sighed in relief, resting her head on Filipo's back.

"Good Tulio. He's an old vaquero's mount," he said, patting the horse's neck. "A cow pony. Best investment I ever made."

Coraza turned and looked back up the slope but could no longer see the garden. At that very moment, she imagined, the light in the Chapel rose window would be revealing the heavenly messengers. For a moment, Coraza wished she were there to see it one last time. And then the moment passed. She was out into the great world now.

Have I done a wise thing? The exhilaration of freedom swirled within her.

"Are you all right back there?" asked Filipo as he pulled off the domino mask. Now that Coraza could see all of his face, he appeared to be only a little older than she. The evening

sun glinted in his sandy hair, and there was a wary kindness in his hazel eyes.

"Yes, I am fine, señor. Now, please, tell me about my father! You were truly his apprentice?"

"Yes, for five years, as I have said. What would you know of him?"

"As I have said, everything! I am nearly mad with jealousy. You lived and worked with him, while I know nothing!"

"Yes, of course, of course, your pardon. Well...er...he was a sword maker, as you know. Some have said the finest magical sword wright in all the New World. Erculeo Salamago could fashion a blade from any metal but mercury, and more than once, I heard him musing on how to accomplish that someday. He was a fine sorcerer as well, and he put subtle magics in almost every piece we made. Every sword we made received a name, and if it was a special commission, the sword was made to match the purchaser, though not necessarily in the way the buyer wanted. Some were quite clever—"

"Yes, yes, but no," moaned Coraza, gently pounding her forehead on Filipo's back. "What was he like? I mean, what sort of man was he? You said he was stubborn, as I am. What else?"

"Oh, I see. Well, he had the strength of a bear and the will of an ox. But he was wise as a scholar about many things. His temper could blow like a volcano, and my first mistakes as an apprentice were nearly my last. His roar could shake the forge's roof. Yet he could also be very patient, and some of his metal and spell work was done with such delicacy, you would not think it was from the hand of the same man."

Coraza thought on what the young man had said. She was also stubborn, and her temper could get the best of her. But she had been good at weaving little talismans, as the orphans did for the sisters to sell. And she could see magic fields. Did this mean she could be a good sorcerer too?

"What else?"

"Well, sometimes, on evenings like this, after a bottle of wine, he would sing. He liked songs about melancholy beauty and lost love, and he would sometimes recite the sappiest romantic poetry..." Filipo's voice caught in his throat, and he coughed. "Sweet Madre, it has been more than a year since I last saw him, and I still miss him."

Coraza closed her eyes and sighed. "I never knew him, and your words make me miss him. But then, why did the holy sisters perform the Sorrowful Remembrance for him? What sins did he commit that his soul will not see Heaven?"

Filipo's back muscles tensed, and his hands tightened into fists on the reins. "The holy sisters are wrong. Your father was a good man. Someone has slandered him, and I'd like to find out who."

"And when you find this person?"

"I will demand his reasons. And then I will kill him."

"Oh."

What sort of hothead am I riding with? wondered Coraza. *Will I have to get away from this boy? Or is this just his machismo speaking? No matter, if he can get me to Don Malaguez. Once I am taken as the Don's ward, I can forget him and plan my new life. Someone of the Don's status must be a learned man. Perhaps he knows how Protectadoras are chosen.*

Coraza noted that the road, though winding, headed roughly north to the pueblo of La Escarpa. The lands and hacienda of Don Malaguez were adjacent to the pueblo in the coastal hills to the east and north.

So, at least I am headed the right direction. Perhaps, if I am patient, Señor del Utherio will take me closer to Don Malaguez' hacienda. And I must learn all I can from him while I may.

"Tell me, if you would, señor, how did my father die?"

"I do not know, señorita. It may be some time before anyone knows. Maestro Salamago was wealthy enough to have a Signo de Vida hung in the Cathedral in Los Mesanjeros. When the stone in the talisman turned black the night before last, the word went out at once."

"I see." Coraza understood how such things might work, being a maker of talismans herself. But she no longer quite trusted the word of holy sisters. "Is it possible the Cathedral is…mistaken?"

Filipo's mouth twitched in a half-grin as he looked back at her. "You would doubt the skill of the Holy Sorcerers of the Cathedral?"

"No, no, of course not, only…"

"Only there is nothing that cannot be tainted by politics and greed. Salamago said that once himself. So now, instead of searching for a live master, I must seek to find out if he is truly dead."

"You were searching for him?"

"For nearly a year. At the end of last summer, Salamago disappeared from the forge, leaving me a little bit of money and a note telling me to find other work. I asked all over, but no one had seen him depart or knew where he might have gone. I had no other life to go to. People told me to forget him and go to sea. But my father was a fisherman, and I learned early that I get very seasick. So, instead, I searched. And still do."

Coraza suddenly understood. "And you thought this sword, his last sword, might tell you something about where my father had been."

Filipo looked back over his shoulder at her. "Yes. You're very quick, señorita."

"I know," sighed Coraza. "It got me in trouble all the time at the orphanage. Once, I could tell what instruction spell a holy sister was going to cast, and I said it. She rapped my knuckles with a stick in front of the other orphans."

Filipo snorted. "No teacher likes a student who is too smart."

She paused before her next question. "And…my mother? Do you know…anything?"

"The holy sisters did not tell you of your mother?"

"No. They told me nothing."

"Ai, that is hard. I suppose you must assume the truth is bad, then. Whoever she was, she is either dead or a…lady of convenience. Alas, señorita, I only worked with Salamago five years. He never mentioned a particular love, certainly no child, though he must have had a dalliance from time to time. Many a doña *accidentally* would leave a lace handkerchief when they came by the forge on business." With forced heartiness, Filipo added,

"Perhaps she was one of those, eh? A lady so grand that she had to give you up rather than face a shamed reputation."

"Thank you, señor, for such kind words, but I do not think so." A memory smote her of the other orphan girls taunting her, calling her the daughter of a puta, a whore. And the holy sisters had looked on, doing nothing. Coraza buried her face between Filipo's shoulder blades.

"Are you all right?"

"I...it's memories. Just...memories." She shivered a little as a cooler breeze blew down the arroyo, hissing through the cottonwood leaves. Coraza sat back and rubbed her shoulders. "It will be getting dark soon."

Ai, why didn't I think to even bring a cloak or a shawl?

"You're right. I know of a place we can take shelter and look at the sword in private. Er..." Something seemed to just occur to him, and Filipo turned his head to regard her over his shoulder. "If I may ask, señorita, how old are you?"

"Sixteen."

"Sixteen!" He sucked air through his teeth. "I, myself, am seventeen. But mierde! This could be bad. We will have to be careful and hope no one sees us."

"Why? You said you would not harm me, yes?"

"Yes, but in the eyes of the law, that means nothing. You are below the age of majority, and I'm not your brother or cousin. Mierda. What was I thinking? What were you thinking, running away like this?"

"I am fleeing for my life, remember?"

"Ah, yes. So you said."

"I am not a liar," she grumbled. "It was a holy sister, Sister Phoebe, who sent me word that my life was in danger and told me where and when to get the sword."

"I see." He became very quiet.

The horse's hoof beats were loud on the rock and dirt of the rutted road and louder yet as they crossed a small plank, wood bridge over the stream at the bottom of the canyon. The stream, though barely a trickle now that it was late summer, could still be heard gurgling softly.

Coraza sighed. "I hope Mater Urania does not punish Sister Phoebe too severely."

"Do you fear she might be expelled from the Order?"

"Or worse." Coraza remembered the pain of the Mater's binding spells. "Mater Urania is a powerful sorceress."

"Indeed? And yet you were nearly taken by a tzinn?"

"Somehow, the wards had failed. In fact, Mater Urania seemed angry that I escaped it."

"I see. I find it hard to imagine someone so cruel, yet as your...as Salamago himself said, the world is far darker than most people know. Still...a tzinn, you say? Truly?"

"Yes." Coraza looked up at the darkening sky, at the branches waving in a strengthening wind, and wondered with growing fear if La Llorona might come for her again, despite Gracia's reassurance. "Do you know anything about tzinn, señor?"

"No more than most people. Whoever would use...could use a tzinn to do harm..." He did not finish the thought.

Coraza could hear the edge of fear in his voice. *So, you cannot protect me if La Llorona does come again*, thought Coraza.

"Don Malaguez' hacienda will be warded against tzinn. All the ranches are, to protect their cattle. Once I am there, as Sister Phoebe advised me, I will be safer."

"No." Filipo shook his head. "In this, the good sister is mistaken. You should not go to Don Malaguez. The man is a pig. Your father despised him."

Cautiously, Coraza asked, "What else would you suggest, señor?"

"I don't know. There are other men of means, other clients of Salamago's who might take you in. Let me think."

As twilight settled over the canyon, Coraza doubted there was time for them to reach another haven. Not if she wanted to stay alive.

Chapter Four

Coraza tensed as Filipo turned the horse off the road to head along a lesser rutted track. Once it may have been well-traveled, Coraza thought, judging by the deep depressions caused by wagon wheels, but now the road sprouted dry weeds and grasses. "Where are we going?"

"Don't be afraid," said Filipo, his tone both annoyed and amused. "I told you we were going somewhere safe. And if you are whom you say, it's right that you should see it. After all, it may be yours someday."

"Mine? What will be mine?" Coraza felt too anxious for riddles and surprises.

"You'll see."

The trees around them gave way to stumps. Despite the darkening twilight, Coraza could make out in the near distance a large, brick building—not as big as the orphanage, for this structure was only one story. But it had two massive chimneys at either end of the tiled roof and an enormous double door like a barn.

As they rode into the bare, gravel foreyard, Coraza asked, "What is this place?"

"Welcome to Aliento del Dragón, señorita. Your father's forge."

Coraza stared at it, trying to take in every detail of the piece of her unknown past. "It was so close," she said as Filipo led the horse to a hitching post beside the big doors. "Not more than an hour's ride from the orphanage, and yet he never came to see me. Never sent a letter."

An emptiness opened up within her, too great for mere sorrow, to have been so thoroughly forgotten by one who ought to have been a part of her life. Tears threatened to fill her eyes, but she fought them back. She did not want Filipo to see her cry. She swallowed hard and gripped the saddle until her hands hurt.

Filipo quickly looked down at the reins as he tied them in a slipknot. "I do not know what to say, señorita. I'm sorry. I would like to think that, were my master still alive, he would be sorry too."

Coraza nodded and turned to dismount from the saddle. To her surprise, Filipo grasped her waist and lowered her down. "I should slap you for taking such a liberty, you know," she said, uncertain as to how she felt about it.

Filipo chuckled a little. "You wish me to apologize for being the sort of gentleman who offers a lady assistance?"

"No, no, only…you should ask first, yes?" Coraza mentally cursed the holy sisters for never teaching her how to interact with men.

I suppose they never thought I would have the chance to.

"By the time I had asked, you would already have gotten down, and I would have missed my opportunity, wouldn't I?"

"Opportunity to what, to touch me?"

Madre, what was I thinking, to run off with this boy? wondered Coraza. *Could I not have escaped the orphanage and the tzinn some other way? And yet, and yet…he knew my father. He is strong, and that is reassuring in a way. And, truly, he is not bad looking.*

"The opportunity to prove I can still do some good," Filipo said. "I can still protect my master's legacy, even if I can do nothing more for him. Salamago deserted us both, Coraza. But I must believe he had good reason." Filipo gazed down at her a moment, as if searching for something in her face. Then his gaze shifted to the hilt of the sword on her back. "I'm hoping what you carry will give us the answer."

Filipo turned and began walking toward the enormous doors of the forge. "I'm afraid there won't be much to see inside, señorita. Thieves and vagrants have done their damage." He kicked a bent piece of iron that lay on the gravel. "Let me go in first, just in case."

Coraza looked up at the darkening sky, and though she saw no hint of dust clouds, she still did not wish to stay alone in the foreyard. Coraza followed after him up to the door. "So you've been back here since you first left?"

Filipo swung one of the huge doors aside and strode into the dark interior. "Several times," Filipo called back. "Though I don't know why. Anything of interest was removed when Maestro Salamago left. Probably he took such things with him. Wait there. I'll try to find a candle for some light."

Coraza stayed on the threshold, staring into the darkness. The interior of the building appeared to be all one open room. She could barely make out some tool hooks on the walls, stone troughs, an anvil. In the middle stood an enormous gaping maw of a forge. It reminded her of the Holy Book tale of the three Molochista children who had been saved from dying in the sacrificial kiln by their faith.

Coraza's gaze was drawn by movement to her right, toward the far end of the room. At first, she saw nothing, and then, within the shadows, two hands moved, glowing green to blue. As Coraza continued to stare, eyes adjusting to the dark, shadows resolved into the vague silhouette of a man. But he was wrapped in a haze of sorcerous power, such a dark purple it was almost black.

Coraza froze with fear. "Filipo, someone is here!"

"Who? Where?" Filipo was instantly at her side.

"There." Coraza pointed to the far corner. "A powerful brujo."

"Are you sure? I see nothing."

"I...I have a little talent," Coraza said. "Believe me, he is there."

Filipo narrowed his eyes at her a moment. "So you take after your father in more ways than one." He drew his sword and turned to face the darkness. "You! Whoever you are. If you are there, come forth and show yourself!"

The dark purple cloud moved slowly and silently in their direction.

"I still see nothing. Are you quite sure?" Filipo asked.

"Yes!" Coraza hissed. "He's coming toward us!"

Filipo held out his sword. "Stop! Tell me your name, thief, or by the Madre, I will make you regret you ever lived."

The purple shadows halted. A tiny, round orange light glowed in their midst like a baleful demon's eye. Coraza wondered what sort of spell it might be, until she smelled tobacco smoke and realized it was the lit end of a cigarillo.

"I believe it is I who should be asking this of you, señor," said the shadows in a deep, raspy, voice like the rustling of dry leaves. "Kindly identify yourself and state what your business here might be."

"I don't have to answer to you!" yelled Filipo. Coraza could hear the fear amid his anger. "Get out, vagrant! Find some other lair to leave your stink in." He rushed forward, but he swung his sword into empty air. The shadow had deftly stepped aside.

Coraza heard another faint scrape of steel and saw the glimmer of a silvery blade amidst the shadows.

"To your left, Filipo, be careful!"

Filipo swung hard to his left and sparks flew with a loud clang as his sword was parried by the brujo. Filipo swung again, but his blade hit nothing. "Where is he?"

Coraza saw the shadow moving stealthily toward her. "To your right!" she cried.

Filipo stabbed to the right, and again, the sorceror in the shadows easily parried his thrust. "I need more light!" Filipo shouted. "Open the other door!" Filipo lunged again and missed the brujo by a wide mark.

Coraza stood transfixed, not wanting to take her eyes off the brujo. She acutely felt the pressure of the sword sheathed on her back, and her arm rose slightly as if preparing to grasp its hilt.

Wait. What can I be thinking? I know nothing of sword fighting. I could be sliced to ribbons in moments. She lowered her arm, cursing herself for a coward, hoping not to see bloodshed. But as she watched, the stranger made no direct attacks on Filipo, instead merely deflected the boy's wild, unaimed blows.

Filipo ran back toward her into what dim twilight spilled in from the doorway. "I can just see him now," Filipo panted. "Open the other door! Give me more light!"

Coraza shoved the huge wooden door with all her strength. Slowly, it creaked open. She winced as she again heard the ringing clang of sword against sword behind her and then the duller clang of a sword hitting the stone floor. With a final push, the door fell back against the outer wall, and Coraza turned. Filipo was gasping, holding his upper right arm. His saber lay beside his right foot. Standing before Filipo was a tall, thin man in a leather hat with a flat brim. The man wore a black serape embroidered with red yarn in patterns meant to ward off curses and the Evil Eye.

Filipo stared at him and growled, "Mierda. A vigilero."

Coraza ran to Filipo and pried his fingers away from his upper arm. "Are you all right? Do you need a bandage?"

"Just bruised. He hit me with the flat, not the edge. Effective, though. My whole arm aches."

"Fortunately for the young señor, my training includes methods of disarming without blood or magic," said the man in the black serape. "And you are correct, I am a vigilero. Agente Marzo Palabo, at your service."

Aha, thought Coraza, *the Ministry did send someone. But why is he here in the forge? I should tell him what happened with the tzinn, but...would he believe me? Or will he just try to send me back to the orphanage?*

"I regret having to hurt you, señor," Agente Palabo went on, "but you were rather...enthusiastic in your attack. You defend this place as though it were your home."

"It once was," grumbled Filipo, stepping back to lean against the anvil. "And I suppose, Agente, you are going to arrest me for raising a sword against a lawman."

The vigilero shook his head. "I had not announced myself, so you cannot be faulted for that. I am guessing you are Filipo del Utherio, the apprentice of the man who owned and worked at this forge."

"I am," said Filipo, "and I would like to know why a sorcerer of the law has come to sniff around. I thought it was no longer necessary to validate a man's sorcery licenses once he is dead."

One corner of Agente Palabo's mouth twitched in a wry smile. "Yes, I'd heard your master had…difficulties with the licensing office."

So, I am not the only troublemaker in my family, thought Coraza with a small, strange twinge of pride.

"Difficulties?" cried Filipo, raising his brows. "They harassed us for years!"

"Harassment? Is that what you think it was? Well, I am relieved to see I am not giving you surprising news that Erculeo Salamago has been reported dead by the Cathedral in Los Mensajeros."

"I had heard. May the Madre welcome his soul."

The Agente studied the burning end of his cigarillo. "Apparently, the Madre will not be welcoming his soul, according to the holy sisters at the Cathedral. There remain many questions surrounding your former master's disappearance and death."

So, there was reason to chant the Sorrowful Remembrance, thought Coraza. *Dear Madre, what did my father do to be denied your heaven? And if this vigilero is not here because of the tzinn…?*

Coraza turned to Filipo and said, "Listen, perhaps the Agente can help us with the answers we are searching for."

Filipo glared at her.

"And who is this very observant señorita who accompanies you, señor?"

Coraza felt the full weight of the vigilero's narrow-eyed gaze like a quail in the path of a rattlesnake. She swallowed hard. She had always heard it was unwise in the extreme to lie to a vigilero. "I am…Coraza Salamago, the daughter of Erculeo Salamago."

Agente Palabo's right eyebrow raised a fraction of an inch. "His daughter? Interesting. I'd heard—"

"That Salamago had no children," Filipo finished for him, nodding. "Apparently, my master had everyone fooled. Even me."

"So, you did not know each other from before—"

"We only met this afternoon, Agente."

Coraza was relieved that Filipo did not go on to describe the nature of their meeting.

The Agente scratched his stubbled chin and took a drag off his cigarillo as he studied Coraza. His left hand rummaged in the leather bag hanging at his hip. "I see. And from your clothing, I would guess your father has been hiding you in the nearby orphanage, yes?"

Coraza paused, gazing down embarrassed at her plain, gathered blouse and simple indigo skirt—the same garments all the orphan girls at Nuestra Senora de la Pacifica wore. She nodded. "Hiding, yes. You could put it that way."

"Rather late at night for a ward of the orphanage to be out, isn't it?"

"Um," Coraza looked at Filipo, who glanced away. "I...the young señor and I...we had to get away...to talk. About my father's death."

"Yes, I am sure." Agente Palabo's knowing smirk was almost gentle. "How old are you, señorita?"

Coraza felt Filipo tense beside her. She raised her chin and said, "I am eighteen, Agente."

"Are you?" The vigilero peered down into the leather bag at his hip. A faint, green light seemed to glow within it. "My little amigo here," he went on as he lifted a small crystal skull out of the bag, "says you are perhaps mistaken." The eye-holes in the sculpted skull emitted a sickly olive-green light. Agente Palabo set the crystal skull on the anvil, turning it to face Coraza. "Would you care to reconsider your answer, señorita?"

Coraza swallowed hard. She had heard of these Calaveras Cristales, objects of ancient Aztecan sorcery, brought north by the Spanish brujos fleeing the brutalities of the Nueva Aztecans during the Great Revolt. She'd heard many spells could be contained within the crystal skulls, cut from stone mined in secret volcanic caverns deep within the earth. But she did not know how their magic worked, and she could see no nimbus of sorcerous glow around it.

It might just be a trick, Coraza thought, to frighten me into telling the truth. But she dared not risk angering the vigilero. "Sixteen," she sighed.

The little skull filled with golden light that brightened the dark forge.

"Ah. My little friend likes that answer better," said Palabo. "And tell me your name again, if you please."

"I am Coraza Salamago, and I am the daughter of Erculeo Salamago." She glared at the skull, daring it to change hue. Although a complex pattern of colors sparkled deep within the crystal, it still primarily glowed golden.

"That will only show you that she believes it," said Filipo.

"You think so? Do you believe her, señor?"

Filipo paused, staring at Coraza for a long moment. "I think it is possible, yes."

The vigilero turned his measuring gaze back at Coraza. "And I am sure Mater Urania will confirm your parentage when I return you to her, yes?"

"No!" Coraza cried. At the Agente's surprised expression, she went on, "I can't go back there, Agente. I can't!"

The vigilero narrowed his eyes even more. "I'm afraid my duty under the law is quite clear, señorita."

"No, you don't understand! She'll kill me!"

"Your punishment may be unpleasant, but I doubt—"

"No, Agente, she means it," Filipo interrupted. "Look at your little friend." The crystal skull was glowing brighter yellow.

Agente Palabo looked from the Calavera back to Coraza. "You truly believe you would die?"

Coraza's hands clenched the air in front of her in desperation. "Agente, the tzinn! There was a tzinn. Surely you must have heard about it. It was La Llorona herself!"

"A tzinn manifested in the area, yes. I saw the signs. But by the time I arrived, it had already been expelled. I rode by the orphanage, but the holy sisters said there was no harm done and no damage."

"That's a lie!" Coraza said. "The tzinn nearly took me, and it nearly broke down the back door! I was outside when the tzinn came, and Mater Urania tried to stop anyone from rescuing me. I was lucky that one sister disobeyed her." She stared at the crystal skull. It blazed a deeper gold. "My life is in danger if I return to the orphanage, Agente! You must believe me."

The vigilero grimaced and rubbed his chin again as he chewed on the cigarillo.

"It could be true, you know," said Filipo. "We don't know how Salamago died. Maybe someone is after all of his family."

"Someone who can summon tzinn?" asked Agente Palabo dubiously. "Did your father have such powerful enemies, señorita?"

"I...I don't know."

The vigilero's questioning gaze flicked over to Filipo.

"She never knew him, never met him," Filipo said.

Coraza looked away, feeling her fresh emotional wounds cut open again. A deep sense of shame filled her, now that her abandonment was exposed to the Agente. Her eyes felt hot, and she blinked hard to keep back stinging tears.

"But given Salamago's fame and sorcerous skills," Filipo went on, "of course he had enemies."

"And do you know who these might be?"

"I have been searching this past year for just that information."

Coraza turned to Filipo, feeling sick. "Do you...do you believe my father might have been...murdered?"

"Something frightened him enough to disappear, leaving all he had built, everyone he knew, behind. Anything, anyone that would terrify a man like Salamago so much...well, what do you think?"

"I don't know what to think," Coraza said, running her fingers through her hair.

"Perhaps," Agente Palabo said, "Mater Urania can shed some additional light on Salamago's circumstances, given he left a daughter with her."

"Haven't you been listening?" Coraza protested. "I can't go back! I won't go back!" Coraza flung open her arms in exasperation and stalked away to the open doors of the forge. Stars were already filling the night sky, and she could barely make out the trees across the forecourt.

I could steal Filipo's horse and ride away, thought Coraza. *But it's too dark. I would quickly become lost. And I don't know how to get to Don*

Malaquez's hacienda from here. And I would have no protection if La Llorona should come again.

Coraza was startled out of her churning thoughts by yellow lights bobbing among the trees. For a moment, she wondered if it was a supernatural apparition, another warning of a tzinn's approach. Then she heard the soft murmur of men in conversation and the hoofbeats of horses walking down the road toward the forge.

Coraza turned and ran to Filipo. "Someone else is coming! Men on horseback."

Filipo looked at Agente Palabo. "Are you expecting compañeros?"

The vigilero shook his head.

"More thieves, then," Filipo growled. "Vultures come to feast on the remains." He picked his sword off the floor.

"Before you fling yourself again into battle, señor," said Agente Palabo, "let us give our visitors a chance to incriminate themselves." He scooped up the glowing skull and beckoned Coraza and Filipo to follow him behind the stone hearth.

Coraza crouched down beside the vigilero as he placed the crystal skull back into his pouch. They did not have long to wait before the horsemen rode into the forecourt.

"Look, a horse, Maestro," said one man clearly. "Someone is already here."

"Tulio!" Filipo exclaimed softly. "Mierda, if they take my horse..."

"I will not let that happen," Agente Palabo whispered. "Patience, please, señor."

From behind the hearth, Coraza saw light fill the forge as men walked in with lanterns.

"Well, this place has certainly seen better days," said a man in a deep, purring drawl, the sort of voice a cougar might have if one could speak. "I expect we won't find much. Salamago was tempestuous but thorough."

Filipo's eyes widened with recognition. "What is he doing here?"

"Who is it?" whispered Coraza.

"That's Doctor Saturnin Raimundo, Don Malaguez' pet wizard."

Don Malaguez, thought Coraza, as new opportunity became apparent.

"I hear voices," said Dr. Raimundo. "Who is there? We've seen your horse. Show yourselves. If you force us to come drag you out of hiding, I assure you that you will not find the experience pleasant."

Palabo stood and stepped out from behind the hearth. "No need for that, Maestro. But you cannot fault me for caution. I hear there are rough men in these parts."

Unable to help herself, Coraza peered around the edge. Standing just inside the double doors was a tall, slender man in a fine brown silk suit that was slightly rumpled. His dark, collar length hair was slicked back, and he had a full, slightly drooping mustache. His amber-brown eyes were narrowed in severe disapproval. Most fascinating to Coraza, however, were the man's hands. Though the sorcerous nimbus surrounding them was subtle, it coruscated with many shifting colors. Not so powerful a brujo as the vigilero, then, she mused, but certainly one experienced with a wide variety of magics. Beside the wizard stood two grubby vaqueros holding up lanterns.

"Agente Marzo Palabo," said Dr. Raimundo, carefully accenting every syllable. "I cannot say it is a pleasure to see you again."

"My sentiments as well, Maestro," said Palabo, casually lighting another cigarillo.

Coraza sensed that whatever history the men had, it had not been cordial. They could not be more different, certainly, in appearance. Compared to the dapper Dr. Raimundo, Agente Palabo looked like a vagabond who slept on the ground every night.

"What are you doing here?" asked Dr. Raimundo.

"The business of the Ministry and the law, of course. But what of you? I'd have thought scavenging from a dead man's belongings to be beneath you."

"And so it is," said Dr. Raimundo. "I have perfectly legitimate reasons for being here."

"And those would be?"

"The land this building stands on is adjacent to my employer's holdings. Now that the owner is...regrettably deceased, Don Malaguez is considering the purchase of this parcel. He asked me to give an appraisal of the property."

"After dark?"

"I came as soon as I could," said Dr. Raimundo. "And of course, I wished to get the drop on whatever competition there might be. But given that Salamago left no heirs, and Don Malaguez has good friends in the judiciary, there should be little impediment to the purchase if I decide it's worthwhile."

"Not if I can help it, you bastard," growled Filipo softly.

What would Don Malaguez want with a forge? wondered Coraza.

Filipo stood and pulled Coraza up by the shoulders with him. "I regret to tell you, Maestro, that your plan may not proceed as smoothly as you think."

"What...who...ah, I recognize you," said Dr. Raimundo. "You were Salamago's boy, his apprentice."

"I had that honor, yes," said Filipo.

"You've grown since I saw you last. Have you been living here all this time?"

"Merely returned for the occasional visit," said Filipo. "But you might be disappointed to learn that my master did, indeed, have an heir. And here she is."

Coraza blinked in the lantern light. She'd never had so many men looking at her at once. It was strange, exciting, and terrifying at the same time.

Dr. Raimundo stared at her as if she were a vaguely interesting and highly inconvenient insect. "And who might this young lady be?"

"May I present Salamago's daughter, Coraza," said Filipo. "It seems my master had been hiding her in the orphanage all this time."

"Maestro," said Coraza, dipping her head.

"Señorita," Raimundo bowed slightly, frowning. "Agente, if this is some sort of trick—"

"I have questioned her," said Agente Palabo, "and she believes it. All I need is confirmation and explanation from Mater Urania—"

This reminder was the final push Coraza needed. "No!" she cried. She ran up to Dr. Raimundo. "Please, Maestro, help me. I am in danger! I fear for my life. I am Salamago's daughter, and the sword I bear on my back, the last sword he made, is my proof. Please, I beg you, take me to Don Malaguez!"

Chapter Five

Swiftly, Dr. Raimundo stepped in front of Coraza. He pulled from a cylindrical sheath at his left hip a gleaming ebony wand chased with silver. "Have these men threatened you, señorita?" He looked as though he hoped she would say yes.

Filipo and Agente Palabo stared in astonishment.

Coraza could not take her eyes off the shimmering colors on the sorcerer's right hand. It was as though the energy of the wand and his life force were interacting in some fashion. "No, no, they have not threatened me, but the Agente only wishes to return me to the orphanage. Señor Del Utherio cannot protect me. I can't let the orphanage take me back. I will die there. Please, I have no use for a forge. If Don Malaguez wants it, I will not dispute him if he will only take me in as a ward and protect me."

"Coraza, no! You don't know what you're saying!" shouted Filipo.

"It sounds as though the young lady knows her mind quite well," said Dr. Raimundo. "And I'm sure my gracious and generous employer will be interested in her offer."

Agente Palabo chewed on his cigarillo some long moments before he said, "My duty under the law is clear, Maestro. The girl is underage and cannot make such decisions for herself. She must be returned to the orphanage."

"No!" cried Coraza.

"You pick interesting times, Agente," said Dr. Raimundo, "to choose to follow the letter of the law. The señorita has asked for the protection of the Don's household, and I am duty-bound to extend it to her on his behalf. Don Malaguez has his own resources by which he can determine the truth of what she says. And his relations with the orphanage are cordial, given that he is one of their foremost patrons. I am sure they can come to an equitable agreement."

"But Coraza," said Filipo, "the sword! It was going to tell us about your father!"

"Oh." Coraza felt the weight of her father's last creation on her back. She'd forgotten, in her fear, that Filipo had wished to examine the sword for clues to Salamago's disappearance and death, clues that she might like to know too.

"Ah, yes," said Dr. Raimundo. "Don Malaguez will want confirmation that the sword she carries is a genuine Salamago. However, he has quite a practiced eye at determining such things, and I assure you, he will give her fair value if it proves to be real."

"No, wait," said Filipo. "It is possible this sword could be a forgery. After my master disappeared, at least one weaponsmith tried to pass off inferior blades as Salamago's. I have not yet seen the sword the señorita carries, but I am better qualified than anyone to give an appraisal of it. Please, let me come along and assist."

"Hmm." Raimundo paused and looked down at Coraza. "Would this be all right with you?"

Coraza nodded, relieved. "Yes, I had promised Señor del Utherio a chance to see it. It would be only fair."

"Very well, then," said Raimundo. "Let us be on our way. I've seen all I need to see here. Agente, if you will be so kind as to not interfere with our departure..."

"Not at all," said Agente Palabo, stepping toward them. "In fact, I, too, am coming with you."

Dr. Raimundo placed a hand on Coraza's shoulder. "You are not welcome at the hacienda, Agente," he said coldly.

"Nonetheless," said Palabo, "my duty is clear. The girl has no relatives to negotiate for her. So I must be present to ensure that she is treated respectfully and fairly, in loco parentis."

Raimundo frowned, glancing from Filipo to Palabo. "If this is some sort of ruse to get back onto Malaguez lands—"

"Believe me, Maestro," said Palabo, "this is one social call I would rather not be making."

"Just a stroke of bad luck, is it? Very well. It's your funeral." Dr. Raimundo holstered his black and silver wand and guided Coraza out of the forge. "The girl will ride with me," he announced to no one in particular.

Coraza stepped into the now dark night and glanced at the sky. The stars were very bright, undimmed by clouds. The warm, night air, still and heavy, carried the scent of sage and dry grass. Coraza sensed no sign of La Llorona.

Doctor Raimundo mounted his black horse and lowered his arm to take Coraza's hand. Surprised not to be unnerved by his touch, Coraza slid into the saddle behind him. There was something more brusque and professional in his manner than she had felt in Filipo's hands.

Again, the hilt of the sword knocked her lightly on the back of her head as she settled back in the saddle. "Ai! This thing!" Coraza tugged at the leather bag strap to get the sword hilt pointed above her shoulder.

"Is that uncomfortable, senorita?" asked Dr. Raimundo. "Someone else can carry it for you, if you like."

Immediately, Coraza felt cold reluctance, and her hands gripped the bag strap. "No, no, it is quite all right. I...I feel I should carry it. For now."

"Of course. As you wish."

As the vaqueros raised their lanterns and the party rode out of the forecourt, Coraza glanced back over her shoulder. Filipo had untied his horse and was getting on, glaring at her. Coraza looked away and saw the vigilero leading his own bay horse from around the back of the forge. His weathered face was unreadable, and his sorcerous umbra was dimmed.

I hope he isn't following in order to snatch me away when he has the chance, thought Coraza. *Why doesn't he understand why I am so afraid?*

Coraza faced forward again and asked, "Do you know much about tzinn, Maestro?"

The vaqueros around them laughed, and Dr. Raimundo himself chuckled. "About as much as any man who has achieved the rank of Maestro from the School of Metaphysics at the University of Madrid, señorita. Don Malaguez hired me to ward his land and household against them."

Coraza sighed with relief. "Thank the Madre," she whispered. "I wish to know more about them. Could you kindly tell me, señor, what they are?"

Raimundo replied, "If I knew the answer to that question, señorita, I would be the Dean of Metaphysicians. The true nature of tzinn is a matter of much argument among all who study the arcane sciences. Thaumaturgists argue that tzinn are merely a form of undead, perhaps human spirits trapped upon this plane and twisted by unknown forces. Deiticians have posited that tzinn are diminished former gods, a matter hotly debated with the Church. There is an order of Mariono monks who insist that tzinn are the remnants of fallen angels. Metaphysicians such as myself argue that perhaps tzinn are a natural phenomenon, a life form of its own, if you will, animated dust and stone instead of blood and bone."

"Wouldn't that be Sere Sorcery?" asked Coraza.

"If there is a magical cause, perhaps. Geomancers have an interesting theory that tzinn are spirits coalesced from the earth's own magical energy fields. It's known that water repels them, and sulphur and saltpeter attracts them, which is why gunpowder is highly restricted in Alta Califia but..." He twisted around to glance back at her over his shoulder. "Why do you ask this? The last I knew, tzinn were not an interest of young señoritas."

"Because I saw one this afternoon. La Llorona." Coraza hesitated even saying the name, lest it might bring the tzinn back.

"Did you? From a safe distance, I expect."

"No. She...it was as close as...as him." Coraza pointed at one of the vaqueros riding a few yards ahead.

Dr. Raimundo coughed out a laugh. "Meaning no disrespect, señorita, but had you been so close to a tzinn, you would not be here, alive, to tell the tale."

"I was rescued. One of the sisters threw holy water at the tzinn. We barely escaped."

"Really?" He sounded as though he were humoring her.

"She might be telling the truth," said Agente Palabo, startling Coraza who had not been aware he was riding right behind them. "There was a tzinn reported in this vicinity."

"Yes, my instruments did pick up something of that nature. I was not doubting that, only that it might be one so powerful and that she had gotten so close."

"You, a Master of Metaphysics, knew there was a dangerous tzinn nearby," Palabo said sardonically, "and yet you did nothing to drive it off?"

"My jurisdiction lies solely within Don Malaguez's ranchero," replied Raimundo darkly. "As for protecting the rest of Alta Califia, well, that's your job, isn't it?"

Agente Palabo did not reply, but Coraza saw a faint flicker of dark red light around his shoulders.

"So, tell me, señorita," Dr. Raimundo asked, "what does La Llorona look like?"

"A woman in a long black dress and veil."

"Anything else?"

"She had...bones for arms and hands. Her face was a skull covered with dry skin." Coraza frowned, not really wanting to see the horrible apparition in her mind again.

"These things are widely known in folklore, you know."

"And there were...two little children that came out from her skirts," Coraza went on. "They also had skulls for heads and no eyes."

Raimundo stopped his horse so suddenly that Coraza's face fell against his shoulder. He again looked back at her, his expression unreadable in the dark. "You saw the Twins," he said.

"Is that what they are?" Coraza asked. "They shook their heads at me, as if warning me."

Raimundo was silent a moment before saying, "Forgive me for doubting you, señorita. Very few know of the Twins. Fewer still have witnessed that apparition and lived to tell about it. You are a most fortunate girl. I confess, I envy you."

"Envy me?" Coraza asked, astonished. "Why?"

Raimundo nudged his horse forward again and replied wistfully. "To have a chance to observe such a powerful tzinn from so close...it is a thing many wizards have longed for."

"I see."

Are wizards so brave, Coraza wondered, *or are they blinded by their hunger for knowledge?*

"Couldn't they just capture one?"

Again, the vaqueros laughed, louder this time.

"It's been tried, of course," Raimundo said, "but the results are invariably fatal to the would-be captors."

"But I've heard," Coraza persisted, "that tzinn can be summoned."

"Only Molochista sorcerors have such knowledge, and until one of them is captured alive and forced to spill his secrets, I'm afraid such matters will remain a mystery."

"Not even the Protectadoras know?"

"Not even the Protectadoras, may the Madre bless their ancient, withered souls."

"I see." Coraza hadn't learned anything useful, really, but it was reassuring to hear Dr. Raimundo speaking of tzinn with no more concern than if he were talking about coyotes or pumas.

From what the light of the vaqueros' lanterns showed, they were riding along the wider track of Camino del Real. The road climbed up a hillside and angled northward. Somewhere up the road, Coraza knew, lay the small pueblo of Las Escarpas. But the horsemen turned off before then, onto another track that went northeast, deeper into the hills. Before long, the scent

of sage and manzanita was overwhelmed by the musk of cattle. In the distance, she could hear them lowing. The horsemen stopped, and the vaqueros raised their lanterns. Dimly illuminated ahead of them, a tall iron gateway loomed, blotting out stars in the night sky.

"Welcome to Hacienda Malaguez, señorita," said Dr. Raimundo. "Here you need not fear tzinn any longer, for the estate is excellently warded. You may have complete trust in my handiwork."

"Nothing too good for the cattle, eh?" said Filipo dryly. It was the first time he had spoken since leaving the forge.

"Precisely," said Dr. Raimundo. 'The Don, like any wise man, protects his wealth. Now if you will excuse me…" The sorcerer drew his black wand and pointed it at the bottom of the iron gate. "The warding is so strong that it brings brief discomfort to those who have been imbued with sorcery. So for my sake and that of the Agente, I'm going to lessen the ward briefly." He murmured words softly but with great intent, and Coraza saw umber light shoot from his wand to the gate. The gate itself glowed for a moment, then dimmed. Dr. Raimundo holstered his wand and said, "It's done. Open it."

One vaquero rode ahead and pushed open the iron gate. Dr. Raimundo nudged his horse and guided it beneath the iron arch.

"Thank you, Maestro," said Coraza. "I am glad to know it will be safe—ehhh!" Coraza groaned as a sharp prickle flowed over her skin, front to back, and she shuddered.

Just beyond the archway, Dr. Raimundo brought his horse to a halt. "Really? You must be very sensitive to magic, señorita, Are you all right?"

For a few moments, Coraza rubbed her upper arms, hugging her chest. Her body felt like a chapel bell vibrating after it had rung. "Yes. I think so. I am…sensitive to magic."

"That would make sense," said Filipo, "given Salamago was her father."

"Señorita," said Agente Palabo, riding up alongside her, so close that his horse's shoulder brushed against her leg. "What is it?"

"I'm all right now," said Coraza. "It was just for a moment." She sat up straight and took a deep breath, forcing her hands to stop shaking.

I mustn't ruin my chance for the Don's protection. I mustn't let them think I am too strange.

"The holy sisters always complained I jumped at anything," Coraza said, trying to sound casual. "It is nothing, truly."

"Hmm," said Dr. Raimundo. "Their discipline spells must have been highly effective on you."

"Yes," said Coraza tartly. "They were." She flexed her shoulders, and the sword on her back shifted with her. Coraza realized something—the one place she had not felt the discomfort was along her back, where the sword lay.

Did it protect me? she wondered.

Dr. Raimundo turned his horse and, after the vaqueros rode through and shut the gate behind them, again unsheathed his wand. Coraza winced and chose to look away as he returned the warding to its full strength. She felt a little queasy as it did, but she wondered if she were just overreacting.

No one spoke as they continued riding. The vaqueros expertly flanked Agente Palabo as though he was a lost maverick steer from the Malaguez herd. Coraza stared straight ahead at Dr. Raimundo's back, praying to the Madre that her chances at a hopeful future had not just been ruined. They rode past an outcropping of rock, a dark silhouette against the night sky.

Suddenly, the vaqueros stopped their horses. "This is far enough," one of them said.

Coraza saw the vaquero nearest her pull out from under his leather vest something metal that reflected the lantern light.

A pistol.

But the pistol was not aimed at her. It and four others, held by each of the vaqueros, was pointed back at Agente Palabo's head.

"As I recall, Agente," said the vaquero, "our master insisted that the next time you set foot upon his land, you would have to have a writ from the Protectorado itself. I presume you can present such a paper?" The vaquero held out his hand.

Agente Palabo sat absolutely still, but Coraza could sense he was gathering power. "No more than you," he growled, "can present a license for carrying restricted weapons."

The vaquero laughed darkly. "Ah, we could, Agente, but it is locked in the Don's oficia for safekeeping. As for yours...no? Then we have no choice but to follow the Don's orders, Agente. Your magic cannot stop all our bullets." The vaquero pulled back the pistol hammer with a loud click. "So, say your goodbyes to your friends and your prayers to the Madre."

"No!" said Coraza, confused. "What are you doing?"

Dr. Raimundo sighed. "Forgive us, señiorita, that you must be exposed to such unpleasantness. Why don't we take this up later, muchachos? We should not have our young guest waiting out in the cold."

"Oh, we don't have to take the time to bury him," said the vaquero. "We can leave his body for the coyotes."

Coraza looked at Filipo. He sat motionless on his horse, staring as if stunned.

Isn't anyone going to stop them? Coraza thought frantically.

"Don't shoot him!" she cried. "The Agente is going to tell me about my father!"

"The Don himself can tell you things about Salamago," growled the vaquero. "But Palabo has dishonored the Don and trespassed on his land too many times."

"It is illegal to kill a vigilero!" Coraza cried. She knew it was a stupid thing to say as soon as the words left her mouth. The vaqueros all laughed again, nastily.

"This is a hacienda, Coraza," said Filipo, carefully. "Don Malaguez is the only law here. And now you see the sort of man he is."

Coraza saw the glow of magic potency intensify in the Agente's lower legs and hands. He softly whistled an odd little phrase of notes as if he was trying to seem nonchalant. His horse flicked one ear back and whickered.

Coraza looked up at Dr. Raimundo. "Is the Don so dishonorable that he would permit this ambush of a lawman?" she demanded.

Raimundo said, "It is…complicated, señorita. Worldly matters you would know nothing about."

"Adios, Agente…" sang the vaquero.

A long second passed and then *pap! pap!* Two loud shots rang out.

In that moment, Coraza saw Agente Palabo leap straight up from his horse. The horse jumped forward and reared, kicking one vaquero's gun out of his hand. Another vaquero cried out and dropped his lantern as he received the bullet from the gunman opposite him in his upper right arm. The third gunman fell from his horse, struck across the eyes by the brim of the Agente's thrown hat.

Agente Palabo landed in a crouch in the spot where his horse had stood, arms out to the sides, a blade in each hand, staring at Dr. Raimundo.

Filipo stared agape at the vigilero, eyes wide.

The maestro's hand went to his wand holster. Without thinking, Coraza grasped Dr. Raimundo's wrist and held it to keep him from drawing the wand. "Please, Maestro, no! Enough!"

Dr. Raimundo looked over his shoulder at her. Then he sighed heavily and relented, moving his hand away from the holster. "Ah, very well."

"I trust there will be no more trouble?" asked Agente Palabo.

"I trust the Don's men have made their point? All right, muchachos, you have proven your loyalty. Put your guns away, and let's get moving."

"But the Caballero—" one vaquero began to protest.

"I will explain things to Don Malaguez. If the Agente is indeed merely here on the señorita's behalf, we will see that he stays no longer than necessary."

"But the last time, Maestro—"

"Yes, and I am hoping he remembers it as well." Dr. Raimundo and Agente Palabo stared at each other for a long, silent moment.

Gunsmoke on the light breeze drifted over Coraza's face. The scent was a metallic tang, with an underlying mineral smell. It was strangely enticing, and Coraza leaned into it, breathing deeply. She felt lightheaded, dizzy...and sneezed loudly.

"Excuse me!" she said, embarrassed.

But her sneeze seemed to have broken the tension between all the men. Agente Palabo resheathed his sword and machete, gathered his horse, and remounted it. The vaqueros slowly and reluctantly tucked their guns back into their belts, the wounded one tying his bandana around his arm.

"I can heal that for you," Agente Palabo offered brusquely. "It will leave a scar the longer you wait."

"No, thank you, Agente. I do not mind scars. It will give me something interesting to show the ladies when I next have a night in town."

"Vamanos," said Dr. Raimundo, frowning.

They continued riding across the starlit, rolling grassland toward glimmering lights in the distance. The riders around her smelled of sweat, tobacco, and leather. Cattle lowed in the distance, reassuring one another.

What now? wondered Coraza. She had clearly fallen among rough men, but what choice did she have? Don Malaguez was like a king in his small kingdom; that was simply how things were on the great rancheros of Alta Califia. The holy sisters often held special prayers on the Caballero's behalf, for he was a major patron of the orphanage. There were few Gente Grande in Alta Califia, as few men of wealth chose to leave the comforts of España or the wealth of South America for a dangerous and distant colony. So few that a single man with substantial land holdings could wield great power.

But because of such power, thought Coraza, *if I become his ward, the holy sisters of the orphanage could not touch me. I could get a better education. And when I am old enough, the Don could arrange a proper marriage for me. One of his status would surely not pick anyone unworthy of his regard. Or perhaps, just perhaps, he knows how Protectadoras are chosen, and I can convince him to set me on that path.* Nevertheless, she could not help wondering whether an unpleasant fate might await her in the Don's care. And she now felt increasing guilt for pulling Agente Palabo and Filipo into unintended danger.

After another half an hour of riding, they reached the sprawling adobe casa grande of the hacienda, and stable hands came forth to take the reins of their horses.

"You may retire to your bunkhouse," Dr. Raimundo told the vaqueros. "Pedro, come with me, and I will look at your wound. The rest of you should get some sleep. Good night."

Coraza climbed down from the saddle, relieved to be leaving the company of the rough gunmen. Dr. Raimundo ushered Coraza, Filipo, Agente Palabo, and the wounded vaquero through a wrought iron gate into a pleasant atrium garden. Water sprayed and splashed in a stone fountain carved in the image of dolphins balancing on their flukes. Torches blazed on long iron stakes. Night-blooming flowers released a delicate perfume, and moths fluttered in the branches of ornamental trees.

"Señorita, Señor del Utherio, you will kindly wait here," said the sorceror, "while I inform the Don of your presence. Agente, you must stay here and go nowhere else. You know what will happen if you are found wandering."

The agente replied with a curt nod. "I have some idea."

As Dr. Raimundo left, trailed by the wounded vaquero, Filipo asked, "What did you do to earn the Don's ire, Agente?"

Agente Palabo replied, "Only my duty, señor. Though, perhaps, a little too diligently."

Coraza said, "I am so sorry, Agente. I did not mean to drag you into this."

He waved his hand dismissively. "What's done is done. I hope you find the peace and safety you seek. But I doubt you will find it here."

"If it is not here," said Coraza, with a sigh, "then it is nowhere to be found."

Agente Palabo simply gazed at her speculatively.

Coraza turned away, wrapping her arms around her chest. The chill night breeze was becoming uncomfortable. Her stomach growled because she had missed dinner. She was anxious, and her legs ached from sitting on horseback for so long. She paced the garden to stretch the muscles as her horsemistress had taught, avoiding Filipo and his judgmental glares. She wondered what she would say to the Don when she met him. She was hardly dressed to meet an aristocrat.

Coraza had never imagined she would actually get to see a garden such as his. Girls at the orphanage would often play at being "ice ladies," pretending to be promenading in dresses dripping with lace and flouncing petticoats at a hacienda garden party, driving men wild with their beauty and mad with their indifference. And there Coraza was, in the scene of her dreams, feeling nothing like an elegant aislada. She gazed sidelong at Filipo and wondered if young men like him were truly so foolish as to fall in love with girls who behaved that way. She decided that she didn't want to know.

"We could look at the sword now, Coraza," Filipo called softly to her.

"No. We could be summoned at any moment." She shifted the bag on her back.

Was it her imagination, or did it weigh more heavily upon her shoulder now? *Perhaps I am just tired.* Coraza distracted herself by looking at the sculptures in the garden. One was a proud Eagle of España bearing arrows and thunderbolts in its talons. Another was a statue of King Anibalo the Third, elephants and lions on his heraldic shield.

Coraza walked on to the next statue and stopped, stunned. In an artificial grotto, sheltered by low hanging branches, stood a painted plaster statue of the Madre, but not the kindly, warm personage of the statue in her cellar room. This Madre had the blue robe and the white shawl, yes, and her left hand held the neckline of her robe open to bare the sigil on her chest. But her right hand held a bloody sword, and below her right foot was the body of a young man with a wound in his side. Coraza knew which apocryphal story it depicted; this was the Madre who sacrificed her only son so that he would not be taken by a tzinn. This Madre had tears on her cheeks, but there was an almost demonic ferocity in the statue's eyes.

Coraza felt a hand on her shoulder and she jumped. "Ai!"

"Coraza, what's the matter? What are you staring at?"

"Filipo, you startled me. It...it's this statue."

"Ah. One of the forbidden Madres. Well, I suppose a man as rich as Don Malaguez can get away with a little blasphemy."

"How can he put this in his garden for any guest to see?"

"I did warn you. The Don is his own man and does what he likes. Please, let us look at the sword while we have the chance. Once the Don has it, he might lock it away, and you'll never see it again."

"All right. But not here. There's not enough light." Coraza turned and walked all the way to the other end of the atrium, nearest the casa grande. There was an inviting brick passageway between the house and the garden on which warm lamplight spilled from a nearby doorway. Shivering as another chilly breeze swept over her, Coraza crossed the brick walkway and entered the warmly lit room.

It was a handsomely appointed office, paneled in oak, with a huge redwood desk dominating the room. Behind it was a heavy, carved wood chair with leather padding on back and seat, reminiscent of a throne. Paintings of helmeted heroes hung on one wall—ancestors of the Don, Coraza surmised. On another wall was a map of Alta Califia, from the Golfo de Califia and the Mexican border to the south, to Puerto Francisco and the Russian territories to the north. On the floor was a large carpet woven with Carthaginian designs, no doubt imported at great expense and no little scandal from Al-Andalus, another sign that the Don had no fear of flouting social convention. Two tall armoires stood flanking a closed door. Ornate brass oil lanterns hung on the walls, giving the room its warm light.

Filipo entered behind her. "The Don's office. We should not be here without his invitation."

"Let's be quick, then," said Coraza.

Agente Palabo, who had followed them like a silent shadow, paused at the doorway, then with great caution stepped inside.

The sword on Coraza's back felt heavy again, and Coraza was relieved to pull the strap over her head and lay the sheath on the broad desk. Part of her shirt flopped aside where it had been slit by Filipo's sword, revealing her under-vest.

Madre mia, I forgot. What picture will I present to the Don this way? As Coraza tried to tuck parts of her shirt under the vest to hold it, Filipo untied the thongs holding the leather sheath closed at the top. He gently tugged the sheath open and began to pull it off the sword, revealing a rosette of red stone at the tip of the hilt—

Coraza looked up and gasped as rapid footsteps, sharp raps on the tiled hallway, approached the room. "Wait," she breathed. "Someone's coming."

Chapter Six

A plump but pretty lady dressed in fine russet silk petticoats, a black lace mantilla draped over a tortoise-shell comb in her hair, bustled past the doorway. Coraza almost released a sigh of relief. But suddenly, the lady reappeared in the office doorway, her dark eyes focused only on the Agente. "Marzo!" she breathed and stepped swiftly toward him.

"Doña Malaguez," said Palabo, removing his hat and bowing low, his voice polite but warning.

The lady glanced aside to notice Coraza and Filipo watching. She stepped back. "Agente Palabo. This is an...unexpected pleasure." Turning to Coraza, Doña Malaguez held out her arms and walked up to her, taking Coraza's hands in hers. "So you must be Erculeo Salamago's daughter! Welcome!" Her smile was warm and genuine.

Coraza blushed and bobbed a curtsy. "An honor to meet you, Doña Malaguez."

"No, no, it is an honor that you should visit my household...Coraza, is it? What a curious name to give a girl, 'shield'."

Coraza shrugged, not knowing what to say. "Nonetheless, that is my name."

"Well, your father was an unusual man. And you, Master Del Utherio, look at you! How you've grown!" The Doña smiled at him like a fond aunt.

Filipo bowed also, blushing a little with embarrassment. "The Madre has blessed me with good health, my Lady. And I hope She has done as well for you."

"Oh, I am in excellent health, thank you. My husband will be with you shortly. He is still savoring his after-supper cigar and brandy at the moment. You are all fortunate to have visited now. Hupitero has only just returned from his travels up north to Monterrey. He was meeting with traders from Russia and some important men from Britain and Los Estados Unitos. Very important men. Exciting and, may I say, world-changing ventures may come from his visit."

Coraza nodded politely, unable to understand why the Doña was giving her and Filipo this breathless speech. *Unless I am not the one who is supposed to hear it.*

Out of the corner of her eye, Coraza noted Agente Palabo standing very still, seeming to study a scale-model iron cannon on a shelf.

"Ah, and this must be the fabled last sword of Salamago," the Doña said, letting go of Coraza's hands and walking behind the redwood desk.

"So we believe, señora," said Filipo.

"I always have admired the magics that Maestro Salamago used to put into his work. Such skill he had. I wonder what spells this one is imbued with. I have a little talent as a Sensitive, you know. May I?" She pointed at the sword with an eager smile.

Filipo reluctantly stepped back. "Of course, señora." He grimaced with chagrin at Coraza. Coraza smiled sympathetically at him. He could hardly have refused Doña Malaguez's request.

To Coraza's surprise, the Doña did not remove the leather bag on the sword. Instead, she placed her hands atop it and closed her eyes. "Ah, yes. There is strong magic in this blade. I can feel it. It tells a story. I sense... regret, great loss, and love. A love gone wrong, almost certainly."

Coraza wondered if the story regarded her unknown mother. Or perhaps herself and her father's regret that he never visited her. Then again, those words might also be for ears other than hers. Coraza felt uncomfortable and dared not look at the Agente. Filipo's brows were raised in mild alarm.

"Salamago still named his swords, yes?" the Doña went on. "I would guess the name of this sword is...Regret. And yet it contains within it the hope that one might right what had gone wrong. To find greatness and glory in the end, despite a misguided beginning." She removed her hands from atop the leather bag and blinked at Filipo. "Am I correct in guessing the sword's name?"

"I…I cannot yet say, señora," Filipo blustered. "We have not yet examined it."

"You will see I am right, señor," said the Doña, playfully wagging a finger at him. "I usually am. I come from a long line of—"

"Oh, here they are, señor." In the office doorway stood Dr. Raimundo.

Next to him was a tall, robust, and handsome man in his forties, wearing a short-jacketed silk suit with silver buttons on the breeches, black velvet lapels, and a black bow tie. He looked at Doña Malaguez with mild bewilderment. "Appalonia?"

The Doña was startled but recovered quickly. "Hupitero, there you are!"

With one very dark glance at the Agente, Don Malaguez said, "My dear, why have you brought our guests into my office instead of the parlor?"

Coraza was about to take the blame, but Doña Malaguez spoke first. "Querido, we are honored to have in our home the daughter of Erculeo Salamago himself, Madre rest his soul. Surely she would want to see your estimable collection of her father's work, yes? And see, she has brought another for you, perhaps the last that Salamago ever made."

"Ah. Yes, so I understand." Don Malaguez, seeming mollified, stepped into the room. "Welcome to Casa Malaguez, señorita!" he said to Coraza, suddenly cheerful and hearty. "And you, Filipo! How long has it been since you last delivered one of your master's masterpieces to me? My, what a fine young man you have become!" The Don walked over to Filipo and patted his shoulder with a meaty hand.

"An honor to see you again, too, señor." Filipo bowed, smiling, looking slightly ill.

"My condolences upon your master's passing. He was a great man. The best swordsmith in Alta Califia. The world shall not see his like again."

"Very likely not," agreed Filipo.

"And to you, señorita, my condolences, though I understand you never met your father."

"Thank you. No, I had not," said Coraza.

"A great pity. A splendid fellow he was. It was a privilege to know him as I did and to count him among my friends."

Filipo turned and discreetly coughed.

"Now, my dear señorita, I am told you seek sanctuary from the dreary life of the orphanage."

"Yes, if you will be so kind and willing señor," said Coraza, feeling all too aware of her drab and damaged clothes.

"Well, if you are, as you say, the daughter of the great Salamago, Madre bless his soul, then I would be most honored to welcome you into my household and act as your compadrazgo. However, I find it most curious that I have not heard of you before this. We have, from time to time, hired girls from the orphanage at Mater Urania's recommendation. But she has never mentioned you to me. A strange thing, given that I was one of Salamago's greatest admirers, don't you think?"

Coraza did not know what to say. "I...I was often kept locked in a cellar, señor. I don't think the Mater told anyone about me."

"Truly? I cannot imagine the Mater being so cruel. How can that be so?"

Filipo stepped around the desk and stood behind Coraza. "It is true what she says, señor. Even I had never heard that Salamago had a child until today."

"Indeed? I wonder why such a blossom was kept secret from everyone."

"Many would not wish it known they sired a child out of wedlock," murmured Agente Palabo. "And some will go to extremes to avoid scandal."

Don Malaguez whirled around and suddenly addressed the vigilero, his voice now cold and harsh. "As for you and your unwelcome intrusion into my household—"

"I am only here to see to the girl's safety, Don Malaguez," said Palabo. "As soon as her affairs are settled, I will leave."

"Yes. You will." The two men glared at one another for a moment. Then Don Malaguez turned, and once more the hearty smile was on his face. "So," he clapped his hands together and rubbed them, "let us have a look at this sword you have brought me."

Coraza sighed, unhappy that she and Filipo would not have the chance to examine it privately. "Of course, señor."

Misreading her lack of enthusiasm, Don Malaguez said, "I assure you, señorita, I will treat it with the utmost respect." He bowed and went to his desk. "Hmm, a ruby rosette and black silk cord...the hilt looks promising."

The Doña stepped back from the desk in feminine deference, with a covert glance at Agente Palabo.

Dr. Raimundo approached the desk and stared down at the sword with intense interest. "Actually, señor, I think that rosette on the pommel is not carved ruby but a crystal. A small animite, perhaps."

"Really?" said the Don. "Valuable?"

"Beyond measure, if I am correct."

Don Malaguez chuckled. "That was Salamago's style. Always the best materials. Is that not so, Filipo?"

"Whenever he could, señor," Filipo replied.

Coraza could hear the impatient irritation in his tone. But fortunately, the Don was absorbed in gently tugging down the gathered leather. Filipo tensed, and Coraza leaned forward, eager for the first glimpse of her father's handiwork.

Next to be revealed was a cup guard of filigreed iron, fashioned to resemble twisted thorny vines. "Interesting," murmured Don Malaguez. "Shall we see the rest?" Without waiting for an answer, he grasped the bottom tip of the sheath and pulled it off in one jerk.

Coraza held her breath as everyone stared at the sword.

"Oh," said the Don, at last, and a slight frown creased his forehead.

The blade was short and not straight, as a proper espada ropera should be, but slightly curved. The metal was dark, dull, and smudged with black. "How...disappointing. You said there were forgeries being made, Filipo?"

"Yes. If you will allow me, Don Malaguez?" Before getting an answer,

Filipo lightly snatched up the sword and examined the blade. Coraza thought she saw a subtle glow around his hands, but it might have been a trick of the light. "Here is his signature and sign," Filipo said, pointing to the juncture of blade and cup guard. "There is some clouding along the edge...my master learned that from a Nijonese swordsmith who visited us." He placed the flat of the sword on the edge of his hand, one third of the way down the blade, and let go. It sat horizontal, unmoving. "The balance is true." Filipo spun the sword and held the point between his eyes, staring down the blade toward the hilt. "The spine is straight with no flaw." Filipo cradled the sword in his hands and sighed. "I believe this is, in truth, my master's work."

"Then I regret to say it is a fortunate thing he stopped with this," the Don said. "Is it unfinished, do you think?"

"No. But perhaps he had to complete it with a forge and tools unfamiliar to him and not of the best quality. I know this was not made at Aliento del Dragón."

"Does it have a name?" prompted Doña Malaguez.

"Eh? Oh, let me see." Filipo again examined the juncture of blade and hilt. "Here it is. The name is...Sorrow."

"Ah," said the Doña with quiet satisfaction. "I was close."

"An appropriate name," said the Don, "for I must confess this is a sorry piece of work. The blade and hilt seem to be from two different projects. The blade is short. The guard is too small. My hand could not possibly fit inside it. The iron filigree is rough on the inside of the guard. And the balance seems intended for a weaker arm."

"Perhaps it is meant to be a child's or a lady's sword," suggested Dr. Raimundo.

Coraza and Filipo looked at one another. *Is it possible the sword was made for me?* she wondered.

"But it is too ugly for a lady and too elaborate to be a child's sword," said Don Malaguez. He sighed and, shaking his head, took a handkerchief from his jacket pocket. He took the sword back from Filipo, wiped the blade, and set the sword down on the desk. Turning to Coraza, he said, "It is sad, señorita, that your inheritance should be a work such as this. Even a dedicated collector such as myself would only offer you two hundred reales for it, and that only out of respect for your late father."

Coraza raised her chin and narrowed her eyes. "It is just as well, then, that the sword is not for sale."

He locked gazes with her a moment and then chuckled. "Of course, of course. Then again, if the hilt stone has such value as Dr. Raimundo says, you could pry that off and keep that alone for your dowry—"

"No!" Coraza cried.

"Yes, yes," said Don Malaguez, raising his hands in placation. "You have no wish to desecrate his work. But know, señorita, that your father was capable of much better than this. Come, see the superior work your father has done, and try to remember him by these." The Don strode over to the carved armoire, pulled a key on a chain from his pocket, and unlocked it. He flung open the doors to reveal two long swords hanging within. One was a rapier with a gleaming gold-leafed folly of a basket guard and a hilt studded with turquoise and rubies. Gold filigree arabesques ran rampant down the blade. Don Malaguez reverently took it down from its hooks and held it out. "Now this is a sword!"

"Ah, yes, I remember that one," said Filipo. "I believe my master named it 'Pride.'"

"And proud he should have been," said the Don. "This is a masterpiece." He hung up the gold sword and took down the other—an evil-looking broadsword entirely of black iron, with a straight bar guard and silver cabochons in the pommel. "This he called 'Nemesis.'"

"Indeed," said Filipo, apparently with fond memory.

"The edge is so fine and sharp that I, myself, am cut by it if I do not handle it extremely carefully. I always thought this work deserved to contain a powerful spell, but your master wouldn't hear of it. I couldn't convince him. He simply said, 'some swords are dangerous enough by themselves.'"

"As are the men who wield them," said Filipo.

"Yes, yes, he said that too," laughed Don Malaguez. "Ah, too soon he has left us. What a pity. You see, señorita, your father was a master of his craft, sorcerer and sword maker."

"That is pleasing to know, señor. Thank you," said Coraza with a little smile. A thought tugged at her. "Filipo...did you notice...whether there was any magic in that sword?" She pointed at Sorrow lying on the desk.

A strange look came into Filipo's eyes. "Well, um, it can be hard to tell. Salamago's spells could be subtle and sometimes attuned to a particular person or situation—"

"Excellent question, señorita!" said Don Malaguez. "Let us find out what last enchantment, if any, Salamago cast. Maestro, would you do us the honors?"

Dr. Raimundo gave a slight shrug and stepped up to the desk. "You understand, I do not have all the proper instruments with me. But I will find out what I can." He rummaged in his jacket pocket, finally bringing forth a round object in a brass casing, rather like a compass. He placed it on the sword blade and watched it for long seconds. Momentary surprise flickered on Dr. Raimundo's face. A shimmer flowed over the sorcerous umbra on his hands. He picked up the instrument and flicked it lightly with a finger, then placed it back on the blade. After a few seconds, the sorceror cast a quick, wary glance at Coraza. Finally, with a shake of his head, Dr. Raimundo said, "No, I see nothing much. I register a magical field, but it is inconclusive. I fear my calibrator may be malfunctioning."

He is either incompetent, thought Coraza, *or lying. Even I can sense there is magic in the sword.*

Doña Malaguez spoke up in her rich, sprightly voice. "Maestro, why don't you try a laying-on of hands?"

"Señora?" He looked as though she had suggested he thrust his fingers into a bucket of earthworms.

With a tone of wicked enjoyment, she continued, "Surely a scholar of such...sensitivity and discernment as yourself will be able to receive some sort of impression, yes?"

"I am not a brujo, madam."

"Humor the Doña, if you will, Maestro," said Don Maquez.

The sorceror's smile was brittle. "As you wish, señor." He placed long, tapered fingers lightly on the blade and closed his eyes. "I get a sense of failure. Disappointment. Matters have not turned out as they should." He removed his hand quickly. "Perhaps these were the thoughts Salamago had upon viewing his finished piece." Dr. Raimundo stepped back and wiped his hand on his jacket. "Perhaps the rumors were true," he murmured.

"And what rumors might those be?" demanded Coraza.

"Forgive me, señorita, but it has been said that Salamago may have gone mad before his death and dabbled in...forbidden magics."

Everyone else spoke at once:

"How dare you!" Filipo cried.

"Maestro, have you no sense of propriety?" declared Doña Malaquez.

"And where have you heard these rumors?" asked Agente Palabo.

Dr. Raimundo cleared his throat. "Why else would he have vanished with no word to anyone? Perhaps, señorita, the best thing you could do to preserve the honor of your father's name is to keep this sword in a safe place. Hidden. Do not let anyone else see it. Ever."

Coraza covered her mouth, striving to hold back tears of fury. *Hidden like I was,* she thought, a sour taste in her mouth.

"Thank you, Maestro," she said flatly, "for your advice." She was distracted by a sudden commotion beyond the atrium garden. She heard the rumble of a carriage, the nervous neighing of horses, and anxious voices. Her heart nearly stopped in her chest as she recognized one voice in particular.

"Where is she? Where is the girl?"

"Mater, if you please, she is in the Don's officia, if you will permit me to announce you—"

"No, no, there is no time. We must find her at once!"

Coraza glanced around, wondering if she could hide or run, knowing that it was foolish. Within a minute, Mater Urania bustled through the door.

"There she is! There is our lost lamb!" Mater Urania headed straight for Coraza, arms outstretched in dramatized yearning.

"Don't touch me!" Coraza cried as she ducked behind a startled Filipo.

"Mater Urania!" boomed Don Malaguez. "Why, what a timely visit. So this girl is indeed one of your charges?"

"She is," said Mater Urania, with a brief, angry glare at Coraza, "and she must come back at once."

Coraza saw Sister Mercuria and Sister Phoebe enter the office shyly. Sister Phoebe appeared to have a bruise on her right cheek. When Coraza tried to catch her gaze, Sister Phoebe looked away in shame.

I'm so sorry, Coraza thought sadly, *that you suffered for my sake.*

"And is she indeed the daughter of Ercuelo Salamago?" asked Agente Palabo.

Mater Urania whirled around at the sound of his voice. He was holding the little crystal skull in the palm of his hand. For the first time ever, Coraza saw fear flicker across Mater Urania's face. Urania quickly gathered her poise and replied. "If you must know, yes. She is. Though a vigilero surely has greater matters to concern him than a runaway child. We will handle this matter ourselves."

Coraza noted the skull glowed golden at first, then a darker tint flowed through it.

"Ah, so the girl has spoken the truth!" exclaimed Don Malaguez. "Excellent! Mater, why did you never tell me you had Salamago's child in your care? The girl has just now asked me for my guardianship, and you know there would be no greater honor for me than—"

"I'm sorry, Don Malaguez," snapped Mater Urania, "but that is quite impossible. She must come back with us at once."

The Don's affability slid off him like a discarded cloak. He was clearly not used to being denied. "How, impossible? Nothing is impossible, Mater Urania. Is there a troublesome mother in the picture? Surely a few reales would see that there is no question—"

"That is not the concern, Don Malaguez. Now, if you please, it has been a long evening and we must go."

"But why the hurry? What is the concern, señora?" Don Malaguez began to slowly circle Mater Urania. "I have never seen you in such a state. Has someone been telling you lies about my fitness as a guardian?"

"Not at all, Don Malaguez," replied Mater Urania. "Rather, it is the opposite. The girl is entirely unsuitable for your household."

"What?" gasped Doña Malaguez, hand to her ample bosom.

"How, unsuitable?" asked the Don. "If you mean because she was born out of wedlock, well, that is not such an unusual thing for an orphanage waif. That is not the girl's fault, and I would not intend for her to marry one of my nephews or to present her to high society. Perhaps one of my vaqueros may someday find her suitable for a wife. I cannot see how conditions of her birth should be a barrier to my wardship."

With obvious strained patience, Mater Urania said, "It is better that you do not know, señor. I understand you are a man of some...ambition. And there are some things beyond the pale, even for a man of your stature."

Don Malaguez frowned and rubbed his moustache.

Coraza saw Dr. Raimundo's gaze on her intensify. "She's a chimera," the sorceror breathed.

"What?" said Don Malaguez.

Everyone in the room seemed jolted by Dr. Raimundo's statement except Coraza, who was merely baffled. She tugged Filipo's sleeve.

"What's a chimera?" she whispered.

He glanced down at her, then swiftly looked away. "A child that is magically altered in the womb. But it's a lie. Salamago would never do such a thing. Never!"

Coraza looked down and pulled her bodice tighter around her chest. *Is that why I am so sensitive to magic? Is that why I see odd things and act unlike other people? Did my father try to mold me like one of his swords before I was even born? Is that what the holy sisters regard me as...an abomination?* Coraza felt a little sick and wished she could sink into the floor.

"I quite agree with Master Del Utherio," said Don Malaguez. "You may not approve of his work, Maestro, but do not slander Salamago's name."

Coraza felt like everyone seemed to be staring at her, and she wished she had the magic to vanish in a flash, though she had no idea where she would go. She looked across the room at Sister Phoebe, whose silent face was full of despair.

"Is it true, Mater Urania, what Maestro Raimundo says?" asked Agente Palabo.

Mater Urania looked down at the crystal skull in his hand, then up into his face. "What would you have me say, Agente? If I agree, then I have doomed the girl to death. Let her return with us and let there be no more said on this matter."

The crystal skull displayed a glow of dirty yellow. The Mater spoke the truth, as far as it went, but there was much more unknown and unspoken. To Coraza, it was like gazing into a muddy pond on a cloudy day—pale sunlight glinting off it, but the dark depths invisible.

The temperature in the room seemed to drop considerably, and the Don and Doña Malaguez looked at Coraza with wary concern. "I see," said the Don at last. "If such a thing is so..."

"It is not!" insisted Filipo. "The Mater is mistaken."

Mater Urania narrowed her eyes at him but did not speak.

"If it is so," said Dr. Raimundo crossing the room toward Coraza, "then you must consider such guardianship all the more worthwhile, señor. Think! No chimera is known to have survived to near adulthood. There are scholars at the University who would pay you a king's ransom for the chance to study her."

"Study me?" cried Coraza in alarm.

The Don held up a hand. "No, no, if you are right..."

"He is not right!" Filipo insisted.

"Aren't I?" purred Dr. Raimundo. "Is it not inconceivable, young señor, that a man who would imbue his inanimate creations with magic might attempt the same with a living creation of his own flesh and blood?"

"How dare you!" growled Filipo. "My master would never commit such a crime."

"It is such arrogance," said Mater Urania to the sorceror, "that leads to mortal sin and the creation of abominations!"

"And to prison," Agente Palabo interjected. "Perhaps that is why Salamago vanished. He feared that evidence of his crime would soon be revealed."

Seeing her chances slipping away, Coraza ran to stand before Don Malaguez. "Please, señor, do not listen to them. You are a powerful man, above any suspicions. You...you need not care what anyone thinks of you. I swear that I will bring no shame to your household. No one need know—"

But already, the Don was shaking his head. "I regret, señorita, that even a man of my importance must keep his name free of certain kinds of shame. I wish there to be no questions of my honor. It would seem your best chance to stay alive is to return with the Mater. A life within four walls is still a life, is it not? I am sorry, señorita, truly. To know this about your father—it is a blow."

"No. Please." Coraza felt as though a large stone had been dropped in her stomach. To have almost achieved a new life, with hope for a future. Now, the very father who gave her life might have doomed her, if what the Mater said were true. *But the Mater might be lying. I must find a way! A way to live, to find out the truth!*

Mater Urania nodded once. "So that is settled then. Coraza, come with us."

"Not so fast," said Agente Palabo. "If she is truly a chimera, then she is evidence of a crime. I will have to take her into my custody and begin an investigation."

"And have her be destroyed when your investigation is done?" asked Mater Urania. "Or will you sell her to the University or one of those Yanqui traveling shows? Are you so cold of heart, Agente?"

"The girl fears she will die if she returns to the orphanage."

"Nonsense. She was merely traumatized when the tzinn appeared, that is all. Come on, Coraza."

"No!" Her gaze fell on the sword lying on the Don's desk. Crazed with desperation, Coraza lunged across the desk and grabbed the hilt, jamming her hand into the iron basket guard. She felt pain in the web of skin by her thumb but ignored it. Raising the sword named Sorrow, she jumped back into the center of the room. She held the blade straight out, turning this way and that to point it at everyone. "Don't touch me," she gasped. "Nobody touch me! I will cut anyone who comes close! I am not going back to the orphanage!"

Chapter Seven

A long moment passed as Coraza stood, breathing hard, in the center of Don Malaguez's study. She held her father's sword straight out before her, her arm shaking. "Stay back!" she commanded. The sword seemed to hum, and she saw a glimmer of orange light flow over the blade.

Everyone stared at Coraza in shock. Then they all began to speak at once.

"Coraza, be careful!"

"Senorita, I advise you to put the sword down—"

"You see, already her altered nature begins to manifest—"

"Now, now, chica, let us not be rash—"

"Stay calm, senorita, and no one will hurt you—"

The babbling voices pounded on Coraza's mind, distracting her, increasing her fear. She saw the open door onto the atrium, and before anyone could stop her, she turned and ran.

Coraza dashed past the statue of the sword-wielding Madre, past the dolphin fountain, to the iron gate. She pushed it open and shoved it shut behind her. Coraza was surprised that no one had been right on her heels, giving chase. She heard the holy sisters still back in the house, exhorting someone, anyone, to hurry to capture Coraza. Taking no chances, Coraza turned and dashed into the forecourt of the hacienda.

A nearly full moon had risen over the hills to the east, casting a dim light. She remembered that the stables were somewhere to her left. It was awkward to run with her hand still jammed in the iron bell guard and her skirt wrapping around her legs. Coraza stopped to lift its hem in her left hand, then turned to her left and ran for the stables. Coraza thought she heard voices and footfalls behind her, but she dared not slow down to look.

The growing smell of hay, horse sweat, and manure was unmistakable. She could make out a paddock and water troughs. Low whinnies came from a tall building ahead, lamps burning by its huge wood doors. Fortunately, one of the doors had been rolled aside. Horse theft was a serious crime in Alta Califia, but Coraza decided to worry about that later.

She dashed in, blinking in the light from the lanterns that hung on the stall posts, startling a stableboy who had been dozing on bales of hay.

"Ai!" he cried, leaping to his feet and stumbling back.

Coraza swung up the sword and pointed it at his nose. "Get me a horse!" she commanded. "A saddled one. At once!"

"S-sì, señorita!" The boy rushed down the center aisle, stumbling once again in his hurry to get away.

Coraza felt regret at frightening him so, but she was desperate. She glanced once back over her shoulder but saw only darkness outside the barn. "Hurry! Please."

"A-aqui, señorita. Here is a horse that still has bridle and saddle."

Coraza ran down the aisle to where the boy was leading a dark bay out of a stall. It was Agente Palabo's horse.

Now I will be truly an outlaw. Nonetheless, she took the reins from the shaking stable boy's hands. The horse tilted its head to look dubiously down its long nose at her.

She heard voices at the barn doors, Mater Urania saying, "I saw her come in here."

"Mierda," sighed Coraza.

The three holy sisters came running up the center aisle of the stable, red-cheeked and puffing. They stopped as they saw Coraza with sword in one hand and the reins of a large and unsettled horse in the other. "You... hold...right...there," gasped Mater Urania.

The stable boy, knowing an impending battle when he saw one, ran past them and out the barn doors.

"Please, Coraza, we don't want to hurt you," said Sister Phoebe gently.

"I told you. I'm not going back!" Coraza growled. She took two steps backward, Palabo's horse on her left side. Coraza glanced quickly behind her, but there was no other way out of the stables except the way she had come in.

"And where do you think you will go?" asked Mater Urania. "The world thinks of those like you as abominations, Coraza. Once your secret is known, your life is forfeit."

"As the caballero said," added Sister Phoebe, "at least life in our orphanage is a life."

"Better to die free than locked up in a cellar all my days!" said Coraza. Her words sounded braver than she felt. Mere hours before, she had assumed she had no other fate than to live in the orphanage cellar. Now, she could not imagine enduring it. "I am more than that! I want to see more of the world! To do good in the world! Whatever my father gave me, it was for a purpose!"

Mater Urania clicked her tongue. "Prideful, stubborn, willful. You are your father's child. But he gave you to us for your care. You are disobeying his will if you resist us."

Over Mater Urania's right shoulder, Coraza saw Agente Palabo silently striding down the stable aisle toward them. Coraza prayed the vigilero had not decided to take the holy sister's side. If he had, she was finished.

"Please calm down, Coraza," said Sister Phoebe. "It's for the best." She raised her right arm. A blue glow began to appear in her hand.

Coraza swiftly raised the sword again to point at Sister Phobe, though to do what she was not certain. She had no wish to hurt her. "What has the Mater done to you? I thought you were my friend!"

Sister Phoebe's eyes were full of pain and sorrow, but she did not reply.

Meanwhile, Agente Palabo's horse jerked its head away, pulling the reins out of her hands, and danced aside until its flank was pressed against the stall gate. Agente Palabo held up one hand and whistled a quick, complex series of notes that seemed to calm the steed.

Coraza took a step to her right, realizing she had trapped herself.

There was no way out behind her, an anxious horse beside her, and two sorceresses in front of her, intent on her capture.

What can I do?

"Yavash!" cried Sister Phoebe, and the blue light flew from her arm toward Coraza.

With no more thought than if she were swatting a fly with a fan, Coraza struck the flow of energy with the flat of the blade. Deflected, the energy flew into a nearby stall. The horse inside shrieked and bucked as the spell tried to find purchase before the magical energy dissipated like a dissolving blue snake.

Coraza stared at her sword in amazement as the sacerdotas gasped, horrified.

Agente Palabo raised his brows. "It seems there can no longer be any doubt that the sword contains magic."

"It is an evil sword," said Sister Phoebe. "Coraza, for the sake of your soul, you must put it down at once!"

"Why?" demanded Coraza. She felt light-headed with victory. With possibilities. *I can do more! I can be more!* She no longer need bow to the holy sisters' demands. "Because my father's legacy protects me? My father meant this sword for me. Now I am beginning to see why! What can be evil in that?"

"Perhaps we should listen to her, Mater," sighed Sister Phoebe. "Perhaps there may be another way."

"Nonsense," said Mater Urania, and she summoned up from her chest a pulsing red light. "Siyasat!" she cried as the energy was flung toward Coraza.

Coraza swung the sword up, batting the scarlet mass of energy toward the barn roof. Piercing cries of pain came from the rafters, and two pigeons and a bat dropped down to flop helplessly upon the stable floor. Coraza winced, wishing she hadn't harmed them.

"You see what damage untrained magic can do," grumbled Mater Urania. "Let us have an end to this foolishness." She brought forth a glow of dark purple from within her chest and aimed her arm at Coraza. "Ranj—"

This will be bad, thought Coraza.

"—sahab!"

But I don't want to hurt the horses or birds or anyone. Time appeared to slow as the cloud of dark energy flowed toward her. Coraza aimed the sword point right at its center and winced with dread. The sword gently vibrated, almost humming, as the purple energy flowed up the blade. But it did not reach Coraza's hand. The energy was absorbed into the sword, shimmering and changing to a lavender light that coruscated over the blade as if it were made of glowing mother of pearl. A different sort of energy flowed up Coraza's right arm, into her chest, jangling her nerves, making her more alert and alive. It was even more intense than the time she had stolen and eaten a handful of coffee beans she had found in the orphanage kitchen.

The holy sisters looked pale. "The sword can absorb and transform magic," breathed Mater Urania. "Agente, you must do something. The sword clearly contains Sere Sorcery."

"And what would you have me do?" asked the vigilero calmly. "I see the senorita is defending herself from sorcerous attack. She is not doing any violence upon you."

"Are you mad?" cried Mater Urania. "The girl is a monster with a sword more powerful than she has any right to own. You must stop her! She has no right—"

"She is no longer your charge, Mater," said Agente Palabo mildly but firmly. "I told you, she must now be taken into my custody as evidence, and victim, of a crime. The sword is evidence as well. I suggest you all calm yourselves and return to your orphanage and leave this matter to the Protectorado."

"You have no idea what you are involving yourself with, Agente," warned Mater Urania.

"Really?" asked the Agente with a sardonic smile. "Why don't you tell me? We can do the formal questioning here and now, if you wish."

The Mater glared at him, her face filled with barely controlled fury. "You will regret this, Agente. I have nothing more to say to you. Come," she said to Sister Phoebe. With a wary glance at Coraza, Mater Urania turned and strode back down the stable aisle.

Sister Phoebe gazed sadly on Coraza. "I am sorry. I was…She told me…But take no mind of me. The Madre will guide us both. I hope you will find safety and happiness. I will remember you always and pray for you every day. Take good care of her, Agente," she said softly to Palabo. She gave Coraza one last quick smile and hurried off after Mater Urania.

Coraza wiped tears on her sleeve. She wished she could call Sister Phoebe back, to have at least one friend by her side. There were a thousand things Coraza wished she could have said to Sister Phoebe, but they caught in her throat. To tell her how much her kindness had meant. How it had kept her alive and hopeful. To take care. To leave Mater Urania and find her own life. To help others the way she had helped Coraza.

She was the only one in my life who ever cared about me, and now I will likely never see her again.

Filipo, pushed aside as Mater Unrania marched out like an indignant quail, entered the barn doors just as the holy sisters were leaving.

"That," said Agente Palabo turning to watch them go, "was very interesting."

"Thank you, Agente," Coraza breathed, lowering her sword. "I will pray to the Madre one hundred times each night to bless you."

Palabo shook his head and held up one hand. "Do not thank me yet. I could not help but notice that you were trying to steal my horse."

"I'm sorry," Coraza sighed. "It was the one the stable boy led out for me, the only one still saddled."

"It is just as well you did not try to get far with it. My horse is trained to resist being stolen." He whistled again, a set of sharp chirps. The horse flicked its ears forward, stepped smartly to the right, and swung its rump hard against Coraza's left shoulder.

"Ai!" Coraza fell aside, her hands flung out to break her fall. Her sword flew from her grip to drop into a pile of musty hay.

Agente Palabo gracefully stooped as if bowing at a society dance and caught her elbow with one hand. He said, "Forgive me, señorita. I hope you are not unduly injured."

Bruised and embarrassed, Coraza awkwardly allowed him to help her to her feet. "Only my pride," she sighed softly.

Filipo rushed up the aisle to them and gently grasped Coraza's other arm. He was carrying the leather bag that had sheathed the sword. "Coraza, are you all right? Was that necessary, Agente?"

"Would you have preferred that I disarm her by more violent means?"

"Well, no, of course not."

Coraza felt sad to be mistrusted. "I would not have hurt you, Agente."

"Perhaps not, but I have stayed alive as long as I have by learning caution."

Coraza nodded. "I understand. May I...have the sword back?" She found herself wishing to grip the pommel again, to feel the weight of the blade challenging the muscles of her arm. She felt weaker without it.

"In time, perhaps." He drew a dagger from beneath his black and red serape and slipped the blade into the ironwork of the basket guard of the sword Sorrow. As if it were a contaminated thing, the Agente lifted the sword with the dagger blade and held out his other hand for the sheath. Filipo handed the leather bag to the vigilero, who deftly maneuvered the sword into the leather bag and closed it without ever touching the sword itself.

"I will gladly carry it for her." Filipo held out his hand to take back the leather sheath. The Agente glanced askance at him. Clearly, he did not entirely trust the former apprentice. After a moment's pause, the vigilero finally gave the sword to Filipo. "I shall want to look at it again," he said.

"Of course, Agente," said Filipo as he slipped the strap of the sword sheath over his shoulder and across his chest. Coraza watched the sword change hands with desperate longing. She scarcely noticed that she had reached out her own arm as if to take the sword back from Filipo.

"Your hand, señorita. It is hurt," said the vigilero.

Coraza looked at the blood trickling down her wrist from a small, circular wound in the web between thumb and forefinger. Strangely, there was very little pain. "Yes, one of the iron thorns in the guard cut me." She instinctively put her hand to her mouth and sucked on it.

Filipo frowned. "How strange. Salamago was never sloppy about the grip or guard. He always crafted them for the best comfort and control."

"Perhaps he had other motives this time," said Agente Palabo, taking Coraza's hand in his and looking at the wound. With his other hand, he swept the flat-brimmed hat from his head and removed the black bandana he wore underneath. He wrapped the bandana around Coraza's hand and pressed down on the wound. With that peculiar intensity Coraza had heard used to utter Words of Power, he murmured, "Bastoosh." Warmth flowed from his hands into hers, the energy barely visible.

Coraza hissed, sucking air through her teeth, as she felt the skin painfully draw together and close.

He swiftly removed the bandana and tucked it into his belt beneath his serape. The wound on Coraza's hand was now nothing more than a pale, circular scar. "Do you think I will be safe from the sacerdotas now, Agente?"

"Hard to say, señorita. They have close association with the Protectadoras and could cause us trouble."

"But I heard that the Protectadoras' powers are fading because they are so old."

Agente Palabo placed a hand on her shoulder. "Never assume that age equals weakness, señorita. As the saying goes, 'an old house may stand while a new house may fall.' The Protectadoras are still mightier than can be imagined. Thank the Madre."

Coraza nodded. "I...I would like to meet a Protectorada someday."

Palabo barked an odd laugh. "Well, it is said the Madre performs miracles, does She not?"

"How does one become a Protectadora? Could someone like me, with magic power...?"

Palabo tilted his head and looked down on her with a speculative gaze. "Well, when you meet one, perhaps you can ask her."

Filipo turned his head toward the barn doors, and Coraza followed his gaze. Dr. Raimundo stood at the far end of the aisle, watching them intently. "I think we'd better go," said Filipo.

"Yes," said Agente Palabo. "I am sure we have outstayed our welcome." He grasped the reins of his horse and mounted into the saddle. He held out his arm to Coraza. "Señorita, if you would do me the kindness of riding with me."

Coraza took his hand and allowed him to help her onto the back of his saddle. His black wool serape smelled of sage and sweat, tobacco and dust.

Filipo found his horse, Tulio, still bridled, in one of the stalls and swiftly saddled it. When they rode out of the stable doors, Dr. Raimundo was sitting on his black horse, waiting for them.

"I suggest you take up one of the lanterns, young señor," Raimundo said to Filipo. "I expect the way will be dark."

As Filipo grasped one of the lanterns hanging by the barn door, Agente Palabo said, "I am sure we can find our way to the gate, Maestro."

"Nonetheless," said Dr. Raimundo, "Don Malaguez has ordered me to escort you to the hacienda boundary to ensure that you leave."

"Why should we want to stay?" asked Palabo.

"It was my impression," Raimundo responded dryly, "that you might have had insufficient private...conversation with the Doña, Agente."

Coraza felt the vigilero's back stiffen, felt power gather at a spot just below his waist, and from the ripple of his shoulder muscle sensed that his right hand was moving beneath his serape toward his sword hilt. "It would be unwise in the extreme," said Agente Palabo, "to impute any dishonor to the Doña Malaguez."

They cannot be thinking to duel here and now, can they? wondered Coraza. She had heard it said at the orphanage that some men held honor so dear, or enjoyed the fighting arts so much, they would duel on any provocation.

"Please, señores," Coraza asked, "can't we just go?"

The vigilero sighed heavily. "The young señorita wisely reminds me of my duty. Perhaps we may discuss our differences another time, Maestro."

Dr. Raimundo glanced from Palabo to Coraza. She thought she read frustration and annoyance in his face. "Very well. Another time," growled the sorceror. "Vamonos."

They rode out on the road to the gate in tense silence. Coraza watched for signs of the gathering of sorcerous power in both Dr. Raimundo and Agente Palabo. Even Filipo's hands and arms dimly flickered, as if he felt he should be prepared for action. When they were well out of earshot of the hacienda's casa grande, Dr. Raimundo finally spoke again.

"You know, you have always struck me, Marzo, as a sentimental fool."

"So pleased to have your approval, Maestro," growled Agente Palabo.

"I tell you this because it is the only reason I am allowing you to leave with this immeasurable treasure in your care."

"The señorita?"

"Just so." Turning to Coraza, Dr. Raimundo added, "Senorita Salamago, please know that if it were in my power to offer you safe haven without the knowledge of my employer, I would do so. It is the unfortunate case that, before long, too many eyes may be focused on Don Malaguez and his qualities, and he must exercise caution."

Filipo snorted and said dryly, "Is it not too late for that, Maestro?"

In the dim lantern light, Raimundo narrowed his eyes. "I remember your departed master's opinion of Don Malaguez. Whatever my employer's shortcomings may seem to be, he may yet be the only man who can save Alta Califia."

"Then may the Madre save us all," murmured Agente Palabo.

"Alta Califia is truly in danger?" asked Coraza, remembering her dreams and the talk of impending war.

"More than you may wish to know, señorita," said Dr. Raimundo.

"Do you know something we don't?" asked Filipo. "It might be important for all of us to know."

"I don't wish to frighten the senorita, so I will only say that it is rumored Molochistas have been active in the north of Mexico, stoking the resentments of those who lost the Great Revolt. Training them in their dark arts. Even instruments as simple as mine hint that they are building a great work down there."

"You have told the Presidio of this, I expect?" said Palabo.

"Heh. I am sure those august brujas know far more than I. I can only hope they are up to the task ahead. As for you, Master Del Utherio, you might consider joining a ship's crew and sailing before all this comes about."

"Do you imply that I might be a coward?" snapped Filipo.

"I said no such thing," droned Dr. Raimundo. "I speak only from respect and concern for your young life."

The ride continued in silence until at last they were back at the iron gateway, its black filigree blocking out the bright stars. Coraza shuddered as she remembered the discomfort she had felt crossing beneath it earlier that evening.

Again, Dr. Raimudo took his ebony wand and lowered the ward with a spray of umber light. "Here I must bid you adios," said Dr. Raimundo, "but I wish to say this: If I hear that the señorita has been mishandled by your bungling compañeros in the Protectorado, or by those withered witches of the Governadora, I will come looking for you, Marzo. And, señorita, should you ever have need of assistance, I have a townhouse on the plaza in Los Mesanjeros, across from the tavern called Oso D'Oro. Do you know where that is?"

Coraza nodded uncertainly. "I have been to the plaza once or twice." The holy sisters had taken the orphans there now and then, regaling them with tales of how the gutters ran red with blood during the Great Revolt.

"Go there, or send word to my manservant in residence, and I will do all I can to help you. Promise me you will remember this."

"Yes, of course," said Coraza, unable to conceive of any circumstance in which she would want the sorcerer's aid. "Wait! I remember that last time my father's sword protected me, a little bit, when I wore it. Filipo, may I please use the sword again?" Agente Palabo and Filipo shared a momentary look.

"I won't even take it out of its covering," Coraza went on. "I'll just hold it in front of me. All right? Please?"

Then Filipo smirked at Dr. Raimundo. "Of course, señorita. Good to know that some do not consider my master's work to be a useless 'trinket.'"

He took the sword bag off of the hook on his saddle, urged his horse forward, and handed the bag to Coraza. She smiled as she gathered it into her arms.

Agente Palabo glanced, worried, over his shoulder at her. Even Dr. Raimundo seemed warily alarmed.

"I won't hurt anyone with it, I swear," Coraza said.

"It is not what the sword may do to me, but what it may do to you, that I fear," Palabo said.

"I regret to admit the Agente may be correct," said Dr. Raimundo. "Something is not right with that piece. If only I could submit it to my better instruments at my townhouse, we could learn so much more…Well, that is for you to decide, if you choose, someday."

"I will be careful," said Coraza. "Here, I will get off the horse and walk across so that I won't fall. And I will only hold the tip of the pommel so that the thorns on the guard won't hurt me." She slid out of the saddle and slipped her hands inside the top of the leather bag, grasping the animite rosette at the top of the pommel. She held the sword straight up in front of her, just ahead of her nose. Chin up and resolute, Coraza marched into the darkness under the gate. That time, she could see a curtain of white sparks rise up and flow over her, but parting like water where they struck the sword. Coraza hissed as her upper arms, hips, and legs prickled fiercely as she walked through. Once on the other side, the discomfort ceased.

Itchy tears leaking from the corners of her eyes, Coraza lowered the sword. "There, you see señores, I…was…protect—"

Her strength drained out of her like water, and darkness swallowed her before she finished speaking.

Chapter Eight

Coraza awoke to the smell of hay, horse sweat, and dust. Doves burbled and rustled overhead. She blearily opened one eye, then two. Bright sunlight knifed in through gaps in the wood walls and roof. Coraza sat up, her muscles aching. She had been lying on bales of hay covered with a blanket. Below her, a horse whinnied softly and whuffed as it stamped a hoof.

I'm in a stable loft, she thought. *Did they take me back to the hacienda? Surely they didn't return me to the orphanage?* Coraza heard murmurs, and she peered through a gap between the flimsy wall slats beside her. Agente Palabo and Filipo stood in a stable stall below, talking softly. The vigilero handed a small cloth-covered bundle to Filipo, then led his saddled bay horse out of the barn. Filipo sat down on a wooden stool as he watched the Agente leave. The far wall of the barn only went halfway to the roof. Beyond it, Coraza heard a wagon rumble by and women walking past chatting and gossiping.

Coraza sighed and got up, still disoriented. *Neither hacienda nor orphanage,* she thought, grasping a support post. *For the moment, I seem to be safe*. She took a deep breath to steel herself for whatever the day might bring, knowing that at least it would not bring Mater Urania's punishment spells or long hours weaving talismans. She felt strange, tired yet strong, as if her passage through Dr. Raimundo's warding had toughened her the way a sword is tempered in fire.

Coraza stood straighter and stepped forward. Her blouse sagged open, revealing her undervest, damaged hopelessly from Filipo's sword cut the day before. *Ai, me, what will I do about this?* She saw some folded cloth by the wooden gate that served as a door to the loft. Hopeful that someone had anticipated her problem, Coraza picked up the clothes. They were, indeed, a skirt and blouse, but made of a rough cloth dyed a dark indigo, the sorts of clothes a native working in the missions might wear.

Coraza sighed, spirits falling. She'd hoped that acceptance by Don Malaguez would make her feel like a person of worth in society. Now that dream seemed gone forever. *I could run, but a young girl on her own faces so much danger in this world. So said the holy sisters, anyway. How can I learn about my father, my mother, about the Protectadoras, on my own? I suppose I must wait and look out for my chances.*

With a sigh, Coraza changed her clothes, clucking over how the blouse and skirt were a bit too large and the leather slippers too worn. She turned to pick up the sword sheath to slip it over her back. But there was no sword on the hay bale.

Frantic, Coraza looked between the bale and the wall, beside it and all around the tiny loft room. The only furniture was a small table that held a tin bowl, a man's straight razor, and a boot polishing cloth. But the leather bag containing the sword Sorrow was nowhere to be seen.

Coraza flung open the gate and hurried down the ladder to the stable floor.

Filipo stood. "Ah, you are awake, señorita."

"My sword, Filipo, it is gone! Have you seen it?"

"Good morning to you too," said Filipo with a wry smile. "It is safe."

A stab of fear struck Coraza's heart, and she curled her fists. "Filipo, where is it?"

He furrowed his brow. "Don't be so suspicious, Coraza. It is not damaged or sold."

"It is all I have, Filipo!" Coraza insisted. "It is unkind of you to keep it from me."

"It would be more unkind to give it back to you."

"Filipo, it protects me!"

"At the expense of your strength, it would seem, Coraza."

Coraza paused, noting the utter seriousness on his face. "What happened last night, Filipo? After I passed through the gate."

"When you fell, the Agente took the sword from you at once. Dr. Raimundo examined you and determined that you were drained but would recover. I suspect that bastard knows things he is not telling. Dr. Raimundo and the Agente argued. Raimundo wanted you to stay on the hacienda, claiming he would find a way to hide you safely. The Agente, of course, does not trust him and insisted on taking you away. They nearly came to blows then and there."

"Madre be praised they did not," said Coraza. "But why did I faint?"

"Dr. Raimundo claimed the sword must have needed great energy to withstand his oh-so-excellent warding sorcery, and that the sword took that energy from you."

Coraza tried to remember, but it had happened so fast. "What does the Agente think?"

"He said the sword was not protecting you, but itself. Agente Palabo said you must not handle Sorrow unsheathed again. He fears it could be very dangerous."

"I see," said Coraza, fear and confusion welling up inside. "Why would my father bequeath to me a sword I cannot hold?"

Filipo shrugged. "I cannot say. Not every Salamago creation was perfect. And he must have been working at an unfamiliar forge. Perhaps he only meant for you to sell it."

"Or, perhaps, if he changed me, made me…a chimera, he thought I would be able to handle it."

Filipo looked around quickly and then grasped her shoulders, gazing at her with solemn intensity. Coraza again wondered what he was searching for in her face. Softly he said, "Coraza, you must never say that word again. No one must think that of you."

"But why?"

Filipo leaned close and whispered, "Did you not hear Mater Urania last night? Chimeras are not permitted to live. One way or another, at birth or when their difference is discovered, the Church, or those of strong faith, kill them."

"Then why am I still alive?" Coraza whispered back.

Filipo shook his head. "I do not know. I am not a very religious person but...perhaps the Madre watches over you."

Coraza thought about Sister Phoebe...something she had said after the attack. "My father was paying them, the holy sisters, for my care. Maybe they wanted to keep me alive...for the money." She felt a little sick at the thought.

"That is very cynical of you, Coraza. But, from what I have seen in this world, I cannot say you are wrong."

Coraza looked down at the scattered hay on the brick stable floor and sighed. The world she had flung herself into was so confusing. She was, however, certain everyone was wrong about the sword Sorrow. Coraza did not feel damaged. Other than a slight soreness in her right hand where the iron thorn had stabbed it, she felt as though banked fires now warmed her blood and that, when needed, she would blaze with vitality.

Perhaps the fault is mine, and I simply do not know enough. But I can learn how to wield the sword. Someday, I will learn. Perhaps someday, the sword will tell me why it was meant for me.

Coraza lifted her eyes and fixed her determined gaze on Filipo. "So. What happens now?"

"I was hoping we could situate you properly in the household of an older woman, but the Agente says we do not dare. You must stay with him to ensure your safety and to not endanger others. But a girl traveling with two men unrelated to her...well. I regret to say, señorita, that people may think the worst of you. I am so sorry. You deserve better than this."

Coraza sighed. She was no stranger to cruel gossip. It had been the primary entertainment of the orphan girls. "Deserve better? That is the most useless thing I have ever heard," she said. "What does it matter? I am here now, and this is my life now. I must do the best I can, yes?" In truth, she was glad she would be able to go with Filipo and the Agente on their investigations.

Filipo nodded. "That is admirable, Coraza. You have your father's courage."

Coraza wanted to shout at him, *No! It is my courage. Mine. I am not just an echo of my father, your lost master! Stop looking for him in me!* Coraza turned away and paced to another corner of the barn. She found herself wishing that Filipo looked upon her a different way. *Madre mia, am I becoming fond of him?*

She called back over her shoulder, "It is good you have decided to work with the Agente, despite what you think of vigileros."

Filipo shrugged. "What choice do I have? You have seen how powerful he is. Oh, here, he brought you something." He picked up from a nearby hay bale the cloth-wrapped bundle she had seen Agente Palabo give him and handed it to Coraza. She unfolded the gingham bandanna.

"Some bread," she murmured, "and an orange! How generous of him! Just like Navidad morning!" Her stomach growled to remind her she hadn't eaten since yesterday. Coraza sat on a hay bale and dug her nails into the orange rind, not minding when the juice spurted out and dribbled over her hands. "Mmm," she said, inhaling the tangy sweet scent. "I shall not wash my hands for days." She teased out an orange section and popped it into her mouth, savoring it. Oranges had been a once-a-year treat at the orphanage.

"It is my experience with oranges," said Filipo, "that even if one washes, the scent stays with you for days." In a quieter tone, he went on, "We should be cautious of the vigilero, Coraza. We do not know his intentions. He may be treating us well so that we might trust him more than we should."

"Why are you still so suspicious?" asked Coraza around a mouthful of bread. "Did he not risk his life to go with me to the hacienda? Has he not safely brought us to this place...wherever we are? Where are we, by the way?"

"In Las Escarpas, just off El Camino Real, a few miles north of the orphanage. I've been staying in that loft you were in for the past couple of months. And for your information, I guided us safely here. The Agente was still fuming too much about Dr. Raimundo to think straight."

Coraza noticed Agente Palabo leaning casually against a support post just inside the stable door. From the wry smile she saw beneath the brim of his hat, he seemed amused. Coraza decided to mention his presence before Filipo said something even more stupid. "And there he is! Thank you for the orange, Agente!"

Filipo turned suddenly, blinking at the vigilero. "Aha. Sneaking up on us again, were you? I should think such tricks were no longer necessary, since we've chosen to cooperate."

The Agente ambled toward them. "I was merely enjoying the sight of the señorita being awake and well, señor, and did not wish to interrupt. I see the clothes I found fit you, more or less."

"Yes, thank you," said Coraza, looking down at the dowdy blouse and skirt. "They, well, they do what they must."

"I'm afraid it is beyond a vigilero's pay to purchase finery for a lady, and even if I could, it would raise uncomfortable questions. Señor Del Utherio, I have news."

"News for me? What is it?"

"I have found someone, a trader passing through, who knew you and your late master. A Gabrielito native named Juan Sanchez."

Filipo rubbed his chin. "Sanchez. The name is vaguely familiar, but I cannot place it."

"Come see him. He seemed eager to talk to you. He may have information concerning Salamago. You come too, señorita. This stable sees too many travelers for me to leave you here alone."

Coraza nodded and wiped her hands on her skirt. She smoothed back her hair, certain that she must look a mess, then her hands went to her chest to adjust the strap of the sword sheath...that she remembered was not there. "Agente," she asked, "where is my sword?"

"It is safe, señorita."

Coraza sighed in exasperation.

Filipo raised his brows as if to say, "Told you so."

A grizzled, mustachioed man strolled into the stable and ambled over to the Agente with expectation on his face. The Agente paid the stablemaster and told him, "We have one more errand to run, then we will be back for our horses."

Coraza noticed the vigilero's bay horse was saddled and bridled and a familiar bit of butter-colored leather peeked out from the blanket roll behind the saddle. She felt a weight lift from her heart. In time, she decided, she would, one way or another, get her sword back.

Coraza followed the two men out of the stable into the bright morning sunlight. There were quite a few people on the broad dirt track of El Camino Real. A Russian rider in a fur hat went by. A Yanqui man with a tall hat atop a shock of blond hair rode past with a long rifle hanging from a holster on his saddle. A couple of soldiers from the Presidio, in their distinctive leather vests and broad-brimmed hats, sat at a table, calling out to men who passed by to join and bring glory to Espania and the king. Everywhere, there were horse or donkey carts bearing furs, bolts of cloth, fresh cut lumber, coal. The varied smells were amazing. Coraza watched people of every age striding up and down the dusty road, bearing baskets, leading children, moving forward in lives that were known and purposeful. Coraza found herself deeply envious of them.

Poor women with baskets on their backs glanced sidelong at Coraza as if trying to determine her heritage and where she fit on the social ladder. Coraza kept her head down and was relieved that, due to her clothing, she was mostly ignored.

Las Escarpas was a little town of fishermen's shacks, hunter's cabins, a couple of inns for thirsty travelers, and a small open-air market just off the road. The Agente led them to the marketplace, past tables laden with salted fish, beef jerky, beaver and coyote pelts, and leather goods. A scrawny tinker at one booth sharpened knives. An old indio woman sat behind a table of woven wool serapes and blankets. Palabo headed directly to one table holding buckets of onions, squash, and melons. Coraza saw that it must have been where the Agente had gotten the orange, for there was a small crate of them as well.

A wizened little native man at the table stood at their approach and took off his straw hat. His short-cropped hair was entirely white. He bowed a little and said, "Welcome back, Agente! Ah, Señor Del Utherio!" His eyes lit up as he saw Filipo, and he smiled a gap-toothed smile. "How good to see you again."

"Señor Sanchez, now I remember you," said Filipo. "You used to work for Don Pico."

"I still have that honor, señor. As you see, he now lets me travel to sell some of the fruits of his fine fields. Although much is being preserved and sent to the soldiers at the Presidio. There is talk of war, you know."

"So I have heard. And is Don Pico still pleased with the swords we made him?"

"He is, señor, although, alas, he had to sell the one, Endeavor, to pay for his daughter's wedding."

"I am sure my late master would not have objected," said Filipo.

"Don Pico treats you well, I trust?" asked Agente Palabo.

A wary look came into the old man's eyes. "Yes, of course. Life is much better at the hacienda than it was at the mission where I was raised."

Coraza thought that was saying little, given the stories she'd heard of the treatment of natives at the Mariano missions. Their enslavement had been one of the causes of the Great Revolt.

"But Señor Utherio," the old man went on, seeming eager to change the subject, "I see time has treated you well. You no longer a boy, but a young man. And you have become prosperous, with servants of your own." He glanced briefly at Coraza.

Coraza blinked but said nothing.

"Uh, no!" said Filipo, startled. "No, she is not my servant. She is… um…she is…" Filipo looked at her, but apparently, his wits deserted him.

After a few long, awkward moments, Agente Palabo leaned over and whispered something in the old man's ear.

"Ahhh," said Sanchez, with a trace of a smile. "I understand, Señor del Utherio. As they say among my people, a hard working woman is better than the daughter of a chief."

"Um…"

"But a bit of advice, señor. As soon as you can, you should buy your pretty new bride some better clothes. Show her some respect."

"Er, yes. Of course. I will," mumbled Filipo as he glared at Agente Palabo.

Sanchez turned to Coraza and said, "Congratulations, señora. You have made a fine catch."

"Um, thank you," said Coraza, deciding that saying as little as possible would be wisest.

"Here," he handed Coraza two oranges. "Please take these as a wedding gift."

"Oh, no, I couldn't possibly," Coraza protested. It seemed improper to accept presents for a lie.

"I insist."

"We...may need the food, Coraza," said Filipo. "It's all right. Take them."

"Very well. Thank you." She gathered the oranges into her arms, feeling wealthy and guilty at the same time.

"Señor Del Utherio," said the old man, "I still carry the knife your generous master Salamago gave to me." The old man took from his pocket a leather pouch. From inside it he brought out a short knife with a deer antler handle that he held like a religious relic.

"I am glad to see it," said Filipo. "Now, speaking of my late master, the good Agente tells me you may have some news."

"Well, señor," the old man leaned forward and spoke quietly as if afraid to be overheard. "In my travels, I have spoken to those who still live in my family village. They say they have seen the great Salamago riding in the foothills of the mountains to the northeast."

"How long ago was this?" asked Filipo

"The last time was weeks ago. I cannot say for certain. But they said they have seen him several times over the years near Cañon de Los Espiritus, the Canyon of Ghosts."

"I have not heard of this place," said Filipo.

"Nor should you have, señor. My people do not go there, save for the young and foolish. The canyon has caves that are said to be haunted. They say if you stay too long, it will capture your soul. The one who told me he last saw Salamago claimed that one day your master went in, but he never came out again."

"Forgive me, but this haunted canyon could be merely folk tale," said Filipo, glancing at Agente Palabo. "And there are many ways a man might leave an area unseen."

Palabo looked away, sighing and wiping a hand across his mouth.

The old man stood straighter, and Coraza saw his bearing become more distant, as though a door closed across his eyes. "My people do not tell tales, señor."

"Oh, no, no, forgive me. I meant no offense," said Filipo, but the old man remained silent, unmollified.

Coraza stepped forward. "I thank you for your words, Señor Sanchez. Please, forgive Filipo. He has been hoping so long for information about... his missing master, that he does not know what to believe. But I believe you."

The old man brightened and smiled at her. "Thank you, señora. You are fortunate, señor, to have found yourself so gracious and humble a bride."

"But please tell me," Coraza went on, emboldened, "this Cañon of Ghosts sounds like an evil place, and yet you say Salamago went there often?"

"So it is, and so he did, over many years, and for that, my people thought him very brave or"—he glanced sidelong at Filipo—"not right in the head."

A muscle twitched in Filipo's jaw. "Many years, you say?"

"Yes, although not as often as he used to. Not as often as when he was bringing that woman there."

Filipo's brows shot up. "A woman? When was this?"

"A long time ago, señor. Ten, fifteen years, perhaps."

A strange feeling circled in Coraza's gut. "Do your people know who this woman was?"

The old man shook his head. "She was apparently always in beautiful lace veils. Some say she must be a high-born lady, but..."—he glanced significantly at Filipo—"that may just be a folk tale. But now that I have told you my story, tell me señora, which household were you working in when this bold young man stole you away for his own?"

It was Coraza's turn to stammer. "Um, uh…"

"Forgive me, Senor Sañchez," said Filipo loudly, "but I'm afraid we really must be going." He put an arm around Coraza's shoulders, more for control than affection. "Mustn't we, querida?"

"Oh, yes, you are quite right. Caro mio," Coraza responded, glancing warily at his hand on her shoulder.

"I understand," said the old man, putting a finger beside his nose. "The master does not know you have taken her away. Or perhaps her father does not know or approve either?"

"Good day to you, Señor Sanchez," said Coraza firmly. "And thank you. May the Madre keep you well."

The old man bowed and smiled in return. "Good luck to you both. May you have many good years together and many healthy children."

"Before we go," said Agente Palabo, "allow me to purchase one of these small sacks of excellent beans for our travels." He picked up a two-pound sack off the table and handed the old man a handful of reales. He turned and, with a sweep of his arm, guided Filipo and Coraza away from Señor Sanchez' table.

"Wait, Agente!" called the old man from behind them. "You have forgotten your change."

"No, Señor Sanchez," said the vigilero over his shoulder. "I have not."

When they had left the market and were back on the dusty road, Filipo pointedly removed his arm from Coraza's shoulders.

"Just what did you tell the old indio about us, Agente?"

"Just that Coraza was another man's servant you eloped with. Since you would not accept the ruse that she was your own menial, what other story could I tell that would not shame her?"

"I will not have my master's daughter taken for a servant, Agente. Perhaps next time you'll allow me the chance to invent my own story."

The Agente murmured, "Your own folk tale, you mean?"

"I did not intend to offend Señor Sanchez," Filipo said with a frown. "I just…I knew Salamago sometimes left on trips to get supplies, but he never told me—"

"We already know there was much he did not tell you," said Palabo, glancing at Coraza.

"Didn't he trust me?"

"Perhaps he wanted to protect you."

"Protect me from what? I am not a child!"

"You were when he took you as an apprentice. And you may find that you regret learning what he protected you from."

Filipo paused. "Is there something else you know?"

"Tell me, señor, what do you think Dr. Raimundo might have been looking for in Salamago's forge in the dark of night?"

After a long moment of silent walking, Filipo replied, "Tools left behind, perhaps. Or materials. Things a sorcerer might find useful."

"Might there have been such things?"

Filipo shook his head. "Salamago took everything that would interest someone like Dr. Raimundo."

"You seem certain about that."

After an awkward pause, Filipo said, "Well, I searched the place completely after Salamago left. *I* couldn't find anything."

"Do you know why Salamago began refusing to renew his manufactory licenses with the Protectorado?"

"Because he hated the meddling of the authorities in his work?" replied Filipo, a bit heatedly.

"Or was it because such renewal requires a thorough inspection of the premises?" suggested Palabo.

Filipo stopped dead in the street. "You think he was hiding forbidden materials. Something he may have found in this Canyon of Ghosts. Materials for practicing Sere sorcery."

"There, now. You have some imagination after all."

"I expect, Agente, that it is your imagination that has run away with you. Salamago was an honorable man." Filipo scowled and walked faster, away from them, toward the stables.

The vigilero shook his head as he took Coraza's arm and escorted her across the dusty Camino to the wooden sidewalk. "I fear this journey will be difficult for him. As for you, señorita, how are you bearing up?"

"I am fine, Agente. Merely a little tired. Truly, the sword did me no harm."

He gave her a thoughtful glance. "I think I know this Canyon of Ghosts, but it is a long ways away. Many days' ride. Do you feel capable of the trip?"

"Yes, of course," said Coraza quickly. In truth, she had no idea, but what choice did she have? "I want to discover what happened to my father, and...I am wondering..."

"If the veiled woman seen with Salamago might have been your mother?" the vigilero finished for her.

"Well, yes. What do you think?"

"We have no way of knowing that yet, señorita. And given that the woman was veiled, it may not always have been the same woman."

"Oh," sighed Coraza sadly. "Yes, I suppose you're right."

"Although, why Salamago should have to travel so far for his dalliances is a puzzle," Palabo added.

When they finally reached the stable once more, Filipo was finishing the cinch on the blanket roll behind his horse's saddle, perhaps more roughly than he ordinarily might. Agente Palabo retrieved his saddled bay, and Coraza noticed the stable master giving her an odd look. Coraza went up to Filipo and said loudly, "I forgive you for our little spat, husband. Now shall I ride before or behind you?"

"Very funny. Stop it," grumbled Filipo. "Ride with him for all I care."

"Young marrieds," the Agente said knowingly to the stable master. "It is so charming when they fight, no?"

Filipo raised his head to glare at Palabo. He opened his mouth, paused, shut it. Then he turned to Coraza. "Well, mi esposa, clearly you must ride behind me, like a proper little wife, yes? And next time, you will not burn the beans, and you will mend my stockings the right way so they do not come unraveled, yes?"

Coraza felt heat coming into her cheeks. But she managed a tight smile. "Yes, so long as you do not fling your discarded clothes on the floor all the time, making them harder to clean, mi esposo."

"Very well. And don't pinch my waist while we're riding. You know how I hate that." Filipo put his foot in the stirrup and swung himself onto the horse, reaching down to haul Coraza up behind him.

The stable master chuckled and walked away.

Chapter Nine

As they rode the dusty El Camino Real north out of Las Escarpas, Coraza said, "I am sorry, Filipo. I did not mean to annoy you so."

Over his shoulder, Filipo growled softly, "And I meant no disrespect, señorita. But you see why we must be wary of the Agente. Who knows what he will have us doing next? He acts as though he has no respect for your father, thinking only the worst of him."

Perhaps the Agente has reason to, thought Coraza. But she did not speak it aloud, deciding it would be better to let Filipo cool down. *Are all young men such hot heads?* she wondered. *No wonder the holy sisters constantly filled our ears with warnings.*

Around a bend, out of sight of the town, Agente Palabo abruptly turned his horse to the right. He rode between two live oak trees onto a narrow dirt track that led up a dry arroyo strewn with sandstone boulders.

"What now?" muttered Filipo. "Agente!" he called out. "Where are we going?"

"This is a faster route over the mountains to Valle Fernando, and less traveled. It may be safer this way."

"Do you expect trouble, Agente?" asked Coraza.

"Always."

"I mean for us. Now."

"The threats I know of, Dr. Raimundo or Mater Urania, are unlikely to strike. But it is the threats I do not know of that concern me."

"I don't understand."

"You are but one mystery in a very complex riddle, señorita. Events are turning that may overshadow our personal concerns." The vigilero fell silent, and the only sounds for the next few minutes were the soft clopping of the horses' hooves on the narrow trail and the wind sighing through the leaves of the oaks.

"You mean the war from the south?" asked Coraza.

"What do you know of that?" asked Palabo, scowling over his shoulder.

"Only that I have heard people fear one is coming. And...I have had frightening dreams."

"Huh? Dreams?" said Palabo.

Fearing he was not taking her seriously, Coraza said nothing more.

Filipo looked around and finally said, "This is leading us into native territory, isn't it?"

"Yes," said Palabo. "There are a couple of Topanga Chumash villages in the region. Among the few remaining."

"Isn't that leading us into trouble?"

"My compañeros and I do our best to stay on cordial terms with the Chumash. After all, they are Califians too and under our protection. We will respect their sovereignty and not enter a village unless invited. I expect they will let us pass in peace. They just want to be left alone, save for those so debased by past slavery in the missions that they have turned to banditry."

Coraza anxiously eyed the crest of the narrow canyon above them. The holy sisters, in their history lessons, claimed that the friars who first came to Alta Califia two centuries before had been bringing the light of the Madre and the ways of civilization to a savage people. Yet Coraza had heard other stories, murmured in secret by the indio servants at the orphanage when the holy sisters weren't around. Stories about grandparents, uncles, and aunts who had been enslaved at mission compounds where the friars forced them to mine the hills or work the fields until they dropped from exhaustion. And for their thanks, the friars treated the natives no better than dogs.

After the Great Revolt, the holy sisters taught, even the King of Spain had been horrified to learn of the harsh treatment of the indios. He had ordered the missions disbanded and the church land sold. But the indios of the kitchens thought it was more to do with the friars setting themselves up like barons of their own fiefs than any kindness toward the natives. And fear that the Chumash, Serrano, Diegueño, and Gabrielito, if not appeased, might make common cause with the Nuevo Aztecans to the south.

During nights in the dorms, when the orphan girls would whisper scary stories, one said that evil Molochista wizards from far Cartago had infiltrated Mexico and were making the demons of the ancient Aztecas come to life. It was after hearing those stories that Coraza had begun to dream of the black serpent. Even now, the thought of it made her anxious.

Coraza jumped a little in the saddle as she saw the silhouette of a man atop the canyon side, staring down at them. "Agente..." she warned.

The vigilero did not even look up. He began to whistle an odd series of notes, like no tune Coraza had ever heard. The man at the ridge lifted his hand, nodded, and then turned away. Coraza sighed and rested her head on Filipo's back.

"Are you frightened, señorita?"

Coraza sat upright, suddenly remembering she was taking liberties with a young man she did not know well. "No, I'm fine. Only...there are so many dangers in the world. More than I ever knew."

"Do you wish you were still back at the orphanage?"

"No. Never."

Filipo pulled his horse to an abrupt halt, and Coraza's face nearly plowed between his shoulder blades. "Agente, why are we stopping?" Filipo asked.

"Because it would seem our way is blocked."

Filipo leaned to the right, and Coraza leaned even farther to see past him. Ahead, in the trail in front of Agente Palabo, stood a short, stout Chumash woman, her black and grey hair in a long braid over her shoulder. She appeared as unmovable as the sandstone boulders to either side of her. She began to speak to the vigilero in a language Coraza recognized from the kitchens of the orphanage. But the woman spoke too softly for Coraza to understand what she was saying.

"What does the old woman want?" grumbled Filipo. "Is she begging for money?"

"You will kindly shut up, young señor, or I will knock you from your horse," said Palabo. He indicated to the woman that she should continue.

She rambled on for some time, as Coraza felt her head and back become hot from the sun. The horse Tulio shook his mane and stamped his feet. Filipo shifted in impatient irritation on his saddle. Finally, the Chumash woman ceased speaking. Agente Palabo lifted his hat to her and said a few words in her languange. The woman stepped aside from the path, and the vigilero rode forward.

"At last," sighed Filipo, and he nudged Tulio's flanks. As they rode past, Coraza noticed the Chumash woman's narrowed gaze following them up the trail. "What did she want, Agente?"

"Apparently, Coraza is not the only one having interesting dreams," replied Palabo.

"The indio wanted to tell you a dream?" echoed Filipo sardonically. "That's all?"

"The same disturbing dream, several nights running. She believed that to free herself of the nightmare, she must stand in the road and tell the dream to the next person she saw, which, to our good fortune, was me."

"How lucky for you," said Filipo.

"What was the dream?" asked Coraza. An eerie feeling swept over her that made the hair on her arms stand on end. The feeling had come upon her before, and she thought of it as wind blown from the hand of the Madre. Coraza had once asked Sister Phoebe if all events meant something, if nothing happened by chance. Sister Phoebe had replied that all things were related within the spirit of the Madre, though one might never know their meaning in the grand scheme of things.

The Agente turned his head to look back at her, and she thought she saw a slight smile on his lips. "Thank you for asking, señorita. The woman dreamed that a huge boulder on a hillside threatened to fall down and crush a native village below. But this boulder was of two colors. One side was natural stone, and the other was the orange of sandy clay but brighter… unnatural. In the dream, the boulder always falls. But sometimes, it falls one side down, sometimes the other. If it falls with the natural side down, the village is crushed and all die. If it falls with the strange side down, the boulder stops in mid-air. The people below are frightened but not harmed. In fact, the floating rock protects the village from a landslide that follows behind it."

"What does it mean?" asked Coraza.

"I don't know. Dream-reading is not one of my skills," said the Agente.

"Then this encounter was singularly pointless," said Filipo.

"Not at all," said Palabo. "The woman may be cured of her nightmares. And she went on to tell me of some suspicious men riding the northern boundary of Malaguez's land, and that, if we do not wish to encounter them, we should take the way to the left in the fork in the trail just ahead."

"Oh." Filipo fell silent.

Coraza covered her mouth with her hand, finding it all she could do not to laugh aloud at his expense. But she could not help turning the Chumash woman's dream over and over in her mind. *Am I committing the sin of pride to think this dream is somehow about me? It speaks of a thing that is changed and is strange, but that might protect rather than destroy. Am I the stone, containing unnatural magic? But why would I crush a village? How would I protect one? It doesn't make any sense.*

It was early afternoon by the time Coraza, Filipo, and Agente Palabo rode to the top of the canyon and the trail began to angle down again. To their right, to the south, distant smoke rose from the village of the Topanga Chumash. To the north, the Santa Monica Mountains rose higher. To the east, before them, the land sloped gently downward in hills covered with long golden grasses, dotted with the dark green of live oak trees. In the farther distance, the land opened up into a broad, flat valley, in which Coraza could dimly see the green of orchards and pastures.

She stared in wonder, having never before seen just how big Alta Califia was. "Where is this Canyon of Ghosts we are seeking?" Coraza asked.

"Is it that way, to the north?" She pointed to the closer mountains.

Agente Palabo replied, "No, señorita. Do you see that line of mountains over there, on the north side of Valle Fernando? That bare one in the distance is San Gabriel, and the range is named after it. If the canyon is where I believe it to be, it is in the foothills to the west and south of that mountain."

Coraza stared at the blue-gray sierra of mountains he pointed to. "But...those are so far, Agente!" Already, her hips and back were aching, and her inner thighs felt chafed and sore.

"That is why I asked if you felt ready for such a ride, señorita. I'm afraid we can't turn back now to find you a place to stay. Unless you'd like to live with the Chumash for a while."

"No, no, I'll be all right," Coraza lied. "Only, it is a bit...farther than I expected." She shifted in the saddle to ease her discomfort, trying not to brush against Filipo as she did so. And failing. "Pardon me, señor."

"Not a problem," said Filipo, too quickly. "Agente, would it be possible to rest soon?"

"Yes, that would be wise. The horses need cooling down, and I need some time to reflect on our situation." Agente Palabo chose the top of a low hill midway down to the valley floor with only three live oak trees for cover.

"Agente," said Filipo, "aren't we too visible to potential enemies here?"

"The idea," Palabo responded, "is that our enemies will also be visible to us." He dismounted in the shade of one live oak. He loosely tethered his horse to a low branch and poured water from his canteen into his hat for his horse to drink. Filipo rode up beside him, dismounted, and helped Coraza to slide from the saddle. Coraza groaned, her thighs and hips aching, and she staggered a little as her feet touched the ground.

Filipo caught her around the waist. "Are you all right, señorita?"

Coraza sighed and leaned against him for a moment. "Just...tired. That is all. This is a good time to rest." Suddenly embarrassed, ashamed, but a little pleased as well, Coraza pushed away from him gently and hobbled over to the shade of the nearest tree.

What am I thinking? I am behaving so inappropriately. I don't even know if I like Filipo. Ai, mi, it is true what the holy sisters warned...Without a duenna, a girl becomes her worst self around men. She sank slowly down to sit on the ground, then leaned back against the rough tree trunk behind her. As the men tended the horses, giving them water and feed, Coraza stared out over the broad valley at the distant mountains, the hot wind blowing strands of her hair across her face. She was too tired to brush them away. *If I am this saddle-weary now, how will I survive this journey? I must somehow, but can I endure such pain?* She felt as though she didn't want to move her legs ever again.

Filipo stretched out in the shade next to Coraza, close enough to both please and dismay her. He put the blanket roll from his saddle beneath his head and closed his eyes. "A siesta is just what is needed."

"If you will please not disturb me for a while," said Agente Palabo, "there is something I must do." He walked a few yards away from them, and at first Coraza assumed he was going to pass water. But the vigilero stopped and lifted his face to the sunlight, eyes closed, and stood very still. Then he crouched suddenly and pressed his hands into the ground, head bent in concentration.

"What is he doing?" asked Coraza.

Filipo opened one eye and watched for a minute. "Hmmm. Salamago used to say that some vigileros have mastered a bit of the native magics as well as some geomancy. Those vigileros, like the Protectadoras, can read the earth, sense the future, that sort of thing. Or maybe he's just doing stretching exercises like any serious man of the sword."

"Oh. How long do you think he'll be doing that?"

"I've no idea. Please be quiet and rest, Coraza. We have a long ride ahead."

"Oh. Sorry." Coraza sat and listened for long moments to the wind hissing through the long grasses, to the cheery chirping of sparrows in the distant trees.

Filipo began to snore softly. The Agente was kneeling, eyes still closed, his cupped hands filled with yellow dirt. Coraza's gaze flicked to the vigilero's horse, which stood with its head down, dozing. Her gaze shifted to the blanket roll behind the vigilero's saddle and the bit of yellow leather that stuck out of it. The soreness in her legs seemed no longer a hindrance as Coraza cautiously, silently, stood and walked over to Palabo's horse, making sure the animal was between her and the Agente.

The horse raised its head to look at her and rumbled low in its throat.

"Shh, I'm not going to hurt you," Coraza whispered. She swiftly leaned forward, grasped the leather bag, and with a mighty tug, pulled it from the blanket roll. Hands shaking with excitement, she opened the top of the leather sheath bag, reached in with her right hand, and grasped the hilt. The sword felt warm and welcoming to her touch, like the feel of Sister Phoebe's hand in those days at the orphanage when Coraza had been so lonely. She drew the sword from the bag and held it up, smiling.

The blade of the sword blazed with reflected sunlight, almost hurting Coraza's eyes. The iron basket guard seemed brighter as well, no longer the lightless black of midnight that it was before.

A hand came from behind Coraza and grasped her right wrist, pulling her arm straight out to her side.

"Ai!" she cried, trying to pull her arm away, but it was like fighting a serpent of steel.

"Forgive me, señorita," said Agente Palabo, right behind her. "But I believe we have discussed the matter of you not touching this sword again. Señor Del Utherio, if you will be so kind as to take the sword from her hand."

Filipo, startled awake by her cry, leapt up and snatched Sorrow from Coraza's hand, darting her an annoyed and disappointed glance.

Coraza hung her head, her cheeks growing hot in shame. "I just wanted to look at it again."

"Huh," said Filipo, examining the sword. "Very clever of you, Agente. You had a close copy made. Not exact, but of course that would not have been possible. A workable copy, nonetheless." He tilted the sword this way and that in his hands, frowning.

The Agente, still as a stone, let go of Coraza's wrist. "I made no copy, señor."

"Well, this is not the same sword," said Filipo. "Who put it on your horse if not you?"

"It is the same sword," said Coraza, confused. "I could feel it when I touched it. I...I know it. It is the same."

Agente Palabo was instantly beside Filipo. "What is different?"

"Well, here, there are many fewer thorns on the bell guard filigree. And look, the black is flaking off. The guard isn't iron, but carbonization over...what might be a coppery bronze. The basket seems to be a little larger. The blade, as well, is longer but narrower. The balance is different."

Coraza stared at the sword, as understanding struck her. "It changed for me," she whispered. "To fit my hand. It knows who I am now."

"That is supposed to be impossible," said Filipo. "No metal can hold a magic powerful enough to change its shape after it is forged. Blacksmiths talk about such things, but—could Salamago have really done it? Is this why he forged this sword in secret?"

"Apparently, he found a way, señor," said Agente Palabo, grabbing the sword from Filipo and jamming it back into the leather sheath bag. Palabo thrust the sheathed sword back into the blanket roll and leaned against his horse, clearly unnerved.

"Agente?" asked Coraza. "What is the matter?"

"If he did...if he truly achieved this," Filipo insisted, "he would be the greatest forgemage the world had ever seen!"

"And the most diabolical," growled Agente Palabo. "Only life can change its shape and its nature through its own will. To imbue metal with that ability is to join life to non-life."

"Sere sorcery," whispered Coraza.

"And the only wizards cultivating such knowledge," Palabo went on, "are the Molochistas."

"The holy sisters taught all the Cartago Molochista wizards had been destroyed long ago," said Coraza. "Did they lie?"

"Perhaps they meant to be reassuring. But some ancient sorcerers survived the Punic wars and spread themselves around the world, awaiting the chance to rise again. Alas, even now there are Molochistas in Mexico, perverting what remnants of the ancient culture of the Aztecas remain, using their own foul sorcery and its need for sacrifice."

"I thought the Aztecas performed sacrifice too," said Filipo.

"The destruction España brought to Mexico three hundred years ago ensured that we may never know what the true Aztecans believed. But the Molochistas have taken advantage of the myths passed down about the ancients and are making them true. And my compañeros report that these wicked practices have slipped northward. Therefore, I regret to say, señor, that if this is the same sword, not only was Erculeo Salamago trafficking in evil magic, he was also a traitor."

Coraza heard the ring of metal against metal and looked at Filipo.

Filipo stood with his own short sword drawn, glaring at the vigilero. "You will take back those words, Agente. Salamago was no Molochista. He would give his life before sinking so low."

"Perhaps that is what he ultimately did." Agente Palabo turned to face the young blacksmith. "It speaks well of you, señor, that you honor your master's memory with loyalty. I understand that he was like a father to you and taught you well. But my loyalty is to the truth. And I will not deny or retract what the evidence is telling me."

"Then you will defend your slander with your blood, Agente."

"Filipo!" Coraza shouted, astonished at his bravado and foolishness. He had already fought the vigilero once and lost quickly. What did he think he would accomplish dueling the Agente again?

The Agente narrowed his gaze and slowly drew his long sword from its scabbard. "If that is how you will have it, señor."

"No!" cried Coraza. "Stop! This is crazy!"

"Stay out of it, Coraza," said Filipo. "I must defend your father's name from being dragged in the dirt, as he is no longer alive to defend himself. Are you the one who has been spreading lies about him, Agente? Did you tell the holy sisters to perform the Sorrowful Remembrance, announcing his soul was damned? I don't know who hired you to destroy Salamago's reputation, but I will see this stops here and now or spend my last breath trying."

Agente Palabo stepped away from his horse and out into an open area beyond the trees, swinging his sword to warm up his arm. "My allegiance is to the king, to the Protectorado, and to the truth, señor. No one hired me to look into your master's affairs. In fact, some tried to discourage me from this investigation. Which has made me all the more curious. Because those of my profession are granted some autonomy, I have followed my own path."

"Then you follow it to your death, Agente!"

"If the Madre wills it," said Palabo, calmly.

The two men stood facing one another a moment. Then, sudden as a flash of lightning, Filipo leaped forward, slashing his sword in a great sweep from right to left. Agente Palabo jumped back and parried the blow but did not offer attack of his own. Again and again, his face contorted in rage, Filipo drove the vigilero back with powerful blows that, had they connected, would have done great damage to flesh and bone.

Coraza stood with the horses, fists pressed to her mouth, wishing there was something she dared do. Tulio, Filipo's palomino horse, strained against its hitched reins, whinnying in distress. Palabo's bay horse merely watched, ears forward, but did not seem particularly alarmed.

On and on the sword duel went, the ringing of the blades on one another echoing loud against the hillsides. Agente Palabo spun and swirled his arm as though in a dance, but sweat beaded on his face, and he was clearly being hard pressed. Filipo moved closer to the vigilero, now attempting thrusts as well as slashes, grunting with each attempted blow, his face bright red from exertion.

Why doesn't the Agente disarm Filipo like before? Or is Filipo truly fighting that well? Coraza wondered if she could stop the duel if she, too, was armed. *I could grab my sword again now. But whom should I side with? Filipo fights for my father's name, but he is being a fool. The Agente fights for the truth, but I don't know what he intends for me.* She side-stepped toward Palabo's horse, but it turned to face her, neck extended, ears back, upper lip curled, ready to bite her.

Coraza looked at Tulio, considering riding off on the sorrel to distract the men from their fight. *But what if only the Agente is distracted, and Filipo succeeds in killing him? Or if Filipo is distracted and the Agente does him grave harm?*

Coraza gave up and fell to her knees on the ground, watching as Filipo, now staggering with weariness, swung his sword at the Agente in wild, unaimed attacks. For his part, the Agente still parried, ignoring wide open opportunities to do harm to Filipo.

Filipo noticed this as well. "Go on, Agente! Cut me if you dare! What, are you afraid? Unable to back up your truth with steel? Have you no stomach for the sight of blood?"

But the vigilero would not be goaded and continued to merely parry and dance out of the way of Filipo's blows.

He's deliberately wearing him down, wearing him out, Coraza realized. But why?

As the sun lowered to the ridgeline of the mountains to the west, Filipo, gasping, could barely lift his sword. Agente Palabo raised his blade one last time and struck Filipo twice, with the flat, on each arm. Filipo dropped his sword and, with a great cry, fell forward. Palabo caught the young man as he fell and eased him down onto his knees. Filipo buried his head in Palabo's shoulder, his back shaking.

Coraza stood and ran over to them, falling to her knees beside the Agente. "Filipo? Filipo, are you—" But she silenced herself as she heard Filipo loudly sobbing.

"He was...he was a great man," Filipo gasped. "A great man."

"He was," Palabo agreed, "once a great man." The Agente looked over at Coraza and moved aside to let Filipo's head slip onto her shoulder. Coraza instinctively wrapped her arms around Filipo's back and stroked his hair, as Sister Phoebe used to do for her. Agente Palabo said to her, "Be proud of him. He fought well. There is no shame in this."

As Palabo got up and walked discreetly away, Coraza held Filipo, rocking him gently as he cried. Her sympathetic tears joined his, flowing down his cheeks. "Thank you," she whispered. "Thank you for defending my father's honor. I am so proud of you. I know he would be proud too." Coraza did not know if pride was truly what she felt for what Filipo had done. But she understood now the depth of his loyalty and love toward her father. And what a worthy person her father must have been to bring forth such feelings. In that way, she was grateful to Filipo to be the mirror to her father's goodness, even if that mirror was now tarnished and shadowed.

She laid her head on Filipos' shoulder, and they held onto one another until well after the sun set.

Chapter Ten

As the first stars appeared in the indigo sky, Coraza sat with her back against a live oak, her chin resting on her knees. Filipo lay on his bedroll, snoring, exhausted from his duel with the vigilero. They had had a quick meal of beans rolled in tortillas heated over a small campfire. Now Agente Palabo was walking a slow circle around the fire, chanting tunelessly as his boots scuffed a pattern in the dirt.

When he finished and sat on his own bedroll beside his horse, Coraza asked, "What were you doing?"

"A spell to contain the fire. In this region, with these dry grasses and the desert wind, a brush fire can do more damage than an army of tzinn."

"Oh." Reminded of tzinn, Coraza could not help asking, "Agente, do you think La Llorona will come for me again?"

"I think she should be the least of your worries right now, señorita." He leaned back against a rock, pulling the brim of his hat low over his face.

Coraza studied him a moment, wondering what he knew that he wasn't saying. "Agente, Filipo said that you have studied the native magics and geomancy. Is that true?"

A brief smile twitched his lips. "Enough to be useful."

"This afternoon, when you went off by yourself, is that what you were doing?"

"Something like that."

"Can you foretell the future?"

"No. But I can tell which way the wind blows."

"Oh." This didn't sound like any senses Coraza had felt about oncoming danger. Hesitantly, she asked, "Which way does it blow? For us?"

After a long pause, the Agente replied, "Danger lies ahead."

Coraza sighed. She knew such a thing without magical skill. But she persisted. "What sort of danger?"

After another long pause, Palabo asked, "Have you ever been in a fight, señorita?"

Coraza tilted her head, frowning. It seemed an odd question. Yet she remembered nights in the orphanage, being jumped on by the other orphan girls who thought it would be fun to thump on strange little Coraza. Especially after she would persistently question some of the holy teachings or talk too long about tzinn. It would lead to hair pulling, biting, kicking, and shrieking, until the holy sisters would rush in to break it up.

"Yes," she answered finally. "I have."

"Did you ever win?"

Coraza paused at this also. In truth, it was her tendency to win such bully-battles that had helped lead to her periodic lodging in the orphanage basement. Though it seemed unladylike to admit, Coraza finally answered, "Yes."

"Good," the Agente said.

"So...there are fights ahead?"

"Do your dreams not tell you this is true?"

Coraza remembered the black serpent. "I think so."

"Now, señorita," sighed Agente Palabo, "I suggest you get some sleep so that we may face whatever the future may bring us well-rested. Buenos noches."

"Who is keeping watch?"

"My horse."

"Your horse?"

The bay turned its head, ears forward, and whuffed as if to say, "You doubt me?"

"His sight and hearing are far keener than yours or mine, and he needs less sleep than we do. Now kindly hush and try to get some rest. We have a very long ride tomorrow."

At the reminder of riding, Coraza groaned and curled up on her side. She closed her eyes and tried to sleep.

Slumber came fitfully at best, punctuated by dreams in which a gruff man, disappointed with her, was exhorting her to do something. But when she awoke, she could not remember what he had said. Or what she was supposed to do.

Though she ached all over and shivered in the chill, Coraza was glad to see the sunrise. She was not surprised to see that Agente Palabo was already awake. He was drinking coffee from a tin mug, staring out at the valley below in thoughtful silence.

Coraza sat up, groaning. Every rock beneath her seemed to have made an impression on her back during the night.

"Good morning, señorita. Did you sleep well?"

"No," Coraza said. "And you, Agente?"

"As well as I needed to."

Filipo still lay on his bedroll, snoring loudly. "Will he be all right?" Coraza asked.

"That is up to him," replied the vigilero.

Coraza excused herself to go pass water behind some bushes. When she returned, Filipo was sitting up, his arms draped over his bent knees. Agente Palabo handed him the mug of coffee, which Filipo accepted listlessly without speaking.

Coraza went over to him and put her hand on Filipo's shoulder. "Good morning, Filipo. How are you feeling?"

He flicked a glance at her and shrugged one shoulder. "All right, I suppose. I ache all over. And you?"

"Me too." She smiled at him encouragingly. To her surprise, he returned a wan smile that warmed her heart.

"I do not mean to be brusque, mes amigos," said Agente Palabo, "but we should saddle up and go soon."

Filipo nodded and stood. With no further words, he went to his horse, Tulio, and fed and watered him. Coraza rolled up her blanket and returned it to Palabo, who tied it behind his saddle. She tried to smooth out her hair and clothing, but she was certain it was useless. She wished she'd been allowed to at least bring a hairbrush. *I must look frightful.*

"I apologize, señorita," said Palabo, "for not getting you a mount of your own. But the horses at the stable in Las Escarpas were already spoken for, and I could not afford the time to seek others of reasonable quality and price."

"It's just as well," Filipo grumbled good-naturedly as he adjusted Tulio's saddle. "That stablemaster would have tried to sell you a broken-down nag for a king's ransom. He charged me two reales in rent for that filthy loft."

"It's quite all right," Coraza said quickly. "I do not mind. I was never that good at directing a horse. I am content to ride as I did yesterday."

The Agente gave her a pointed glance, and Coraza swiftly looked away to hide her blush. She now truly did not mind at all riding behind Filipo. She began to plan how often it would be seemly to rest her head on his muscular shoulder and just how much she should let her arms encircle his trim waist.

A young man can be heartened by a girl's interest. *Perhaps I can buoy his spirits.* She found herself almost actually looking forward to the long ride ahead.

Through the morning, the Agente and Filipo kept their horses walking at a brisk but not too taxing pace. The trail sloped gently downhill, which helped. The day warmed quickly as the sun rose, filling the air with the scent of sage and damp grass. Clumps of bright orange poppies adorned the hillsides. Quail burbled and scurried out of the way of the horses' hooves, chest-forward like offended magistrates. Coraza spotted a small fox and a couple of rabbits bounding through the brush. Hawks circled overhead in a sky of brilliant blue.

For a time, the trail followed the borders of the ranchero of Don Pico, and the vaqueros graciously allowed Agente Palabo and Filipo to water their horses at the cattle troughs. By mid-day, they had ridden down to the floor of Valle Fernando, where the temperature was quite warm, and the horses slowed to a plodding pace.

Coraza allowed her head to droop onto Filipo's shoulder as the warmth sapped her strength. "Ai, mi, it is so hot!"

"Alas, there are no pleasant sea breezes here in the interior to cool us off," said Filipo.

Palabo's horse, walking beside them, twitched one ear back, then raised its head to stare south, whuffing its nostrils. The vigilero let his horse stop, and Filipo pulled Tulio to a stop as well.

"What is it?" asked Filipo.

Coraza sat up and peered southward. The valley sloped gently upward in a series of rising hills ending in a range of low mountains about ten miles away. There was a line of dust in the air amid the hills and then, coming over the rise of the hills, a clump of dark dots.

"Riders," said Filipo.

"Yes," agreed Palabo, his eyes narrowed to slits. "Soldiers of the Presidio, if I'm not mistaken."

"They won't have any business with us, will they? Should we get off the road?"

"One hopes their interest lies elsewhere. Let us keep riding east and see what they do. But let's not press the horses in this heat."

Palabo turned his horse, but the beast seemed jittery and began to trot. Tulio did the same, bouncing and jarring Coraza against Filipo's back. With no shame at all, Coraza wrapped her arms around him and hung on tight. The air was suddenly filled with distant thunder, and Coraza looked back. The dust cloud was larger, and the riders were clearly approaching, at fast speed.

"They're gaining on us!" Coraza cried.

"Let's run then!" said Filipo.

"No!" commanded Palabo. "Let those idiots kill their own horses, if they wish. We aren't fugitives. Let's wait and see what they want."

So the Agente, Filipo, and Coraza waited, sweltering, on the trail as the soldiers rode ever closer.

"I count twelve," said Filipo.

"Fifteen," said Palabo.

"Think we could take them?"

The Agente paused. "It is treason to attack lawful soldiers of the Governadora, señor." But Coraza saw dim flickers of light around the vigilero's hands and arms. He was thinking about it.

Presently, the unruly cohort of men rode up to them, their horses sweating and foaming at the bit. The men indeed wore the flat-crowned hats and heavy leather vests and chaps of the soldiers of the presidio. Most of them were not much older than Filipo, and the young men were flushed and laughing, jostling each other as if they were out on a pleasurable excursion.

The man in front was an older, portly fellow with a drooping bushy mustache. He walked his horse up to Palabo and said loudly, "Am I addressing the Agente Marzo Palabo of His Majesty's Service?"

"You are," responded Palabo flatly. "And whom do I have the pleasure of meeting?"

"Permit me to introduce myself. I am Colonel Silenuso Gonzalez. I have reason to understand that you have a prisoner in your custody, a girl who claims to be the daughter of the sword maker Erculeo Salamago."

"She is the daughter of Erculeo Salamago," said Filipo.

"Aha!" cried the Colonel, fixing his gaze on Coraza.

All eyes of the other soldiers turned to her as well. She did not like how some of them were staring at her, like hungry wolves catching sight of a rabbit.

"So, you admit that you do have this person with you."

"She is not my prisoner," said Palabo, with a chiding glance at Filipo. "She is evidence and witness for my investigations into the activities of her late father."

The Colonel laughed loudly. "Ah, you vigileros have such strange ways, Agente! When we have a witness, if they are of good character, they are permitted to stay in their home, or if they are scoundrels, we put them in jail. We do not bring them tagging along with us like the entourage of royalty."

"It is true. My ways differ from yours," said Palabo. "What do you want with us?"

The Colonel drew himself up in his saddle. "We have orders to take the girl from your custody and deliver her to the Protectadoras of the Presidio as soon as possible."

Coraza sat up straight. Her first excited thought was, *Truly? I actually get to meet them!* But then the hope quickly curdled to fear. There could be only one reason the ancient brujas of the Protectadora would ask for her to be brought to them. Mater Urania told them she was a chimera. They intended to kill her.

"No!" Filipo shouted.

The Agente held up one hand to silence Filipo. "Colonel, you understand I cannot simply hand over a defenseless young girl to any squadron of men who demand it."

The Colonel drew himself up even further. "Agente! Do you imply that I and my men are of unsavory character?"

"I imply only that you are men, Colonel. If you cannot give me proof of these orders, I must respectfully decline."

"Ah, the proof." The colonel fished within his leather vest as the sweat dripped from his brow. He pulled out a rolled up, somewhat crumpled piece of paper tied with a wilted red ribbon. He handed it to the vigilero. "Here you are, Agente. My written orders. I am told they are signed by the Protectadora Doña Vincenza herself."

Palabo took the proffered paper and unrolled it, reading it carefully. At the very bottom, he seemed to pause a long time over the signature. He rolled the paper back up and returned it to the Colonel. "I'm afraid this writ appears to be entirely in order."

Coraza shrank further against Filipo's back, as if she could hide behind his muscles.

"Ha. You see, Agente. Colonel Gonzalez does not lie."

"I did not mean to imply that you did. Only that Colonel Gonzalez might be mistaken. I notice, for example, that the Doña Vincenza only says she wishes to ask questions of the señorita, and that great care should be taken when bringing her to the Los Mesanjeros Presidio."

"Indeed, Agente. But that term, great care, is often used when we are escorting a prisoner who is likely to be dangerous. Though I cannot imagine how the Doña would think such a thing in the little chica's case." The Colonel smiled through his broad mustache at Coraza, although the smile did not reach his eyes.

"Perhaps the Doña only meant what she said," suggested Agente Palabo. "Though I am surprised that you felt so many men were necessary to escort one young girl."

Colonel Gonzalez scowled beneath his bushy brows. "I understand it was the Doña's concern that a certain vigilero might be uncooperative. Besides, it is good for the men to get out and about now and then. Sitting idle in the Presidio for a long time is taxing to men of spirited blood."

Several of the other soldiers nodded enthusiastic agreement.

Unable to stop herself, Coraza said, "Why do you stay in the Presidio, señores? Why aren't you patrolling the desert, protecting Califia from the tzinn?"

The soldiers stared at her. One of them said, "Will you listen to the mouth on that one?"

"Does she mean to chide us? To say we lack manly courage?"

"Someone should give her a good slap to teach her she cannot address soldiers of the Governadora in this way." The man looked pointedly at Filipo.

Filipo glared back in silence.

"You must forgive the señorita," said Agente Palabo. "She has recently survived an attack from a tzinn. As you might guess, this event has made an abiding impression upon her."

Silence fell on the soldiers. A couple of them made the sign of the fig, thumb extended between middle and ring finger, to ward off evil. The Colonel frowned at Coraza as though unsure what to make of the new information.

Finally, he burst out in a loud "Ha! But she is still alive, Agente, so what has she to fear?" He leaned forward, his elbows on the front rise of his saddle, and addressed Coraza as though she were a child of five. "Listen, chica, and I will tell you a state secret. The tzinn, they are our friends."

"Friends?" asked Coraza, horrified, causing some of the soldiers to chuckle.

"Yes! It is the wild spirits of the desert who truly protect the borders of Califia. Not stalwart men at arms, like us, or the wily vigileros. We are brave, chica, but few. What else do you think keeps the savage Nuevo Aztecans at bay, or keeps the land-hungry Yanquis from boiling in like locusts? So, the next time you meet a tzinn, you should curtsy and say 'Gracias.'"

"Before she offers it her soul," said Filipo dryly, "for the good of the colony?"

The Colonel frowned and nudged his horse to stand directly in front of Filipo. "I am not certain I like your tone, young señor. Just who might you be?"

"I am Filipo Del Utherio, blacksmith and former apprentice to Erculeo Salamago."

"I see. While that is commendable, it does not make you a gentleman of noble blood, and therefore, you have no right to speak to us with disrespect. I will let it go this once, but I remind you to keep a civil tongue when addressing soldiers of the Governadora."

"I will remember this, Colonel," said Filipo.

"Good. See that you do."

"Is it true?" Coraza softly asked Agente Palabo. "About the tzinn?" She was heartsick to think that her homeland's protection lay in such monsters.

"Certainly many think it so," responded the vigilero, "though I expect the Protectadoras still do their share."

"Yes, yes," said the Colonel, waving a dismissive hand, "a few of the old brujas have some power in them, but they age, no? What else have we against savages who have made common cause with the Molochistas? How many was it we heard were sacrificed to their pagan gods this last year?"

"Five hundred, Colonel."

"Five hundred!" The Colonel leaned forward on his saddle again and said to Coraza, "And you know how they were killed, chica? The living hearts were cut out of the victims' chests, still beating, and the bodies tossed down the steps of their infernal temple." The Colonel smiled with relish. "You know what else? In springtime, their ceremony is to flay men alive and dance around in their skin. Isn't that a jolly way to welcome the flowers and birds? So, do not recoil in horror, chica, that we should welcome tzinn at our borders. The alternative is far worse. Now Agente, we have stayed and chatted long enough. I hope the Doña Vincenza was mistaken, and that you will be swift and cooperative in delivering your pris—your charge to us."

Coraza looked at Palabo, trying to plead through her eyes that he do anything but hand her over.

"I cannot imagine," said Palabo, "how the Doña acquired such a poor opinion of me. I will be more than cooperative, Colonel."

"Good!"

"In fact, I will assist you. I and the young señor will accompany you and your men in escorting the señorita to the Presidio."

Coraza's spirits lifted just a little at the news.

"Now wait a moment!" said the Colonel, drawing himself up in umbrage. "The Doña said nothing about you coming with us!"

"I read the orders most carefully, and she says nothing against it either," said Agente Palabo. "And if the Doña has questions about Salamago, the young señor may have even better answers to offer her than the señorita. So, we shall all accompany you, and the Doña Vincenza cannot be other than pleased with your service."

The Colonel chewed on the ends of his mustache a moment before grumbling, "Very well. Come along then. We are bid to return to the Presidio as soon as possible."

"Let us be on our way at once," agreed Agente Palabo.

Filipo turned in the saddle and gazed one last time toward the far sierra to the north.

Coraza did as well, understanding that, for him, the search for clues to her father's fate would be delayed a long time. For herself, she now might never know.

Surely, the Agente would not willingly escort me to my death, Coraza thought. *But perhaps he is delaying, to wait for a moment when we might escape. Would he do that for me? Defy a direct order from the Protectadoras? Filipo might, but is it right that I should ask that of him? Or does the Agente hope to speak before Doña Vicenza on my behalf and thereby spare my life?* Unlike the vigilero, Coraza had no way to know which way the wind blew, so she tried to counsel herself to patience.

The soldiers turned their horses and began riding west again. Although they returned to jostling and laughing with one another, it was muted, and they kept glancing back over their shoulders at Agente Palabo, as if he were a cloud of fog dampening their high spirits. To Coraza's dismay, the Colonel dropped back to ride alongside Filipo and her.

"You seem to be a strong young man. And a blacksmith, you say? Tell me, señor, have you considered coming to work in the Presidio? Our horses are in constant need of shoeing, and our swords are always losing their edge. We could use a blacksmith of skill."

"I...had hoped, Colonel, to one day set up a forge of my own," responded Filipo, clearly choosing his words with care.

"Of course, of course, you had dreams for greater things. As do all young men. But we go where fate takes us, do we not? And now that your master is deceased, and it appears you do not have other sources of wealth, perhaps you should be more practical about your future. It would reflect well on you to choose to serve the Governadora. I would put in a good word for you, and the Doña Vincenza would doubtless take you more seriously were you to demonstrate your loyalty in this fashion."

Filipo responded merely, "Your offer is more than generous, Colonel. Thank you. I will give it thought."

"You do that," said Colonel Gonzalez, more iron in his voice. "You would do well to assure yourself that you will have a future, young señor."

"Thank you, Colonel," Filipo repeated flatly.

Coraza looked at the Agente. The vigilero was watching the Colonel with narrowed eyes, saying nothing.

But Colonel Gonzalez was not dissuaded. "Think of what a refined influence your learning might have on the arms of the Presidio, young señor. Tell me, do you think damascening will ever return as a decorative art, or perhaps blue steel etching? Did your master ever make daggers? I am quite fond of the cinqueada, myself." The Colonel prattled on well through the early afternoon as they picked their way through the bouldered chaparral. Coraza rested her head between Filipo's shoulders and allowed herself to doze.

She raised her head at the sound of the soldiers' barking laughter. They were riding down a road going south, toward the mountains that separated Valle Fernando from the valley of Los Mesanjeros. A native man, perhaps in his forties, had come riding up to them on a trotting burro. As the indio stared at the soldiers, the rage burning in his eyes was unmistakable.

"Well, look who has found us!" cried one of the soldiers, voice filled with disbelief and wicked merriment.

The native man's gaze raked across them until it came to rest on the Agente. At once, the man kicked the burro and trotted up to Palabo. The vigilero bent low over his saddle, and they spoke in tones too soft for Coraza to hear, but the indio pointed at the soldiers often. At last, Palabo raised his head and gave the soldiers a withering glare.

"Don't believe him, Agente, whatever he told you," said the Colonel. "You know how these people lie. His wife refused to give us food when we rode past their house, and his son would not show us the proper respect. We taught them an appropriate lesson."

Palabo said nothing to the Colonel but rode up to Filipo and Coraza. "I am sorry, but I must leave you for a time."

"Agente!" Filipo protested.

"I would choose not to go, but someone's life hangs in the balance. I will catch up to you as soon as I can. Be careful, both of you. I will see you again soon." Without waiting for a response, the vigilero wheeled his horse around and rode away with the indio toward the southeast. The soldiers laughed and shared with each other various quite nasty remarks concerning vigileros and natives.

Coraza clutched at Filipo's waist as she watched Palabo depart. "Filipo..."

He reached down and squeezed her right hand. He softly said, "We'll be all right, so long as we head straight to the Presidio. They wouldn't dare violate a Protectadora's orders." But the breathlessness of his voice betrayed that he did not quite believe his own words.

The Colonel rode back to them, his face unabashedly smug. "Well, as I said, young señor. Fate does not always hand one the future one wishes. Does it? Vamonos."

The group of soldiers surrounded them very much like a pack of wolves, grinning hungrily. All but two narrow-faced men, one in his twenties, one somewhat older, who rode together a bit behind the rest. These two were watching Coraza and Filipo with concern.

Coraza buried her face in Filipo's back, hoping the Presidio was not far.

But they had not ridden more than another half hour when Coraza heard Filipo say, "Colonel, why are we stopping?"

She sat up, back aching, and saw they had come to a roadside tavern. The painted sign above the door read "Cantina La Encina."

The soldiers laughed. Colonel Gonzalez said, "Has the sun blinded you, young señor? What does it look like we are stopping for?"

"But...but your orders were to return to the Presidio directly. As soon as possible." There was a hint of panic to Filipo's voice.

"As soon as possible," the Colonel replied affably, "does not mean we should kill our horses to get there, señor, or drive ourselves until we fall out of our saddles from hunger and thirst. It is the heat of the day, and time for a rest. A long climb up the road to El Segundo Pass is ahead of us. Let us gather our strength while we may."

As the soldiers dismounted, Filipo hesitated, and for a moment, Coraza thought he might kick Tulio into a gallop to attempt escape.

"What's the matter?" she whispered.

"Your father once said that bored men and drink is the most dangerous mixture of all."

Two soldiers grabbed Tulio's bridle and led the horse to the hitching post. "Come on and be sociable," one of them said. "You mustn't insult the

Colonel by refusing his company."

"It would seem we have little choice," Filipo said. He dismounted quickly and gestured at Coraza to do so as well. She leaned out of the saddle and let him swing her down, before any of the soldiers could put their hands on her. She allowed Filipo to take her hand and guide her into the tavern.

The room was dim and dusty, poorly lit by lanterns hung on wall posts. Coraza and Filipo looked at the table nearest the door, but it was already filled with soldiers. The only other place available was a trestle table across the room. Filipo guided her onto the bench seat beside the wall, and he sat close beside her.

"Now what do we do?" breathed Coraza.

"We wait and hope the Agente finds us soon."

"Inkeeper!" cried the Colonel. "Wine for all my men! We have completed yet another important mission for the Governadora and deserve our reward!"

"The mission is not completed yet, and he's already boasting," grumbled Filipo.

The innkeeper, a pudgy little man with an anxious expression, bustled quickly to fill mugs for everyone. Coraza wondered what would happen to his tavern if he had not been so obedient. She wondered if he was even going to be paid. She sighed and leaned her head on Filipo's shoulder. He took her arm in his, grasped her hand, and did not let go.

An hour passed, and then another. The afternoon darkened. And still the Agente did not come. The talk among the soldiers in the tavern had become loud, fueled by drink. Coraza tried to pay no attention to what they were saying. Finally, the Colonel got up a little unsteadily from his chair by the fireplace and walked over to their table. He sat heavily on the bench across from her. His eyelids were red from the wine.

"Señor," he said to Filipo, "perhaps you are not aware that there is a quite comfortable outhouse at the back of the building. Please feel free to make use of it to refresh yourself."

"Thank you, Colonel, but I do not feel I have need of it at this time," said Filipo.

The Colonel squinted at Filipo, his lips in a disapproving pout. "Perhaps you are somewhat dim, young señor. Therefore, I will be more straightforward. I have things to say to the chica that are for her ears alone. Now go."

Coraza clutched tighter at Filipo's hand.

"Perhaps you have not observed, Colonel, that she is under my protection. Whatever you have to say to her you will say to me too."

Colonel Gonzalez stared at Filipo, tapping his finger noisily on the table. Finally, he blew out a great sigh and said, "As you will."

Turning to Coraza, the Colonal reached out and snatched her other hand before she could take it off the table. He gazed at her and stroked her wrist with a false pity that disgusted her. "Señorita, perhaps by now you have come to understand that you are in a difficult situation."

"If we leave now for the Presidio," Filipo interjected, "there need be no difficulty at all."

The Colonel narrowed his eyes at Filipo, reached down with his left hand to his waist, still not letting go of Coraza, and drew forth a long dagger that he pointed at Filipo's throat. "You will be silent henceforth, young señor. Or I will tell the Doña Vincenza that you resisted arrest."

Filipo said nothing more, but his eyes were eloquent with disgust.

Coraza tried to pull her hand away, but the Colonel's grip was like iron.

"Now, as I was saying, chiquita," he went on, placing the dagger on the bench beside him. "You may be in a bit of trouble. And as I have demonstrated to your friend here, I am also a man of some generosity and understanding. My men can be a little...rambunctious at times. And the Protectadoras can be cold and cruel in questioning those they think might be their enemy. But I am a man of some authority, certainly with my men, and respected by the Protectadoras. If you are sweet to me, and do a small favor or two, I am more than willing to take you under my protection. I will see that your journey to the Presidio continues smoothly, and I will put in a good word for you with the Doña. I will tell her that you are cooperative and no traitor to the Governadora. Once all the nonsense is cleared up at the Presidio, I will even return you to your young friend's embrace"—he looked pointedly at Filipo—"little the worse for wear. Now, what do you say, eh?"

Coraza stared at him. She had no doubts of the sort of favor the Colonel was asking. In her world, a girl's honor was all that she had of value. To lose it was to doom herself to a future of sorrow and misfortune. One might as well be dead. She was raised on the holy sisters' stories of saints who had died rather than surrender their virtue. And her guts roiled at the thought of being used by the vile, unctuous man.

I may be a chimera, but my father valued me enough to make a sword of great power for me. What would he think if his soul can look upon me? What would Filipo think of me? Surely, the Madre would not intend this for me. The Agente asked if I could fight. Did he, in some way, foresee this?

Shaking, Coraza glanced over at Filipo. His jaw was set, his teeth clenched. A muscle twitched in his cheek as he turned and stared meaningfully at her. It was as though both he and her father were watching, judging, through his eyes.

Coraza looked back at the Colonel. She lifted her chin a little and said, "No, señor. I will not do as you ask."

The false kindness drained from his face. He let go of her wrist and slapped the table with a heavy hand. "Well, then." He stood and announced to the room in general, "I do not understand it! No one can say I have not been generous. I have offered these two all the help I can, and yet these ungrateful ones refuse. The Madre knows I could not have done more. Now the Madre help them both." He snatched up the dagger and re-sheathed it at his belt. Then he shambled back to his chair by the fireplace without looking back.

As the speculative gaze of the other soldiers turned to them, Coraza realized, as her stomach turned cold, that she and Filipo were now to be thrown to the wolves. She was startled as two soldiers rose swiftly and instantly sat across the table from them. But these were the two men who had watched her with concern before.

"Are you both fools?" said the older one, more in despair than in anger. "Why didn't you take his offer, girl? The Colonel would have given you the only protection that matters."

"But at what price?" growled Filipo. "If you are seriously saying my late master's daughter should have...prostituted herself, then you are no better than your Colonel."

The soldier paused, then looked down into his wineglass, shamefaced. "Forgive me, señor. We once were of better quality, my brother and I," he said, indicating the younger soldier beside him.

"We are of genteel blood," said the younger man, "but do not ask our family name. Our father fell out of favor with the Governadora, and we were forced to join the Presidio in exchange for his life."

"More of the Colonel's 'generosity'?" asked Filipo sourly.

"Just so," the soldier admitted softly. "And because you have not accepted it...now anything may happen."

"Why would the Colonel let me be harmed?" asked Coraza.

"Yes," added Filipo. "Is he not violating his own orders to bring her in as soon as possible and with great care?"

"If the señorita is not of wealth or noble blood," said the older one, "and she has the cloud of suspicion over her, what do the Protectadoras care if she is roughed up a little before arriving for questioning? She won't be killed, señor. You may at least rest assured of that."

"She may merely wish she had been," muttered the younger one.

"Good quality may still lie within you, caballeros," Filipo said. "Will you help us?"

The two brothers stared at Filipo with wide eyes. "What you are asking, señor," said the older one, "is that we give up our lives for you. To raise arms against our compañeros would be treason. We would be cut down now or hang after, but either way, we would be dead men."

"And what are our lives worth now, brother?" asked the younger one. "What have we become? You and I saw what they did to those Indians. Do real men do such things? Will we do such things ourselves when someday we are ordered to?"

"The Colonel told us," responded the elder, "that the Governadora wants the natives cowed and obedient so they will not join the Nuevo Aztecas if they come north."

"Cowed?" scoffed the younger brother. "I rather think it will drive them into the invaders arms." He looked up at Filipo. "I would rather not see that day. My sword arm is yours, señor, if it is needed. Better that my life be destroyed today than my soul destroyed tomorrow."

"Thank you!" Coraza breathed, scarcely believing their kindness.

After a moment, the older brother nodded. "Very well. Mine, too. I have seen too much for this life. I fear my soul is already doomed. Madre help us."

"Thank you, señores," said Filipo. "Perhaps whatever sacrifice we make today will redeem you."

Coraza heard the scraping of chairs on the stone floor, and three inebriated young soldiers swaggered over to the table.

Now it begins, she thought. Coraza could hear in her memory the Agente's voice asking, "Did you ever fight? Did you ever win?" Why could he not be here to help us? She glanced involuntarily at the door.

The swaggering soldier followed her gaze. "Well, well, it appears your friend the Agente will not be joining us tonight."

"Perhaps," said one of the youngbloods behind him, "the indios he went to help killed him for his horse."

"Or the harm you did took longer to repair," growled Filipo.

"Compañeros," the swaggerer said to the brothers at the table, "you heard what the Colonel said. Why do you drink with these ungrateful wretches?"

"Perhaps they have interesting things to say, Carlo," suggested the elder brother.

"What, because the fellow was apprentice to the great Salamago?" The blustery Carlo placed his hands on the table and leaned toward Filipo. Coraza could smell the wine on his breath. "Salamago was a pretty good blacksmith, I hear, until he started making magical trinkets for rich people."

Filipo's hand tightened on hers.

Smiling with cruel glee, Carlo leaned closer. "Is it true what they say, señor? That your master went mad before the end? Or perhaps he was crazy all along?"

"You would be wise," said Filipo, his voice amazingly steady, "to show no further ignorance of my master's character."

Carlo laughed. "How can you call it ignorance, señor, when he has left us proof, in the form of his little bastard here." Carlo looked directly at Coraza.

Filipo stood, stepping back from the bench, pulling Coraza up with him. "No man may say such things concerning my master or his daughter without paying a price." He gently pushed Coraza to stand behind him, and for a moment, their gazes met, his eyes filled with fear and a terrible resolve.

In that moment, Coraza understood that Filipo knew his life was over—he was going to die this night. He was going to die attempting to protect her honor and her father's name. And although he might do these things more for her father than for her sake, Coraza felt her childish infatuation blaze into a fierce love. A love all the sweeter that it never would be spoken aloud, would never find completion. She squeezed Filipo's hand one last time, a tiny embrace he returned. Then she stepped behind him, and Filipo drew his sword.

"Aha!" cried Carlo. "The traitor draws against us! To me, compañeros! Help me avenge this insult to the state!" As the soldier drew his saber, exultation suffused his face.

"Carlo," said the older brother, "don't let the wine talk for you. You made insults to the young señor's face, so he drew as any fellow of manly blood must. Put your sword away."

"Well now," drawled Carlo drunkenly, "look who has sided with the traitors. I always felt you two were disloyal in your hearts."

"We only want to see our guests treated fairly," protested the younger brother. "There is no need for more fighting. Didn't you slake your blood-lust enough this morning with the indios?"

"Them? Ha! How can a man prove himself against savages armed only with sticks and rocks? No, here is true sport. Guard yourself, señor." He raised his sword point at Filipo, hungry for the fight.

Filipo turned his head a little and said softly to Coraza. "Get to the door. Run when you can. Find the Agente and tell him what happened. Go."

As she heard more steel rasp against scabbards and more chairs scrape across the floor, Coraza sidled toward the east wall of the tavern. The three soldiers at the table by the door, however, stood as one and blocked her way.

"Not so fast, chica!"

"You would not insult us by leaving so soon, would you?"

There was a shout behind her, and swords rang against swords. The soldiers in front of her were distracted a moment by the sound. Her moment of fear past, Coraza felt a surge of rage and determination rise to supplant it.

As the heroes of the stories would cry, if I must die this day, let me die bravely and well. Coraza snatched the empty wine bottle from their table and smacked the nearest one on the side of his head.

He staggered back, holding his ear, crying, "Mierda! Madre de Dios!"

His tablemates reached for her, and Coraza swung again with the bottle. She remembered what helped her win those fights in the orphanage. *Give them little to grab onto. Do too many things for them to react to.* One man grabbed her wrist, and then Coraza let her rage turn from hot to cold.

There, in the eye! There, to the neck! There, to the groin! She shrieked, she bit, she scratched, she punched. For Filipo! For Salamago! The soldiers near Colonel Gonzalez at the fireplace hesitated, uncertain which fight to join as their commander roared with laughter.

Coraza seized the moment and leaped onto a table to avoid the clutch of another soldier, then jumped to the floor. In a moment, she was at the door. Unable to help herself, Coraza turned for one last look at Filipo. He was thrusting and parrying like a demon, eyes wide with fury, but he was being pressed back into the corner, the brothers close beside him. Against the drunken soldiers, they had made their strikes, and two, three, four soldiers staggered back with deep cuts on their arms, cheeks and legs.

Filipo's gaze caught hers, and he yelled, "Run!" And then a thrown beer jug struck his head, and he went down.

With a gasp, Coraza pushed the latch and flung herself out the door. The cool evening air slapped her face, and she welcomed it, drinking in the sweet fresh air. But her loving glance had cost her. She was not five paces from the door when two men grabbed her from behind, their fingers like iron bands digging into her upper arms. They carried her back toward the tavern.

"Ha! Such spirit in this one!"

"Let us tame this wild colt!"

They lifted her off the ground, and Coraza kicked with her legs, but she was tiring, unable to put force into it. Instead of carrying her inside, the men took her around to the side of the building and slammed her back up against the wall.

A resounding *no* rose to a crescendo in Coraza's soul. The blade of her father's sword appeared in her mind, and she called upon its strength, its protection. *I am more than this. I am stronger than this. If I am a chimera, let the magic my father imbued me with save me!* She felt a strange power billow up from her guts, a strange orange glow. She felt the taste of dust and ashes in her mouth. She stared at her attacker in the face and growled, "You. Will. Not. Have. Me." From the center of her gut, power flowed out to fill her limbs and face like liquid fire. She watched as dark orange light flickered over her chest, arms, and hands, until she was covered with flames of pure Sere sorcery.

"What's going on? What are you doing?" demanded the soldier holding her.

Coraza focused her gaze on him. And suddenly, she went cold. Or, rather, she no longer felt any particular temperature. She seemed no longer weighed down to the earth. She felt light, like a flake of ash dancing in the smoke of a campfire. Coraza opened her mouth, but she did not scream. Instead, a torrent of hot ash and smoke poured out of her throat into the soldier's face. He screamed and staggered back, hands clasped to his cheeks.

Coraza raised her arms, and a howling circle of wind raised the dust around her. She could hear eerie whispers in the wind, though she did not understand what they said. Thunder rolled the cloudless sky above.

"What is it, Pedro? What is she doing?" cried the other soldier.

The first one fell to the ground, moaning.

Coraza turned to the second soldier, as all pain, all personality, drained out of her, discarded, unnecessary. She rose on the air to tower over him. She heard screams of terror from the building beside her, blending in beautifully with the howls of the wind.

"Ai, Madre! A tzinn!" he cried. He spun and began to run down the road.

She could see him plainly, a glowing red silhouette, like a fleeing, dancing, enticing flame. Feeling a vague hunger, Coraza gave chase.

Chapter Eleven

Filipo came awake to the sound of a low drone, as if an enormous wasp hovered nearby. The scent of ash and burnt wood stung in his nose. Dull pain pulsed through his body.

Hell must have claimed me, he thought, with an ache in his stomach. At first, Filipo did not wish to open his eyes, fearful of what Stygian terrors he might see. *But if what the holy sisters believe is true, and my master's soul has been denied Heaven, then Maestro Salamago himself may be here, and I have much to ask him.* The thought gave Filipo the courage to open his eyes and sit up.

He blinked in the bright sunlight spilling through a doorway. The droning stopped, and when his sight cleared, Filipo saw it had come from an old Indian woman sitting in a chair beside the doorway. He was clearly no longer in the roadside tavern. She gazed at him a moment without expression, then stood up and went outside. Moments later, a figure strode in through the doorway and grasped Filipo's left shoulder.

"Filipo, how do you feel?" asked Agente Palabo.

Filipo did not answer for some moments, as his gaze focused on the vigilero's gaunt face. "I...I am alive?"

"Yes, but it was a near thing."

Filipo looked around, confused, dimly seeing the rough walls and plank floor of a rustic hovel. "This is not the inn."

"No, you are at the farm of the indios whom I went to assist. I am so sorry for what happened, Filipo."

"How am I here?"

"Two soldiers brought you. They were brothers, I think."

"Brothers? They are good men, Agente. Did they bring Coraza, too?" Palabo shook his head.

Horror swept over Filipo, and he grabbed the Agente's arms. "Did they say where she is? Is she still alive?"

The vigilero sighed. "They saw her run out of the inn but did not see her after. There was much confusion, they said."

"Are they still here?"

"No. They would not stay, even wounded as they were. They feared for their lives, so they left at once for Tejas, hoping to catch a ship to the West Indies."

Filipo swallowed hard and stood up despite lingering weakness and dizziness. "I wish they would have stayed, so that I may have thanked them for saving my life. Perhaps Coraza's too, if...Unless Coraza has been shamed or killed..."

Intense regret threatened to wash over him. He remembered the courage shining on her face when Coraza rejected the Colonel's "assistance." How beautiful she had seemed in that moment. He remembered how fiercely she had fought against the soldiers in the brawl. The room spun slightly around him, and Filipo leaned against the Agente to regain his balance. "We must search for her at once. If she is dead or dishonored, I will avenge her," Filipo growled.

"You are not fully healed, my friend," said Palabo. "You have lost some blood. Perhaps you should rest. I will look for Coraza—"

"No!" Filipo pushed off him. "Why did you abandon us? Why did you leave your duty to attend to these...these..." There were no words to match the darkness of Filipo's thoughts.

"These self-same indios who used their skills to help you cling to life?" Palabo snapped. "Filipo, if you had seen...no, it is best you did not."

"If the indios have such skills, why could they have not fought off the soldiers and looked after themselves?"

Palabo covered his face and shook his head. "It is a shame Spanish

Califians choose to know so little. The missions disallowed the natives in their so-called 'care' to learn the old ways. Much has been lost and forgotten. What little knowledge the indios retain is hard-kept and mostly kept to themselves, lest it be forbidden to them again."

Filipo staggered to the doorway and leaned against it, blind in the sunlight. "If you say. But if Coraza is dead, you will have wished that you had let me die as well." With every ounce of will, Filipo walked into the dirt road in front of the hovel. Back over his shoulder, he shouted, "Bring me a horse! Is my horse here?"

A shadow rushed past him as his eyes were still adjusting to the light.

"Filipo—" the Agente began.

"No, I am no longer listening to you! Just bring me something to ride and let me go. I'll bet those bastard soldiers have stolen my horse too. Mierda, I wish I were dead!"

Filipo heard the soft clopping of hooves approaching, and he squinted toward the sound. He saw a native boy of about nine years, whose right arm and leg were bandaged, another bandage wrapped over his right eye. The boy was leading Tulio.

"Tulio!" Filipo cried, and he staggered to embrace his horse's neck. Tears came to his eyes, but he fought them back as the horse nuzzled his shoulder.

"He is a pretty horse, señor," said the boy, patting Tulio's shoulder. "The two men who brought you brought him too."

Filipo looked down and saw the edges of the still raw wounds not entirely covered by the bandages. *What had been done to this boy?* The brothers who had fought at his side had said, "Do real men do such things?" Feeling a severe discomfort unrelated to his injuries, Filipo said, "Thank you. I hope...I hope your family is well."

The boy only nodded and limped back to the doorway where the old woman placed a protective arm across his shoulders. Filipo turned away and hauled himself up onto Tulio's saddle, fighting back nausea, trying to dismiss the pain in his shoulders and abdomen.

Agente Palabo came riding around the hovel and stopped his horse next to Filipo. The vigilero handed him a round canteen. "Here, drink. You need liquid. It may keep you upright in the saddle a while longer."

Reluctantly, Filipo accepted the canteen from Palabo and took a long drink. He handed the canteen back and wiped his mouth on his torn sleeve. "Thank you."

As they rode out of the farm, Filipo saw a barn nearly burnt to the ground and two goats dead and hacked up in the corral. The scored dust in the road hinted that something had been dragged, something that had left spots of dried blood. Filipo thought back to the boy and found he could no longer hate the Agente for his moral lessons quite so much.

Palabo led the way south and west, over two miles of rolling, grassy hills toward the low mountains that separated the valley from the Valle de los Mesanjeros. And there was the inn, looking smaller and even more decrepit somehow.

So close, thought Filipo. *Only five miles.*

They tied up their horses, Agente Palabo eyeing the ground, noting footprints and hoofmarks. "Too many. Tracks have been lost."

Filipo pushed open the inn door, his stomach tightening with dread. But the tables were neatly placed, the chairs upside down on the table tops. The rodent-like tavern master was sweeping up remnants of broken glass on the floor. He stopped and stared as Filipo and Agente Palabo came in.

"Buenos dias, señor," said Filipo, careful to keep all friendliness from his voice.

"B-b-buenos dias, señores," said the innkeeper. He put aside his broom and humbly shuffled over to them. "I'm afraid my establishment is closed for the day, so I may offer no services. If you would like to return another time—"

"I am here on official business," said the Agente. "I understand there was a disturbance in this inn last night, and I am duty-bound to investigate."

"Yes, yes, of course, Agente," said the innkeeper, "but…it was merely a drunken brawl of idle soldiers. Such things happen often—"

Anger overrode Filipo's patience. "Where is the girl?"

The innkeeper jumped as though he'd seen a ghost. "What?"

"You saw her. The señorita who came in with me. What happened to her?"

"I-I do not know, señor. She ran out, and some men ran after her, and one of them came running back in shouting about a tzinn. He...he did not look well, señor. This panicked everyone, and the soldiers ran away. I did not see the señorita again."

"A tzinn?" the Agente demanded, scowling.

"So they said, Agente."

Filipo turned to Palabo and said softly, "Coraza was still afraid that La Llorona would return for her."

"Did you see or hear any sign of a tzinn?" Palabo asked the innkeeper.

"Well, I thought I perhaps heard some wind and dust rattling against the walls and roof. But I was inside, and with all the noise of the soldiers shouting..." The inn master shrugged. "Who could have heard anything else?"

"It would not have been La Llorona in any case," Palabo said to Filipo. "She of all the tzinn likes to arrive with great fanfare. I would have sensed something even as far away as I was."

Filipo's gaze darted around the main room, looking for any sign of Coraza. He saw a familiar sword leaning up against the wall behind the bar. "My sword!" Filipo went and picked it up, examined it. The blade edge was deeply nicked and scored. It was going to need sharpening.

"S-Sí, señor, I was holding it in case...for your return."

Filipo turned and frowned at him.

The innkeeper shrugged again with an embarrassed smile. "I saw it was a Salamago and obviously valuable, so clearly someone would be wanting it..."

Such as yourself, so you could sell it, Filipo thought sourly. He slid the sword back into the empty scabbard at his side. "Thank you for your thoughtfulness, señor."

"Yes, of course," the innkeeper said with regret.

"Con su permiso, señor," said Palabo. "We will have a look around."

"No, no, there is no one. Nothing to see!" cried the innkeeper, louder than he needed to. "I have been cleaning all night, so there will be nothing to find! You may as well be on your way, Agente."

Palabo stared at the tavern master a moment. Then he put his hand on the man's shoulder. "Señor, I have relatives who are simple businessmen such as yourself. I understand how difficult it is to make a living here on the frontier and in these troubled times."

"Yes, yes, truly," said the innkeeper, bobbing his head. "You understand."

"I feel, in part, responsible for the damage you have suffered." Palabo reached down to his belt and pulled from a hidden pocket some paper bank notes. Carefully he smoothed each ten-reales note on the bar until the stack reached one hundred reales. As the innkeeper goggled at the money, Palabo softly continued. "I sincerely hope I can make amends, and if there is anything further I may do for you, I hope you do me the kindness of letting me know."

The innkeeper swallowed hard. "Well. If the Agente would be so kind, I do happen to have a problem at the moment with… rats."

"Rats?"

"Yes. Big ones." The innkeeper's gaze began flicking unnaturally toward a small, narrow door on the north wall. "It may seem beneath you, Agente, but if you would kindly…deal with them, I would be most appreciative."

"But of course, señor. It is the least I can do."

The innkeeper snatched the bills off the bar and stuffed them into an apron pocket. "Madre bless you, Agente."

Conversationally, Palabo said as he strolled toward the narrow door, "Rat infestations often can be traced to one's storeroom, I believe."

Filipo came up behind Palabo, already suspecting what they might find. Palabo tried the door latch and found it locked. He raised his leg and kicked the door in.

Inside the small storeroom sat Colonel Gonzalez on a rough cot, both his arms in slings and three long lines of welts on his left cheek, as if fiery claws had raked his face. On a second cot against the far wall lay another man huddled beneath a blanket.

The Colonel started in surprise but recovered his composure quickly. "Ah! Agente! You have come at last. And I see you have recaptured the traitor who attacked me and my men and summoned a tzinn upon us." Fixing his gaze on Filipo, the Colonel added, "You will hang for this, young señor. Mark my words, you are a dead man."

"You must forgive my hesitation, Colonel," said Palabo, "but I have been told a different version of the events that occurred last night."

"You would doubt me, a soldier of the Governadora? You would take this traitor's word over mine?"

Palabo took from his satchel the small crystal skull which he placed on top of a barrel. "Rest assured, I am most interested in hearing your version of the truth."

The Colonel eyed the crystal skull. "I have nothing more to add," he said quickly. The skull turned a dubious shade of green.

"Where is the girl?" Filipo demanded.

"I have no idea where your little puta is," snarled the Colonel.

Filipo drew his sword and placed it at the Colonel's throat. "Since I am, as you say, already a dead man, it does not matter what further crimes I commit. So, I have no qualms about doing you additional harm. Where is Señorita Salamago?"

The Colonel sputtered, "Agente, help me! Are you just going to let this ruffian threaten me?"

The vigilero did not move from where he stood. "He seems a dangerous man, Colonel, and I do not think it wise to upset him further. Perhaps, for your safety, you should humor him and answer his question."

The Colonel glared at Palabo. "I already told you, I don't know! She ran away, and then a tzinn came along. Maybe the tzinn took her. I hope it did, for all the trouble she caused."

Filipo glanced at the crystal skull, which, to his dismay, was turning golden. "We have reason to doubt a tzinn was ever here," Filipo said.

"Do you?" snarled the Colonel. "Then how do you explain what happened to Leando there?" He nodded toward the figure on the other cot.

Switching his sword to his left hand, Filipo cautiously leaned to his right and snatched the blanket down from the head of the cot. He gasped and stepped back. The face that stared back at him seemed to have been boiled, withered, and sandblasted at the same time. The man whimpered, shivering, unable to speak, and pulled the blanket back over his head.

"You see?" said Colonel Gonzalez. "If a tzinn did not do that, then you tell me what did."

Filipo felt the serpent of doubt stir in his belly. "Agente?"

The vigilero picked up the crystal skull, placing it back in his satchel. "Thank you for your assistance, Colonel. You have been most helpful."

"Of course, I have."

"In fact, in gratitude for your cooperation, I am going to do you a great favor."

"Agente?" asked Filipo in disbelief.

Ignoring him, Palabo leaned toward the Colonel. Quick as a striking rattlesnake, his hand dove into the Colonel's leather vest and pulled out the rolled and sweat-stained document of orders. "Since you are indisposed, I am going to finish your assignment and return this document at once to Doña Vincenza at the Presidio. I intend to give her a complete account of what has happened. I will, in particular, inform her of how the señorita, whom the Doña *urgently wished to question* on important matters of state, seems to have been lost, perhaps fatally, while under your care."

For the first time, Filipo noted, the Colonel turned pale, and fear was evident in his eyes. "Agente, please. You will kindly give good account of what I have suffered and explain it is the fault of this miserable miscreant here!" Again, the Colonel glared at Filipo.

"As I said, Colonel, I will simply state what I have observed, as will the young señor. Whom I will bring with me to the Presidio. And I am certain the Protectadoras will send someone to hear your version of the story. They have methods even more efficient at divining truth than I do. And they are, you understand, very firm with those who disappoint them. So, rest well, Colonel. I will take care of all matters for you. Come, Señor del Utherio.

We must get to the Presidio as soon as possible."

"But...but wait, Agente!" The Colonel tried to rise, but his legs failed him, and he sat heavily back down on the cot. "Surely, there are matters more pressing than this little misunderstanding? I could put in good words for you, yes? Perhaps arrange with my Capitan to find you a good post back in España. Better than this dirty, good-for-nothing colony, eh?"

"You are too kind, Colonel," said Palabo with narrowed eyes. "As it happens, I love Alta Califia and would be happy nowhere else. Unlike some men, I consider my duty to this land and its people a sacred thing. And I put my duty before all other matters. Adios, Colonel. Rest well."

Filipo followed the vigilero out of the storeroom, trying not to smile. The Colonel's punishment was assured, at least. But was Coraza still alive?

"Good day, señor," Palabo called out to the innkeeper. "Your vermin problem will be dealt with soon."

"Thank you, Agente!"

Filipo and Palabo stepped out of the tavern and headed toward their horses. "You don't suppose she might be hiding nearby?" asked Filipo.

"Surely, she would have heard us arrive and come to us if so," said Palabo.

"Still..." Filipo wandered toward the south end of the tavern. A small patch of indigo blue on a low, scrubby tree caught his eye. Filipo strode to the shrub and pulled from its thorny branch a swatch of cloth matching that of Coraza's skirt. The edges of the cloth were burnt, and it had been roughly torn away. Filipo closed his fist around the tattered rag, feeling tears welling in his eyes.

Palabo's hand fell on his shoulder. "It does not mean the worst, Filipo."

"It does not speak of the best, either."

If only there was some way to know if she yet lives, Filipo thought desperately.

"Agente, do you still have the sword named Sorrow?"

"I do," Palabo replied. "But I would not put your trust in such a thing."

"Even so," said Filipo, "we ought to look at it."

Palabo paused. "Very well. But unlike Doña Malaguez, I do not have the skill of reading objects."

Filipo nodded. He tucked the scorched indigo rag into a pocket and walked with Palabo to the Agente's horse. Palabo pulled the yellow leather sheath from his bedroll behind the saddle. He held it a moment, then held the hilt out toward Filipo.

Filipo reached inside the leather sheath bag and grasped the hilt, pulling it out. He blinked in astonishment as the curved blade glowed and coruscated with orange and golden light, shining in greater glory than he had ever seen captured in a Salamago sword. The blade seemed to pulse with life. Filipo also could not "read" objects, though he could sense when a sword was crafted right or wrong. This sword felt righter than it ever had. The bell guard was now smooth, ready to accept the hand to wield it. The metal of the blade showed no faint lines of tempering, as if it had been molded whole. He had not believed that the sword was magically attuned to Coraza. But now, he could think nothing else.

"I think," he said, "that Coraza lives."

Palabo nodded. "We may find out for certain when we reach the Presidio. The Doña Vincenza can examine the sword herself, I am sure, and tell us more."

"To the Presidio, then." Filipo handed the sword back to Palabo, who re-sheathed it. "Though it doubtless means my imprisonment and death."

"Matters may not fall out as you think," said Palabo, mounting his horse.

"Even so," said Filipo as he got onto Tulio, "I have faced death once already. What more have I to fear?"

The vigilero chuckled darkly. "You have never met a Protectadora."

They put heels to their horses and galloped south toward the Valle de los Mesanjeros.

Chapter Twelve

Coraza returned to awareness, standing on a hillside. The long dry grasses around her hissed in the wind like disapproving women. It was midmorning, and the sun beat down brightly, the air already hot. She could smell sage and dust. A valley stretched out before her, and to her right, a few miles to the west, she could see the spires of the Cathedral of the Madre standing above the Pueblo de Los Mesanjeros.

She felt warm breezes across skin that was unused to feeling the open air, and she looked down at herself. Her blouse and skirt were shredded, scorched tatters. Coraza wrapped her arms around her chest so that the wind would not reveal her body to the world. *Where am I? How long have I been here? What happened to me?*

Closing her eyes, Coraza tried to remember the last thing she could. She and Filipo waiting in the tavern, the fight, Filipo's valiant swordplay that brought him down. She had run, soldiers had grabbed her, and—the last thing she had heard—one of the soldiers, staring right at her, had cried, "Tzinn!"

So, a tzinn came for me. No...wait. She slowly recalled her transformation, the wind, the cool fire in her blood, the surge of power in her bones, a vague hunger...*Madre mia! The tzinn, was it me? Not a chimera, but a tzinn? Is that what I am?* A sick iciness congealed in her stomach. *I am...a demon? The creation of a Molochista? If that is so, no wonder Mater Urania and the Protectadoras want me dead.* She searched her feelings within, to find that otherness, the way a child might explore a loose tooth with a tongue. But she did not feel wretched, sinful, or denied the love of the Madre. She was simply...herself. Calm, in fact. At peace. *How can this be?*

She tried to gather her thoughts, but it seemed her past, her understanding of the world and herself, were as shredded as her clothing. *Filipo is probably dead.* Devastation hovered over her at the realization, and she fought it back with whatever hope she could muster. Perhaps the good soldiers who are brothers saved him. *But even if they did, Filipo will surely no longer think well of me. Even the Agente abandoned me. I must begin anew, or I will not survive. But where can I go? Surely, I can no longer become a Protectadora now. Must I go out to the desert and live wild as the tzinn do?* A part of her liked that thought, but another part did not. *But I can only be part of society if I keep the strange part of myself hidden. How can I possibly do that? Did my father intend for me to be this way? Is this the shape he created in me? Madre mia, why?*

Coraza suddenly became aware she was being watched. There was a road some yards off to her right, winding down the hillside into the valley. There was a donkey cart standing in the road. A white-haired old man with a well-trimmed white beard, wearing a battered straw hat, was sitting at the front of the cart, watching her, as was the burro.

Ai, mi. How long has he been there? An abuelo, no less, who will doubtless want to stick his meddlesome nose into my business. The old ones treat every boy or girl as their grandchild.

As she feared, the old man waved and called out to her. "Hola, mi hija! Are you lost?"

Coraza shook her head and lifted her arm to wave him off. But the wind caught the tatters of her blouse, blowing it every which way, and she had to pull her arm back down swiftly and bend down to retain any hint of modesty.

Unfortunately, that alarmed the old man, who got off the cart and came across the hillside at a run to Coraza's side. "Hija, hija, what has happened to you?" He removed the sarape that had been neatly folded on his shoulder and flung it over Coraza. It smelled a little of sweat and soap and hay. He tugged it down until her head popped through the center hole.

Coraza was grateful but looked away, ashamed at what the old man might have seen.

The old man glanced around the hillside, then fixed his worried gaze back on her. "Please, hija, I mean only to help you. What happened to you?"

Coraza felt it would be wrong to reward his concern with rudeness. "There...were soldiers..." she began.

"Ah! Say nothing more. These truly are not safe times for a young one like yourself to wander alone. I am Diego Salbatore. I am taking some vegetables from my farm into town to sell. Would you like to ride with me? Perhaps there is someplace in the pueblo I can take you, yes?"

Not having any other plans at the moment, Coraza nodded. "Where am I?"

The old man placed an arm across her shoulders and gently guided her toward the cart. "Ai, mi. You are on the Rancho La Brea, the property of Don Antonio Rocha."

"Is he a good man?"

Salbatore shrugged. "He is rarely here and leaves us alone to work the land for him. That, to me, makes him a good landlord. And we are permitted to use the pitch in the tar pits on the rancho for our houses if we wish. It is a good thing you did not stumble into one of those pits, señorita, or you would become stuck and turn to bones like the ancient dragons we have found there. Here, let me help you up."

If only you knew what you were befriending, a chimera, a half-tzinn, Coraza thought sadly. She got onto the narrow buckboard at the front of the cart, maintaining her modesty as well as she could, given the state of her skirt. The old man pulled an empty burlap sack from the back of the cart and flung it across her lap.

"Thank you, señor," Coraza said softly.

"It is nothing, no more than a good Mariano should do," said the abuelo as he climbed onto the other side of the buckboard. The old man's eyes creased with concern. The brown burro looked back at them curiously, twitching an ear. The old man shook the reins. "Onward, Miguelito!" The burro blew air out its lips and trudged ahead.

Coraza sat, legs tight together, hands clasped primly in her lap. She smelled the vegetables in the back of the cart warming in the sun, and her stomach rumbled.

"Ah, would you like something to eat, mi hija? Here…" Salbatore turned and pulled a tied-up kerchief from the cart behind him and handed it to Coraza.

She tugged open the kerchief knot and found within a wedge of cheese, some dates, and corn bread. Coraza surprised herself with how fast she ate it all. And then she realized she had just devoured the poor farmer's entire lunch. "I am so sorry. Thank you, señor. Thank you so very much."

"It is nothing. The Madre has given me a good life, and I have all I truly need. It is a pleasure to share with others. Is there some house I may take you to? You have a relative in town, yes? A mother? An aunt?"

Coraza shook her head. "No. I…was in an orphanage." She began to wonder if it was wise, to get so close to the city, where there were more eyes to see her and mention her to authorities.

"I see. Should we perhaps return you to the care of the holy sisters?"

"No!" Coraza blurted out. "They will kill me!"

Salbatore gave her a pained smile and did not speak for some moments. He faced straight ahead, but Coraza could tell he was still examining her from the corner of his eyes. "If this is a matter for the law," he said softly, "I could take you to the Office of Justice."

"No!" Coraza said. "Please, no."

"Ah. Yes, the constables are not always understanding of…women's troubles. And magistrates are reluctant to hear complaints against the Presidio. Unless you have a lot of money." Salbatore fell silent again.

For long moments, Coraza listened to the rattle and squeak of the cartwheels and the clopping of the burro's hooves. She wondered if she should just leap out of the cart and make a run for it. *But where would I go?*

"I tell you what. I have just decided to visit my eldest niece," Salbatore announced suddenly, with a broad smile. "Would you like to visit her too? She fancies herself a curandera."

A healer, thought Coraza. *I think my condition is beyond healing.*

"I have no money, señor."

"Ho, do not let that concern you! Serena is generous to a fault. And she likes meeting new people. Only, she is also a bruja. I hope you won't mind?"

Coraza considered this. A bruja could be just a woman selling herbs or a witch of considerable power. "Is she with the Protectorado?"

"Oh, no, no! Serena is, shall we say, far too independent."

This sounded better. Coraza nodded. "Yes, that should be all right." With some rest and time to think and consider her situation, she might better be able to decide her future course.

"Good! We can be there soon. Much closer than Los Mesanjeros."

Coraza relaxed a little. It was a comfort to have somewhere to go, even if just for a short while. As the burro cart rattled down the road, the old man hummed to himself. Mockingbirds, mourning doves, and bluejays sang and cawed from the bushes along the way. As the foothills gave way to the floor of the valley, Coraza could detect the acrid smell of hot tar on the air.

Salbatore turned the cart onto a narrower track to the right that led to a pueblito of houses and a tiny church. To the south, Coraza could see a grander adobe building with a red tiled roof.

"Yes," said Salbatore, answering a question she had not asked, "that is Don Rocha's grand hacienda. He built it two years ago but, as I said, never lives there. Only his mayordomo inhabits the place. I understand the Governadora has her eyes on using it for government functions."

Soon they entered the first block of shanties and cabins. Dried chiles and garlic hung from the eaves. Women were sweeping the porches or beating rugs hung on lines. Salbatore waved and called out a cheery "Good Afternoon, Señora!" to each one, and they each smiled wearily and waved back. Then they would notice Coraza and stare with great curiosity. Coraza hunched down on the buckboard, wishing she were invisible.

Perhaps this wasn't such a good idea.

Scruffy, thin dogs stared and sniffed the air as the burro cart passed. Coraza wondered if even the animals could sense her changed nature. But something else was strange.

"Where are the children?" Coraza asked. The few times she had been out in the world before, she remembered there would always be some little ones playing hoops or pelota in the street. She had been jealous because the children looked so happy and had homes to live in and a mamma and papa to take care of them.

Salbatore raised a bushy brow at her. "The women have been keeping them inside. There is all this gossip of tzinn being seen walking. Some whisper that La Llorona herself, Queen of the tzinn, has returned. They have heard her wailing in the night, and children have gone missing from this area."

"Missing?" Coraza felt guilt encircle her heart.

Madre mia, please tell me I have had no part in harming any child, please! I do not think I could bear to live if I had. Was it another tzinn? Has La Llorona come back again? What would I do if I see her again? Should I run or greet her as an equal? Did she come for me that day because she knew? Surely, I cannot be such a monster as she.

Salbatore shrugged. "One or two, none recently. And those might have only run away or been taken by a more human form of monster. Some say Molochistas have returned to Alta Califia. Some say they may bring an army from the south."

"Yes, so I have heard," sighed Coraza, all too aware she was living proof that they had. Lectures from faith classes at the orphanage came back to her. Despite the spread of the Church of the Compassionate Madre, who refused to give her son in sacrifice to the greedy ancient god Moloch, there remained sects of that ancient religion of Cartago who would bring back the Old Ways, some of which included child sacrifice, sere sorcery, and the control of tzinn.

Like her.

"The holy sisters taught that the Molochistas were destroyed years ago." Coraza said carefully.

"Who knows? Perhaps the last auto da fé did not catch all of them. And there are still dark parts of the world where the gentle arms of the

Madre do not reach. Ah, but listen to me, gossiping like the old man I am. Please, forgive me."

"Of course," said Coraza, happy to drop the subject. The air was still in the pueblito and felt oppressive.

What am I doing? Is there any hope for me at all?

The burro and cart ambled down a lane that was cluttered with small houses of slightly better build. Some were made of wood, a few of adobe. The lane was shaded with fig and lime trees, poplars and acacias.

Diego Salbatore drew up the cart beside the broad porch of a rustic log house. Colorful flower baskets hung from the eaves, draped with bleeding-hearts, nasturtiums, and morning glories. An herb garden in terracotta pots cluttered its front yard, bound within a woven twig fence. Agave and prickly-pear cactus grew alongside the house, as did the pale trumpet flowers of tronadora and toloache.

Not bothering to tie up the burro, Salbatore jumped down from the cart. "Wait here just a moment, hija, if you please."

Coraza sighed and nodded. As the old man bustled into the house through a back door, Coraza huddled on the buckboard, all too aware that a woman across the dirt street was staring at her. *She's trying to figure out what my story is, where I fit in. She sees a damaged girl, and she's going to make some wrong guesses and judgements. Bad as those judgments may be, they're nowhere near as bad as the truth.*

There was shouting within the house. "You brought me a what?"

"A surprise, Serena. I have brought a lost girl whom you can help."

"You are always bringing me lost things, Tio Diego! Kittens, puppies, birds that fall out of nests—"

"But you are so good with them, Serena. The Madre blesses you with so many opportunities to show compassion."

"I will be blessed into starvation! You never think about what it costs me, Tio Diego! You never think first at all!"

"But Serena, you should see this girl. Your heart would melt for her."

"Hah! Some chica who got in over her head and now doesn't want to go home?"

"Who better to counsel her then, Serena?"

Coraza heard the crash of pottery breaking, followed by enthusiastic swearing.

Diego Salbatore trotted out the back door again, brushing terracotta flakes off his shoulders. "Come. We are fortunate. She is in a good mood." He reached up a hand and guided Coraza down from the buckboard as if she were a society lady.

"Are you sure?" asked Coraza as her feet touched the ground. Part of her torn skirt caught on the rough wood of the cart, tearing it further. Coraza sighed and tugged her skirt off the cart, wondering if she could bear any more indignity.

"Oh, yes, yes. Serena has the will of an ox, but when that will is used to make you well, that is all to the good, yes?" Salvatore guided Coraza in through the door, his hands on her shoulders. The interior of the house was cool and dark. The place smelled of sandalwood, oranges, mint, and other odors that made her nose pleasantly tingle. Coraza's eyes took some moments to adjust in the dim light.

"Here she is, Serena."

"So, chica, you—" and then the woman in front of her stopped, staring at Coraza.

Coraza stared back as a long, uncomfortable moment passed. Serena had what the orphanage girls would have unkindly called a "horse face," long and with big teeth. She had wavy black hair streaked with gray, which cascaded down past her shoulders. She wore many necklaces of heavy silver over her black velvet vest and high-necked blouse. Her blue, tiered velvet skirt blended into the darkness of the room. Serena's eyes were dark as well, and Coraza feared whether the woman was enough of a bruja to see below surfaces. Coraza was relieved to note that Serena's umbra was just a faint purple haze on her hands. This was not a witch of great power. With any luck, she would not discover Coraza's terrible secret in the brief time Coraza would be there.

"She said," Salbatore added softly, "that there were soldiers."

"Soldiers!" Serena flung up her arms and rolled her eyes. "Ai, the

Governadora has much to answer for." She turned and began to savagely rummage through the drawers of a huge credenza that dominated one wall.

"Now, Serena, be careful…"

"Why? All the hacienda knows how I feel."

"But the mayordomo—"

"The mayordomo can stuff his ambitions up a goat's ass! He wants to be Alcalde so he sucks up to her. If the Governadora spent more time governing than having parties and affairs, Alta Califia would be safer." She pulled some clothing out of the lowermost drawer, turned, and faced the old man. "Now, don't you have somewhere to go, Tio Diego?"

"I was on my way to market, yes, when—"

"Then you should be going, before your vegetables rot. Shoo!"

"But—"

"Go!"

Smiling, Salbatore bowed a little to Coraza. "May the Madre bless and protect you, señorita."

"Thank you, señor. Um, your serape…"

"No, no, keep it for now," he said, patting her shoulder. "Serena will return it to me later."

"After I have let all the stray cats you brought me sleep on it. Begone!"

"Yes, yes, Serena. Goodbye." Salbatore bustled out the back door, humming to himself again.

Serena took Coraza by the hands and drew her deeper into the big room that took up most of the house. Every flat surface Coraza could see was cluttered with prayer beads, candles, dried flowers and herbs, and statuettes of familiar holy messengers and saints. And one unfamiliar one whose head was a haloed skull. Licenses to use sorcery were prominently displayed on one wall, between a silver mirror in the shape of the sun and a tapestry of spiral shapes meant to ward off the evil eye. A pair of cats contentedly licked milk from saucers beside the kitchen doorway.

"Your uncle seems very nice," Coraza said, carefully.

"Yes. A saint. An angel." Serena grumbled. "And he expects the rest of his family to be saints too, the poor fool. What is your name, chica?"

Not knowing what else to say, Coraza told the truth. "Coraza." At Serena's frown, she added, "Yes, I know it is an odd name."

"No matter. Listen, Coraza." Her tone became softer, more concerned. "I can, if you wish, make a potion so that...there will be no baby. It will make you sick for a little while, but that is all."

"What? No, I mean, that isn't...I mean they didn't...I fought them off."

"You fought them off?"

"Well, they were drunk."

"Of course."

"And then I...fled."

"Good for you! Smart girl. Here, let us get you out of those rags, eh? Do you want a bath?"

Coraza recoiled at the thought and then wondered why. *Is it my tzinn nature that has caused me to always dislike water?*

"No, thank you."

"Just as well. It takes forever to draw and heat the water. Go on and undress. The neighbor women will give me at least an hour before their curiosity will bring them knocking on the door."

Grateful for the dark curtains over the windows, Coraza pulled off the shredded blouse and skirt. The undervest fell off of its own accord. Coraza looked down at herself and then turned away from Serena. *She will see my trisigil. What might she make of that?*

As if reading her thoughts, Serena said, "Do not be shy about your sigil, chica. I see them often in my work. You will likely have nothing I haven't seen before. And I will keep anything I see a secret. You cannot imagine how many of my neighbor's secrets I bear: who is unfaithful, who wants to be unfaithful, who wants his neighbor cursed, who wants a curse broken. It is one of the burdens of a bruja."

"Do you know what they mean, the trisigils?" Coraza asked.

"Of course. Sigil readings are one of my services. Would you like me to read yours?"

Fear and hope warred in Coraza's heart. *What could she tell me? What might she learn? Then, again, I need all the knowledge I can get to survive.*

"Yes. Yes, I would. Although, I have no money to pay you."

"Of course not. Well, I will have Tio Diego give me a sack of vegetables for my trouble. Sometimes, I live whole months on his carrots and squash. Now then, let us have a look at you. Quickly, and then you must dress."

Coraza summoned her courage and turned to face Serena. She lowered her hands from her chest.

"Ah. The artisan hand in the Father's Seat. You are of a family of makers. And the lattice in the Seat of Self, a structure upon which things are grown. And the..." Serena stopped.

"The big black blot," Coraza finished. "Have you seen that before?"

Serena stepped toward her. "Silly girl. That is not just a blot."

"No?"

"It is a holy seal. I have seen them before. The holy sisters of the Cathedral put such a mark over the original tattoo, if there is some reason to keep it hidden. Since the seal is in the Mother's Seat of the sigil, it was either for your protection or the protection of your mother."

"Why?" asked Coraza.

"Come, now, not everyone would want their parentage displayed upon their person. Tio Diego said you were an orphan. Were you told who your parents were?"

"Only my father."

Serena nodded. "Perhaps he wished to spare you shame."

"You mean, if my mother had been...a woman of convenience."

"Exactly. How old are you, Coraza?"

"Sixteen."

"Past your quinceaña, then. Good. Would you like me to remove the holy seal for you?"

Coraza stared and blinked, astonished. "You can do that?"

"Yes. The holy sisters might not be happy about it, but we shall not tell them, shall we? You are of an age that you have the right to know, if you choose. But the truth may not be a pleasant, or even an interesting, one.

The choice must be yours, Coraza. Do you truly wish to know what lies beneath the seal?"

"Yes, yes, of course!"

"Do not say of course, chica. I have known some to regret their decision. The knowledge haunts them until death. So, I will ask again, are you sure you wish to know?"

What can be worse than what I already know? thought Coraza.

"Yes, please!"

"Very well. Start dressing, and I will make the poultice to dissolve the mark."

Serena swept off to the kitchen, and Coraza heard the sound of jars and pots being pulled from the shelves. Coraza pulled stockings from the pile of clothing at her feet and put them on. She plucked up a serviceable petticoat of stiffened linen and tied that around her waist, then a skirt of gingham.

Serena returned to the main room, stirring a pale green mixture in a bowl. Setting the bowl down, she fetched a long strip of white cloth out of a drawer and smeared some of the herbal paste onto the middle of the cloth. She brought the long bandage over to Coraza and said, "I will put this on you, and it will take until morning to dissolve the seal. It may sting just a little at first. Raise your arms, please."

Coraza nodded, smelling agave, lemon, and mint in the ointment. Serena slapped the ointment-slathered portion of the bandage onto the trisigil on Coraza's chest and wrapped the two ends under her armpits, tying them behind Coraza's back.

At first, the ointment felt pleasantly cool on Coraza's skin. Then, it began to sting. Then, it began to burn. Coraza looked down and saw the skin on her chest begin to glow with a burnt-orange light. The edges of the bandages were steaming and turning brown. The pain became intense as her body fought the magic of the ointment, as if a battle were being waged across her skin just below her collarbone. Coraza sucked in her breath and moaned as her body shook and a chill stole up from her belly. Her body wanted to change.

"No," she growled through gritted teeth. "I mustn't. I won't!" She had to control her nature somehow. Serena deserved no harm. Coraza's pain was not the bruja's fault.

"Chica, are you all right? Look at me!"

Coraza faced Serena, and the bruja's eyes shot wide. Serena jumped back, making the sign of the circle. "Dios mio. Your eyes..."

"I won't hurt you. I swear, I won't." Coraza felt the pain spreading into her arms. She shut her eyes and breathed in and out rapidly.

I can control this. I can stop it. I must. I don't want to hurt her. I don't want to turn tzinn. She clenched her fists and concentrated on the magic in her skin. Bit by bit, she forced the energy in her skin to ignore the pain, ignore the magical fire. By sheer strength of will, she fought down the chill in her belly, the dark spirit that wished to possess her. Shivering like a frightened Chihuahua, she contained the pain and heat in the small area of skin just below the ointment. And it cooled until the pain was no more than a light burning, as if that one spot had been in the sun too long.

Serena looked at each window as if fearful of prying eyes. She rushed forward and snatched up the blouse from the floor, pulling it over Coraza's head. "Put this on, quickly!" As Coraza tugged her arms into the sleeves, Serena grabbed Coraza's shoulders and propelled her into a windowless storage room in the back. "Stay here!" Serena commanded.

Coraza felt so weakened from her battle with herself that it was the easiest thing to obey. Serena dragged in a long wooden bench that filled most of the center of the storeroom.

"I am afraid you must stay in this room and sleep here the night as well. No one must see you. Madre mia, chica, do you know what you are?"

Coraza nodded. "I am a chimera." She decided not to add the rest.

"No wonder your mother's sign on your sigil was sealed. What was done to you...it is a great crime, Coraza. If your mother's name was known, she would be taken to the Grand Tribunal in Madrid and burned at the stake."

Coraza sat on the bench as Serena took a clay pot off the shelf and removed its lid. Serena reached into the pot and pulled out a handful of dried beans. Walking around the bench, Serena began to scatter the beans on the floor.

"Why are you doing that?"

"Speaking of evil things often draws the attention of Evil, chica. I am just taking precautions. Someone like you is the reason a bruja like me is not permitted to have children. The church fears there is too much temptation to...magically meddle with a child in the womb."

"Why would anyone do this?" Coraza asked softly, wrapping her arms around her middle.

Serena snorted a bitter laugh as she flung more beans to the floor. "Because people always want more than they have, chica. Many women come to me, asking me to ensure that their child will be born a boy or girl. Or that it will have fair skin or be very strong or smart or beautiful. Even if I had such power, which I do not, I cannot legally do such things. You are example of the reason for such laws. Such magic, if it were used, can so often go wrong. Life is its own kind of magic, and it fights what man wants to impose on it. Chimera infants usually come out monstrous and do not live long. You are very, very lucky, chica, to have lived as long as you have."

"I do not feel lucky," said Coraza.

"No. I suppose you do not. Perhaps tomorrow your sigil will reveal what your parents wanted to make of you."

Coraza amassed the courage to ask, "And then what? Are you going to report me to the Cathedral? I will not blame you if you do."

A long moment of silence passed. Finally, Serena said, "I will not betray you, hija. That would be sending you to certain death, and I will not do that. Such matters are for the Madre to judge, not I. Tio Diego brought you to me to keep you safe. You fought down the urge to do harm, so you have proven you are not evil. You clearly have much inner strength, Coraza. I will do what I can, but you cannot stay here beyond tonight. I have too many nosy neighbors. Sleep here, and in the morning, we will look at your sigil and hope it gives you guidance. We must think of someplace you can go, someone who might have the power to protect you."

Coraza nodded. "Thank you, Serena. It is more kindness than I deserve."

"Pish!" said Serena, some of her archness returning. "We are all confused and crazy people, chica. Let us not speak of what is deserved. Let us only give each other what we can, what is needed. Rest now. I will bring you some food and a pillow while I think about what to tell nosy Rosa across the street about you."

Chapter Thirteen

The sun was setting between the spires of the Cathedral de Los Mesanjeros, to the west behind them, when Filipo and Agente Palabo rode wearily up to the adobe gate of the Presidio, the great fort built to protect the city of Los Mesanjeros.

Filipo noticed that the soldiers on guard duty barely glanced up from their boot polishing as he and the vigilero walked their horses in. A strange mixture of anxiety and nostalgia washed over Filipo as they entered the Presidio's large courtyard and smelled the horses, leather, iron, and sweat.

His father had brought Filipo there when he was only eight years old. Filipo had been impressed by the uniformed officers in their polished helmets and boots and admired the rough-riding soldiers in their leather vests and hats. He had briefly wanted to run away and join the army then and there. But his father had needed Filipo to help him in fishing, and Filipo had grown strong hauling nets and dexterous in repairing them. Only a predilection for sea-sickness had kept Filipo from following his father's vocation. And a sensitivity and tolerance for magic, plus the connection of a-friend-of-a-friend to Señor Del Utherio, had gotten Filipo the fortunate position as Salamago's apprentice at the age of thirteen.

Salamago had been an impressive, almost frightening man, with great muscles, wild hair, and a smile that promised secret knowledge, practical wisdom, and the chance he'd knock you flat on the floor if you crossed him. Once established in his service, Filipo felt with great pride that he would never be anything else but a blacksmith..

So now, Filipo would rather die at gunpoint than become a soldier, and he watched the men around him with narrowed eyes. But he saw no one who was involved in the fight at the tavern. Those soldiers who looked up to watch them pass mainly stared at Agente Palabo with curiosity. Though the daylight was dimming, Filipo could see that the walls of the garrison were in poor repair, adobe flaking, wood rotting, bricks broken. There was a strange unease in the fort, quite unlike the atmosphere of his childhood visit.

The Agente led the way across the yard to a large wood outbuilding with a tiled roof. Farmers in their straw hats, women in plain-woven skirts, and workmen in leather trousers sat by the steps at the building doorway. Some watched the door with hopeful eyes; some sat downcast, dejected. Palabo dismounted, and Filipo followed his lead. The vigilero pulled the leather sheath holding Coraza's sword out of his bedroll and strapped it across his back.

A sergeant's boy ran up to take their horses' reins. At first, Filipo resisted, but Palabo waved his hand to indicate it would be all right. "If we are not safe here, then we are safe nowhere," he murmured. The Agente gave the boy a coin, and Filipo reluctantly let the boy lead Tulio off to the fort stables.

As Agente Palabo ascended, the poor folk on the steps around him called out, imploring, "Agente! Please speak for me! Agente, please give my request to the Captain! Agente, please take my complaint to the Protectadoras! Agente!"

Palabo kept his gaze to the ground and waved them off. From the set of his jaw, Filipo could tell that this cruel, feigned indifference hurt him.

They stepped inside the Captain's office, dimly lit by two wall lanterns and a large candle on the desk. Behind the battered oak desk sat a pale, balding man with a thin, drooping mustache. Despite his uniform, Filipo doubted the man had ever seen battle.

He glanced up at them, quill pen poised in hand. "I am finishing my business for the evening," he said in a bored voice. "Kindly return in the morning."

"I am afraid this cannot wait, Captain Antaides," said Palabo striding forward.

"Oh. It's you." The Captain sighed and set his quill carefully down on blotting paper. "What do you want, Agente Palabo?"

"We need to speak with Doña Vincenza at once."

The Captain blew a laugh out between his lips. "You must be joking. You know as well as anyone that the Protectadoras see no one."

"I believe this time will be an exception. She will speak to us."

"I understand you have a reputation for nonconformity, Agente, but really, this is too much. Give me a message, and I will see that it is passed to the Doña."

Palabo leaned over the Captain's desk. From beneath his serape, the vigilero brought forth the rolled up orders he had taken off Colonel Gonzales and slapped the paper down before the Captain. "We bring word of the fate of Colonel Gonzales and the vital informant he was charged to escort here. His expedition has failed. I believe Doña Vincenza will wish to know the details at once. I also believe she will be most upset with anyone who delays this news getting to her."

The Captain delicately picked up the orders and unrolled it. "Colonel Gonzales..." he muttered. "Yes, we had been expecting him and his men back today. I'd wondered why they were late."

Something in the Captain's tone implied to Filipo that the Captain had very good guesses as to why the Colonel might be late. Filipo stepped forward. "Captain, I must voice an official complaint—"

Palabo swiftly held up a hand to silence him. "Another time, Filipo. We must speak to the Doña first. Well, Captain?"

With a suspicious glance at Filipo, the Captain stood. "Very well, I'll take your request to the steward of the Protectadoras. But you must prepare yourselves for disappointment, señores. I cannot remember the last time Doña Vincenza met with anyone personally. Wait here."

He gathered his dignity and strode out of the office, accompanied by the cries of the petitioners, to whom he shouted, "Go home! Go home!" The door banged shut behind him.

Filipo sighed, feeling the weariness of his long ride and recovery. He sank into a chair beside the desk, too tired to summon the fury he ought to have felt toward the Agente. "Why did you stop me? I have a right to air my grievance to the Captain. We owe it to Coraza."

Palabo stared out the window, watching something. "In these troubled times, one should be cautious about denigrating an officer to his superior. The superior might choose to take the wrong side. The truth will come out soon enough. How are you feeling?"

"Terrible."

"Mmm. Perhaps we can ask the Doña's help in that. But you must pull together what stamina you can. You will find the Protectadora's appearance a bit...startling."

Filipo wondered what could be so strange about the sight of a very old woman. As a boy, he had seen an aunt and a grandmother on their deathbeds. Distressing under the circumstances, but he hadn't been startled. "You are certain she will meet with us?"

"Yes."

Sure enough, some ten minutes later, the Captain returned, even more pale of face than before. "You are to come at once," was all he said.

Filipo and Agente Palabo followed him across the courtyard to a squat adobe tower that sat astride the eastern wall of the Presidio. The Captain unlocked the heavy iron-banded door and let them in. But he did not follow. "One last thing, Agente. Where are Gonzales and his men now?"

Palabo turned. "The last I saw of them, the Colonel and one man were resting at the El Camino Tavern on the north side of the Tujunga pass. As for the rest, I don't know."

The Captain gave him one curt nod, then shut the door.

Filipo and Palabo were inside a square room, bare except for two secretary-style desks and a strange metal cage in the back. Before them stood a woman of perhaps fifty, dressed all in black. Filipo began to bow, but Agente Palabo kicked his boot.

Without preamble or greeting, the woman said, "The Doña Vincenza awaits in the room below. Understand, your time with her must be brief."

"Very good, señora," said Palabo. "We will be brief."

The woman led them back to the cage, slid open the barred door, and gestured for them to enter. Filipo hesitated, but Palabo said, "It is all right."

Filipo cautiously stepped in behind the vigilero.

"Pull down the lever when I have closed the gate," said the woman, and she slammed the metal gate back across the cage.

Palabo grasped a large iron bar sticking up on the back wall and shoved it down. The whole cage began to descend with a disconcerting *chunka-chunka* sound.

"What magic is this?" asked Filipo, looking wildly around.

"It is called an ascensor," replied Palabo. "I have heard there are buildings in Yanqui cities that use these contraptions to reach higher floors."

"Are Yanqui legs so weak," asked Filipo, "that they cannot use stairs?"

Palabo shrugged.

To hide his discomfort, Filipo went on, "Besides, I thought sorcerers lived at the top of towers, not beneath them."

"Those wizards whose arts require knowledge of the stars do, certainly. But the Protectadoras practice the arts of the geomancer, and thus find their inspiration below ground."

The cage finally shuddered to a stop. Palabo stepped forward and slid the cage door aside. Ahead of them was a smaller room than the one above, lit by candle sconces on the walls. In the middle of the room was a lone chair. On it sat a bent figure, her head and face hidden beneath the drape of a black lace mantilla.

Agente Palabo stepped out, murmuring to Filipo with a small smirk, "Now." He bowed deeply, and Filipo did as well. "Thank you for the honor of speaking with us directly, Doña Vincenza," said the vigilero as he straightened up.

"Normally, I would not, but I understand your news is most urgent, Agente." The woman in the black mantilla rose from her chair. And continued to rise until her feet dangled below the hem of her black skirt, no longer touching the floor. With hands so thin and bony that they belonged on a wraith, she lifted the edge of the mantilla and draped it across the back of her head. The old sorceress's face was sunken and slack, a skull draped in skin. Her rheumy eyes shone with a sickly green-yellow light. She seemed physically as fragile as a snowflake yet emanated enormous magical power. Filipo swallowed hard and fought not to look away. "What has happened to the girl?" Her low voice, to Filipo's surprise, was strong and steady.

"I gave Coraza over into the care of Colonel Gonzales, as you instructed, señora," said Agente Palabo. "I accompanied them for a time, but then I was called away on other business."

"What happened then?"

"That is Señor del Utherio's tale to tell."

The wizened old woman turned and drifted to hover before Filipo. "And who is this?"

"He was the apprentice to the late Erculeo Salamago, señora."

"Was he? How interesting. Well, young man?"

Filipo struggled hard to maintain his composure in the sight of such a ruin. He noticed the Protectadora's thin, withered lips twitch in the semblance of a smile. She was enjoying the effect she had on him. *This is the sort of creature we have as our ultimate protector?* Filipo thought, his horror now tinged with anger.

Filipo cleared his throat and began. "The Colonel insisted we stop at a tavern, señora. While there, he demanded...favors from Coraza. When she refused, he allowed his men to harass us. I was challenged and forced to defend our honor. While I was fighting, she escaped...I hope. Then I was struck down and remember nothing else until the Agente revived me."

"You are courageous, young señor. Fear not, Colonel Gonzales will be punished for his corrupt behavior."

"Perhaps," Agente Palabo interjected, "if the señora had chosen to trust me and merely informed me that the Protectorado had wished to see the girl, none of this might have happened."

"Do you chide me, Agente?" said the old woman, turning to him and tilting her head at an almost coquettish angle. "You who have such a reputation for unreliability? Can you not understand why I put my trust in someone more under my control?"

Filipo nervously wondered why the Agente was speaking so boldly. *Does he have bigger cojones than I thought, or does he have some scheme in mind?* Then Filipo caught sight of the rage seething behind the vigilero's eyes and realized that, indeed, Palabo had meant to chide the Protectadora. *Good for him.*

Fearing, however, that the Agente might be magically struck down any moment, Filipo added, "Indeed, if you had merely told the Colonel of Coraza's importance, perhaps he would have thought twice before behaving as he did."

The sorceress turned back to face Filipo, her head tilting in the other direction like a cat discovering new, enticing prey. "Because of the many, many questions that might then be asked, young señor. And I see that Salamago's infamous lack of courtesy has been passed on to his apprentice."

Filipo gulped down his pride and bowed again. "Forgive me, señora."

After a long, uncomfortable moment, Doña Vincenza said, "Well. Let us turn to more productive pursuits. Have you determined whether the girl still lives, Agente?"

"We have reason to believe she does, señora."

"And what reason is this?"

"Salamago left to his daughter a sword. We believe there is a magical link between this blade and Coraza." Palabo pulled the leather sheath off his back and held it between both his hands.

"So that is the troublesome legacy Mater Urania mentioned. Let me see it."

As Palabo loosened the leather ties to the sheath, Filipo said, "We were hoping, señora, that you might have the skill to read Coraza's location from the blade itself."

"I will attempt it."

But as Palabo drew the sword Sorrow out of the sheath bag, Filipo moved to stand between it and the Protectadora. "Wait. It has changed again."

"What?" asked the Agente.

"Look. The metal of the blade has more of a greenish sheen. It is as though it's been through another annealing or tempering, another pass through the fire and cooling to make it stronger."

"I am concerned as to what that may mean," murmured Palabo.

"Indeed," agreed Filipo.

"What are you talking about?" demanded Doña Vincenza.

"Your pardon, señora," said Filipo. "This sword seems to change its appearance, which is unlike any other blade my master ever made. We think it has something to do with changes in Coraza." Reluctantly, he took the sword from Palabo's hands and held it out horizontally before the ancient sorceress.

She raised her hands, which drooped like dead things from her wrists. Her fingers twitching like the legs of spiders, she slowly lowered her palms onto the flat of the blade. She closed her eyes and sighed. "Hmmm…" Suddenly great orange sparks crackled out of the blade, lashing her hands and wrists. Dona Vicenza shrieked and lurched back. The sword slipped from Filipo's hands and fell clattering to the stone floor. "That fool!" the Protectadora shouted, rubbing her hands against her black skirt.

Filipo stooped to pick up the sword, first tapping the blade cautiously a couple of times to ensure it would not attack him as well. He was unsure as to whether the Doña's outburst referred to Salamago or Coraza.

Agente Palabo reached out to her asking, "Are you all right, señora?"

"Yes, yes, yes, yes, yes, now put that cursed thing away."

Filipo slipped the sword back into the leather bag. "Forgive us, señora. We had no idea it would do such a thing."

"I'm sure you did not."

"Were you able to learn anything from it, señora?" asked Agente Palabo.

"I have learned Salamago is…was more clever than I gave him credit for."

"But regarding Coraza, señora—"

"Other than she is alive and nearby, somewhere in the valley, no. I was…forbidden to look deeper than that."

Filipo fought to keep a smile off his face. He felt a familiar pride well up at the skill of his master. Salamago had feared what the Protectadoras might do with it, his last creation, and he had somehow implanted a defense against it.

"Agente," Doña Vincenza went on, "I now charge you and the young señor with the task of finding the girl. Find her as soon as possible and bring her to me at once. Do not allow yourself any more distractions, Agente. I cannot tell you how important this duty is. The Governadora has come to town for the Dragon Ship Fair, and I will have to inform her of this turn of events."

Filipo narrowed his eyes at the Protectadora. "I thought you wanted Coraza's existence kept secret. Why should the Governadora be informed about her?"

"I am sure," said Agente Palabo, with an odd look at the Protectadora, "that the Governadora would be concerned to know there may be Moloch-istas active in Alta Califia."

"Questions, questions, too many questions," murmured Doña Vicenza as she drifted closer to Filipo.

"I will accept your orders, señora," Filipo went on, amazed and a little frightened at his own bravado, "only if you solemnly swear that Coraza will not be harmed or killed."

"Filipo," the Agente said in a warning tone.

"No!" Filipo insisted. "What would be the purpose of finding Coraza alive only to bring her to her death? I will not do such a thing."

The Protectadora hovered closer until her nose was just a couple of inches from Filipo's. Summoning all his courage he stared back, unblinking, into her yellow-green eyes.

Her lips quirked again. "You have feelings for her."

Filipo jerked back, startled. "Uh, well, she is my master's daughter. I am duty-bound to protect her."

"Is that what you tell yourself? How charming. Very well, if it will ease your conscience, I will swear that I have no intention of harming Coraza, let alone killing her. She is far too important."

"Do you? Coraza said several times that Mater Urania meant to kill her."

"The Church and the Protectadoro do not always see eye to eye. We operate in the realm of the practical and the necessary, not the sacred. If there is truly a hell, I am surely bound for it. As for Coraza, it is fortunate that Mater Urania did not entirely know what she was housing, and she was all too willing to take Salamago's money. However, I must council; you must put aside whatever tender thoughts lie in your heart toward the girl. Coraza was not made for any sort of normal life, and she will never be a wife and mother."

Filipo's gut clenched at the Protectadora's choice of words. "Made? She is a person, born like any other!"

Doña Vicenza backed away, her eyes narrowing to slits. "She was not conceived and born like any other human person. Now that is enough questions."

Agente Palabo's hand fell on Filipo's shoulder. "Forgive him, señora," the vigilero said. "Filipo is still recovering from a long ride and the many grievous wounds he suffered last night defending Coraza. My healing skills could only do so much. He is still a bit light-headed. My magic reserves have been drained, so I can do no more. We will need at least a night's rest before beginning the search again."

Filipo wanted to argue, but better sense finally got a grip on him, and he held his tongue.

"Hmm." Dona Vicenza stared at them for long, silent moments. At last she added, "Follow me." She turned and drifted to a narrow door at the far end of the room. Without raising a hand, she somehow opened it and floated into the room beyond.

"Where is she going?" Filipo softly asked Palabo.

The Agente slung the sword bag containing Sorrow over his back once more, murmuring, "I believe you are about to be accorded a great honor. Go on. Follow her."

Uncertain, Filipo went after Doña Vincenza. Beyond the doorway was a short earthen tunnel, and Filipo's nose filled with the scent of damp sandstone and clay. Out the other end of the tunnel, Filipo entered a large, circular room, two stories high. Along the curved earthen wall stood chairs, many of which were empty. Those that weren't were inhabited by ancient women slumped over, immobile. Filipo wasn't certain they were all alive. Attached to each Protectadora's wrists and ankles were silvery wires that led into the wall, as if each sorceress were caught in a web that lay just beyond the room.

"What are the wires for?" asked Filipo. "Do they keep you from falling?"

A dry laugh emerged from Doña Vincenza's throat. "They are everything, young señor. Another of Califia's blessings and curses. Deep scars run through this land, where the earth wars against itself, and rocks grind against each other. Some call these scars ley lines; some call them faults, as if they were like the flaws that give gemstones such character. These create and carry enormous energy. We draw on that energy to sustain us and support our sorcery. Doing so not only prolongs our life, it prevents earthquakes as an extra benefit. Now, sit there," Doña Vicenza directed him, pointing at an unoccupied chair.

"What? No! What are you going to do?" For a moment, Filipo feared his remaining energy was to be drained by those wires, and he would become dried like a snake's dead skin.

"Foolish boy. You will receive some of the energy I just spoke of. It will help you heal and clarify your thoughts."

Reluctantly, Filipo sat in the dusty wood chair, the ancient leather seat creaking under his weight. He couldn't help wondering whether some bruja had recently died in it, thereby causing it to be available.

"Agente, some assistance if you please," Dona Vicenza called out, and Palabo emerged out of the tunnel.

Without a word, Palabo walked up to Filipo and began to wrap silvery wires around Filipo's wrists and ankles.

"Agente, are you sure—"

"Hush."

Doña Vicenza draped her limp, cool hand over Filipo's head. "Rest now. Remember, we give you this gift so that you will be able to bring Coraza to us. Do not let it be wasted."

"What will hap—" and then a wave of power rolled into him like the breakers he knew as a fisherman's boy, and his mind drifted away.

And then Agente Palabo was slapping him. "Wake, Filipo, you have had enough."

Filipo blinked his eyes open and stood. He felt as though he had stood at the head of a flood with his mouth open. He felt beyond full of…something. He expected his body to slosh when he walked. But he felt awake, alert, alive. All memory of the wounds he had received the night before were gone. His body had never felt better. "Ai, Agente, this is amazing!"

"Isn't it? Come, we should leave the Protectadoras to their work." He nodded his head toward Dona Vincenza, now sitting slumped in a chair across the room, wrists and ankles bound with the silvery wires, like a dead fly in a spider's web.

"Why doesn't this energy help her as it has me?"

"How do you think she and the others have lived so long?"

"Oh." Filipo nearly danced from one foot to the other. "How long was I asleep?"

"Almost two hours."

"Only that long?" It had felt like only a second. It had felt like a lifetime. Filipo found it strange that both could describe the experience. He turned in place, arms out, now sensing the magical power that flowed into the room, power that poured down the cracks in the earth that crisscrossed the region like scrimshaw hatch marks on ivory.

"Do you think they would allow me to come back for this treatment again, should I need it? You know, if I should be wounded in another sword fight?"

"It is enticing, isn't it?" said Palabo. He grasped Filipo's shoulder and propelled him toward the tunnel passageway. "But do you really want to join the Protectadoras, never to leave this chamber again?"

"Ah, perhaps not at this time. Have you ever drunk from the wires, Agente?"

"Once, when I was about your age. When I became a vigilero. That was enough for me."

Through the tunnel, back into the antechamber and into the acensor they went, questions caroming around Filipo's mind. As Palabo raised the lever and the elevator chunked slowly upward, those questions began to spill from Filipo's mouth. "I wonder how or why my master would have forbidden Doña Vicenza to touch the sword he had made. I don't think they were even acquainted. How did he know she might someday attempt to read it?"

"Good questions, Filipo. I don't suppose you have some good answers as well?"

"No, no. Not yet. But if all the Protectadoras are so old, why don't they bring new brujas...Wait, you don't suppose that is what they intend for Coraza, do you? She once said she'd like to be one."

Palabo shook his head. "The way she has been treated is all wrong for that possibility. If she were to be a Protectadora, they could have escorted her with honors from the orphanage at a younger age and trained her. Instead, they locked her away, fearful of what she was, and gave her no training at all. The Protectadoras were formed during the Great Revolt, and they do not want to let in outsiders, no matter how necessary that may become. They wish to hold on to political power as well, as it is certain that is why Lucita Remedios became Governor."

"I don't understand," said Filipo.

"Governadora Remedios is Doña Vincenza's granddaughter. Didn't you know that?"

Filipo shook his head. Politics had never been an interest of his. Maestro Salamago had mostly kept silent on such matters himself, which Filipo had thought wise for an artisan whose customers were the rich and powerful. Finally, the ascensor slammed to a stop, and Palabo pushed the metal cage gate open. As Filipo stepped out, his stomach growled loudly. "Forgive me, Agente, but I am ravenous!"

"I have anticipated this," said Palabo. He led Filipo out of the adobe tower and over to the captain's office. Upstairs from the office was a room with simple small beds and a large table, heavily laden with bread and roast beef and even bottles of wine.

"Soldiers eat well," said Filipo, his mouth watering.

"Officers do. Sit and eat. Then we will plan our search. It is good to have confirmation that Coraza is in the area, but the Valle de los Mesanjeros is a big place."

For the next few minutes, Filipo ate his fill, and it all tasted wonderful. When at last he could speak again without being rude, Filipo said, "You know, there is one other who can successfully read that sword."

"Indeed? Do I know this person?"

"You were in the same room when she last did so. The Doña Malaguez."

Hope flitted across the vigilero's gaunt features, only to be replaced with regret. He shook his head. "A good thought, but impossible. Too dangerous. You know I cannot venture back onto the Malaguez hacienda without risking death."

"But we need not go back to the hacienda," said Filipo, warming to the discussion, "and it need not involve you at all. Remember the Dragon Ship Fair? Every lady of good blood goes to get first pick off the Cathay merchant ships. I am sure Doña Malaquez will be among the shoppers—she's been there before. My master took me to the fair a few times. It's a good place to find the people of quality, when you need to speak to them or sell them something. She regards me kindly, and I am not suspect as you are. I could approach her myself and pretend I have another Salamago sword for her husband's interest. What do you think?"

After a pause, Palabo replied, "I think the ley lines have done more than just heal you. They have managed to make you intelligent."

Filipo set down his fork, wondering if he should bother to be insulted.

"I will agree to this plan on one condition," said Palabo. "That you will also take a note from me to her, and that you swear upon your honor that you will not read it."

Filipo smiled. He had a pretty good idea of what would be in the note anyway. It was...reassuring, somehow, to see that human side of the vigilero. "You have my oath, Agente."

"Then we have a plan, amigo."

Chapter Fourteen

"Wake up, chica. It is nearly dawn."

Coraza sat up, her body sore from sleeping on the hard bench in Serena's storage room. The only illumination was one lit candle on a shelf. Dark wisps of disturbing dreams still lingered in her mind. Dreams—or was it memory—of a man at her feet, begging for his life. She had gazed down upon him without pity, or triumph, or any sort of human feeling.

"Here, eat this." Serena placed a cloth napkin wrapped around something warm in her lap.

Coraza was startled—the bundle felt alive for a moment. But then the scent of cooked beans and rice reached her nose, and her stomach growled. Coraza unwrapped the napkin, finding a tortilla stuffed with beans, rice, cabbage, and shreds of chicken. She bit into it carefully.

"Every woman in the neighborhood, nearly, came by yesterday. All trying to find out who you are, to hear your story," said Serena as she bustled around the storeroom, sweeping up the circle of beans that had served as Coraza's protection, or cage. "There is so little to entertain us here, every stranger becomes a drama."

"Thank you again for your kindness," Coraza rasped, her mouth dry.

"Psht," said Serena with a dismissive shrug of one shoulder. "We will look at your trisigil, and then we must go. Have you thought of anywhere you could be safe?"

"Yes," Coraza answered. "There is one person who has offered me protection."

"A relative?"

"No. A man who knows what I am. He said if I ever needed help, I could call upon him."

Serena put her broom aside and snatched a clay jar from a shelf. She took off the lid and dabbed a cloth into the jar. "Do you trust this man?"

Coraza shrugged this time. "I know he will not kill me. Or return me to the orphanage. And his interest is not like Colonel Gonzales. He is more interested in my being...strange, than my being a girl."

"I am not sure that is better. But at least it is someone. Here, let us have a look at you." Serena knelt down beside the bench, unlaced Coraza's undervest, and lifted up the blouse until it was wrapped around Coraza's neck.

The ointment-covered cloth was cool against the skin of Coraza's chest. The muscle below it seemed to hold an ancient ache, beyond pain, as though the magical salve Serena had applied the night before had burned through to the bone.

Serena wiped the spot vigorously with a dry corner of the cloth. "Ah, yes. It has worked very well. Keep holding the blouse up like that." Serena dropped the cloth and plucked the lit candle from the shelf. She held the candle near. "Madre!"

"What is it? What do you see?" Coraza asked anxiously.

"I have never seen anything like this, chica. You have not one, but three symbols in the Mother's Seat. It is like a trisigil within a trisigil."

"Three? How is that possible?"

"The marks are magical, you know, so that they grow with a person as he or she ages and never fade. The holy sisters make a stencil, then for the tinting use a powder whose composition they keep utterly secret, so that the marks can never be removed. It is entirely within their skill to make an intricate sigil like this, but I have never seen it before.

"Ah. But tell me, please, what are the three symbols?"

"One is the sign of the Eye with a sword as the pupil. That is the symbol of the Protectadoras."

"The Protectadoras?" Again, Coraza felt a surge of hope and longing, soured by fear and disappointment.

"Yes, and beside it is a heraldic lion. This is a sign of noble family. Your mother was no mere woman of convenience, chica. That should be of some comfort to you, I suppose."

Coraza was not sure what to make of it. What hope would a lineage of wealth mean, given that she had been abandoned to an orphanage? "And the third?"

"I do not recognize it, but my intuition tells me it is a magical symbol. It is like...a mountain transfixed by a lightning bolt. If your protector is a sorcerer, he might know more. But I would be very cautious, chica."

"Yes, of course. You said you can 'read' someone's trisigil. Is mine beyond reading?"

Serena sat back on her heels, her face grim in the candlelight. "I have never read for a chimera, so I cannot say for certain. What your sigil tells me...a mystical artisan's sign in the Father's Seat, a lattice framework in your Soul Seat, and the marks in your Mother's Seat, all point to a...deliberateness about your being. Your situation is not that of a child who was merely enhanced on a whim to be prettier or smarter. It is more as though you were..."

"Built? Like a house?"

"Yes. And at least one of the Protectadoras knew of you from the very beginning." Serena stood and turned away. "If one of them had a hand in your creation, then we are all lost."

"Lost? Why?"

"It means there is a Molochista amid the Protectadoras."

Coraza stared at the candleflame in shock. Such a thing was beyond comprehension. Much of the history she had been taught at the orphanage centered around the battle between Roma and Cartago and how the rise of the Church of the Madre lead to the defeat of the detested Molochistas and their use of human sacrifice in their sorceries. Eventually, the Molochistas were scattered to the dark places of the world, but the Church had remained ever vigilant. The rise of the Nuevo Aztecas, however, showed that the vigilance had not been enough. If the Molochistas now had a champion in the coven that protected Alta Califia, then their colony was doomed. The war of sorcery that was to come would be horrific. And if the evil sorcerers succeeded, they could use Alta Califia as yet another base for further conquest. Perhaps to strike back at Roma, Espana, and eventually all of the world, would fall under their murderous darkness.

Coraza relaced her undervest and lowered her blouse, smoothing it into place. "So. What should I do?"

"Pray with all your heart that I am a foolish woman who is all wrong. Now get yourself ready. I hear Tió Diego at the front gate." Serena bustled out of the room.

Coraza did her toilet and brushed her hair. She felt numb inside. If the Protectadoras knew of her birth, why had she been permitted to live? Unless only one Protectadora knew and had hidden Coraza away in the orphanage to protect her. As Serena returned with a large serape to drape over Coraza's shoulders, Coraza determined that, if nothing else, she would insist that Dr. Raimundo help her find out the truth. If she could learn her true nature and power, she could plan how to find her way in the world, find out how to be a "Coraza."

 As Serena gave her a basket that smelled like it held chopped carrots, Coraza paused and looked at the floor. "I am finding hard to say the right words to say goodbye to you and thank you, for all your help."

"A good thing, then, that you do not have to, chica, not yet anyway, for I am coming with you. A girl your age draws far less curiosity with a duenna by her side. Come on, let us not make Tio Diego wait."

Serena put her arm across Coraza's shoulders and guided her out to Diego Salbatore's donkey cart. The old man nodded to her and softly wished Coraza good morning as she climbed onto the buckboard to sit wedged tight between him and Serena. Salbatore lightly flicked his long switch against the burro's backside and clicked his tongue. With an annoyed bray, the burro strained against the harness and pulled the cart forward. Coraza became aware of curtains in the surrounding house windows being pulled slightly aside, watching her depart the Hacienda La Brea.

Although the central plaza of Los Mesanjeros was only a few miles from the hacienda, the donkey cart was slow. And when they entered the narrow, cobbled streets of the city itself, they often had to stop, waiting as merchants clogged the streets, preparing their shops and booths to open. The trip took hours, and the sun was well above the horizon by the time Diego's donkey cart emerged into the great central plaza of La Reina de Los Mesanjeros.

Coraza's emotions were in turmoil, seeing the Plaza again. When she was much younger, the holy sisters had brought the orphan girls into the city as part of their history lessons. It had seemed so grand, so amazing, to the eyes of a child. In the center of the plaza stood a tall stone statue of Queen Califia herself—a muscular warrior-woman with indio features, bearing a golden spear in one hand and a round white stone representing a pearl in the other. The holy sisters had said Queen Califia was probably only a legend. But a popular book written in the sixteenth century describing Califia's fabulously wealthy island kingdom of amazons had spurred expeditions and the eventual founding of the colony. Although Califia and her amazons were never found, the colony was nonetheless given her name.

Two large ironwork gazebos stood at the north and south end of the enormous plaza. Coraza remembered hearing musicians play cheerful music there on a Sunday afternoon. There had been candy merchants, puppeteers, and toy sellers. Such childhood joy felt at odds with the stories of blood running in the gutters of the plaza that were told by the holy sisters with such grim relish.

On the western side of the plaza rose the great twin-towered Cathedral of The Madre. Coraza had been awed by it as a child. Now she wanted to cower between Diego and Serena, hoping that no clergy of that holy place had the sensitivity to notice and identify her. Surrounding the plaza were narrow buildings crammed together, the finest shops and townhouses of the wealthy and would-be-wealthy.

Coraza saw a painted sign of a golden bear swinging from the eaves of a building across the plaza to her left. "There! From what Doctor Raimundo told me," she said to Serena, "his townhouse should be among these here." Coraza pointed to their right.

"You don't know which one?" asked Serena.

"I am sorry, no."

"Well, then. I have made a fool of myself for worse causes. Wait here in the cart with Tió Diego. Dr. Raimundo is his name, you say?"

"Yes. He works for Don Malaguez."

"Don Malaguez? I have not heard good things associated with that name. I hope you know what you are doing, chica."

"So do I."

With an imperious swirl of her skirt, Serena marched through the gate of the townhouse beside them. Coraza could not hear what was said when someone opened the door, but Serena returned quickly to the cart. "Come, your guess was close. It is the next house up."

Coraza turned to Diego Salbatore. "Thank you so much for all your help."

"To what better use can I put my remaining years than to help others? Go with the Madre, señorita."

"You too, señor."

Coraza let Serena guide her off the cart and walked arm in arm with her up the sidewalk to the house, just as though they were mother and daughter or aunt and niece. They strode through the low iron gate and up to the carved and polished oak door upon which Serena rapped loudly.

In moments, the door was opened by a thin, fussy looking man with a narrow mustache. He frowned disapprovingly at them. "Yes?"

"Is this the residence of Dr. Raimundo?" asked Serena imperiously.

"It may be. And who is asking?"

Serena looked at Coraza. Coraza stepped forward and said softly, "My name is Coraza Salamago. Dr. Raimundo once said if I ever required help, that I should seek him here."

The majordomo stared down at Coraza for a long moment. And then a light seemed to dawn behind his eyes. "Come in at once," he demanded. He ushered them into a foyer no larger than a short hallway leading to a rising flight of stairs. "Forgive my hesitation, señorita, señora," said the majordomo with a slight bow. "The Maestro had explained to me the possibility of your arrival, but it had seemed an unlikely event to him. Dr. Raimundo is not here at present, but I will send him a message immediately. Kindly proceed upstairs to the salon and make yourselves comfortable. I will rejoin you shortly." With that, the majordomo ran up the stairs as fast as his spindly legs would take him.

"I truly hope you know what you are doing," Serena said.

Coraza sighed. "This is the only chance I have left."

"I would stay longer if I did not have other promises to keep," grumbled Serena. "But neighbors can be so demanding and can turn so nasty when you don't meet their expectations." She kissed Coraza's forehead. "May the Madre be with you, chica."

"I am no longer certain that She is," Coraza said softly. She was sad to lose Serena's company so soon, but she understood. Coraza did not want to endanger anyone else.

They heard footsteps running and a door slamming at the back of the townhouse.

"She must be," said Serena. "Or you could not have lived so long. Listen, if this man does you harm, send word to me, and I will set such curses on him that he will regret ever being born. Good luck, Coraza."

"Thank you," Coraza said with a sad smile.

Serena swept out the door, and Coraza shut it behind her. Not knowing what else to do, Coraza walked up the stairs to a narrow landing. To her left stood an open door into what appeared to be a salon or study. She cautiously stepped in.

Perhaps, in some other person's house, it would have been a salon. There was an upholstered settee, although it appeared dusty and never used. A high table took up much of the center of the room, and sideboards lined the walls save one. The south wall was filled with a large window that overlooked the great Plaza. Every flat surface in the room was covered with some sort of mechanism, device, or oddity: brass clockworks with pendulums swinging frantically, beautifully cut prisms held by ornate bronze pincers, polished fossils, huge crystals, lumps of obsidian, carved ivory from Asia. On a low shelf was a large jar in which some monstrous dead creature floated, preserved in a viscous liquid. Coraza did not want to look at it too closely.

She straightened as clattering footsteps announced the return of the majordomo. "I have sent a messenger to the Maestro—oh. What has happened to your duenna, señorita?"

"She had other pressing duties and had to leave," said Coraza.

"Ah. Well, do not worry. The Maestro is the complete gentleman in his behavior. May I bring you some lemonade or tea?"

"Lemonade would be wonderful, thank you," said Coraza, trying not to laugh at the description of Dr. Raimundo as a gentleman.

"Excellent. I have some freshly made. Make yourself comfortable, but, ehm, try not to touch anything, if you please. The Maestro is fussy about the settings of his instruments."

I can imagine, thought Coraza.

The majordomo scurried off again, but Coraza was too unsettled to sit. She wandered the room, hands clasped behind her back, and peered at one thing and another. *Have I done the right thing?* she kept wondering over and over. *Could I trust him if I tell him I had turned into a tzinn? Would he send me to Espana to be studied? Would that be so bad? It would be a life...or maybe it would just be a different cellar to be locked in? Could I instead convince him to help me find out more about my father? About why Salamago wanted me to be the way I am?*

The Cathedral de Los Mesanjeros was so near—it was as though she could feel its looming proximity through the walls. On one of her childhood trips to the city, the orphans had been permitted a tour inside. The Cathedral had been so beautiful, with its stained glass windows and statues of saints. It had filled Coraza with awe, and she remembered smiling so much her face had ached. That such admiration must now be replaced with dread brought a dull ache of a different sort to Coraza's heart.

She wandered to the darker southwest corner of the room and bent down to peer at a pretty brass concoction of etched gear wheels that was spinning within a bell jar. As she stared, a slender filament at the mechanism's center began to glow red and a soft, high chime began to ping over and over. At first delightful, Coraza began to become alarmed as the sound did not stop and became increasingly irritating.

She heard the majordomo enter behind her and spun around. "I didn't touch it, I swear!"

The majordomo set a small silver tray bearing a glass down on the settee. He came over to her, clicking his tongue. "Oh dear, oh dear." He frowned at the instrument. "I am terribly sorry. The Maestro is so enthusiastic about melding the ancient sorcerous arts to more scientific methods. But not all his endeavors are successful. If you will excuse me." He plucked up the bell jar and hurried off with it.

With a sigh, Coraza returned to the settee and picked up the glass of lemonade. She sat and sipped at the cool, tart sweetness, but it did not please her as much as it ought. She felt unsettled, waiting in the bizarre room. She did not wish to be so close to the Cathedral. Coraza wished desperately that Agente Palabo had not abandoned her and Filipo. She hoped that Filipo was somehow still alive. If they were, might they have been successful in finding Salamago's secret forge? *Could I convince Dr. Raimundo to go there too?*

Coraza did not know how long she sat waiting, but the sun was considerably higher in the sky when the door downstairs banged open and running footsteps rumbled up the stairs. Dr. Saturnin Raimundo, slightly disheveled in his dark brown vested suit and hat, paused in the doorway and stared at her. Coraza stood slowly, warily, hands clasped in front. She nodded to him. "Maestro, I have come, as you once invited me to."

Dr. Raimundo glanced suspiciously around the room. "You are alone?"

"Yes, Maestro."

"Where is Agente Palabo?"

"I do not know, Maestro. He surrendered me and Filipo to soldiers from the Presidio. Who did not treat us kindly."

"That stupid bastard," Raimundo growled. He came up to Coraza and grasped her shoulders. "You did right to come here." He ever so lightly caressed her cheek with a trembling hand. "Were you harmed in any way?"

"I...I managed to escape harm."

"That is good. But that meddling vigilero will have much to answer for!"

The majordomo appeared in the doorway behind him. "Ah, you have returned, Maestro. I fear there is another urgent matter I must inform you of."

"Let it wait."

"I fear it cannot wait, Maestro."

Dr. Raimundo shut his eyes with an exasperated sigh. He spun around and strode to the majordomo's side. "Very well, but quickly."

"Maestro, you have received yet another invitation from Governadora Remedios to attend the banquet she is having this evening in honor of the Dragon Ship Fair. Her messenger was most insistent that your attendance is expected."

"Damn that woman. Doesn't she understand some of us have more important things to do than attend dinner parties?"

"Need I remind you, Maestro, that we have turned down her invitations three times already this year? If you rebuff her again without an honorable excuse, she will consider it a personal insult. You recall what the Don said regarding bringing scandal to his household—"

"Yes, yes. Damn. I shall have to come up with some good excuse to leave town."

Coraza felt a light shine within, as if the Madre herself had blessed her with opportunity. There was the chance to continue her interrupted search. "Maestro, perhaps I can help?"

"Eh?" Raimundo turned to her, frowning.

"Forgive my eavesdropping, Maestro, but I could not help overhearing. I can suggest to you a place to go. Before the soldiers of the Presidio intercepted us, the Agente, Filipo, and I were on the way to see my father's second forge. A secret forge, where he may have been practicing forbidden magics. Perhaps it is where the sword you saw, the sword named Sorrow, was made."

Raimundo stared at her again for a long moment. "A secret forge? And you have learned where it is?"

Coraza nodded with as much confidence as she could muster. "An indio told the Agente that my father was sometimes seen in a certain place."

Raimundo walked back to her. "If this is true, where might this place be?"

"To the east, and then north, in the mountains north of the Valle Fernando."

"Can you not be more specific?"

Coraza shook her head with a knowing smile. "I could, but I will not tell you until we are well on our way, Maestro. I must insist that we go together. I intend to see it for myself."

Raimundo paused, with an appreciative smile growing on his lips. "Clever girl. But then, of course, what better place to hide you than a place few even know exist? Very well. Anibal, bring me the latest schedule for El Dragón and hire the light hansom carriage from the stable down the street. We must be on our way as soon as possible."

Chapter Fifteen

Filipo del Utherio waited beside the cloth barrier that separated the Dragon Ship Fair and its aristocratic customers from the common folk outside. Coraza's sword hung heavy on his back. Overhead, in the morning sky, sea gulls wheeled with eager, piercing cries. The air held a sweet smell of the sea, bringing back memories of helping his father on the fishing dory.

Out in the harbor, Filipo could see amid the three-masted European traders the enormous Dragon Ships of Cathay. Twice a year, they would arrive at the coast of Alta Califia, bringing the most wondrous of goods for sale. Salamago had discovered that the merchants aboard the ships might also be in a mood to buy if offered items unusual enough and well made. Filipo smiled at the idea that perhaps one of his master's creations now graced some gilded Imperial chamber in the Forbidden City of Peiping.

"Señor del Utherio?" The hired guard startled him out of his reveries. "The Doña Malaguez has agreed to see you. You may enter."

"Thank you." Filipo noted the direction in which the guard pointed and spotted Doña Malaguez. He wound his way over to her, past booths laden with porcelain, silks, brassware, incense, teak carvings, and jade jewelry, dodging Asian merchants in long black robes with braids hanging down their backs. When at last Filipo arrived at Doña Malaquez's side, he was dismayed to discover she had her dour maidservant with her.

The Doña was admiring a bolt of beautiful royal blue silk studded with embroidered silver stars. "I do so wish Jupitero would be less miserly!

Wouldn't this make a divine dress—ah, young señor, there you are!" She turned and smiled at him with large, bright, hopeful eyes and Filipo had a sense of what might have plucked at the grizzled heart of Agente Palabo.

Filipo sketched a quick bow. "My deepest thanks, Good Lady, for allowing me to inconvenience you."

"Oh, don't be silly. Your master, the Madre bless and keep his soul, was so highly esteemed by my household, how could I not agree to see you? Your last visit to our hacienda was under such…unfortunate circumstances. I was concerned about you. The messenger said you have discovered another of Salamago's creations?"

"Yes, señora. I was so embarrassed about the poor quality of the last sword I showed your husband that, when I came across this one, I thought of him at once. It is similar to the last but much higher quality, so that I believe the first was perhaps merely an early version of this one. I would have approached Don Malaguez myself, but as you said, my prior visit was shameful. I feel more comfortable having you seeing the sword first to vouch for me." Filipo's hopes rose as he noted that the Doña's handmaid appeared to be supremely bored, her interest wandering.

"Of course, of course," said Doña Malaguez, airly waving a hand. "Jupitero is so busy these days, it would have been difficult for you to secure an appointment with him in any case. It was wise of you to come to me."

"Thank you, señora. Well. Here it is." Filipo took the sheath off his back and held the sword out, still encased in leather, to the Doña. As she grasped it, their hands met, and Filipo pressed into her fingers the tightly folded up note he had been given by Agente Palabo. He gave her a brief, significant look.

Doña Malaguez raised her brows and, without turning around, said, "Leonora, I have decided. I simply must have those purple silk slippers I admired earlier this morning. The ones with the phoenixes embroidered on them."

"But señora, that booth was clear across the field! I don't even remember which one exactly."

"Oh, you remember. It was the old man with the wart on his cheek."

With one hand, the Dona untied the velvet coin purse hanging from her belt and handed it to her maid. "Hurry, now! Find the booth and buy them before someone else does. Oh, and do please remember to pick something out for yourself. You have a birthday coming soon, do you not?"

Torn between duties, the handmaid took the purse but hesitated a moment more. "You are certain?" She glanced at Filipo with potential disapproval.

"Don't be silly," said Doña Malaguez with a click of her tongue. "I've known Señor del Utherio since he was a boy. He is an honorable young man. Now go!"

Shaking her head dubiously, the handmaid raised her skirts a little and departed through the crowd at a trot.

Doña Malaguez expertly slipped Palabo's note into her bodice as if she were fussily adjusting the lace stole across her shoulders. "Are you truly here to show me a sword, señor?" she asked softly.

"In truth, I am, but not to sell it. I need you to read this sword again. The young girl who was with me at the hacienda is now lost. I, and another, believe the sword can help us find her."

The Doña sighed and glanced anxiously from side to side. "Normally, I sense only intentions or feelings, not...how to find something. This is a difficult place for such a reading, señor. So distracting. And there are some here who would frown on such an activity."

"Please. There is a strong bond between this sword and the girl. She may be in great danger. Or even," it hurt his heart to say it, "no longer with us. Do what you can."

"Very well. I need to touch the steel itself."

Filipo slowly slid the sword out of the sheath.

As others passed within hearing distance, Doña Malaguez said, louder, "Ah, you are right, señor. This does appear to be a sword of good quality. Let me examine it further."

Putting her fingertips on the underside of the blade, she closed her eyes. After a few long moments, she murmured, "Yes, the bond is strong... from the energy I feel...yes, she lives, señor."

Filipo felt a weight lift from his heart. "That is something then. Anything else?"

"Such strong energy…it must be that she is not far." The sword shifted under her hands, almost like a compass. "Wait…she is heading east. Rapidly."

Seeing dark silhouettes approaching, Filipo cleared his throat. "So, you see, señora, I have hopes that your husband will consider this a work of superior quality and perhaps wish to add it to his collection."

Snapping out of her light trance, Doña Malaguez blinked and said, "You are quite right, señor. It is of a quality that might catch my husband's interest. He will be pleased that you showed it to me."

"Speaking of your estimable husband, Appollonia, I am ever so dismayed not to see him here." The speaker was a handsome woman of perhaps forty, surrounded by four well-armed men dressed in black.

Doña Malaguez gasped and curtsied. "Forgive me, Governadora Remedios. I did not see you approaching."

The Governadora? Cursing his spectacularly poor luck, Filipo bowed, glancing aside for a way to slip off unnoticed. Unfortunately, the Governadora's bodyguards were alert and watching. One of them eyed the sword Filipo was holding, and Filipo took great pains to re-sheathe the sword slowly and place it across his back again. Fortunately, all of the Governadora's attention seemed focused on the poor Doña Malaguez. The hint of a cold smile on the Governadora's lips reminded Filipo of the Protectadora Dona Vincenza. *If I did not already know they were related, that would suggest it to me enough.*

"I hope all is going well for you this day, Governadora," Doña Malaguez went on as she rose from her curtsy.

"Not as well as I would like," replied the Governadora, fussing with the silver bracelets on her wrists. "It dismays me that your entire household seems intent upon snubbing me."

"Oh, no, Governadora, I am certain you are mistaken. It is only that Jupitero is so busy with his trade transactions in the north—"

"Yes, I am aware of his…transactions," the Governadora said darkly.

"But now it seems even your household wizard will not deign to accept my invitation to tonight's banquet."

"You mean Doctor Raimundo?" asked Doña Malaguez.

"Are there other sorcerers in your husband's employ?"

"No, I meant I am surprised that he would allow himself to appear so rude—"

I'm not, thought Filipo.

"As to miss an opportunity to be in your gracious company. But he does get caught up in his...projects."

"The excuse we have just received from him," huffed Governadora Remedios, "is that he has a niece who is very ill whom he must escort to relatives outside of the city. I was not aware that Dr. Raimundo had any blood relatives in Califia. Is this true, Appollonia?"

"The Maestro and I are not close," said Doña Malaguez, staring at the ground. "I am afraid I would not know whether it is true or not."

A niece? thought Filipo. He remembered what Doña Malaguez had said she felt in the sword. Nearby but moving east. *It's not a niece; it's Coraza! Of course. She must have remembered his offer of protection, and she had nowhere else to turn.* Filipo glanced from side to side, looking again for an escape so that he could run to inform the Agente.

The Governadora clicked her tongue. "And here I expected more sympathy from you, Appollonia. One woman to another. You disappoint me. No matter. I have one of my men following him to corroborate this information."

Filipo could see Doña Malaguez's intense discomfort beneath the Governadora's withering gaze. Before he could stop himself, the gallantry his blood demanded surged forth. "If you please, Governadora, I am acquainted with Doctor Raimundo myself, and he does seem a most secretive man. I am certain the Doña Malaguez is not misleading you regarding her ignorance of his activities."

Suddenly, the full weight of the Governadora's serpentine stare fell upon him, and Filipo deeply regretted having spoken.

"Are you?" she asked in her low, honey-mixed-with-venom voice.

"And just who might this strapping young man be, Appollonia?"

"Governadora, may I present to you Señor Filipo del Utherio who, as you may know, was the apprentice to Maestro Salamago, may the Madre keep his soul."

"Was he?" replied the Governadora, the rising and falling tones of that one syllable conveying a wealth of interest. She glanced at the sword on his back, at the Doña, and then back at him. "My condolences upon your master's passing, young señor." She held out a limp hand. "A pleasure."

Filipo placed his hand beneath hers with as little contact as possible and bowed over it. "An honor, Governadora."

"And I," said Doña Malaguez, "should offer belated condolences to you, Governadora. I understand you and Maestro Salamago were...well acquainted at one time."

Governadora Remedios cast a thunderous glare at Doña Malaguez, and Filipo wondered what price the Doña would eventually pay for revealing that information. He remembered Salamago once saying that the wars women waged amongst themselves were no less cruel than those of men, the difference merely that ladies used words to cut their foe instead of swords. "My brief acquaintance with Maestro Salamago was many years ago," snapped the Governadora. "What you have heard was doubtless exaggerated by gossips." Her gaze returned to Filipo and she frowned. "I sincerely hope you are not denigrating what is left of your late master's good name to somehow enhance your own, young señor."

Filipo bared his teeth in an embarrassed attempt to smile. "Not at all. In fact, this is the first I have heard of any such association. My master was a gentleman in regard to his...acquaintances and never spoke of any such thing. Whether such a thing occurred or not." Though he kept his outward expression cool, inside he felt like bursting into surprised laughter. *The Governadora herself! Oh, Salamago, you old rascal!*

"Oh." The Governadora pursed her lips, and her features softened with perhaps a mixture of relief and disappointment. She raised her chin, and her nostrils flared with a sharp intake of breath. And in that moment, in a blend of sun and shadow that for an instant granted youth to her face,

Filipo saw another resemblance that nearly took his breath away.

No...it cannot possibly be..., he thought. But from what had just been said, it was, indeed, possible. Coraza was no mere child of a lady-of-convenience. She was of the nobility, of the Governadora herself! And changed in the womb, the holy sisters said. Was that Salamago's idea or the Governadora? Did Remedios even know she might have a daughter? Filipo's thoughts spun like a dust devil.

After a very long, uncomfortable moment, the Governadora said, "Isn't there some other duty you are supposed to be doing, young man?" It was a clear dismissal.

"Of course, Governadora. Again, it has been a great honor to meet you." Filipo bowed to her and then to Doña Malaguez. "Good day to you both, señoras." As casually as possible, Filipo strolled out of the tented booth, then turned and ran through the fair as fast as his legs could take him without colliding with anyone. He had to get back to the Agente at once.

Chapter Sixteen

Coraza clung tightly to the seat of the two-wheeled, one-horse hansom carriage as it careened through the streets of Los Mesanjeros, the hard leather rough against her hands.

"Driver, can't you go any faster?" demanded Dr. Raimundo.

"Your pardon, señor," said the elderly driver on the buckboard just in front of them over his shoulder. "But you see, señor, the traffic."

The narrow, cobbled streets held the usual random assortment of horsemen, women bearing baskets, burro carts, barking dogs, and children. Such streets might be easily negotiated on foot or horseback, but in a carriage, there was constant danger of collision. Dr. Raimundo kept looking back through the oval glass window set in the canvas. "At this rate, we will miss the train."

Coraza could not believe her turn of fortune. Dr. Raimundo had decided the fastest way to get them both out of the city and nearer their goal was to take El Dragón, the most elegant train in the Americas. Financed by the royal crown of España, it ran from Los Mesanjeros to the former colony now called New Orleans. Never had Coraza ever dreamed she would have the chance to ride it. And now, in less than pleasant circumstances, she would. *Does the Madre at last smile upon me? Or does She laugh at my foolish dreams?*

"I am terribly sorry, señor," said the driver. "I am going as fast as I safely can."

"How about if you throw caution to the winds?"

"I would be throwing my employment away with it, señor."

"Damn, I should have just rented a horse," Raimundo grumbled.

"What is the matter, Maestro? Why do you keep looking behind us?" asked Coraza.

"Because we are being followed."

Coraza's stomach went cold. "By whom?"

Do the holy sisters still seek me? Did the soldiers of the Presidio send out warning I might be a tzinn?

"I don't know. But he's a determined bastard. Driver! Crack the whip some more, if you please."

"As you wish, señor."

And then, as though by the blessing of the Madre, the street cleared, and the horse and carriage leaped forward. Within minutes, they pulled up beside the grand, domed gold and blue brick edifice of the Los Mesanjeros Railway Station. Dr. Raimundo pressed several paper reales into the driver's hand. "This transaction is private, you understand?"

The driver looked wide-eyed at his fist full of bills. "You shall have my utmost discretion, señor."

"Very good. Come on!" Raimundo grabbed Coraza's wrist.

Coraza let go of the carriage strut as Raimundo pulled her off the seat. She hitched up her skirts with her free hand and ran beside him into the station. The building was long and narrow, and the air was noticeably cooler inside. Through an archway beyond, Coraza glimpsed one of El Dragón's elegant cars waiting on the tracks. A loud *chuff-chuff-chuff* sound filled the air, and she could smell a hint of burning coal. Coraza had heard people describe the mighty engine pushing out steam as El Dragón breathing, and it truly did sound like a monster panting.

A whistle issued a long, shrill blast, and a man outside shouted, "Boarding! Last call for boarding!"

"Damn!" swore Raimundo. He rushed to the ticket window.

Coraza hurried to catch up to him. A small, balding man wearing a green eyeshade stared blandly up at them.

"Is there a private car available?" Raimundo demanded.

"Señor," the ticketmaster nasally intoned officiously, "for a private car, you must make arrangements two days in advance."

"I don't have two days. We must board the train now. There is always a private car attached to El Dragón."

"Yes, but it is for the convenience of dignitaries only."

"Are there any dignitaries using it today?"

"As it happens, no, señor."

"Then I will lease it. As far as Pomona."

"Señor, this is highly irregular—"

"How much?" Raimundo began to unfurl paper reales.

"I will have to confirm with the management—"

"Last call for boarding!" came the cry from outside.

"We don't have time for that! You will lose money if it runs empty. How much?"

"Oh, very well. One hundred reales, señor."

"One hun—that is robbery!"

"There are still seats available in third class if the señor prefers."

"Never mind! Here!" Dr. Raimundo slammed down a pile of reales and slid them under the window.

The ticket master slid back a large piece of green cardboard. "Fourth car from the end. But you will have to get this approved and signed by the station manager."

The chuffing became louder and more rapid. Through the breezeway, Coraza saw the elegant car begin to roll forward. She tugged Raimundo's sleeve. "Maestro—"

"Stuff the manager! He can deal with me later." Dr. Raimundo snatched up the green ticket, grabbed Coraza's hand, and took off at a run out onto the platform.

Unable to keep up with Raimundo's long strides, Coraza tripped on a raised bit of brick and fell with a loud cry.

"Get up! Hurry!" Raimundo demanded.

"I can't run as fast as you!" Coraza said as she stood, her palms burning from breaking her fall.

"Oh, dammit," grumbled Raimundo. He grabbed Coraza around the waist, hoisted her onto his shoulder, and took off at a run again alongside the train, which was now rolling at a good clip out of the station.

Coraza felt supremely embarrassed bouncing along on Raimundo's shoulder. To think she was about to board El Dragón, carried like a sack of grain onto the most elegant train in the west, the most protected, heavily warded—*oh, no!*

Raimundo lifted her off his shoulder, swinging her up to the hands of a conductor at the door to the private car. As she crossed over the edge of the track ties, pain smote her, as if she'd been flung into a wall of solid fire. Her mouth opened wide, but she could not breathe, could not scream. The magic of the warding flowed over her, stabbing down to her bones, making pain her entire existence. The moments seemed eternal until she was carried into the center of the private car. As the pain leaked away, she began spasming and flailing, her body not entirely under her control. She screamed, and the conductor set her down on the floor. Coraza rolled over, crying, and vomited. The lemonade she had drunk earlier in the day was now acrid and harsh in her mouth.

"Señorita, señorita, what is the matter?" cried the conductor, bending over her.

Coraza curled up tight, her body humming from bathing in the magic, every nerve jangling from the memory of the pain. But worse yet was a growing fear. A chill seeped up from her belly, promising relief from the pain, from the nausea, if she would relinquish her mortal flesh. As it threatened to overwhelm her, Coraza clenched her fists. *No! I mustn't change, mustn't change, mustn't change—*

"My niece is ill!" Raimundo declared. "She has fits, as you can see. I am taking her east, into the desert mountains, for her health."

"Señor, this does not appear to be any minor ailment. Shall I send for the train physician?"

"No! It is a metaphysical condition. I shall look after her. Can you not see why we must use the private car? Just leave us in peace."

Coraza felt a wave of cool air sweep over her, and her muscles ceased their spasming. For a moment, she feared the tzinn transition was upon her. Then she saw Raimundo running the ebony and silver wand across her back. He picked up her feet, and the conductor lifted her by the shoulders. They carried her down the swaying train car and set her on a long, plush upholstered settee.

"Your pardon, señor, but we must maintain our customary level of service. I will send someone to clean up the mess."

"I'm so sorry—" Coraza began, coughing.

"Do not fret, señorita," said the conductor, patting her shoulder. "El Dragón has weathered many things in its travels. Rest, and we will see to everything."

As the conductor departed, Raimundo murmured, "I would wager El Dragón has seen nothing like you, señorita. Are you all right? I should have remembered about the warding. I'm sorry. If I had, I would have better prepared you."

Coraza nodded, feeling weak and drained, but no longer in pain or discomfort. Though she doubted any preparation he could have given would have helped her withstand the pain. *Perhaps all will be well. If I can suffer that and still control myself, perhaps I need never change again.*

As Raimundo continued to gaze down at her, she became a bit self-conscious. "What is it, Maestro?"

"My majordomo told me of a certain mechanism that became active in your presence. The one with a small red light that chimed."

"Oh. I hadn't touched it. I didn't mean to set it off! I'm sorry."

"No need to apologize," Raimundo said, patting her arm. "But if what it indicated is accurate, señorita, then you are the most remarkable thing in all the history of sorcery."

The door at the end of the car opened again, and a squad of three white-gloved young men in gaudy red and gold uniforms came in. One of them worked at Coraza's mess with a brush and pan. Another had brought a blanket and pillow for Coraza, as well as a glass of cool water. She drank eagerly from the glass as the steward fussed with the blanket and plumped the pillow behind her. The water washed away some of the burn in her throat, but it was not satisfying.

Another steward entered, bearing a glass of wine, a newspaper, and a cigar for Dr. Raimundo. As they departed, behind them entered the train physician, wearing a black coat and carrying a small leather case.

"Señorita, I am told you are not well." The physician said, glancing suspiciously at Dr. Raimundo.

"Ah, yes, it is true," Coraza said, trying to sound earnest. "For a few weeks now, I have been having painful fits. I have been told there are mineral hot springs out in the desert. My uncle is being so kind as to take me there to see if they will help."

"I see," intoned the physician. He proceeded to examine Coraza's eyes, ears, and mouth. He then gave Coraza one end of a long, rubber "listening tube" to hold against her chest. After listening for a few moments, the physician shrugged and placed the tube back in his satchel. "She is healthy enough for travel. I or someone will be checking on her from time to time, to make sure she is comfortable. The railway has a reputation to uphold. You understand, señor." "Do what you must," said Dr. Raimundo. "So long as the rest of the train does not hear of her...unfortunate condition."

"Of course, señor. We are nothing if not discreet."

"Good." Dr. Raimundo took a seat at a small table across the car and sipped at his glass of wine.

Coraza looked around, now that she had the chance. The car was furnished like she imagined the fanciest of high society salons might be, oddly in contrast to the brick homes and shacks speeding past the window outside. The carpet was plush; the wallpaper was green velvet, as were the fringed curtains on the windows. Crystal oil lamps hung, gently swaying, on the walls. The tables and chairs were polished teak. The rumble of El Dragón's engine in the distance was like the heart of a great beast. The chuffing of steam from its stack was its breath.

One of the uniformed young men entered the private car again and approached Coraza, holding a small, gaily painted chest. He knelt beside her settee and opened the chest to reveal a treasure of toys within. "With the compliments of the rail company, señorita, please feel free to choose an item for your amusement."

"She's not a child," grumbled Dr. Raimundo.

"Oh, let me look," said Coraza, enchanted by the sight of things she could only long for in the orphanage. There was a porcelain doll in a white lace dress, a tin soldier, a painted sailboat, a small book of poetry, little wooden chess pieces in a box that folded out to become a board. But what attracted her eyes was a mysterious red velvet drawstring bag. She pulled it out and undid the drawstrings. She reached in and found a few perfectly round polished spheres of stone, some transparent crystal, some banded rock of white, black and grey. "How pretty!" They felt cool against her skin as she rolled them around in her hand.

"The señorita likes the marbles? Consider them yours, with our compliments. May you enjoy your journey on El Dragón." The steward closed up the chest and, with a bow, departed.

"By the Madre, I thought they'd never leave," said Dr. Raimundo.

Coraza let some of the marbles roll onto her blanketed lap. She liked the way light glinted off the flaws in the transparent quartz ones. But there was something else, something in the nature of the stone spheres beyond just their beauty, that fascinated her. "What are these for, Maestro?"

"Hmm? Oh. Marbles are a boy's game. An ancient pastime, old as the Romans if not older. Boys play with them, using them as weapons to knock another boy's marbles out of a circle drawn on the ground."

"Weapons? Why would anyone use pretty things as weapons, or play such rough games with them?"

Dr. Raimundo glanced oddly at her. "Part of human nature, I suspect."

Filipo stood on the tracks beside the platform, staring at the receding caboose of El Dragón in the distance. "Damn," he muttered to himself. "We're too late."

Agente Palabo came trotting out of the station. "The ticket master confirmed that a man and girl matching their description boarded the train. Caused quite a fuss, apparently."

"Now what do we do? I won't run Tulio to death trying to catch them," said Filipo.

"No need to tire the horses." Palabo patted Filipo's shoulder, then continued running to a large repair shed on the other side of the tracks.

Filipo followed, noting the smells coming from the repair shed reminded him of the forge: hot iron, sweat, leather. But there was an additional unfamiliar overtone of oil and coal dust. The large doors were open, and several men in leather coveralls were lounging about.

"Excuse me, señores, but I need your help," Palabo announced.

"Certainly, Agente," said one of the men, his face weathered and brown as a leather saddle. "How may we help the Protectorado?"

"There is a person of interest aboard the train that just left. The safety of Alta Califia may be at stake. We need to catch El Dragón."

This was greeted with hearty laughter all around. "I am sorry to tell you, Agente, that you have just missed it. And El Dragón is the fastest train on the continent. I do not recommend chasing it on horseback. Perhaps you could send word ahead to have it stopped if the matter is urgent."

"That would not serve our purpose," said Palabo. "And rather than use our horses, I was hoping we could borrow your mule."

Filipo looked around but saw no animal or stall.

"Our mule? Oh. The Mule!" The foreman nodded at a contraption consisting of a platform set on four small rail wheels, with a double T-bar on a post in the middle connected to a rocker-arm. "You are welcome to borrow it, Agente, but I do not think it can help you catch El Dragón."

"Wait, now," said one of the other men. "There was that time Erfeo and I raced the Mule on a bet. We got up to good speed. Several men pumping it can go fast as a horse and for longer."

"Yes," chimed in another man. "And, you know, El Dragón must slow down when it reaches the curve and upgrade at the San Jose Hills. That will give us a chance to catch up."

"Well, then, compañeros," said the first fellow jovially, "for the sake of the colonia and the Protectorado, let's see if we are as fast as El Dragón!"

Clearly eager for the diversion, the railway workers grasped the edges of the Mule's platform and rolled it out of the shed. With every man hefting, they lifted it onto the tracks. The Mule's platform was just wide enough for three men to stand, tight together, at each T-bar, six in all.

Agente Palabo gave one of the men a few reales. "If you please, look after our horses. I don't know how long we'll be gone.

"The company stables are at your service, Agentes," he said, handing the coins back. "Your mounts will be well cared for until you return. They are posted in front of the station, yes? I will see to them myself." He hurried off.

"I believe we can fit six men on the Mule, for maximum strength," said the foreman.

Two of the railway workers got on one side, their backs to the way they would be headed, as did Palabo. The foreman and one other squeezed onto the other side, facing forward. Filipo stepped up onto the platform beside the foreman, trying to adjust the sword on his back so that it did not touch the man beside him.

"One word of advice," the foreman said to Filipo, "while we are moving, do not let go of the bar. Erfeo did that, and the bar knocked him in the chin. Lost three teeth. So, let's go. On the beat of my voice. Hey-yo! Hey-yo!"

Pushing down the T-bar in time with the workmen's chant, Filipo, Agente Palabo, and the others got the Mule rolling down the tracks at ever-increasing speed. It felt good to be using his muscles again, and it was not unlike working the large bellows at Salamago's forge. The railroad workmen were grinning at each other, daring each other to push harder, go faster. Even Palabo smiled a little, caught up in the enjoyment of the chase. Filipo looked ahead, down the track, focused on the thin column of steam in the distance.

Hold on, Coraza. We'll be there soon.

Coraza dozed on the lush settee, the marbles rolling around in her lap. The heavy scent of the cigar smoke that Dr. Raimundo was enjoying made her nose itch. The rear door to the car opened, and another conductor whom she hadn't seen before strode in.

"Señor, I have come to check on the señorita."

Raimundo flung the paper he was reading down onto the table in disgust. "She's fine! Can't you people leave us—" He turned and froze as he saw the conductor's face. "You." Raimundo stood, grasping for his wand holster.

"Fatoosh," said the conductor with a wave of his hand.

Raimundo stood, frozen in place, a vortex of violet strands encircling him, holding him upright like a wax statue.

The conductor plucked the ebony wand from Raimundo's hand and turned toward Coraza. "Señorita, you must come with me at once."

Anger overriding her fear, Coraza cried, "No! Who are you? What do you want?"

The man sighed and said, "This will go better if you cooperate. I have no wish to harm you, but I will do what I must." Purple light flickered down his forearms and gathered in his hands. Coraza jumped up from the settee, spilling the marbles in her lap, and stepped backwards toward the forward door of the car. "Leave us alone!"

The man lunged toward Coraza, his foot landing on the marbles. His leg slipped out from under him, and he fell hard onto his side with a surprised grunt. Raimundo's wand flew out of his hand and clattered to the floor near Coraza's feet.

Coraza snatched up the wand, turned, and dashed out the forward car door. The dry air smelled of hot metal and coal smoke. A wood bridge connected the railcars, but Coraza could see the car ahead was crowded. To her left, an iron ladder led up to the roof. Without a moment's more thought, Coraza put the wand in her teeth, grasped the ladder with one hand, gathered her skirts with the other, and swung herself onto the rungs. She climbed up as fast as she could go. The railcar door banged open again below her just as she reached the roof.

The wind whipped her hair and skirt about her, and the car beneath Coraza's feet swayed as she imagined the deck of a ship might. She crouched onto the hot metal roof, turned to face into the wind, and lay flat on her stomach. She prayed to the Madre, *Please, let the man not think I have come up here.*

But her prayers were not answered, for in just a few moments, the head of the man appeared at the top of the ladder. He scowled at her and shouted, "Come down at once, chica!"

"No!" Coraza shouted back.

"Do not force me to come get you. It will not go well for you."

"Go away and leave me alone!" Coraza felt frustration and anger begin boil within her again.

Does the Madre seek to test me? Do I have to fight for any good fortune in this world?

Grimacing, the man pulled himself up onto the rocking railcar roof. As he stood and began walking toward her, Coraza raised Raimundo's wand and aimed it at him.

The man stopped, arms out for balance. He stared at the wand and then back at Coraza for a few moments. "That wand will do you no good," he finally said. "It isn't charged. Put it down and give up now."

Coraza glanced at the silver-chased ebony wand in her hand. One of the tiny gem bezels along the side was glowing a faint green.

The man lunged for her. Coraza pressed the green bezel with her thumb. Energy crackled out of the wand like a green bolt of lightning, striking him on his left side. The man cried out as his left leg buckled beneath him. His left arm hung useless as he fell over. Just inches in front of her, his face contorted in confusion and fear as he tumbled off the railcar.

Carefully, Coraza peered over the side. The man had fallen free of the track, but he was slow to get up, obviously hurt. He glared at Coraza as the train pulled her swiftly away.

Who was he? Coraza thought. *Who does he work for? How many enemies do I have now?* She crawled back toward the ladder. Swinging her leg over, she stepped onto the rungs, her legs and hands shaking. She carefully descended, trying not to look at the landscape speeding by, trying not to let panic overcome her. Coraza slipped back through the door to the private car, hoping no one had seen her.

Dr. Raimundo still stood, frozen in place as he was when she'd left him. *What should I do?* She wondered. There was possibly a spell in the wand to release him from the agent's sorcery, but it would surely be unwise to experiment with the wand to find it. Coraza set the wand on the table, held her hand out toward Raimundo, and said the word she had learned from Sister Phoebe, "Nekpar!"

Nothing happened. Remembering that sorcery had to come from a deeper place, Coraza let her inner anger and fear rise to the surface. Again she shouted, "Nekpar!" Her voice, throaty, almost alien, surprised her enough to make her jump. An orange glow flowed out of her arm and spilled over Raimundo.

He shuddered, lips twitching. His hand scrabbled at his wand holster, and he looked wildly around. "You, what? Where did he go?"

"He...fell off the train," Coraza said.

"When? How?"

"He froze you with a spell and chased me up to the roof. I used your wand, and he fell off." Sheepishly, Coraza handed Dr. Raimundo the ebony and silver wand.

He looked at her, looked at the wand, and swiftly re-holstered it. "Well. How very resourceful you've turned out to be. Is he dead?"

"No. He was hurt, but alive."

"Pity. He might have a chance to communicate to others."

Coraza winced at the sorcerer's callousness. "You seemed to recognize him, Maestro. Before he froze you."

"I did. He is one of Governadora Remedios' private bodyguards. I've had a run-in or two with him before."

"The Governadora's bodyguard?"

"Clearly the Governadora cannot trust the army or the Protectadora to succeed, so she's set one of her pet fighter mages on the job. She wanted to hire me away from Don Malaquez for such a position once but—never mind."

"Was he sent by the cathedral? The holy sisters, or the Protedadoras?"

Raimundo sighed and rubbed his chin in thought. "Might be any or all of them. I'm afraid, my dear, this turn of events is going to require a slight change in plans."

"Oh." Coraza's shoulders slumped in dismay.

"Hey-yo! Hey-yo!" His arms beginning to burn from the exertion, the sword on his back beginning to chafe, Filipo was pleased to see the caboose of El Dragón coming nearer as it began its climb up the San Juan curve. Agente Palabo and the railroad men had nearly matched Filipo in vigor, and the Mule had indeed rushed along at the speed of a galloping horse.

"I think this is going to work, Agente!" he gasped to Palabo.

"Man on the tracks!" shouted the rail foreman beside Filipo.

Filipo looked past Palabo's shoulder and saw in the distance a man standing in the middle of the track, waving his right arm. His left seemed to be held tight against him.

"Stop! Stop!" came the man's faint cries.

"Get off the track! Get off the track!" yelled the rail men, waving their arms.

As the Mule careened closer and closer to the man, his eyes visibly widened. He shouted, "In the name of the Governadora, stop!"

"We can't stop!" yelled Palabo over his shoulder. "Move, señor, move!"

The man, close enough now that Filipo could see he wore a conductor's uniform, extended his right arm and yelled, "Fatoosh!"

As a ball of violet light hurtled toward them, Palabo drew a circle in the air and said, "Samah!" A shield of white light appeared on his arm, and he batted away the oncoming spell.

As the Mule bore down on the hapless wizard, he leaped off the tracks just in time. Filipo turned his head to watch the man dwindle in the distance.

"I will have your heads for this!" the man shouted, shaking his fist at them. "The Governadora will hear of this! You will all pay!"

"The Governadora?" said the foreman with a frown. "Should we stop, Agente?"

Palabo shook his head. "He could be lying or mad."

"At the Dragon Boat Fair," Filipo gasped to Palabo, "the Governadora said she was sending someone after Raimundo. Maybe that was him."

The vigilero frowned. "This does not bode well."

"The train is slowing, señores," said the rail foreman, "But the hills will make us slow too. We must catch the train quickly, or we will fall behind again."

"All our strength then," said Filipo.

"Once again, we are indebted to you, señores," said Palabo to the railmen.

"It is nothing!" said the foreman with a big grin. "If we catch El Dragón, we will have tavern boasts for years!"

Each man bent his back and pushed on the bar with all the strength left in him. The rear of the train's caboose inched closer and closer. Filipo could feel the grade begin to rise beneath the wheels of the Mule.

When he next looked up, the rear platform of the caboose was only a few feet away. The rearmost door opened up, and a conductor wearing braid on his shoulder and cap came out. "Who are you?" he shouted. "What are you doing?"

"I am Agente Marzo Palabo," the vigilero shouted, panting in exertion, over his shoulder. "I must request...your permission...for us to come aboard the train, Capitan."

"Very well, permission granted." The captain of conductors reached out his hand. With careful timing, Palabo let go of the bar, twisted around, grasped the conductor's arm, and vaulted onto the caboose rear platform.

In a moment of panic, Filipo realized his chances of getting onboard were much trickier. "Agente!"

"Who is that?" asked the conductor captain.

Without pause, Palabo said, "That is my deputy. We must help him board as well." He grasped the balustrade and leaned out as far as he could.

"Come on, Filipo."

Filipo paused a moment, finding himself oddly pleased to be called Palabo's deputy. Then necessity broke in on him. While the rocker arm was moving, he couldn't move around the Mule, but if it stopped, he'd fall behind too fast. He'd have to run for it. "Get me as close as you can," he said to the rail men.

They nodded grimly and put forth one more burst of effort. When the front end of the Mule was nearly touching the back of the caboose, Filipo leaped from the Mule's platform. He hit the tracks running and pumped his legs with all of his might, reaching up his left arm.

Palabo and the conductor captain reached out and pulled Filipo up onto the caboose step. Filipo grasped the banister, collapsed against it, gasping to catch his breath, his head swimming with spots before his eyes. The men on the Mule relaxed and let the rocker bar slow at its own speed. As they fell behind, Palabo waved his thanks.

"Adiós, Agente. Good luck to you!" they shouted back.

As Filipo worked at getting his breath back, the captain of conductors asked, "So what is this about, Agente?"

Palabo answered between gasps. "I...understand there is a Dr. Raimundo aboard...accompanied by a young girl. I believe he hired a private car...at the last minute."

"Ah, yes," said the captain, knowingly. "We have had our suspicions about this fellow. What is he wanted for?"

Palabo shook his head. "We just want to talk to him."

The door to the caboose banged open, and a frightened young steward said, "Capitan, I found Alonso. He was locked in the water closet, and his uniform had been stolen."

"Was it this Dr. Raimundo who took it?" asked the captain.

"No, Capitan. It was someone he had not seen before."

Palabo said, "We may have passed the unfortunate thief behind us. It appears he fell off the train. Could you please lead us to Dr. Raimundo's car?"

"Yes, of course. But enlighten me if you would, Agente, as to what is going on? You understand, I am responsible for the security of the passengers of El Dragón."

Palabo shook his head. "I'm afraid it is a private matter. But your passengers are in no danger. Ready, Filipo?"

Filipo did not feel ready. Every muscle in his body burned from exertion, and his lungs still felt unsatisfied with their measure of breath. He nodded. "Of course, Agente," he gasped.

"Good. Capitan, if you will lead on."

The captain of conductors led them through the caboose, through a horse car and two luggage cars, finally reaching the door to the private car. The captain turned the handle, but the door didn't budge. "Bless me, it's locked!" He fished around in his pocket for keys, taking over a minute to find the right one. At last, he flung open the door and burst in, shouting, "Maestro, an agente of the law has come to speak with you!"

But his words echoed in the empty car.

"We're too late," sighed Agente Palabo. "They're gone."

Chapter Seventeen

Coraza sprawled on the hard ground, her body shuddering. Dr. Raimundo had his hand clamped over her mouth. El Dragón chuffed away, just beyond a low, rocky ridge that hid them from view of the passengers. "I am truly sorry, my dear. But we can't take the chance of anyone hearing your cries."

She felt no pain. A spell from Raimundo's wand had seen to that. But her body, nonetheless, felt ravaged, violated by the magic energy of the warding spell she had passed through once again. Coraza fought with every ounce of her will to keep back the changes her body demanded. And yet, in some way, she wanted to let go, to let that other part of her take hold, to feel the peace of no feeling. Her eyes leaked tears. Her jaws ached from clenching. Every tendon in her arms and legs felt ready to snap. She glared at Dr. Raimundo as she tried to draw enough breath through her nose. At last, after minutes that felt forever, the tremors subsided, and her muscles relaxed. Even so, a quiet voice within said, *Enough. I shall not bear this again. Never again.*

Bizarrely, she heard men chanting, "Hey-yo! Hey-yo!" passing by on the tracks beyond. One seemed a familiar voice, but her mind was buzzing so that she could not be sure. *Am I hallucinating now because of my reaction to the warding spells?*

Dr. Raimundo frowned and turned his head toward the tracks, clearly hearing the voices as well. He continued to hold Coraza down, not moving until the voices were well past. "A good thing we left when we did, my dear.

The train was followed by others, as I'd feared. The Governadora is known to be persistent."

At last, Dr. Raimundo released her mouth. Coraza rolled over, coughing. She would have vomited, but her abdomen felt too weak, and there was nothing left in her stomach to release. Fury hummed within her, yet she knew everything the sorcerer had done was for good reason. *He doesn't yet understand how dangerous that was. I might have turned tzinn and killed him!*

Raimundo sat up, rubbing his arm. The leap from the linkage had been a hard fall for both of them, even though the train had slowed on the hills.

"Now what do we do?" growled Coraza.

Dr. Raimundo narrowed his eyes at her but did not chide her for her rudeness. "Now we hurry to our destination in the hope that our pursuers haven't deduced where we are going. Which brings me to a very important question, my dear. Where, exactly, are we going?"

Coraza sat up and rubbed the back of her neck. "There is a place called the Canyon of Ghosts…" She told him everything she had learned from the Indian farmer in Las Escarpas and what Agente Palabo had thought it meant. Then she waited for Dr. Raimundo's anger at being led so far afield on so little information.

But he merely gazed at her for a few long moments, then nodded. "Although I would have preferred a specific point of reference on a map," he said at last, "I believe the Agente's logic is sound. For a reason most people would be unaware of."

"And what reason might that be?"

"That sword you had been carrying, remember it had a stone at the tip of the hilt which I said was carved from animite crystal?"

"Yes?" said Coraza, confused.

"Geomancers have long known that animite has the property of attracting the same energy that animates souls, hence its name. And that is why it is of value in Sere sorcery. In small amounts, the attraction of the crystal is negligible. In large amounts, such as a major vein, spirits are drawn to it like lodestone to iron shavings. Where there are rumored to be many ghosts, there might well be a vein of animite in the earth beneath. Do you feel well enough to move on?"

Coraza nodded. "I think so." In truth, she ached all over. But she didn't want to appear weak to Dr. Raimundo. Though she trusted him to escort her to her father's secret forge, she still did not know what he intended to do with her after. And she did not trust him to be honest about his intentions, so she assumed there was no point in asking. Once she learned whatever there was to discover in the Canyon of Ghosts, then she would decide whether to remain in his company.

Dr. Raimundo caught her arm and helped her to stand. "What happened to that sword of yours, anyway?"

"I don't know. The last I saw, Agente Palabo had it."

Dr. Raimundo blew air out his lips. "That fool. He's probably stashed it away in some Presidio storeroom by now."

This seemed unlike the vigilero. But thinking about Agente Palabo made Coraza remember Filipo and how bravely he had died for her, and she did not have time to grieve. She straightened her back and said, "Let's go."

Filipo and Agente Palabo waved their thanks to the captain of conductors as they stepped out onto the flimsy wood platform at a village in the middle of nowhere.

"Good luck, Agentes," the captain of conductors shouted, waving from the door of the caboose as El Dragón pulled away.

Filipo felt absolutely spent. He staggered wearily behind Agente Palabo as the vigilero took stock of their surroundings. The train had let them off at a stop that was rarely used, a pueblo of perhaps five or six houses clustered around a square of beaten earth. The only witnesses to their unplanned arrival were three wary housewives sweeping their porches and a couple of very excited little boys crying, "Mamá! El Dragón! El Dragón!"

There were no benches on the platform and no ticket window either. Apparently, purchases of that sort were to be made at the ramshackle tavern across the open square. Agente Palabo began to amble in that direction.

"So, it was all for nothing!" Filipo sighed, exasperated as he staggered behind the vigilero.

"Not at all," said Palabo, more heartily than Filipo would have expected. "They are off the train, and we remain close to our quarry. This region has plenty of farms and small pueblos like this one. Raimundo and Coraza can't stay hidden long. Someone will see them. Now I think I will investigate what beverages this fine establishment has to offer."

"Agente, I have given my all in the chase to catch the train. I can go no further today."

"Rest, then. I'll go around and ask questions."

With a groan, Filipo sat in front of the tavern on a hard weathered chair at a table made from a barrel and wood pallet. He pulled Coraza's sword off his back and put in on the table, then crossed his arms over it and laid his head down to rest. As his muscles relaxed, and the warm, dry wind caressed his face, he drifted into sleep, and from there into dreams.

He was standing in the old forge, as in years past. He was letting the summer air flow through the great doors, trying to cool off a little, work paused for siesta. Out of the corner of his eye, he could see Maestro Salamago stretched out in a hammock, head thrown back, left arm flung out. Filipo smiled. The old man rarely rested, but when he did, it was with abandon. Filipo sighed and stared out through the doors at the familiar cottonwood and oak trees. "Where is she? What am I going to do?" he murmured.

"She's looking for me," Salamago muttered from the hammock.

"Don't be silly, Maestro," said Filipo, fondly. "Why would she be looking for you? You're dead."

"She's coming to find me," Salamago insisted.

Filipo strolled over to the hammock. "How on earth would she do that?"

"She's coming to find me," the man in the hammock repeated.

Filipo thought it odd that Salamago's lips did not move, and yet his voice was as clear as if he'd spoken in Filipo's ear.

"But consider where you are, Maestro," said Filipo.

"Yes," replied Salamago, his voice rich with irony. "I am in my forge, am I not?"

Filipo shrugged. "Of course. What of that?"

"Idiot boy."

As Filipo felt warmly nostalgic at the insult Salamago so often had hurled at him, the world around him shook and a voice from without called his name.

"Filipo!"

A vigorous pull on his arm brought Filipo out of his dream and back, blinking, into the world. "What?" He raised his head off his arms.

Agente Palabo sat atop a barrel beside him and plunked a dusty bottle down on the table. "I've brought refreshment, such as it is. Though it is possibly more vinegar than wine. You were muttering in your sleep."

"Oh." Filipo ran his right hand through his hair. "I dreamt I was talking to Maestro Salamago. We were in the old forge, in Las Escarpas. He kept insisting that Coraza was coming to find him."

"Coming to find him in his forge," Palabo murmured. He uncorked the bottle and took a swig, swished the wine in his mouth, then spit it out on the ground. Then he stopped, staring at nothing. "The secret forge," he whispered. His gaze met Filipo's. "Coraza has told Raimundo about the secret forge."

"It was just a dream," said Filipo. He glanced down. His left hand was gripping the naked hilt of Coraza's sword, the leather bag having somehow slipped down. A chill swept over his skin, and his stomach did a somersault. Filipo jerked his hand away from the sword.

"Perhaps you have a touch of talent after all," said Palabo. "Or Doña Vincenza granted you some of hers. Either way, I think you are on the right track."

"So...perhaps Salamago truly spoke to me?" Filipo murmured. Palabo only shrugged. "Come, let us find some horses and be on our way."

Filipo hastily bundled the sword back into its leather sheath and flung the strap over his shoulder. He shuddered as the blade fell against his spine.

"This is as far as I go, señor," said the gray-haired Gabrielito Indian, defiance in his eyes.

"Come now," said Dr. Raimundo. "Are you afraid of some foolish ghost stories?"

The native merely stared at him as if the sorcerer were mad.

"Oh, very well," grumbled Dr. Raimundo. "We will guide ourselves from here."

They were on a ridge in the foothills of the San Gabriel Mountains. Coraza sat behind Raimundo on a bony nag they had hired the day before at the same hacienda where they had found their guide. The landowner had apparently owed debts to Don Malaguez, which Raimundo used to their advantage. Coraza felt grimy, sweaty, thoroughly unkempt. Yet she also felt a measure of triumph. If the indio stories were true, one piece of her life's puzzle was soon to fall into place.

"I should take the horse too," said the Gabrielito.

"We'll return it when we're finished," snapped Raimundo.

The Indian made a dubious snort, turned his burro, and rode back the way they had come.

Ahead of them lay the entrance to a deep arroyo that wound its way into the mountains. Even though it was mid-day and the air was warm, the sun bright, a faint mist rose from the arroyo like a June fog at the seashore.

As soon as the Gabrielito was out of sight, Raimundo kicked the horse's flanks, urging it down the juniper dotted ridge to the arroyo's mouth. Raimundo turned the horse east to follow the floor of the canyon as it wound deep into the foothills.

There was no creek flowing out of the arroyo, though Coraza could see from the shape of the stones and the dirt that one had flowed there in years past. There were no trees, no grasses, no weeds. The canyon itself was utterly bare sandstone and rotting granite. The clop of the horse's hooves against the rocks echoed loudly between the canyon walls.

A few yards up the arroyo, the air turned chill. Coraza could see her breath misting, joining the fog surrounding them. In the shadows, the mist began to coalesce, forming the hint of a face, an arm, a hand. Coraza shrank against Dr. Raimundo's back. "Maestro?"

"I see them. But it's what we expected, isn't it?"

"Do they know we are here?"

"Do they sense our presence? I suppose we will eventually find out. The fog is thicker up ahead."

"Shouldn't you have your wand out? What if they try to stop us? Or hurt us?"

Raimundo chuckled. "You know, it's strange, but for all the frightening ghost stories through the ages, genuine spirits have never been proven to kill anyone. The fear of ghosts may cause a witness to have an accident or stop his heart, but they are otherwise powerless to manipulate the material world."

"So, they are not a form of tzinn then?"

"No, they are not tzinn."

The horse slowed, its ears flicked back. The air became colder, and a pale shape rose up beside Coraza. The face appeared to be an old native woman, her eyes wide, mouth gaping, toothless. She reached toward Coraza.

"Are you certain?" Coraza asked, pressing herself against Raimundo's back. Her stomach tightened, and she shivered, wide-eyed.

"Yes, of course I'm certain," he replied with annoyance.

The old spirit drifted alongside them, staring at Coraza, the spectral hand coming closer.

Coraza raised her arm to fend the phantasm off. The ghost woman's hand passed through Coraza's skin, muscle, and bone. The sensation was strange, hot and cold at the same time. Without thinking, Coraza thrust her arm into the spirit's chest, as if to grasp its heart.

The ghost looked down at Coraza's arm. White filaments streamed from the spectre's form, flowing into Coraza's skin. The spirit's mouth widened in a silent scream. Instead of fear, Coraza was overcome with a curious euphoria. The energy streaming from the ghost into her hand and forearm was pleasant, invigorating, like the aroma of her favorite tea. Coraza leaned closer to the spirit, wanting to drink her in.

Somehow, the spirit found the energy to pull away and flee, disappearing into the mist from which she had coalesced. Coraza's arm suddenly became cold as ice. She clasped her right fist close to her chest with a whimper, guilt flowing over her.

Raimundo sighed with exasperation and said, "For the last time, Coraza, the ghosts cannot harm you!"

No, Coraza thought sadly. *But I can harm them. I even enjoyed it. Just who is the monster here?*

"So, have you an answer to your question as to whether they are aware of us?"

"Yes," said Coraza. "They are."

"Interesting. If I had any skill at necromancy, I could have gotten one to speak to us. Could have been useful if one of these shades lived when Salamago worked here. A pity the University insists on its students choosing a specialty. My studies were in the College of Natural Metaphysics. Ah, well. Looks like our spectral audience is taking pity on us. The mist is lifting, and I think I see a building up ahead."

Coraza peered around his shoulder. The air in the arroyo ahead was indeed clearing. Coraza suspected it was because the spirits of the canyon wished to be as far away from her as they could manage, not from any kindness. The fog parted to reveal a dark, rectangular shape ahead. As the horse plodded closer, Coraza could make out a wide, squat stone chimney, a shingled roof, a narrow porch. The arroyo broadened for a few yards in front of the building and became a level, flat area, almost like a natural courtyard. The building itself, however, was just a shack, built up against the rock wall of the canyon. Raimundo pulled the horse to a stop in front of it.

"This can't be the forge, can it?" asked Coraza, disappointed.

Raimundo stared at the rustic hovel for a long moment. "I think this must be the place."

"How can it be?" asked Coraza, remembering the enormous brick forge she had seen at Las Escarpas.

"That chimney is far larger and more substantial than a cabin of that size needs. I'd be willing to wager the shack is just a front." Raimundo kicked his feet out of the stirrups, pulled the horse's head down with the reins, and swung a leg over. He slid down off the horse and strode up onto the hovel's porch. Raimundo tried the knob and found the door opened easily. He walked in.

Coraza dismounted as fast as she could in her tattered skirts and tied the bony nag's reins to one of the porch pillars. She cautiously entered the shack. The light inside was dim, the cabin's only window was covered by a threadbare swatch of gingham. The interior smelled of dust and ancient fire and animal nests. The only furnishing was an iron bed frame with a thin, stained mattress. Dr. Raimundo was crouched on the floor, his head stuck into the fireplace. "Aha!" his voice came back, muffled and echoing as if it had issued from an infernal plane. "Just as I thought. This hearth has a false floor, and the chimney descends well underground. I smell charcoal and iron in the ash."

Coraza folded her arms across her chest and rubbed her shoulders, more for reassurance than for warmth. Something odd on the roughhewn wood floor caught her eye. Between a large, braided rag rug and the nearest bed leg, a faint, dark arc seemed drawn on the floor. Coraza knelt and touched one end of the drawing with her fingertip. Dark red powder came away, sticking to her skin. Coraza's hand shook. "Maestro?"

"Yes, what is it?" He must have heard the distress in her voice, for he emerged from the fireplace and came over to her. Coraza lifted her hand to him.

"Is it...dried blood?" she asked.

He grasped her wrist and pulled it closer, sniffing at her fingers. "No," he replied, frowning. "It's crushed cinnabar."

"Oh," Coraza felt slightly relieved. "I found it scattered near the bed.

See there, it looked almost like a design."

"Did it?" He looked this way and that around the bed with excited interest. He released her wrist and drew his wand from its holster. Raising the instrument up, he thumbed a blue bezel on its side. A faint blue glow flowed out of the wand tip, filling the shack. Its light revealed a faint but highly complex design on the floor all around the bed, intricate as a spider's web, adorned with half-erased symbols. "Madre," Raimundo breathed with astonishment.

"It's a spell, isn't it?" asked Coraza, stepping back from the diagram, fearful of what it might trigger.

"It was a spell, or rather the focus of one, but its occasion has long passed."

"Sere sorcery?" Coraza asked.

"Without a doubt. And quite sophisticated too. A sort of circle of summoning, but with many protective wards woven in."

Coraza stepped back again.

"Oh, don't worry," said Raimundo. "This spell was long ago spent and disabled. It shouldn't set you off."

"What was it for?" Coraza asked, unsure why the faint tracery disturbed her so.

Dr. Raimundo stared at the pattern for long silent moments.

"Well?" Coraza prompted.

"I don't wish to shock you," Raimundo began, tentatively. "But there are stories. Some say practitioners of the Sere arts like to...invite daemons in, temporarily, for their pleasure."

"They...they want to be..."

"Possessed."

"Why?" asked Coraza, horrified.

Dr. Raimundo rolled his eyes. "Why do misbegotten people smoke foul-smelling weeds or drink foul-tasting spirits or ingest near-poisonous mushrooms? Because they enjoy the experience. Perhaps it makes them feel happy or powerful or wise for a little while. They believe it will give them insight. In any case, this thaumagram was a highly complex summoning spell of some sort."

Coraza frowned at the floor, her skin creeping. "Someone would doom their soul for this...enjoyment?"

"You would be amazed, my dear, at the lengths to which people will go for their entertainments. Now, there must be a hidden entrance to another chamber somewhere." Raimundo walked to the back wall and began tapping gently on the wood with his wand.

Was my father a...demon addict? wondered Coraza. Her insides curdled at the thought her father might have been of even worse character than the holy sisters let on. *And was I...was I...brought into being during such a...*She hardly dared finish the thought. Filipo hadn't hinted of any such behavior, but perhaps Filipo hadn't known. *Perhaps Filipo was blessed to have died before learning such horrible things about his master*, thought Coraza, though she couldn't really convince herself.

She stepped around the bed to join Dr. Raimundo. Her heel scuffed the rag rug aside. Stumbling back to catch her balance, Coraza saw what appeared to be the corner of a trap door. "Maestro, look."

Dr. Raimundo turned and saw where she pointed. "Aha! Of course, the forge would be below. Much more efficient for venting." He kicked the rag rug aside and knelt beside the trap. There was a rosette at one end that was clearly a lock or latch of some sort. Raimundo made some adjustment to his wand and touched the rosette. It glowed red for a moment, then gold. Raimundo pulled the wand away, touched the rosette, and lifted up the hatch door. "Only a simple locking spell. I'd have thought Salamago would have gone to greater lengths to protect his secrets. Perhaps he felt the location was protection enough."

Coraza stood beside Raimundo and looked down into the tunnel beneath the hatch. A wooden frame ladder led down into darkness. A smell of old rust, coal, and dust drifted up. Raimundo readjusted the setting on his wand to emit light again and swiftly descended the ladder. Swallowing hard, gathering her skirts in one hand, Coraza followed after.

Dr. Raimundo's light vanished down a short, narrow tunnel for a moment, and then she heard a muffled exclamation.

"What is it?" Coraza asked, hurrying to catch up to the sorcerer, bumping against the rough rock walls of the tunnel. "Is it the forge?"

As she reached the end of the tunnel, Dr. Raimundo blocked her way and caught her in his arms. "No, no, Coraza. You shouldn't see this."

She'd caught a glimpse of a body lying on the stone floor. "Let me see. Let me see!" She beat her fist on Raimundo's shoulder. "I have a right to know!"

"He's dead, Coraza."

"Of course, he is dead. I know that. Let me see!"

"Very well. But you've only yourself to blame for your nightmares, then." Raimundo released her and raised his wand to illuminate the chamber.

A man lay stretched out on the floor, wearing plain brown trousers, tunic, and a long leather apron. His head, still covered with a tangled bush of dark, grey streaked hair, was tilted back, lips drawn back to reveal yellowed teeth. His left arm was flung out at an awkward angle over a deep rut cut in the stone floor. There appeared to be a gash in his wrist. His eyes were closed, orbs sunken into the sockets, but his skin was intact, mummified, and there was no smell of decay. Behind the remains of what had been Herculeo Salamago, a recess had been cut into the rock wall, a hearth directly beneath the fireplace above.

Coraza breathed deeply, horrified but also fascinated. She was not afraid. She stared at the body, trying to memorize every inch of the man who had been her father. *Why?* she mentally asked him. *Why did you abandon me to the orphanage? Why didn't you live to tell me who or what I am? Why did you do...whatever it was you did? Did you ever feel any caring for me, or was I just a magical mistake to you?* Tears leaked from her eyes. Her hands curled into fists. She could not truly grieve for the father she had never known, but sadness and anger filled her for what she would never know.

Dr. Raimundo stepped away from Coraza to more closely examine the wall above the stone trough. The light from the wand revealed more symbols, but they were crudely drawn, unlike the delicate tracery of the thaumagram above. One of them she recognized…the mountain struck by lightning, just like the symbol on her trisigil. Coraza's hand went reflexively to her chest. "So…he was a Molochista," she said.

"Perhaps, but not an accomplished one," said Dr. Raimundo, frowning with bewilderment. "The way this spell is drawn conveys haste and desperation. Events were closing in on Maestro Salamago, and he had to work fast with what little knowledge he had. Apparently, the spell cost him his life. Or he was dying already and had to hurry to complete his work before the final darkness."

Coraza put her knuckles to her mouth. "Can you tell what the spell was meant to do?"

The sorcerer was silent for long moments. "Tell me again, what happened to that sword you inherited?"

"I don't know. I thought Agente Palabo had it."

"Hmm. If he had caught on to what the sword is, I'd expect he'd have destroyed it. But something tells me this spell is still active, and the sword still exists."

"Then what spell did he put into it?"

"He put himself into it, señorita. That is Sere sorcery, the binding of life to unlife. Giving a soul to matter that was not meant to have one. Perhaps Salamago thought he could better guide you in undeath than he had in life."

Coraza stood still in shock. The sword she had been carrying. That she thought had protected her at Malaguez's hacienda. That she so wanted to keep in her hands. He was there! *If only I'd known…If only I'd known while I had it! Did the holy sisters know…I don't think so. They knew, somehow, he had done forbidden magic, but they didn't know all of it.*

"But why?" asked Coraza. "Why put himself into a sword instead of… just staying alive?"

"I have no answer," said Dr. Raimundo. "It makes no sense to me. But rumors did say he had gone mad before he disappeared." The sorcerer moved on to examine another part of the wall. "This part looks like it was painted in blood. Poor desperate fellow."

Coraza wrapped her arms around her chest. She had longed for the truth, but each part of the truth she learned felt fouler, cut deeper, until her heart wanted to twist with unknowable sadness and revulsion over the bizarre darkness of it all.

"Madre, look at this," murmured Raimundo, moving to the farther end of the egg-shaped chamber. "A vein of animite, small but still enough to make a man wealthy for life..."

Coraza heard another voice then, so soft that she wasn't sure she was truly hearing it. The voice was familiar in a way that tugged at her heart.

"I think we've found them," said the distant voice. An indecipherable murmur answered. "Look, there is a horse. It must be theirs."

Filipo! Coraza thought, her heart turning over. *Has his ghost been trapped in this canyon too? Why would he have come here?*

"Shouldn't we go in?" Filipo said, a little nearer. The voice was now clearly echoing down the flue of the fireplace.

Or maybe he is still alive! thought Coraza.

"Hm? Did you say something?" muttered Dr. Raimundo.

"But who knows what he's doing to Coraza in there," said Filipo.

Finally, she could contain herself no longer. "Filipo!" Coraza cried. She turned and dashed down the short tunnel.

"Wait!" Raimundo shouted, following after.

Coraza flung herself up the ladder, through the shack, and out the front door.

And there Filipo stood, in living flesh, next to Agente Palabo. Both blinked in astonishment to see her.

"You're alive!" Coraza cried, her heart filled with joy, her eyes filling with tears. She opened her arms and started to run toward Filipo.

And was suddenly yanked back as Dr. Raimundo grabbed her upper arm. "What are you doing, you stupid girl?" He held his wand pointed threateningly at Filipo's heart. Filipo stepped back, arms raised. "These men are not your friends."

"Yes, they are! Let me go! Filipo, he's here! My father is here!"

"What? Is he alive?" cried Filipo.

Coraza noticed, then, the hilt of the sword Sorrow behind Filipo's right shoulder. "No, I mean. His body."

Raimundo shook her roughly. "Aren't you listening to me? Don't talk to him!"

"Let her go!" Filipo demanded.

"So that you can escort her to her execution?" snarled Dr. Raimundo. "Isn't that what you've come for?"

"No!" insisted Filipo.

Dr. Raimundo looked at Agente Palabo. "Who sent you then? Why are you following us?"

The vigilero seemed to consider his words carefully before answering. "The Doña Vincenza wishes to speak with Señorita Salamago and asked that we find her."

"Hah!" said Raimundo. "You see, my dear, these gentlemen intend to finish the job the soldiers were sent to do. Working for the Protectadoras now, are we, Marzo?"

"The last thing we want to do is harm her!" Filipo insisted.

"Oh, really? So, you might, but the Protectadoras have no such affection for the girl," said Raimundo.

Coraza had suspected the Protectadoras might want her dead, but it was another cut to her already aching heart that Filipo and the agente might be helping the old witches.

Filipo glanced back and forth between Coraza and Raimundo for a moment before saying, "Listen to me carefully. Doña Vincenza is the Governadora's grandmother..."

"What has that to do with anything?" asked Raimundo.

"It matters because Governadora Remedios," Filipo went on, "is Coraza's mother."

Coraza stared at Filipo, open mouthed. It was a statement so far from any possibility Coraza could have imagined that she wondered why Filipo would attempt such an outrageous lie.

Dr. Raimundo began to laugh, and then he turned to look at Coraza, and his laughter died away. He frowned in thought. "What an interesting supposition. Do you think the boy's right, Marzo?"

"Señor Utherio has explained his reasoning to me," replied the Agente with a shrug. "He could be right."

Dr. Raimundo began to chuckle again, this time with an edge of mad absurdity. "So, Governadora Remedios, daughter of heroes of the Great Revolt, is a secret Molochista? You know, I wouldn't put it past the scheming bitch. If this is true, you've no idea, young señor, what a gift you have just given your old friend Don Malaguez."

"You think it's true?" Coraza softly asked Dr. Raimundo. All those years, dreaming in the orphanage of secretly being the child of a wealthy parent of noble blood. And now it might be true, but in the ugliest way possible. Coraza began to feel a little dizzy and numb and sick.

"I don't care about politics!" Filipo shouted. "I just want Coraza safe."

"She is safe," growled Dr. Raimundo, "so long as she's with me. So, get out of here, before I blast you both to ashes."

A bolt of indigo light erupted from Agente Palabo's hands, knocking Dr. Raimundo down. Filipo rushed toward Coraza, but Dr. Raimundo was still aware and fired his wand. The spell struck Filipo in the chest, sending him sprawling clear across the clearing. Violet bands encircled him, and his back arced in pain as they tightened.

"No!" Coraza cried, her heart torn as she saw him fall again on her behalf. She started to run toward him—and Raimundo fired again.

The spell struck her side, knocking her to the ground. Violet bands of energy hummed around her, tightening, the magic biting into her skin and bones, making breath harder and harder to draw. She couldn't tear her gaze from Filipo as he writhed under the punishment of the binding spell. The spell made her blood feel as though it burned.

She remembered thinking, *Enough. Never again. It was too much, this world. Too much ugliness and pain.* Filipo had been the one good thing left in it. She would save him, even if it meant revealing her true nature to him. He would never love her once he truly knew anyway. But at least she could save him. She felt the creature within her demand release.

Coraza closed her eyes.

She let go.

Chapter Eighteen

Filipo grimaced and writhed on the hard canyon dirt as the violet bands of sorcery tightened around his chest. Maestro Salamago had once spoken of these—binding spells that fed off the strength one used to resist them. It was best not to struggle, Salamago had said, but Filipo could not help himself. Not when he had just seen Coraza shot with the same spell by that amoral snake of a sorcerer. *If I get my hands on him, I will kill him,* Filipo thought savagely, his breath now reduced to a wheeze. Coraza's sword on his back ground into his spine, and the hilt pressed hard against the back of his head.

Filipo turned his head aside. Coraza lay just a few yards away. He wondered if he could roll over to her, if it would help. She wasn't moving. Either she was unconscious from the pain, or she was wiser than he and not fighting the magic. Dr. Raimundo and Agente Palabo had squared off, Raimundo with wand at ready and Palabo dancing from side to side, his hands performing mysterious motions.

Raimundo growled, "Give up, Agente. You're on the wrong side. The Protectadora is nothing but a damned Moloc—"

Palabo's fist slammed into the sorcerer's face.

Raimundo staggered back, left hand to his jaw, but he stayed on his feet. He raised his ebony and silver wand again and pushed a bezel. Blue and white flame jetted out of the wand.

Palabo yelled as he was thrown upward and back, crashing into the sandstone scree of the canyon wall. The Agente slid down to the ground, holding his left arm.

Blood dripping from his mouth and chin, Raimundo cried, "You idiot! I would prefer not to kill you, but you give me no choice." He raised his wand and aimed it at the vigilero's head.

"Shakat!" Palabo shouted, and a transparent ball of wavering air flew from his outstretched hand into Raimundo's stomach. The sorcerer doubled over, eyes squeezed shut in pain.

Wordlessly, Raimundo raised the wand again and pushed another bezel. A grey-purple miasma formed around Palabo. The Agente coughed and choked in the poisonous cloud. "Nekpar!" he rasped. The purple fog faded, but he did not rise from his knees.

With a death's-head grimace of triumph, Raimundo staggered across the clearing toward the gasping, vomiting vigilero.

Mierda! They will destroy each other! thought Filipo, enraged at his helplessness to defend Palabo or Coraza. He perceived movement out of the corner of his eye.

Coraza was getting up. She was no longer enveloped in violet bands—the binding spell on her had broken somehow. No, she was rising up, lifting into the air with sorcerous power like Doña Vincenza. Her clothing had turned ash black and seemed to be flaking away. Her skin was pale as porcelain, like a mask, and as she turned toward him, her eyes were entirely black, orbs of obsidian.

"No", breathed Filipo, his stomach cold with fear and sorrow. *What has that bastard done?*

Perhaps at the sound of his voice, the creature that was once his master's daughter drifted slowly toward him. Her face was beautiful and terrifying all at once, like a precious doll brought to horrific life. Closer and closer she came, her left arm stretching out toward him.

"No", Filipo gasped again, and he tried to push himself back from her with his legs, but his muscles seemed weak as damp string, and he could not catch enough breath. He looked over at Raimundo and Palabo, but they were still caught up in their battle.

Palabo threw something at the sorcerer which flung Raimundo's right arm aside, just as a fireball blasted from the wand's tip to explode in a shower of flame high on the canyon wall. Raimundo cried out as a sheet of blue sparks enveloped him, and he fell back, dropping the wand.

"Stop! Look! Help!" Filipo called out to them, but his words were scarcely a whisper.

Coraza now hovered beside Filipo, and her hand reached down toward his chest. It was a beautiful hand, as if carved by the most skillful artist from the finest marble. Filipo wondered if the Coraza he knew and had protected and cared about and admired was still there. Was she just temporarily transformed? Did the sorcerer make her a monster? Was she was going to choke him, or draw his soul from his body and drain his life away?

"Pleasedontkillme," Filipo gasped at her, as if it were all one word. "Pleasedontkillme-Corazapleasedontkillme-Iloveyou-pleasedontkillme-please."

She tilted her head to one side, like a bird or a cat. Sound came from within her, as if from a great distance. It sounded like the hissing of sand and the wind in dead tree branches, sensual and alien. "Love...you..." Her hand reached down to just above the violet bands of sorcerous energy binding his chest. "Nek....par..." the Coraza-tzinn intoned.

In a flash of purple light, the bands vanished. Filipo gasped hard, drawing in as much air with each breath as he could. He was amazed to still be alive.

Coraza-tzinn withdrew her hand, and the ghost of a smile appeared on her porcelain face. She turned away and drifted toward Dr. Raimundo.

The sorcerer had finally noticed Coraza. He sank to his knees, staring at her rapt and openmouthed as if she were a statue of the Madre come to life.

Agente Palabo watched as well, his face stricken and remorseful. He brought his hands up, as if to cast a spell.

"No, wait, Agente!" Filipo called out, waving at the vigilero.

The Coraza-tzinn noticed the wand on the ground, dipped low, and scooped it up with her marble-like hand.

Madre, what is she going to do? Filipo got to his feet unsteadily.

She drifted close to Dr. Raimundo, who continued to stare at her in wonder. Coraza lifted the wand and pointed it at his head. Then she shook it at him like a teacher rebuking an unruly student. "Stop...fight..." she moaned in her otherworldly voice.

"Yes, yes, of course, my dear," breathed Dr. Raimundo, nodding. "Whatever you wish."

Agente Palabo stepped stealthily toward her. But she turned and shook the wand at him as well. "You...too..."

Palabo froze. "You can speak. You are aware?"

After a pause, Coraza-tzinn said, "I...am here."

"Don't you see, Agente," said Dr. Raimundo, "She is a miracle. She is the Great Amalgamation. She is what sorcerers have sought for centuries to achieve."

"Molochista sorcerers," Filipo growled.

"Do not speak of what you don't understand," Raimundo began.

Suddenly, the Coraza-tzinn jerked sideways, then she bent backwards at an unnatural angle. Her arms flailed out as a white burst of light engulfed the clearing, momentarily blinding Filipo.

He blinked as the light faded and lowered his arm. Coraza, now in her previous form, lay unmoving on the ground.

"No," breathed Dr. Raimundo. He reached out toward her.

Agente Palabo's fist slammed into the side of the sorcerer's head, knocking him to the ground. Raimundo groaned and then shut his eyes, unmoving.

Filipo slid to his knees beside Coraza's fallen body. He placed a shaking hand gently on her neck to feel for a pulse.

Palabo crouched on the other side of her and carefully rolled her onto her back. Other than her clothes being scorched to a ruin, she appeared uninjured.

Filipo couldn't detect a pulse. "Agente, is...is she dead?"

The vigilero took a flat oval stone of clear crystal from his pouch and placed it on Coraza's chest over her heart. A faint green light appeared in the stone. "She lives, just barely," Palabo said, faint amazement in his tone.

"The change must have taken all the strength she had. We must get her to the Presidio as soon as possible."

"You can heal her, can't you?"

"Some, perhaps. But her nature is a mystery to me. Doña Vincenza will understand what she needs."

"Perhaps the silver wires, the power of the earth…" Filipo rambled, trying to keep despair at bay. He lightly touched her left cheek, realizing he had meant what he said, that he loved her. But he no longer knew if the Coraza he loved still existed. Or if she had ever truly been the girl he loved, or if he had loved an illusion. Still, he felt committed to continue to protect her, to stay at her side, no matter her nature. Not just because she was his master's daughter—although that was part of it—but because of what he had learned of her strength and courage. He would see it through.

"Give me a moment." The Agente placed the palm of his right hand over the flat stone on Coraza's chest and closed his eyes.

Filipo took the sword off his back and placed it in Coraza's left hand, folding her fingers over the hilt. She had spoken of the sword's protection before. "Protect her now," he whispered. The animite stone at the top of the hilt, protruding from the sheath bag, glowed a perceptible scarlet. Filipo looked at the abandoned cabin. "I'll be right back."

"Where are you going?" asked Palabo.

"She said my master was here."

"She said he was dead, Filipo."

"Still…I must see him. I must know." He got up and ran toward the shack.

"Filipo!"

"I have to know! I'll just be a moment!" Filipo ran inside and blinked in the dim light. After a second, he saw the square hole in the floor. He ran to it and scrambled down the vertical ladder into the tunnel.

It was utter dark, and Filipo spent a moment in desperate frustration. *If only I could do magic.* Then he remembered what Agente Palabo had said, that perhaps Doña Vincenza, by filling him with the sorcerous power that fed the Protectadoras, may have given Filipo what nature failed to. He had watched his master's casual spells carefully over the years. Perhaps it was time to try.

Raising his right hand, fingers curled as if holding an orb, he intoned, "*Golnar*". He was startled as golden flames sprouted from his fingertips, brighter than he had ever managed before. He allowed himself a brief smile of triumph before, emboldened, he pressed on down the earthen tunnel.

He stopped in the entrance to the forge chamber, shocked by the sight of Salamago's mummified form. Filipo's former master lay on the floor in precisely the attitude as in Filipo's dream. Filipo's mouth dropped open as he took in the evil symbols on the wall that had been painted in Salamago's blood.

Palabo grabbed him from behind. "Come on! Her life hangs in the balance!"

"Do...do you see?" Filipo stammered. "Do you see what he's done?"

"Sere Sorcery. Yes, Salamago has much to answer for," growled Palabo, "but we must go now!"

Torn between the man who raised and sheltered him and the girl who needed him above, Filipo wavered. "I must bury him," Filipo said, "before his shame is discovered."

"It is too late for that!" cried the Agente. "Salamago must make his own peace with the Madre. You can come back for him later, but right now, we must see to his daughter."

Tears began to fill Filipo's eyes. He wanted to scream "Why?" at the old man, to shake the body to pieces, demanding what had turned a good and skillful man to such evil. He wanted to deny the truth, but what he had seen, what Coraza had shown herself to be, would not allow him to lie to himself. He had loyally served and learned from a man who practiced Sere Sorcery. And Filipo would now bear some of that shame forever. He lowered his hand to put out the light and let Palabo lead him back to the ladder and out into the fog-shrouded canyon.

"I see you've discovered a talent for magic after all," said Palabo. "The Protectadora's earth-flow can have that effect. That's good. We may have need of it."

Still dazed and fighting back tears, Filipo nearly tripped over Dr. Raimundo's fallen form. "What do we do with him?" he asked roughly.

"Leave him be."

"Shouldn't we kill him?"

Palabo frowned at Filipo. "Kill a man while he is unarmed and helpless? That would be murder."

Filipo shook his head. "What about his wand then?" Filipo picked up the fine ebony and silver instrument.

"So, you would merely steal from a helpless man?" Palabo asked.

"He might use it against us again."

"He might use it to defend himself against thieves. Here." Palabo snatched up the sword from where it lay on Coraza's chest. "You want to bury something? Bury that." He flung the sword at Filipo with surprising force.

Filipo caught the sword, staggering back a step. Palabo picked up Coraza, positioned her on his shoulder, and carried her toward the horses.

Feeling that his master's last sword more than deserved its name, Filipo slung Sorrow across his back and followed the Agente.

Coraza traveled through a series of dreams. The first took place in a gray, colorless desert where the stones spoke. Skeletal forms drifted, chanting, "It is coming. It is coming." She could not tell if they were hopeful or frightened.

In the second dream, she was in the midst of a landslide, a rockfall, tumbling and bumping endlessly against boulders and cliffs. In the next, a man who resembled the mummified Salamago was shouting at her and gesticulating—the way the holy sisters would when she had slept late and had important chores to do—but Coraza could not understand what he was saying. She dreamed again of a great black cloud writhing like a serpent. It's movements beat the air, creating a thunderous heartbeat. She could feel its hunger, insatiable and constant. Then, at last, she lay in a chill riverbed, arms outstretched, water flowing over and through her, invigorating her. In the last, she reclined on soft clouds, regarding a dark, starry sky across which, at times, a gray-green comet would fly.

In each place, a small part of her mind would wonder, *Is this Death? Is this Heaven? Is this Hades? Where am I?*

But the starry sky was now dim and static overhead. And her nose itched. Unthinking, Coraza reached up a hand to scratch it and realized she must be awake and alive. She turned her head. The bed beneath her was covered with a cream-colored lace counterpane, and the pillow beneath her head was soft. What she had taken for a starry sky was a canopy over the bed, bedecked with sequins. The air held a strange scent of damp earth and rosewater. With great caution, Coraza sat up.

She wore a long, white cotton nightdress, simple but far finer than anything she had worn in the orphanage. She was in some fine lady's bedroom, but also underground. How she knew, Coraza wasn't sure. There were no windows. Perhaps she could feel the weight of the earth through the walls. Perhaps having spent a year in the cellar of the orphanage had made her accustomed to it.

The only illumination in the room came from bronze oil lamps in each corner, each in the shape of an owl. They made her feel as though she were being watched. The room was furnished with a large wardrobe, a chest of drawers, a small desk, a long table, and a coat-rack on which hung a long gray-green cloak. There were no mirrors. Coraza swung her legs over and stood, finding she could stand steady. As before, when awakening from the change, she felt healthy and whole. But this time, she sensed her safe return had been a near thing.

On the long, narrow table sat a bowl of fruit. Coraza snatched up an apple and bit into it, finding herself ravenously hungry. She finished the whole thing, seeds and all, and was licking her fingers when the door banged open. Coraza jumped back as a middle-aged woman dressed in black bustled in, carrying folded cloth.

The woman blinked, unsmiling, at Coraza and said, "Ah. You are awake. Good." She had the air of a high-status servant, so Coraza felt comfortable addressing her.

"If you please, señora, could you tell me where I am?"

"You are in the Presidio at Los Mesanjeros."

"Am I a guest or a prisoner here?"

"Does this look like a jail?" She gestured to take in the room.

A low throaty voice came from the far corner. "Some of us sometimes think of it as such." The gray-green cloak rose from the coat rack, shimmering as the illusionary façade dropped away.

Coraza cried "Ai!" and backed into the table, setting the fruit bowl a-wobble. She nearly cried out, "a tzinn!" as the incredibly ancient woman draped in gray organza floated across the room toward her. But Coraza could see the sorcerous power glowing, nearly pulsing off of the wizened creature. Not at all like La Llorona, the woman, frail as she might be, was alive and more powerful than any holy sister or sorcerer Coraza had ever met.

The old woman tilted her head and regarded Coraza with rheumy grey-green eyes. "Is this how you greet your great-grandmother, child?"

The servant fixed Coraza with a steely frown. "Show some respect for the Doña Vincenza, girl."

"Your pardon, señora." Coraza did a small curtsy as well as she could in the nightdress.

Doña Vincenza looked at the servant. "Go fetch Lucita." The servant bobbed a curtsy and bustled out the door.

Coraza's hands were shaking as the wraith-like Protectadora drifted closer. "How are you feeling?" the Doña asked.

"I'm...fine. I feel quite well."

"Hmm. You show remarkable resilience. Agente Palabo was not at all certain you would survive."

"Are he and Filipo here?" Coraza asked, suddenly feeling an urgent need to have friends nearby. "May I see them?"

The old sorceress shook her head. "I am afraid I had to send the vigilero and his...deputy off on another important errand."

"Will they be back soon?"

"That is impossible to say. You had best not think about them, as there are many important things for us to discuss about you and your nature."

The door burst open again. Accompanied by the maidservant, a woman of severe beauty, dressed in a fine gown of midnight-blue velvet, swept in. Coraza knew this must be Governadora Remedios herself, and she lowered herself again into a curtsy. Still, Coraza could not keep her gaze from the woman's face, searching for resemblances to her own, searching for signs of love, recognition, and approval.

But the Governadora merely looked over Coraza with a dissatisfied frown, and Coraza's heart sank. The Governadora said to the servant, "Leave us." The black gowned servant nodded and hustled out, shutting the door behind her. Turning to Doña Vicenza, the Governadora asked, "Well?"

"I have good news, Lucita. The vigilero told me she made the change completely and yet was able to retain her awareness." Doña Vincenza spoke in the fond tone of a doting grandmother reporting her grandchild's first babbling words.

"Indeed?" Change flowed over the Governadora's features, surprise, pride, and hope. She stepped back. "Well, then," she said with an encouraging gesture. "Let's see it."

Coraza's mouth dropped open in dismay. She looked back and forth from the Doña to the Governadora. "But...but I..."

"Apparently," the Doña said, "some sort of shock is required to bring about the change, from what the vigilero reported. He observed that Coraza was reacting to a binding spell thrown by Dr. Raimundo."

The Governadora nodded, impatient. "That is to be expected, I suppose. Well, then, give her a shock."

"What?" Outrage overrode whatever good sense Coraza had left. Hands balled into fists, she stepped up to the Governadora. "How could you? I am told you are my mother! Are you my mother? Why did you want me to be something evil? Why did you do this to me? Why did you abandon me? Why don't you care—"

The Governadora slapped Coraza's cheek smartly, just hard enough to sting. "Listen to you," she said, her voice heavy with disgust. "Yes, I bore you within my body. The blood of my father, your grandfather, flows within you. Your grandfather and grandmother were heroes of the Great Revolt. Doña Vincenza, your great-grandmother, is also a hero of the Great Revolt. The blood of heroes flows within you, and yet you whine and whimper. Is this the way a hero speaks?"

Coraza clasped a hand to her aching cheek, too stunned to speak or cry. She felt as though the Holy Madre had dealt her a vicious joke.

"Now, now, Lucita," said Doña Vincenza, gently laying a cold, limp hand on Coraza's shoulder. "You are being unfair. Coraza does not yet know the reason for her nature, or why we created her. You must give her time."

"We don't have time!" the Governadora shouted. And Coraza saw something else behind the woman's imperious manner. She saw fear. "You received the message from the oracle at the Cathedral?"

"Yes, of course. I am still waiting for confirmation of her visions, however," said Doña Vincenza.

Coraza fought back the tears trying to flow. *I will not cry in front of this woman who claims to be my mother,* she thought. *I must not let her think I am weak.*

"I know events are rather pressing," Doña Vincenza went on, "but if we are to have any hope of training her, she has to be prepared properly, don't you think?"

"Do we have any hope at all, abuela?" asked Governadora Remedios, and to Coraza's surprise, the Governadora took a lace handkerchief from a purse at her waist and began to dab at her eyes and nose.

"Here we have the embodiment of hope," Doña Vincenza said, patting Coraza's shoulder. "And now, it is you who are talking unlike a hero. We must be strong to be deserving of hope."

"Yes, yes, of course," said the Governadora, and she straightened, taking a deep breath. Once she had command of herself, she began. "In brief, then, Coraza. My mother died in the Great Revolt. My father survived but was wounded both in body and in soul. He had seen and heard things he told no one else but me, his only child. We put down the revolt in Califia, but my father knew the instigators were Nuevo Aztecans from Mexico. He also knew that Molochistas were planning to create tzinn more powerful than any seen in this world in centuries. And they would use such tzinn to conquer the rest of the Americas. Perhaps to even turn our own protective tzinn against us. This is why we needed Sere weapons of our own. Why we need you."

"I thought tzinn could not be created," said Coraza.

The Governadora snorted. "So the Molochistas would have the world believe. But my father knew it could be done and would be done, and he passed this news on to me, his impressionable daughter. When my father died, when I was about your age, I vowed to do all I could to protect Alta Califia from the destruction he foresaw. Doña Vincenza and I decided that, in order to fight a great tzinn, we needed a new sort of hero, one who intimately understood tzinn. I entertained every sorcerer I met to learn what I could, at great risk to my reputation you understand, without alerting the Church. All Doña Vincenza and I had were bits and pieces of the knowledge necessary. And then I met your father, Erculeo Salamago. I don't know where his knowledge came from, no doubt a past he wished to forget. But I charmed him until he told me enough and then seduced him, and Doña Vincenza and I put our plan into action."

So, she was no kinder to my father than she is to me. Coraza remembered the intricate drawing on the floor of the shack in the Canyon of Spirits. Beneath the bed. She did not want to think about what happened there. She wrapped her arms around her chest, wishing she could be anywhere else, even back at the orphanage.

"I had hoped for a son," the Governadora went on. "But Erculeo refused to undergo the rites that would have ensured that outcome."

"Perhaps just as well," interjected Doña Vincenza, "given the tzinn we summoned."

"Yes, yes," said Governadora Remedios, waving the handkerchief impatiently. "I suppose it could have been strange, given that La Llorona answered our call."

Coraza's head snapped up. "La Llorona?"

"Yes, child. You could, in fact, say that she is your other mother. You carry a bit of her soul around with you. Somewhere in your body is a tiny chip of animite. This is like the bit of sand in a clamshell around which a pearl grows. This bit of tzinn nature suffused and directed your growth as you burgeoned within me. You could say it is from La Llorona that you get your tzinn nature."

Coraza put her hands to her head. "Is that why she came for me? I thought Mater Urania had lowered the wards so that La Llorona could kill me."

"I don't know how much that foolish nun knows of your parentage, but she may have hope you would no longer be an irritating problem for them," said the Governadora.

"We were asking a lot of the holy sisters," said Dona Vincenza sardonically, "to hide Coraza in a place devoted to sacred work. I can understand Mater Urania's...discomfort."

"Do you think La Llorona recognized me? As her daughter, I mean," said Coraza. The tzinn's plea for filial love seemed even more poignant.

"Unlikely," snapped the Governadora. "Pure tzinn don't think. Not as people do."

No, but she might feel, thought Coraza. *And how strange that she might feel more maternal attraction than this woman who bore me.*

"But when you were born," the Governadora went on, "you seemed so...ordinary. There was no sign of magical ability or extraordinary strength about you. By then, Erculeo was torn with remorse over what we had done. He broke off our affair and buried himself in his blacksmithing work. He seemed to want to forget all that had happened. I had the Cathedral blot out your trisigil, since your remarkable creation seemed irrelevant. I gave you to the orphanage, only hinting to the Mater that there might be... unusual things to watch out for. I chose to pursue politics in the hope of rescuing Califia in that way. And the rest you know."

Coraza rocked back and forth, holding her rage and sorrow close. "So, I was made...to be a hero. To save Califia. By being a tzinn."

"Why do you think your name is Coraza?"

Coraza could not speak for a moment. It all made sense, and yet so little sense. It seemed madness. "How could you expect such a plan to succeed?"

"Something like it was done once before."

"Careful, Lucita."

"The girl wants to know, abuela. Let her hear the depth of our hubris, our sacrilege. There are some who say the Holy Madre's son was created to combat evil. That he was imbued with a heavenly Spirit and thus had a dual nature. We cannot summon angels, and God no longer performs such miracles. But we can summon tzinn. And we do what magics we may."

Coraza looked back and forth between the Governadora and the Protectadora, scarcely able to voice how appalled she was. "You have doomed your souls for this."

Doña Vincenza nodded gravely. "I am ultimately bound for Hades as is my granddaughter. Why do you think I so unnaturally prolong my life? I know what awaits me. But I would have been more ashamed to have died knowing I could have saved many but did not."

"The attack is coming soon, Coraza, and thousands will die," said Governadora Remedios. "Those who do not die will be twisted by the darkest magic on earth. If Molochistas gain all of the Americas as their territory, then someday all of the civilized world will fall to them as well. What I did, some might call a madwoman's notion. Now, you may be all that stands between the world and that terrible future. But I confess that I still doubt that you are capable. I look at you and see a frightened, disturbed child, hardly ready to face a normal life, let alone an existence requiring extraordinary courage and will."

This is madness, Coraza thought again. *And how unfair to put all their hopes on me, even from before I was born. And yet...if true that thousands may die, that the world may fall if I do nothing, how can I turn away from this calling, this destiny? I did want to become a Protectadora someday. As I am, I cannot, but maybe I can still be a protector. I will not let her disapproval defeat me. I will show her. I will show her that she should have cared.*

Coraza raised her chin. "You are wrong, *Mother*. I will fight the Molochistas," she said. "I will do whatever I can to stop their evil. And if I cannot stop them, I will die trying."

"Ah," breathed the Governadora, a glimmer of pride and approval at last appearing in her eyes. "Now those are the words of a hero."

Chapter Nineteen

Filipo's neck was sore, but he could not help turning his head once again, to look back over his shoulder to the west.

Back toward Los Mesanjeros and Coraza.

He and Agente Palabo had been riding south and east for two days, taking their horses at a steady pace so as not to founder them. They had descended from mountains into an alien desert as arid and empty as Filipo's soul. After what he had seen in the secret forge, Filipo considered himself a man with no past and no future. He had once dreamed to become a great blacksmith, but how could he now, without thinking of his master's shame? He needed time to sort through all he had seen and learned. He felt like a sopping cloth that had been wrung over and over to dry. He felt without direction. Even Coraza, to whom he still felt a caring duty, had been hidden away by the Protectadoras for healing.

Thus, it had seemed the most natural thing when Doña Vincenza had explained to Agente Palabo that she had another urgent mission for him, that Filipo should accompany the vigilero as his deputy. What else was there for him to do?

He had left the sword named Sorrow at the Presidio. It was fitting that father and daughter should be together, wasn't it? He didn't know if Doña Vincenza would let Coraza have the sword or not, but at least it no longer rode his back. And yet, he felt guilty, as if he had abandoned them both. But Coraza, what was she now? Had she always been that beautiful, terrifying creature at the secret forge? Was she the tzinn who frightened the soldiers away at the inn? Filipo's feelings roiled like a pot of boiling water.

"I regret to tell you," Palabo commented wryly as he rode just ahead, "that no matter how often you turn your head, you will not develop the skill of an owl to wear your head backwards."

Stung, Filipo faced forward. "You have gained such wisdom by experience, old man," he said. "There is one difficult thing that I hope you can teach me."

"And what might that be?"

"How do you manage to love a woman you cannot have?"

The vigilero grunted. "I focus on my duty."

"Really?" asked Filipo, dubiously. "And is that enough?"

Palabo looked down. "Of course not."

"So, what then?"

"I try to remember her smile and let that be enough."

Filipo tried to remember if Coraza ever smiled. Yes, there had been times. When they first rode out together away from Don Malaquez's hacienda. He remembered how, after the humiliating duel with the Agente, Coraza had held him and rocked him and told him that he had fought well. The desert wavered before his eyes as he indulged the memory. His heart caught in his chest. "Agente, I am trying this, but it only seems to make it worse."

"Yes," Palabo agreed sadly. "I should have warned you about that."

They rode on across the desert pan through an immense silence broken only by hoofbeats, creaking leather, the wind, and occasional birdsong. The scrubby bushes were only tall enough to shelter tiny lizards that skittered away so fast that Filipo could scarcely catch sight of them. There were cacti in an amazing variety of shapes and "trees" that seemed clothed in shaggy gray fur. "I'm amazed anything lives out here," he commented at last.

"Life is tenacious," Palabo said. "Some days I think stubbornness is life's best virtue."

"Life needs it out here. Is it true this is tzinn territory?"

"We are on the borders of it. True Sere spirit country lies to the east. The desert there is as dry, and the hills as blasted, as the fabled Sahara, where tzinn were first discovered."

"Will we see any tzinn, do you think?"

"I am almost certain of it."

Something in the Agente's tone implied Filipo had asked a stupid question, so he lapsed back into silence.

As day wore on into evening, Filipo spied a grove of cottonwoods ahead at the foot of a hummock of low, bare, rocky hills. In the midst of the trees stood an incongruous pair of adobe bell towers.

"A mission?" Filipo asked, startled at the loudness of his voice. "Out here?"

"Any place there was a chance of mining silver and converting natives was a good place for a mission, as far as the old friars were concerned. This mission used to be on a major trading road to Mexico before the borders were sealed."

As they drew nearer, Filipo could see a corral with a pair of burros, some goats, and some scrawny sheep. There was also a small garden, tended by men in brown robes. "The friars are still there? I thought all the missions were shut down ages ago."

"Officially, yes, all the Marianos were called back to Spain so that the Church would not own all of Califia. The Church no longer owns the land, but Friar Juan-Paolo has been permitted to live here, in gratitude for his service to king and colony. He has been of great assistance to the Protectorado."

A young Indian monk, his hair cut in the traditional bowl cut and tonsure, came running out to them. "Welcome, Agente, señor. Let me take your horses, and please come inside and refresh yourselves."

"Can this be little Brother Miguelito?" asked Palabo. "You have grown like a tree."

The young monk smiled as he took the reins of Palabo's horse. "Indeed, it has been too long since you last visited us, Agente."

Filipo swung his leg over and dismounted. As soon as his boots hit the dust, he felt weariness descend on him like a heavy cloak. He was never happier for a chance to rest. He handed Tulio's reins to the young monk.

"Take good care of him, Brother. He is all I have in this world."

The young monk nodded. "They say a good horse is worth more than a king's gold."

"True words," Filipo muttered, patting Tulio's damp shoulder as the horse was led to the paddock. He followed the Agente to the huge wood doors that served as gateway into the mission compound. Filipo's legs ached and felt disinclined to move, but the pain served as a welcome distraction from other thoughts.

Palabo raised his fist to knock on the doors, but they swung open with a mighty creak before his hand reached the wood. To Filipo's surprise, the man hauling the doors open was a wrinkled, mottled-skin, white-haired old friar. He clasped arms with the Agente, considerable warmth and animation in his eyes. "Marzo, how good to see you."

"And you, Padre. You are looking well."

"It is this dry heat. It preserves. I shall be a mummy before I am even dead."

Filipo did not appreciate how this inadvertent reminder brought back the vision of the horror of Salamago's remains. To banish it, Filipo walked up to the Agente and the friar, presenting himself to be introduced.

"Padre, may I present my assistant, Filipo Del Utherio."

"Welcome, young señor, to my humble chapel in the desert."

"Thank you, Padre, for providing this welcome oasis."

"I am pleased that the Madre allows me to be of service. Marzo, I wish that our reacquaintance could be in better circumstances, but I'm sure you are aware of the crisis. Your compañero awaits in the dining hall to give you a full report."

"Thank you, Padre. We'll speak to him at once."

Compañero? Filipo followed Palabo across the mission compound to a wood building up against the high adobe wall. Inside, at a simple trestle table, sat a gray, grizzled vigilero in the uniform of the black and red poncho. He looked the way Palabo might in ten to fifteen years. On the table before him stood a bottle and a glass of pale green liquid. As the old vigilero looked up at them, Filipo guessed from his red eyes and slack lips that he might have been drinking for a while.

Without preamble, the old vigilero said, "Marzo! Did you know they make wine from cactus? I never thought something so pleasant could come from something so unfriendly."

"It's my understanding, Aciles," said Palabo, as he sat down across the table, "that man can make an alcoholic beverage from anything that grows."

"Such clever devils we are. The trick is being able to drink whatever concoction is made. So, who is your friend?" He looked up with bleary eyes at Filipo.

"May I present Filipo Del Utherio. I have found his assistance useful."

"I see. Is he strong of heart and courageous of blood?"

"He rises to what occasion demands."

"Good. We need worthy men. Have a seat, young señor."

So, it is just like that, eh? Filipo sat, understanding now what he was to become, and finding that not only did he not mind, he felt somewhat honored.

"I am concerned, Marzo, that your young friend looked upon me with dismay. Does he not know that a vigilero is permitted to imbibe some liquid courage when he has seen what I have seen and heard what I have heard?"

"I have not yet briefed him on all the details, Aciles. So tell us, what have you seen and heard?"

The old vigilero put his elbows on the table and leaned forward, suddenly all grim business. "Two nights ago, there was a massive breach in the border wards in Arizona territory."

Palabo nodded but did not respond.

Filipo jumped in. "Is there time to repair the breach before the Nuevo Aztecans bring an army across?"

"Too late," said the old vigilero. "They've already brought the Great Tzinn across the border. It's been sitting just beyond the Rio Colorado with its Molochista handlers for about a day now."

Fear began to creep up his spine. *Great Tzinn?* He wondered what a Great Tzinn might look like. He could only imagine Coraza in her tzinn form but enormous-sized, towering over the landscape. Somehow he didn't think this was the form of the Molochista's creation.

"What are the Yanquis doing?" asked Palabo.

"Nothing. Waiting," said Aciles.

"Bastards," growled Filipo.

"No, no, I'd do the same thing," said the old vigilero. "They know the tzinn is here to take Alta Califia. It is in their interests to wait, to see if we are successful in holding it at bay."

"Or to gobble up what territory they can if we are not. Vultures. But so long as it is on the east side of the Rio Colorado," said Filipo, his thoughts churning, "the Great Tzinn is useless. It cannot cross the water."

Aciles nodded. "So, clearly, the Molochistas have a plan to deal with that obstacle."

"A bridge?" asked Palabo. "The river is broad but shallow north of where it meets the Gulf. A bridge could be built, but it would take time."

"And wood," said Aciles, shaking his head. "There isn't that much wood in this region to build a good house, let alone a bridge of that size. And my informants tell me the Molochistas did not bring wagonloads of logs with them. No, I'm thinking a dam. Built of stone. They're going to divert the river."

"I see," said Palabo. "If they can make it flow somewhere else for a while, let the true bed dry enough to cross, move the Great Tzinn to the west bank, then allow the river to return to its original bed—"

"Easiest," said Aciles with a shrug, "is to divert the river east of their current position and not worry about putting it back, which Nature may or may not correct eventually."

"Are they such powerful wizards," asked Filipo, "that they can move a river?"

Aciles barked a laugh. "You hardly need sorcery, son. Well-placed earthworks will do the job long enough for what they require, and there's plenty of dirt and rock in the desert."

Palabo nodded again. "But they cannot possibly hide such a massive construction. It will take time, and that will give us the chance to interfere.

Perhaps we can delay them long enough to find a way to destroy the tzinn. How are they sustaining the creature?"

"There is talk of whole villages being devoured between Nuevo Tenochtitlan and the border. And I suspect they have brought prisoners with them as…travel rations. Don't look so shocked, young señor. This tzinn has been used to a diet of hundreds of fresh human hearts each month. They are hardly going to starve it now."

"Then how do we stop this thing?" Filipo asked softly.

"That is the important question, isn't it?" said Palabo. "I should send a pigeon with this information to the Presidio."

"I've already done so," said Aciles, "and to another sorcerer or two who might help. In these dark times, we must find all the allies we can."

"Will the Protectorado send the army?" asked Filipo.

"What for?" exclaimed Aciles. "To provide more fresh meat for the tzinn? I am sure the Molochistas are hoping we do. No, young senor. This creature will not be defeated with the might of arms, but with the cleverness of minds." He tapped the side of his gray head with a gnarled finger. "I have served the king and colony in the desert for decades, and I have observed the tzinn in all their many forms, protective and dangerous. Such knowledge is what will be our salvation."

Filipo could not help but wonder what the old vigilero would think of Coraza.

A young monk carrying a bowl of fruit came bustling up to their table. "Here, señores, please refresh yourself. Mañuel is slaughtering one of the sheep so we will be able to provide you with a hearty supper of good mutton stew."

The vigileros thanked the monk, but thinking of the Great Tzinn and its appetites, Filipo found that he himself was no longer hungry.

Chewing on a piece of hay, the goat stared up at her with curious, friendly golden eyes.

"No," Coraza insisted, crossing her arms. The cellar room beneath the Presidio was chill and dim, and she felt as unnaturally captured there as the goat.

Doña Vincenza sighed. "You cannot afford to be squeamish, Coraza. We must find out what will sustain you in tzinn form."

"No, I mean, I don't...when I was in that...form, I wasn't attracted to animal flesh or blood." She scratched the goat behind the ear and patted its head.

"I see. Very well." The Protectadora nodded at the maidservant in the black dress, whose name, Coraza had come to learn, was Elena. Elena grabbed the rope that tethered the goat to an iron ring on the wall and led the docile animal away. "If nothing else, the soldiers will have stew tonight. Please, Coraza, can you remember anything of what you hungered for as a tzinn?"

Coraza tore her gaze away from the goat being complacently led to its slaughter. *What did I hunger for? Peace? Common Sense? Justice?* Coraza wondered, though she spoke none of it aloud. She had been angered by Filipo's suffering and the men's foolish fighting and in that frame of mind had endured her change to tzinn. Memories from her tzinn form were vague, but she remembered that.

"Coraza, the survival of Califia and all in it may rest upon your unique nature and how we may use it to defeat the Aztecan Molochistas. We may only have days to prepare. Please try to be cooperative."

Chastened, Coraza tried to calm her rebellious heart. As her fingers kept trying to tie themselves into knots, she realized what she had been trying not to reveal. "Well, there is something."

"Yes?"

"But I was not in tzinn form at the time, and that is why I did not think of it." Coraza told Doña Vincenza about the spirits in the Canyon of Ghosts.

The Protectadora's eyes widened. "Ah, so you may be a soul eater. Why didn't you tell me this before?"

"Because I was ashamed of it!"

"Shame is a luxury we can ill afford in these troubled times, Coraza. This is excellent news."

Coraza scowled at Doña Vicenza. "Excellent? How can it be excellent? Why are you so cruel?" she blurted out.

A subtle change occurred around the Protectadora's eyes. "Cruel? Coraza, I know the holy sisters taught you to be good in a sinful world. That one should have a kind heart. But we face an enemy that is colder and more heartless than you or I or even the Governadora could ever try to be. We must harden ourselves for the tasks at hand."

"But if we turn to evil because of our enemy, does that not make us their equal in the eyes of the Madre?"

Doña Vincenza looked down at her hands. "I suppose it is our hope, our expectation, that our evil will be temporary. To us, it is the means, not the end. That upon our victory we may return again to the ways of kindness, justice, and mercy. But the Molochistas could not be what they are without their cruel ways. Upon their victory, they would only persist in what they do because it will have brought them success. Now, what you tell me is good news because it means you may be able to absorb the essence of, and thereby destroy, other tzinn. That would be the best outcome of all, would it not?"

"Yes. Yes, I suppose." Coraza turned away and paced the packed earthen floor. If she were part tzinn, would it not mean destroying her own kind? She wondered what it would be like to destroy La Llorona in such a way, to drain the essence of the creature that was, in part, her mother. Coraza imagined unspooling the tzinn like a skein of black yarn. *Would the tzinn feel pain? Would she cry out for mercy? Would her eyeless children, the Twins as Dr. Raimundo had called them, wail at their mother's loss?* Coraza felt a little sick.

"But there must be some other way. Why aren't you teaching me magic too? The Molochistas use magic to control the tzinn, don't they?"

"Yes, but if you are to fight in tzinn form, there is no point. Tzinn, while creatures of magic, cannot wield spells themselves as human wizards do."

Coraza thought about this a moment. "But...I did."

"Surely, you are mistaken."

"No, I did. I broke the spell that was binding Filipo. I used Nekpar."

The Protectodora stared at Coraza, her gaze intense. "Truly? Yes, a negation. That might just be possible. And that might be all you need to break the Molochista's hold upon their terrible creation. This is the best news of all, Coraza. For, believe me, you will only succeed in fighting the Great Tzinn if you are in tzinn form yourself. In mortal form, you would be destroyed in an instant. So you must do whatever you must to sustain yourself, keep yourself in tzinn form, while maintaining your consciousness as well. Only in this way will we succeed."

And there it was, the thing that frightened Coraza the most, filling her nightmares. "But great-grandmother, what will happen if I cannot change back? What if I become trapped forever as a tzinn? Will I become a monster? Will I forget I was ever human? Would I wander the desert like La Llorona? Would you send someone to kill me?"

The old sorceress's eyes crinkled at the edges, and the creases in her forehead deepened. "We are in unknown territory, my child. There has never been anyone like you. I'm afraid we must hope for the best and then deal with the consequences when they occur."

The door opened and Elena peered in. "Señora, the messenger pigeon you were awaiting has arrived."

"Very good, Elena. Let us return you to your quarters, Coraza. I must rest and think on all you have told me. And you must set your mind to acceptance of your tzinn nature."

As Coraza walked back to her room beside the floating ancient sorceress, she knew. *Of course, Dona Vincenza has thought of what will happen if I stay tzinn. She and my mother, the Governadora, must have thought of the consequences of creating a creature such as me. She has probably already chosen who will dispatch me if I become a monster. What if it's Agente Palabo? Might I escape to the desert? Could I enter the Sere realm of my dreams and hide there, giving up my life in the human world forever?* Coraza shook her head, unable to see any good paths in her future.

Screams in the night shocked Filipo awake. He sat bolt upright on his cot. He was disoriented in the darkness, trying to remember where he was, what he was doing there.

The mission.

In the desert.

An unearthly howl, deep and loud as thunder, filled the air. It was answered by another scream, unhuman.

A horse.

Tulio!

Filipo jumped out of bed and ran down a narrow flight of wood stairs to the main hall of the dormitory. The outside door was already open, and a young acolyte ran by with a torch. Filipo followed him.

Behind the mission, the torchlight revealed Tulio rearing and straining at his tether. The palomino's eyes were wide and rolling, and his ears were flat against his head. Screaming again in terror, the horse flailed his hooves against the darkness. Palabo's horse stood still as a statue against the corral fence. It rumbled deep in its throat, glaring at something in the darkness, upper lip raised as if prepared to bite. Behind Palabo's horse huddled two very frightened sheep and a burro.

Filipo looked to his right. Out of a copse of cottonwoods emerged a wolf-like creature twice as tall as a man. Its gray fur was blurred indistinct, as if made of fog, and its eyes glowed a red deeper than any flame. Its jaws gaped, lined with pale stone teeth. Hunger seemed to radiate from the creature as distinct as an odor.

"The tzinn!" breathed Filipo, barely able to coax the breath from his lungs.

The giant wolf bared its fangs at Filipo, then turned its head away, almost with disdain. Its ravenous gaze was focused elsewhere. On Tulio. Like a cat stalking prey, the tzinn padded toward the horse.

"No!" Filipo grabbed the torch out of the acolyte's hands and leaped between his horse and the tzinn. The wolf-tzinn paused, nose wrinkled, eyes glaring. Filipo waved the torch before it like a madman.

"That will do no good, señor!" cried the acolyte, Miguelito. The boy dunked a bucket into the horse's water trough and threw a gallon of water at the tzinn.

The wolf-tzinn leaped back, agile as a real wolf, and shook its fur like a dog. Then it raised its head and unleashed a howl that made every hair on Filipo's skin stand on end.

"Madre!" exclaimed Migelito. "That should have weakened it."

But apparently it did not, for the wolf-tzinn lowered its head and advanced on Filipo, rage in its eyes.

Padre Juan-Paolo and the two vigileros ran into the clearing. "Señor del Utherio, catch this!" cried the friar. "Uncork it and throw it down the tzinn's throat!"

Almost transfixed with fear, Filipo dropped the torch and managed to catch the orange-sized earthenware orb that was tossed to him. He pulled out the cork with shaking hands, just as the tzinn's maw opened wide and fell over him. Filipo tossed the orb down the wolf-tzinn's gullet, praying as he awaited the pain from the stone teeth piercing his flesh.

But the pain never came. The tzinn jerked its head back, choking on the earthenware bomb. It backed up, shaking its head violently back and forth. Its eyes widened, and with a shrieking whine that made Filipo's spine hum like an ill-played violin string, the creature exploded into a ball of gray dust. A gust of wind spun the dust into a column, a small tornado, and it blew away out of the clearing into the dark night.

Shaking, Filipo staggered back, bumping into his shuddering horse. Filipo gently patted Tulio's neck. "It's gone now, Tulio. Calm yourself. It's gone."

"Well done, Filipo!" said Agente Palabo.

The older vigilero walked up and looked at Filipo for a long moment. "You all right?"

Filipo nodded, though he could not at that moment swear it was true. "That...that was the Great Tzinn? Have we defeated it?"

"That? Oh, no, no, my boy. That was one of our native crop. Some poor coyote must have died on a ley line or something. He was just a pup compared to what we are going to face."

"But he was stronger than he should have been," said Miguelito. "Water hardly bothered him."

"It is the presence of the Great One," said Friar Juan-Paulo wearily. "I am not sure how, but it calls to the native tzinn, and they feed off its strength."

"Padre," said Agente Palabo, "do you have any more of those holy water bombs?"

"Perhaps half a dozen," the old friar replied. "I have requested more from the Cathedral, but you know how slow they are about such things."

"And anything could happen to a shipment on the road," said Aciles sardonically.

"May we have three of them?" Palabo asked.

"You may have all of them, Marzo," said the padre. "For if you fail, the rest are of no use to us."

"So," said Aciles to Filipo, "you are the sort of man who will, without thinking, stand between something dear to you and a monster."

"So it would appear," said Filipo, cautiously.

The old vigilero grinned. "Good. Just the sort of madman we need. Try to get some sleep, son. We head out for the border at dawn."

Sleep? thought Filipo, his nerves still jangling. At the moment, given the living nightmare he had just faced, he suspected sleep would be very hard to come by.

Chapter Twenty

Coraza drifted in a grey, stony world. A distant voice wailed, and Coraza drifted toward the sound. She saw a woman in a long black veil; above her spun a dark thunderstorm without rain. The woman turned, and the wind whipped the veil away to reveal a face stretched over a skull. *Mother*, Coraza said.

"Oh, beautiful child," the tzinn intoned, "help us."

"*You are not alone*, Coraza said. *Together, we are not alone.*"

The tzinn raised her skeletal hands to the sky. The churning clouds took on a black, serpentine form. Coraza felt as though she would be drawn into that churn, dissolved and devoured. The head of a stylized black serpent emerged from the clouds, and its breath was a blast of searing cold wind.

In her next dream, she was again on El Dragon, but the tracks lead into the churning cloud and she was certain the train would never reach its destination.

Suddenly, Coraza awoke in utter darkness. She sat up on the bed, sensing it was the dead of night even though the room was deep underground. Her heart pounded from the terror of her nightmares. Even awake, a pall of doom remained wrapped around her like a smothering cloak.

A faint green glow crossed from right to left in front of her. "Great-grandmother?"

"Yes," sighed Doña Vincenza. A flame erupted from a candle on the night-table at the left of the bed, illuminating the skeletal face of the ancient sorceress. She seemed so like La Llorna in that moment that Coraza shuddered. The Protectorada was carrying a long, wooden box tucked under one arm. She seemed even older and sadder than usual. "I...am having difficulty sleeping. I see you are as well."

"Yes. I was having bad dreams." Coraza stammered.

Doña Vincenza nodded. "Something is interfering with the flow through the ley wires. I can no longer sense events in the land. I cannot shake the feeling that something has gone terribly wrong."

"I feel it too," said Coraza. "Do you think it is the work of the Molochistas, or their Great Tzinn?"

The Protectadora frowned. "Perhaps. I don't know. And that disturbs me the most. There is something I should give you." She drifted over to the bedside and let the box she carried fall onto the counterpane.

Coraza knew immediately what it was. "My sword!" She pounced on the box and flung open the lid. There lay Sorrow, it's slightly curved blade shimmering with golden light, it's basket hilt of thorns glowing a pale red. She grasped the iron hilt and pulled the sword onto her lap. The sword flared, a beautiful green light flowing up and down the blade. Stinging, itching tears welled in her eyes.

"Yes. It would seem it has missed you. Your friend Señor Del Utherio left it for you when he departed. I did not trust it, not knowing why your father wanted you to have his sorcerous reliquary. Now, I believe that perhaps I was wrong. In these troubled times, you should be reunited with it."

"I was told," Coraza murmured, lifting the hilt up, "that my father may have put his soul into the sword, in a final act of Sere Sorcery. Connecting life to unlife." It felt warm against her skin.

"Coraza!" A male voice exclaimed, loud and strong.

Coraza jumped, so astonished she nearly dropped the sword. "Great-Grandmother, did you hear that?"

Doña Vincenza blinked and shook her head. "No, child. Are you all right? What did you hear?"

"He spoke my name. The sword...I heard a man say my name." The glow on the blade had dimmed, as if it had spent itself in the effort to speak to her.

Doña Vincenza pursed her lips. "Señor Del Utherio claimed that your father's spirit spoke to him in a dream when he held the sword in sleep."

"Then it is true." Coraza ran her hand over the blade. "I hope it speaks more. I have so many questions."

The ancient sorceress gazed on the flickering flame of the candle, "Lucita once told me that Salamago had greater knowledge of the Sere arts than any student of the University might have received. That was why she chose him. I have often wondered…well. If…you should happen to encounter his spirit, it could be useful…if you could solicit his suggestions for action in this time of peril…" Her words drifted off.

The old woman's hopelessness frightened Coraza, and she held the sword tighter. "Yes, of course, great-grandmother. In fact, I—" A shriek from the corridor outside the room startled Coraza into silence. It was followed by thudding blows and more distant cries of fear.

Doña Vincenza spun, eyes wide, to face the door.

"What is it?" Coraza asked. "What's happening?"

The door burst open and Elena, the servant, stumbled in, her face and black dress smudged with dirt. She fell to her hands and knees. "Treachery!" she screamed. "Señora! We are betrayed!"

"Betrayed?" said Doña Vincenza. "By whom?"

Coraza leaped off the bed, sword in her hand, and knelt by the servant's side. "Elena, are you all right?"

"How can I be all right, señorita, when pigs have taken over the household?" With a glare, the woman jerked her chin back over her shoulder. Coraza looked up and saw a man in the doorway. He held a blazing torch in one hand and an ebony and silver wand in the other, pointed at Elena. Slowly and deliberately, Doctor Saturnin Raimundo walked into the room.

"Good evening, señora, señorita," he said gravely. "Forgive this intrusion into your private quarters. But there are matters and events of which you need to be informed."

"What have you done?" asked Doña Vincenza, her voice low and dangerous.

"I? Personally, very little in the scheme of things. But the people of

Califia have done much. They have grown distressed at the news of a Great Tzinn camped just beyond the eastern border with a small army of Molochistas. The people are distressed that the Governadora and Protectadoras seem to be doing nothing about this situation. They, in fact, believe the Protectorado is no longer capable of offering any protection at all. Therefore, my employer, Don Malaguez, has risen to the occasion to lead the citizens of Califia in this time of crisis. And the soldiers of the Presidio have agreed that he is a more capable leader in whom they can place their trust."

"A coup," Doña Vincenza sneered, wrinkling her nose.

Raimundo shrugged.

Coraza felt heartsick. The floor seemed to drop out from under her feet. "You...the Don would choose a time of such danger to Califia to... to..."

"What better time, señorita? If the Governadora were to succeed in driving away the Great Tzinn, her reputation would be unassailable, her power unshakable. Don Malaguez would never have a chance. If she were to fail in dealing with the tzinn, then all is lost in any case."

"Should Califia survive," said Doña Vincenza, "the king will never permit this unlawful—"

"I'm afraid His Majesty would be all too willing," interrupted Dr. Raimundo, "once he hears of Señora Remedios's dabblings in Sere Sorcery. I understand Mater Urania stands prepared to give evidence, if needed, of just such unlawful activity."

Doña Vincenza's face paled. "That would doom Lucita to the Inquisition."

"And yourself as well, I believe, señora. A terrible fate, to be sure, and therefore, my considerate employer has offered to overlook her offenses if Señora Remedios will willingly resign from the governorship and recommend Don Malaguez to the king as her successor."

Coraza stood slowly, aiming the point of the sword named Sorrow at Raimundo's chest. Dark purple flames flickered along the blade. "Where is my mother?" she demanded.

Dr. Raimundo glanced down at the sword with just a hint of concern on his face. His gaze rose to meet Coraza's intense stare. He flicked his wand upward to point above. "I regret to tell you, señorita, that former-Governadora Remedios is a ward of the Presidio. It is unfortunate that her cell is not as comfortable as her Palacio. But she is alive and safe, and if she is cooperative, she will remain that way."

"You must surely be lying," growled Doña Vincenza. "My granddaughter could never have allowed herself to be captured in a coup."

"She had demanded to speak with me, and so I acceded to her wishes. Alas, I also brought guards with handcuffs with me. It was all too simple, really.

"You beast!" roared Doña Vincenza. A ball of glowing pale-green light appeared in the ancient sorceress' hand, and she flung it at Dr. Raimundo.

With a flick of his wand, he batted the missile aside. It struck the wall in a splash of green liquid sparks and vanished. "It would appear the charges of weakness are not unfounded," he said. "Although, I suspect, the aid of a copper dampening net around the Presidio must take some of the blame."

"Fools!" said Doña Vincenza, visibly drained. "You and Don Malaguez have doomed us all!"

"How are matters any different than before? At least now the people of Califia have a strong leader they believe in, one who will have a plan of attack."

"We have a plan!" Coraza declared, raising her chin.

"What? Oh, yes, I am sure the señora has sent a few estimable vigileros, expecting that their knowledge of native lore will convince the Molochistas to give up and go home. I think their chance of success is...unlikely."

"And what does Don Malaguez intend to do?" asked Doña Vincenza.

"What he does best, señora. Bide his time. Prepare the field to his advantage. In the meantime, negotiate and learn their weaknesses—"

"If you know anything of Molochistas, you know they have no interest in negotiation!" declared Doña Vincenza. "They intend to conquer!"

"Everyone has his price," said Dr. Raimundo.

"So I see," snapped the sorceress.

"Besides," Coraza cut in, "our plan is not merely the vigileros."

"Then please illuminate me, señorita."

Coraza felt a strange buoyancy fill her. The hilt of the sword in her hand hummed with energy, and thoughts filled her head. *It is this. It is you.*

"I am going to destroy the Great Tzinn."

To his credit, Dr. Raimundo did not laugh or sneer. "Do you think you can?"

"It is what she was made for," said Doña Vincenza. "You may think of Lucita as a libertine adventuress. But she sought knowledge of the forbidden arts, knowing what the Molochistas could do. She has always been devoted to the protection of Califia. Coraza is the culmination of Lucita's studies. A tzinn in human form that will have the intelligence any Molochista's tzinn will lack."

Dr. Raimundo paused and then shook his head. "Truly the University of Madrid has never seen a finer Maestro's thesis. And therein lies the problem. If Coraza should be destroyed in the attempt...it would be too great a waste."

"Waste?" asked Coraza. "Why would you preserve me? To be evidence against my mother before the Inquisition? So that we may burn together?"

"No, no, no, my dear—"

"Or do you and your employer fear," Doña Vicenza suggested, "that she might succeed? Were you hoping for an alliance with Nueva Azteca in hopes that the Molochistas might reward Don Malaguez with even more territory to govern?"

Dr. Raimundo narrowed his eyes. "Don Malaguez may be an ambitious man, but he is not evil."

"Don't be so sure," growled Doña Vincenza.

"I can do this. Let me fulfill my destiny," Coraza said to Dr. Raimundo. "Let me try to destroy the Great Tzinn. Let me show that my father and mother's plan has worth. That I have worth. If I fail, then Don Malaguez will have his chance. If I succeed...," Coraza went on, hoping she gauged Dr. Raimundo's personality correctly, "then you may take the credit and become the great hero of Califia."

Raimundo actually laughed for a moment. "You think I am a man of public pride señorita, like my employer. I prefer private renown among my sorcerer peers."

Coraza chided herself but continued. "Privately, then, but my success would make the king look upon your employer more kindly. And if I survive, I can continue to protect Califia for my lifetime at least. And Don Malaguez will not only be able to negotiate with the Nueva Azteca, he will be able to tell them what to do."

Dr. Raimundo sucked in his breath and rocked back on his heels in thought. "What a clever girl you have turned out to be. Just what is your plan to destroy the Great Tzinn, Coraza?"

It came to her in that moment, what her dreams had been trying to tell her. "I will ride El Dragón east to the border. The warding will protect me from attack until I reach the Rio Colorado."

"But the warding gives you great pain."

Coraza nodded. "I am counting on that. I can bear it once more, if I must. But when I disembark, it will help me change and take on tzinn form. It will be the shock I need," she added, turning to Doña Vincenza. The sorceress looked stricken. "Great-grandmother?"

"Yes," said Doña Vincenza, her voice strangely flat and distant. "El Dragón. I have seen it in my visions also. It must be the only way. And I must come with you."

"Come with me? But..."

"Surely you cannot survive outside the Presidio," said Dr. Raimundo.

"I have some strength in me yet," said Doña Vincenza. "And I must go to help my great-granddaughter fulfill her destiny."

Dr. Raimundo bit his lip, his mustache twitching. Coraza imagined his mind full of his finely calibrated instruments whirring, spinning, calculating. Finally, he said, "Very well. I think I can get Don Malaguez to agree to this. I will have him commandeer the train for the run eastward."

"We must go soon," Coraza said.

"I will do what I can," said Raimundo, his tone implying he could promise nothing.

"And one more thing," Coraza went on.

"Yes?"

"I want to speak to my mother."

Raimundo narrowed his eyes and gave her an ironic tilt of the head. "You are hardly in a position to make demands, señorita. And I am not sure that I trust you not to attempt some heroics with regard to the former Governadora."

"Really, Maestro," said Doña Vicenza, "have you no soul? The girl has only recently learned her mother's identity. Now, Coraza is asked to perhaps make the ultimate sacrifice, and you would deny her a chance to say goodbye? If so, I am not sure my opinion of you could sink any lower!"

The Protectadora's grandmotherly chiding must have reached what little soul Raimundo possessed, for his shoulders relaxed a little and he gazed down at the floor. "Very well, I will see what can be arranged. In the meantime, I will have to sequester you securely here, for your own safety, you understand. Please do not abuse my trust by attempting to escape." He turned swiftly and left the room, shutting the door behind him.

Coraza turned to Elena and helped the servant stand. "Can we escape?"

Elena shook her head. "There is only one exit to these chambers."

"We thought it made for a good defense at the time they were constructed," mused Doña Vincenza. "We hadn't planned on our own soldiers turning against us. I'm afraid we must wait upon our would-be-Governor's pleasure."

"How could they?" Coraza asked. "How could they choose this time to turn against their protectors?"

"They are frightened," Elena grumbled. "I grew up on a ranch, and frightened animals do the strangest things."

"Let us hope," said Coraza, glaring at the door, "that Don Malaguez is frightened enough."

Filipo lay on his belly amid the desert scrub. The dirt and sand was still cool from the night, and the rising sun had not yet warmed it. Down at that level, the desert felt much more alive, with insects and lizards and small birds flitting past, startled at the sight of three vigileros lying prone beside the western bank of the Rio Colorado.

Agente Aciles was observing the other side of the river through a tarnished brass spyglass.

Filipo narrowed his eyes, trying to perceive what the old vigilero might be seeing. It was difficult to discern clearly through the wavering warm air, like looking through water. There appeared to be men gathered in small groups, surrounding an undulating black smudge that, on occasion, blotted out the rising sun. "How many Molochistas do you think there are?"

"Not more than fifty, from what I can see."

"So few?"

"They probably started out with more. But when you have a Great Tzinn, you don't need an army," Aciles said dryly. "Besides," Palabo added, "a smaller force moves more swiftly and lightly upon the land."

"Here," said Aciles. He handed the spyglass to Filipo. "Tell me what you see."

Filipo examined the battered designs on the spyglass tube rings. "Is this a magical instrument?"

"Not enchanted, but the lenses are made from the same crystal as our skulls of truth."

"So, it will show me...what is true?"

"The effect is more subtle than that," said Palabo.

Filipo raised the small end of the spyglass to his right eye and peered across the river. Although distant, he could see the figures of the Nuevo Aztecans with a surprising clarity. Some standing at the perimeter of the camp were clearly on guard. Others standing closer to the wavering darkness of the Great Tzinn held their arms raised in supplication, or perhaps control. They seemed confident, patiently waiting.

"It's as though I can sense their intentions," Filipo murmured.

"Interesting," said Aciles.

Unable to resist, Filipo trained the glass upon the Great Tzinn itself. It was like watching a roiling black cloud or serpentine smoke. Light glinted off it, and Filipo caught a glimpse of a huge feline head with pale fangs and dead yellow eyes. Nausea rose in his stomach and chest. Filipo pulled the glass away from his eye. He stared down at the grains of sand on the riverbank and breathed deep to banish the nausea.

"Looked at the tzinn, didn't you?" asked Aciles, dryly.

"It…it's a monster," breathed Filipo. "Like a giant serpent but with the head of a cougar. Like a cloud covered with feathers. Its core is…rotting death."

"Actually," Aciles said, "the head is that of a jaguar. Just to show how foul the Molochistas are, they chose to make the great tzinn in the shape of one of the ancient true Aztecan gods, the feathered serpent Quetzalcoatl. But the original Quetzalcoatl was said to bring peace, wisdom, and knowledge. This ugly mirror of a god brings only death."

Filipo looked at Aciles, "You know a lot about other people's gods?"

Aciles shrugged one shoulder. "You get as old as I, you learn things. Any ideas how to attack it, son?"

"We could lure it into the river," Filipo suggested. "Have it chase one of us thinking it had found a victim. Tzinn hate water. We could throw the holy water vials into it to weaken it and make it drown."

Aciles winced. "That's not a bad plan, except that the Molochista wizards who control the tzinn won't let it get into such danger."

"First," said Agente Palabo, "we must find out where they are going to construct their dam and how."

"That means," Aciles added, "that we must capture one and make him tell us what he knows."

"But there are so many, and they are alert to danger," said Filipo.

"We must pick an outlier. Perhaps those three you noticed who watch the north. You say they appear to be expecting something. Might be useful for us to know what they expect. There's a rocky hill between them and the main force. If we strike fast enough, they will not be able to shout an alarm, and we can deal with them uninterrupted. We'll head upriver, swim across as the current carries us down, and land on the opposite bank just below them."

"But they'll see us!" said Filipo.

Aciles and Palabo looked at each other. "Not necessarily," said Palabo.

"You...vigileros have an invisibility spell?"

"More of a take-no-notice-of-me spell," said Palabo. "I used it the night we first met, in Salamago's old forge. If Coraza had not been so sensitive to magic, you might never have known I was there."

Filipo remembered. It seemed like a lifetime ago.

"It works best in darkness and shadow," Palabo went on, "but also when a person's attention is on something else."

"Yes," said Filipo, "Good. You will teach it to me, then?"

The two vigileros again shared a glance. "It would take too long, son," said Aciles.

"But, then the Aztecans will see me!"

"And that will distract them from seeing us," said Aciles. "Don't worry, young señor. We will defend you."

Filipo sighed. He had intended to never become a soldier. Yet there he was, in the thick of a war. There was no future for the apprentice of a shamed swordsmith. Dona Vincenza had told him there was no future for him and Coraza. Yet now, at least, he might claim some glory for himself and his name, whether he lived or died. Now it was time to show worth where he was needed. Like at the inn, protecting Coraza from the soldiers. He would be helping to protect all of Califia. How would he ever respect himself if he turned that unrequested duty away?

"All right. Let's go."

"Brave lad. Vamanos."

They crouched and ran low many yards upstream. They had left their horses half a mile back in a stand of cottonwoods in the care of Miguelito, telling the acolyte to return to the mission with the horses if the vigileros did not come back by nightfall. Filipo was glad his prized horse was getting nowhere near the Great Tzinn. Although if they did not succeed...

"This is a good spot," said Aciles. They had stopped where the river rippled, flowing over large rocks in its bed. They were around a bend in the river, hiding them from the guards' view. Aciles watched the river, and his arm and fingers wavered as if calculating something. "If we can move steadily across, the current should place us at the base of that hill, out of sight from the outliers and the main camp."

"But they'll see us…me, swimming across," said Filipo.

"Stay underwater," said Palabo. "Pull yourself across holding onto the rocks. Don't let the current carry you too far downriver."

"A good thing you're strong, boy," said Aciles. "The current may look slow, but it has miles of momentum behind it. Another thing, take off your boots and your sword and stow them behind the bushes here."

"What? You would leave me barefoot and defenseless?"

"Wet leather boots will hinder more than help you and dragging your sword through water is no way to treat a good weapon. Besides, any true vigilero is a weapon all by himself."

Agente Palabo slipped off his boots, knelt beside the river, and began to chant softly. Aciles did the same. Filipo tugged off his boots and sword scabbard and put them behind the largest nearby bush. He turned and blinked as the light from the rising sun glinted off the river. Suddenly, he realized he could not see either vigilero. He wondered where they went.

"Go on, son," said Aciles in his ear.

Pretending he had not been surprised, Filipo walked into the shallow water beside the bank. The water was warm just beside the shore but grew colder further out. Filipo breathed deeply three times, then slipped down into the river.

The current caught him and pushed against him like an inexorable wall of water. Filipo's back slammed into a submerged boulder that held him against the flow. He dug his hands into the rocks on the riverbed and began to crawl across. At times, the current pushed his legs to point downstream, but still he reached as far as he could, grabbed what he could, pulled himself across, then reached out again. It was like traversing a cliff face underwater. His breath slowly bubbled out of his mouth, and his lungs began to ache. His hands grew chilled and numb. He grasped a rock covered with slimy moss, and his hand slipped. Filipo panicked, arms flailing, until a hand grasped his wrist and pulled him to the next rock. At last, the water warmed again, and his fingers dug into soft sand and mud. His chest felt like bursting as his head breached the surface.

Filipo crawled up onto the steep bank of the river and gasped for air.

"Well done," Palabo said softly in his ear. "We are just south of where our targets are standing, on the other side of that slope. Catch your breath. Then, when you are ready, charge them. We'll take care of the rest."

Filipo breathed deeply, expecting that, any moment, one of the Nuevo Aztecans would hear him and come running around the hill. His wet trousers and shirt clung to his skin, but the desert air was so dry he could feel the cloth quickly losing its dampness. The dirt felt pleasantly warm beneath his bare feet. After a few long minutes, Filipo stood and nodded at the shadows beside him. He walked up and around the hill.

The Nuevo Aztecans were spread out, two closer to the river, one a few yards east. They were dressed the same, in brown hemp shirts and trousers, sandals and long hair adorned with jade beads and black raven feathers. The fellow farther to the east was crouched down, examining some stones on the ground. He seemed smaller and slighter to Filipo. Filipo gathered himself, then took off running, past the two closer men, to the small fellow beyond. As he expected, the Aztecans he passed turned to chase him. Filipo heard satisfying grunts and thuds behind him as he fell upon the small fellow, driving his knees into the Aztecans chest and his fist into the Aztecan's mouth. Sitting astride his waist, Filipo put a hand over the small man's neck and squeezed enough to cause discomfort.

"Tell me your plans," Filipo growled at him, despite knowing that Palabo would want to do the questioning.

To his shock, the small man grinned with bloody teeth. The Aztecan hissed out laughter. "Poor Califio," he rasped in heavily accented Spanish. "You are too late. The trap is set."

"What trap? Tell me, or I will kill you."

A strange strangling noise behind him made Filipo turn to look over his shoulder. With surprising strength, the small man beneath him pushed

Filipo's shoulder, knocking him on his side. In a flash, the small man wriggled out from under Filipo, leaped to his feet, and took off running around the hill, toward the main Molochista encampment.

Filipo jumped up and ran after the fugitive.

"Filipo, don't!" he heard behind him, but momentum carried him forward. He rounded the hill and charged down the south slope, now in full view of the Molochista encampment.

The small Aztecan ran, yelling, arms waving, toward his compañeros. The closest group turned to see what the fuss was, and their eyes locked on Filipo at the bottom of the hill. Filipo stopped for a long moment. One of the Aztecans loaded a stone into a sling and began whirling it. Filipo willed his legs to turn, and he began to charge back up the hill.

Pain erupted on the back of his skull as a stone struck him and he went down.

Chapter Twenty-one

Coraza clutched her lace handkerchief tightly as Dr. Raimundo escorted her into the Presidio prison. Either he had worked very fast to secure permission for her visit or had chosen to not inform Don Malaguez at all. In any case, it had only been a few hours after he had informed them of the coup. The early morning sun glinted through the dusty windows, reflecting off polished buckles and bayonets. Coraza thought the sun was itself traitorous to shine so brightly on the morn of such a terrible day.

Coraza's petticoats itched, her corset hindered her breathing under her gown of indigo satin, and her scalp ached because her long black hair had been wound into an intricate knot held with many pins. But Doña Vincenza had scoured the Protectadora's quarters for the finest dress, insisting that Coraza visit the prison dressed like a high-born lady. "A woman's clothing earns her respect," the old sorceress had said. "And today you need as much respect as possible." Coraza wondered if Sorrow, strapped in a sheath across her back, helped or hindered that impression.

Coraza's heart felt emotionally split in two. She was fulfilling a destiny she was created for, a destiny she had not asked for. But she felt a need to prove herself worthy of their hopes, worthy of life. She would have to use all of her power, and to her surprise, she welcomed it. Was eager for it. To burst out of an ordinary human shell to become something...amazing. Coraza only regretted that, if she indeed were to face the Great Tzinn that day, the dress was going to be ruined. However, she reflected that if she were going to lose that battle, it was a fine gown in which to die.

The iron-bound door to the main chamber of cells opened in front of her, and the young soldier with his hand on the latch widened his eyes. "A visitor for Señora Remedios," said Dr. Raimundo. The young soldier blinked and stepped aside.

The smell struck Coraza like a wall, a fetid odor of sweat, rotting hay, old urine, and all-too-new offal. There had been some attempt to cover it all with astringent lime wash, but that only made the odor worse. Coraza coughed discreetly into her handkerchief and stepped into the corridor lined with cells.

"I am sorry, señorita, but it is forbidden to bring a weapon into the cell block," said the young soldier.

Coraza glared at him and then at Dr. Raimundo.

Raimundo waved his hand. "It is a keepsake to her only. She is no swordswoman. I will vouch for her. Let her retain it, if you please."

With doubt in his eyes, the young soldier relented.

Coraza looked up and down the corridor. Unlike the prisons she had heard of in history classes, these were not cells that locked prisoners away from sight. These cells were no more than cages, with walls of iron bars, exposing prisoners for all to see like animals in an exhibition.

To her left, in the large cell at the end of the corridor, an entire family huddled together, father and mother, an older daughter and two little sons. Their fine clothing was stained and torn and their faces red from weeping.

A family of good blood who insisted on supporting the Governadora, thought Coraza. They looked at her with distant hope. Coraza gave them a sad smile and a sympathetic nod but turned away.

At the other end of the corridor, in a smaller cell, a woman knelt on the floor, head bowed in dejection. Feeling a sudden ache in her heart, Coraza rushed down the corridor to crouch down outside the bars. The former Governadora, her dark, grey-streaked hair unbound, stared at the floor unmoving, her fists tightly clenched on her knees. The first word to escape Coraza's mouth surprised even herself. "Mamá?"

Lucita Remedios slowly looked up, her eyes slightly unfocused. She raised her hands and gripped the bars. Her wrists were bound in heavy bronze manacles embellished with symbols—wardings to prevent her from casting magic. A similar wide collar encircled the former Governadora's neck, so that any words of sorcery she spoke would be robbed of their power.

"Coraza?" Her voice was husky and rough, as if she had done much shouting recently.

Coraza nodded. She curled her fingers around her mother's hands, fighting back tears.

Footsteps approached from behind, and Lucita Remedios' face suddenly became thunderous. Her full pride returned, she stood up and glared with white-hot fury as Dr. Raimundo stepped up to the bars of the cage. "Have you no honor, señor?" she growled. "Do you think to debase me further by having my only child see me this way?"

Dr. Raimundo stretched his neck a little and swallowed before replying. "Señora, she asked to see you. And it was no little trouble to arrange it. I should think you'd be thanking me for this kindness. After all—"

"Kindness!" Lucita Remedios roared. "You know nothing of kindness, you shameful, pitiful excuse for a man!" She kicked the iron bars of the cell for emphasis. "A dog has more heart than you! A pig has more heart than you! Be glad I am cuffed as I am, or I would curse you and your blood into the seventh generation!"

Dr. Raimundo blanched and turned hastily to Coraza. Amid the ex-Governadora's curses he said, "I will permit you two a few moments of privacy. Remember, no tricks. Señora, señorita." He dipped his head in a quick bow and scurried down the hallway and out the door, to the bemusement of the soldier posted there.

As soon as Dr. Raimundo was out of sight, Lucita Remedios deflated, her energy spent. "Never trust a man, Coraza," she murmured. "They are all scoundrels and thieves."

Coraza took from this that one must be careful of which man one trusted. She quickly changed the subject. Softly she said, "Mamá, I am leaving to kill the Great Tzinn."

The ex-Governadora's eyes widened, then narrowed as she smiled a sad smile. "What is the use of trying, Coraza? Califia is finished. Even if you succeed, Don Malaguez will only sell the land to the Russians or Yanquis, maybe even the Molochistas. The king will do nothing to stop him. We are too far away, too small, too poor. Perhaps it is best that I will be exiled to Isla Catalina, and I will not see what the treacherous Don will do—"

"Mamá," Coraza interrupted, impatiently, "please, we haven't much time. Is there anything you can tell me that might help me kill the tzinn?"

Señora Remedios frowned, then glanced surreptitiously at the soldier at the door. Taking Coraza's hand in hers, she drew with her nail on Coraza's palm. It was the symbol of the mountain struck by lightning. "Like on my trisigil?" Coraza whispered.

Lucita Remedios nodded and put her hands on Coraza's cheeks. Pulling her close to the bars, she kissed Coraza's forehead and then whispered in her ear, "Zhoguroch. It is a bad word, but perhaps you can use it for good, yes? Say it only once, when you most need it."

Coraza practiced the word without speaking it aloud. "It's Sere sorcery, isn't it?"

The ex-Governadora tilted one shoulder in a shrug. "Sometimes one must use the weapons of one's enemy."

Coraza nodded. "I wish we could have talked more," she said. "There is so much I could have learned from you."

Her mother caressed her cheek again. "Ah, Coraza. Seeing you like this, grown up so pretty and brave and fine...I wish we could have been like a normal mother and daughter."

"I wish that too," Coraza said, tears starting to well again in her eyes. She heard the door to the cell block groan open behind her.

"Señorita," Dr. Raimundo called from down the hallway, "we must go. El Dragón will be departing within the hour."

"In a moment, Maestro," Coraza called back.

"El Dragón?" Señora Remedios said as if impressed. "You travel to your battles in style, hija."

Coraza shrugged. "It is the fastest way."

"Then go, and may all the Furies be at your side." Pulling her close one last time, she whispered, "And if you survive, save some energy for vengeance against Don Malaguez, hmm?"

"If we survive," Coraza corrected her, squeezing her hand. "Vaya con La Madre, Mamá."

"Only if She has lost Her memory. Otherwise, it is a warmer place for me. Go now, before I start to cry."

"Yes, Mamá." Coraza turned and hurried down the hallway, handkerchief again pressed to her face. *If my mother is doomed to "a warmer place,"* wondered Coraza, *where might my soul be destined, assuming I have one?*

Dr. Raimundo held the door open for her and followed her out. "Was your visit satisfactory?"

Coraza nodded, rolling the very bad word around on her tongue to commit it to memory. Her palm still itched a little where the Sere rune had been drawn on the skin. But the best gift she had received from her visit to Governadora Remedios, the one that would sustain her spirit should she face the final death, were the few moments when she perceived a trace of love and admiration in her mother's eyes.

Filipo blinked, the morning sunlight so bright it hurt his eyes. He became aware of pain radiating from the back of his skull. He was bound to a post, his arms tied behind him, his feet bound together. He heard voices around him and lifted his head, trying to focus his sight. He felt a warm hand on his bare chest.

"Chalchihuatl," the man in front of him murmured. He was short, broad-chested and swarthy, his long black hair braided with raven feathers. Huge circular obsidian earplugs stretched out his lobes. He wore a deerskin cape or robe, patterned with flowers and butterflies, draping from one shoulder down to his knees. The Molochista saw that Filipo was looking at him, and he smiled, revealing teeth inlaid with turquoise, obsidian, and gold.

He muttered strange words and gave an ironic bow. "*Kenin otimoui-ka?*"

"I don't understand you," growled Filipo. "Do you speak Spanish?"

The man shrugged and shook his head.

Well, the Molochista understood Spanish, even if he would not speak it, Filipo thought.

"Go to hell," he grumbled.

The Molochista chuckled. He pointed at himself. *"Pistiayotl."*

"I don't care what your name is. Let me go!" Filipo demanded, as loud as he could. Filipo wondered if the vigileros were still alive nearby and could hear him, but he dared not betray their existence in case they were.

Pistiayotl wagged a finger at him. *"Itzlicoatl."* He waved his left arm outward.

Filipo let his gaze follow the gesture. To the east, the tents of the Molochista camp were just yards away. Hovering above it, circling languidly, was the Great Tzinn, its black serpentine body thicker than a man's height, covered with shiny feathers like those in the Molochista's hair. It was larger than it had seemed through the spyglass. Filipo's stomach clenched, and his blood ran cold despite the warmth of the desert morning sun.

Pistiayotl made a beckoning motion toward other men dressed as he was. *"Xia!"*

The other Molochistas raised their arms to the Great Tzinn and led it from the tents toward Filipo, like the children of the Chinese merchants at the Festival flying a huge dragon kite.

"No," Filipo breathed as the enormous golden eyes in the jaguar head of the Great Tzinn focused upon him.

Pistiayotl laughed. He held his arms out and stepped back as the tzinn Itzlicoatl drew near.

Filipo began to tremble, and he clenched his jaw shut to hold back the terror. He struggled against his ropes, but they were thick and well-tied. Suddenly, he was enveloped in a cold black cloud that swirled around him like a tornado. The dust hissed, and a clicking, clinking sound filled the air. The feathers, that from a distance appeared soft like a bird's, up close could be seen to be made of obsidian, sharp and glittering black stone. The flashing obsidian feathers circled closer and closer. Filipo shut his eyes.

Sharp points of pain erupted on his shoulders and arms, his calves and thighs, as the knife-like obsidian feathers whisked over his skin. Filipo gritted his teeth tighter against the pain. *Is this it, then?* he wondered. *Am I to die no better than a pig slaughtered for a feast? Coraza, forgive me and stay safe. Salamago, I will meet you in Hell. Madre, bless me. Save my soul. Let my end be swift—*

"Ixachi!"

The snicking and hissing drew away, and Filipo opened his eyes. The Great Tzinn uncoiled itself from around him and turned. Filipo stared into the great ebony jaguar face hovering just above him. There appeared to be a strange, dim intelligence in its golden eyes. Filipo shivered again, feeling the blood oozing from a thousand cuts on his skin. Letting his fear be overridden with rage, Filipo bared his teeth at Itzlicoatl.

"Go ahead," he growled. "May you choke on my bones. May my blood turn to poison in your belly. Eat me whole and alive so that I may tear your guts to pieces as I die. Go on! What are you waiting for?"

Itzlicoatl tilted its head like a curious cat. The air compressed around Filipo's head like two enormous warm hands. He found he could not turn away from the Great Tzinn's gaze. The warmth closed in around his mind, leeching away his fear.

Suddenly, he was somewhere else. Filipo found himself floating high in the air above a great, shining city, with broad avenues as wide as a whole city block in Los Mesanjeros. At its northern terminus stood an enormous pyramid clothed in white stone, painted with colorful murals. There were many, many houses and smaller temples, open markets everywhere one looked. Crowds of prosperous people filled the boulevards, wearing feathered robes and heavy jewelry of silver, gold, and semi-precious stone. Surrounding the city was an enormous lake, and on the lake sat floating gardens attended by gaily painted boats as numerous as bees in summer. It was the most magnificent, beautiful place Filipo had ever seen.

Hovering over the city was Itzlicoatl, undulating like a happy eel. The sun shone overhead, the life-giver, the god above gods, without whom humankind would descend into darkness and death. Blood flowed down the steps of the great pyramid like a crimson river, and it was a beautiful sight, for this sustained the sun in the heavens. The Great Tzinn flew as an intercessor between the humans below and the sun above, as a sort of messenger, an angel...and Filipo had the stray thought that only one tzinn he knew of could rightfully be called an angel. He remembered Coraza's pale tzinn face before him, intoning "Nekpar!" and suddenly—

He was back in the desert, tied to the post. The Molochista in front of him raised his brows. The head of the Great Tzinn drew back as if in surprise. Filipo bared his teeth again, and with all his strength, all his voice, he shouted "Nekpar!" at the tzinn.

The Molochistas all jumped as if they'd been shocked. The Great Tzinn rose and began to drift, as if the invisible strings that bound him to the wizards had been cut. Itzlicoatl turned and began to fly away to the northeast. The wizards shouted and shrieked and began to madly chase after it, waving their arms. All except Pistiayotl, who still stood in front of him.

Filipo felt the barest husk of a laugh escape from his chest. It was only a brief, moral victory. Already, the Molochistas seemed to be regaining control of their runaway charge. Probably, they would return and slit his throat so he could not speak again. But he had shaken their confidence for a moment. It was victory enough.

"Thank you, Blessed Madre," he whispered. "Thank you, Coraza, my angel."

Pistiayotl smiled again without humor and slowly clapped his hands. "Bravo," he said, all friendliness gone from his eyes. Then he glanced for a moment at the sun and looked back over his shoulder to the north, slightly worried.

"What is it?" Filipo asked. "I'm going to die soon anyway. Tell me, what is going to happen to the north?"

"*Heh. Tepotzlicoatl.*" Then he made a sound like *chuff-chuff-chuff-chuff*, followed by a loud "Poc!" His hands flew out for emphasis. With a chuckle, Pistiayotl trotted away to assist his fellow Molochistas corral their wayward tzinn.

Filipo sighed and leaned his head back against the post. He wondered how much longer he had to live...hours, possibly. *Would the time be best spent in prayer?* he wondered. He was surprised to feel a hunger for life he had not felt since he was a child running along the beach in the surf. Now, he was acutely aware of the desert wind blowing across his many wounds, the pain reminding him he was still alive. He wondered where the vigileros were and hoped they were safe. He wished he could have seen Coraza one last time, to tell her goodbye.

Two Aztecans who were standing nearby suddenly stiffened and fell over silently. Filipo wondered what magic or ailment struck them when he heard a voice whispering in his ear.

"As soon as your hands and feet are free," said Agente Palabo, "run for the river."

Filipo felt tugging on his wrists and around his ankles as a knife sawed through the ropes. In moments, the ropes slid off, and he was loose.

"Now!" Aciles' voice urged.

Filipo turned to his left and began running. His skin screamed with pain as the hundreds of shallow cuts left by the Great Tzinn's obsidian feathers all opened up again. Filipo clenched his jaw to banish the agony. Behind him, he heard shouts, and he could almost feel the gaze of the Great Tzinn fall onto his back. Filipo's blood had been promised to Itzlicoatl. It was coming after him to claim it.

"Faster!" hissed Palabo beside him, although Filipo couldn't actually see him. A wave of chill air against his back heralded the Great Tzinn's imminent arrival. He heard the *snickety-snick* of the obsidian feathers draw closer and closer. He felt hot breath against his back and smelled the stench of a thousand rotting hearts. Filipo pushed his legs to their limit, reached the riverbank, and dove in.

The cold water slapped his skin with a different sort of pain, an intense sting that made him shudder. Filipo had to fight not to scream and breathe water. A dark shadow blotted out the sunlight above the surface. An orb was pressed into his hands. *Holy water! My plan can be tried after all!* Filipo tugged out the cork stopper and kicked to the surface, fighting the current pulling him downstream.

"Ai!" he shouted at the tzinn.

Itzlicoatl's head whipped around, fangs gleaming, golden eyes blazing. Filipo threw the holy water vessel as hard as he could deep into the Great Tzinn's open maw. The two vigileros breached the water beside him like dolphins and threw their vessels to smash against Itzlicoatl's face.

The Great Tzinn's eyes rolled upward, and it rose vertically away from the water. Responding to cries from the Molochistas onshore, Itzlicoatl turned, shook its tubular body like a dog, and drifted back to the company of Aztecans. A flight of atlatl spears struck the water around Filipo and the vigileros. Filipo dove underwater again and swam as hard as he could for the western bank.

Filipo crawled up the riverbank, his skin burning with pain. He huddled onshore as old Aciles and Palabo pulled themselves out of the river, their not-noticed spell gone. Filipo shuddered, his jaw clenched as he watched the Molochistas on the opposite shore, tending to their tzinn who appeared to be completely undamaged.

"It didn't work," Filipo growled. "Why didn't it work?"

"The Great Tzinn is very strong," sighed Aciles, slicking his wet gray hair back from his face.

"Perhaps it truly is a sort of god," mused Palabo, gazing across the river.

"Now, now, Marzo, that's enough blasphemy," said Aciles.

The old vigilero patted Filipo on the shoulder, and Filipo flinched. "It was a good plan, son. But our little bottles of blessed water were not enough, it seems. We will have to think of something else."

"Why aren't the Molochistas crossing after us?" asked Filipo.

"I'm sure they expect to deal with us in time, when they are ready. Come, let's fetch our boots and swords and consider what else we can do."

The three men loped back upriver to where they had stashed their belongings before the first swim across. Filipo shook his boots to make sure no scorpions had taken lodging there before putting them back on. The boots felt hot, stiff, and uncomfortable on his feet. And the leather stung the cuts on his calves. He put his shirt back on, aware that it would be blood-soaked before long.

"We should put salve on your cuts," Palabo said. "Or you will become infected from the river water."

"Does it matter?" Filipo grumbled. "We'll probably all be dead tomorrow."

"None of that now," said Aciles. "So long as a man lives, he can act. So long as he can act, he can hope. Did you learn anything from the Molochistas while you were their prisoner?"

Filipo shook his head. "Nothing we can use. The tzinn captured my mind for a time and showed me a magnificent city. But I do not know if the place exists or not."

"I have heard Nuevo Tenochtitlan is being rebuilt to reflect its ancient glory," said Aciles, "but that means nothing to us. Anything else?"

"I asked what they were waiting for to the north. The Molochista only said something like 'tepozlicoatl', made a *chuff-chuff* noise.

Both vigileros looked at each other. "Tepotzlicoatl," Palabo corrected. "It means iron-serpent. The guards we fought with said this word also. Did he tell you anything else?"

"Just a loud noise, like...an explosion."

Both men looked northward. "Diós mio," breathed Aciles, rubbing his grizzled chin. "El Dragón. They're going to blow up the train."

"An iron serpent gives its life for the obsidian serpent," mused Palabo darkly. "The Molochistas always did have a sense of the poetic."

"What? This makes no sense!" said Filipo. "Is it meant to be a diversion?"

Aciles crouched and began drawing in the dirt. "I am an idiot not to have thought of it. But look, the train bridge crosses over the Rio Colorado where it is broad and shallow. To the west are a series of dry lake beds and a canyon leading down to Lake Atualpa, which the Yanquis call the Salton Sea."

"A perfect catch basin," said Palabo, nodding.

"The bridge and train debris should be sufficient at that place to divert the water," Aciles went on. "They'll have their river dam in an instant and more human sacrifice as a bonus."

"We've got to stop it, then!" said Filipo. "We have to ride north and keep the train from crossing the bridge!"

"There's over fifty miles of very rugged territory between here and there," said Aciles. "You'd run your horse to death and still not get there in time."

"Well, we can't just sit here!" But Filipo remembered the Molochista he'd knocked down saying, "*You're too late.*"

"No, I will send Miguelito back to the mission to dispatch a pigeon to the station in Los Mesanjeros. It is the fastest way. With any luck, we can keep the train from leaving the station. The Molochistas may still blow up the bridge, but at least we can keep them from taking lives with it." He ran off toward where the horses and the mission acolyte waited.

Filipo watched the old vigilero go. "What are we going to do?" he asked Palabo.

"We wait," the Agente said. "We consider what may be done. I suspect we have a few hours yet. But whatever may happen up north, the tzinn will be crossing here. So here is where we must make our stand."

Chapter Twenty-two

Coraza winced at every bump on the bricks as she pushed the wheeled chair. The sword named Sorrow, still in the sheath on her back, thumped against her shoulder, as if warning her to stay alert. Doña Vincenza, slumped in the chair beneath a gray lace mantilla, either not caring or without the strength to protest against the jarring ride. The servant Elena walked beside Coraza, also wheeling a chair with another ancient Protectadora. And to her left walked Dr. Raimundo, wheeling an old sorcerer, a hero of the Great Revolt and the only other wizard of the Protectorado capable of traveling. Dr. Raimundo walked with his head down, his face shadowed by the wide brim of his hat. They rolled their charges up the train platform, alongside the puffing iron carapace of El Dragón.

The platform was bustling with stevedores and conductors loading baggage and supplies, efficient but tense. Up ahead, would-be refugees both rich and poor tried to cram their way into the passenger cars, in hopes of escaping whatever fate lay ahead for Alta Califia. There was a smell of desperation in the air. *It might be the last train out for quite some time.*

A private car had been arranged for the venerable sorcerers and standing at attention beside the door to that car were two young porters in crisp dark blue uniforms. Beside them stood the white-haired Captain of El Dragón himself.

As the party rolled up, the Captain doffed his hat with a brisk, short bow. "Señores, señoras, señorita. It is an honor for us that the heroes of the Great Revolt have chosen to ride El Dragón today."

Coraza did not think the Captain recognized her, given that she was dressed in finery and veiled behind a black lace mantilla. But as Dr. Raimundo raised his head, the Captain did recognize the sorcerer. The Captain's expression darkened, his gaze sharpened, and he took one step forward. "You. You, señor, are not welcome aboard my train."

"I beg your pardon?" said Dr. Raimundo, his tone carefully neutral. He stepped out from behind the wheelchair and rested his hand casually on his hip, near his wand holster.

The Captain took another step forward, his arms tight by his side, fists clenching and unclenching. Coraza thought she saw the flickers of sorcery around his fingers. "You heard me, señor," the Captain said. "These others, they are welcome. But you will not board my train."

"Perhaps the Captain had not heard," said Dr. Raimundo, "that it was I who arranged passage for these august personages, and it was I who paid our fare."

"I do not care, señor, what you may have paid or what events you may have arranged to come about, but a man who has set himself against the lawful Governadora will not set one foot aboard El Dragón, and that is final."

Coraza understood, then, that the Captain was a loyalist, true to her mother's governorship, and word must have reached him of Dr. Raimundo's involvement in the coup.

Dr. Raimundo turned his head slightly, the muscles in his jaw tightening. His hand drifted perilously close to the hilt of his wand.

No! Coraza thought. *He cannot be thinking of starting a fight here and now!* She shook her head vigorously at Dr. Raimundo.

A withered hand levitated from the arm of the wheelchair. "If the good Captain pleases," said Doña Vincenza, her weakened voice like the bending of a rusty hinge, "we have use for this one in our endeavors. Will you kindly reconsider your embargo?"

For only a moment, uncertainty played around the Captain's eyes. "With great respect, señora, I am sorry. But I cannot allow it. A man must face himself in the mirror when he shaves. I could never face myself again if I abandoned the principles of duty and propriety." These last words were said directly to Dr. Raimundo.

While Coraza inwardly cheered on the Captain's courage, she was all too aware of precious time passing. "Señores, please..." she began.

"Very well," said Dr. Raimundo at last. "It is a captain's prerogative, whether train or ship, to choose who shall be aboard. I will acquiesce to the Captain's decision so that our heroes may go forward on their journey. Any discussion of politics can wait for a future time." He smartly stepped aside, indicating that the porters might take charge of the wizard in the wheelchair he had been pushing.

Coraza's heart sank. Although she didn't entirely trust Dr. Raimundo, she had relied on his being there to help in defeating the Great Tzinn. And she feared she couldn't look after all of The Protectadora wizards by herself.

With a nod from the Captain, the porters took the wheelchair and lifted the old man, chair and all, into the door of the private car. They took the chair holding Doña Vincenza from Coraza's grasp and lifted it in through the doorway. The porters did the same for the third Protectadora. Elena boarded the train under her own power a moment later. Coraza turned and looked back over her shoulder at Dr. Raimundo.

The sorcerer tipped his hat to her, his expression grave. "May the Madre favor you this day, Coraza," he said, his tone flavored with many emotions.

Coraza turned to the Captain. "Please, señor, won't you reconsider? The fate of Califia may depend upon his assistance."

"Then the Madre help Califia," the Captain growled. "I am sorry, señorita, but my decision is final."

The white-gloved porters emerged from the car again and each took one of Coraza's elbows. "Are you ready to board, señorita?" asked one of them.

"Yes," Coraza replied, and they lifted her up toward the step, over the warding line of the track. Coraza gasped as she hit the sorcerous wall, the magic so intense it glowed as bright as wildfire around her. *They've made it stronger,* she thought, and searing pain teased at her skin. She could feel the sword on her back drawing on the energy, trying again to protect her. Coraza braced herself for the nauseating agony...and then her mind began to fade. *No! I musn't change, not here!* But nevertheless, darkness fell.

"Ah, Coraza. There you are." A man spoke with a gruff, low voice nearby.

Coraza blinked. She was standing in the cavern below the cabin in the mountains, in her father's hidden forge. Erculeo Salamago stood before her, hale and whole now, the muscles on his bare chest gleaming, his dark, bushy hair standing out from his head. The cavern was lit by burning coals in the stone trough, and the Sere sorcery symbols on the rock walls glowed with an intense yellow light.

"Why am I here?" Coraza protested in confusion. "I need to be back on the train! I have to go destroy the Great Tzinn!"

"Calm yourself, Coraza. You have gone nowhere. You are still on the train. This is an illusion, a place that is no-place, a world in the mind. It is Sere Sorcery," he added, with a shrug. "Only moments will pass while we talk. Finally, there was enough power present for me to activate this spell, and it is high time we spoke, don't you think?"

Coraza swallowed hard and tried to calm down. It had been one of her greatest wishes to speak to her father. But she was trying to keep her courage up for the battles to come. And she hoped she was not embarrassing herself on the platform of El Dragón, speaking aloud to someone who wasn't there.

"Don't you have questions for me?" asked Salamago.

"Yes. Of course," said Coraza. A thousand questions crowded her tongue, preventing any from getting out. More than this, however, she felt a growing rage within that went beyond words. If she had let herself, Coraza felt like she would roar and scream loud and long in his face.

"But your main question is 'why', is it not?" asked Salamago. "Very well, I will tell you my story. You see, I am a bad man, Coraza. Doomed from birth. I was a Molochista, born to Molochista parents in Nuevo Tenochtitlan. My blood comes as much from ancient Cartago as it does from España. As a youth, younger than you, my team lost a game of pelota, and I was to be sacrificed. The law was the law. But I was a coward and clever, and I used my knowledge of magics and my parents' help to escape. I came north, learned the blacksmith's trade. I became good at it and used my Molochista knowledge to make magic weapons for the wealthy. So long as I could please them with my work, no one looked too carefully into my past, although there were whispers.

Then Lucita, your mother, came to me. She was so clever, so full of… big ideas. Her family were heroes of the Great Revolt, and I admired her. I'd come to hate what the Molochistas were doing, and I joined in her schemes to save Califia from them. That is how we plotted to create our own tzinn, one that could think, one that would be wise and protect, not destroy. So, I found this place." He looked around at the illusion of the hidden forge. "Here, in the Canyon of Ghosts. We summoned a tzinn, La Llorona, one of the most powerful tzinn in Califia, to ride Lucita while we…while we made you. Lucita was hoping for a boy. But then you were born, a girl, and you were just a normal pink, plump little baby. We thought we had failed.

"We let you be examined by the holy sisters at the Cathedral so you could get your trisigil, just like a normal Califian baby. But somehow, the holy sisters, through their own mystical methods, saw your nature. They put it in your trisigil for anyone with the knowledge to see it. It took a very big donation to the Church to get them to cover it over.

"Very soon, it became clear that Lucita was going to become Governadora, and then there was no chance we could claim you openly. The scandal it would cause! So, we gave you to the orphanage, and I gave the sacerdotas enough money for your care and left it at that."

"Couldn't you at least have…come to visit?" Coraza asked in a breathless voice, her fists clenched.

"You would have had questions, wouldn't you? Questions I dared not answer. People would see me, the great Salamago, visiting an orphanage, and wonder why. I had enemies, Coraza, and jealous men would try to ferret out the truth. Did I not already say I was a coward? There, I have said it. I was afraid. What we did to create you, Coraza, was great blasphemy, sin beyond sin. I dared not have any word of that known. And then, when you at last began to manifest some power, I knew it was finished. It was all going to come out. I would be ruined. Lucita would be ruined. Califia would be in an uproar. The Mater at the orphanage, she…offered to arrange for you to be…"

"Destroyed?" Coraza said sadly.

Salamago's spirit wiped his face and brushed back his wild hair. "I couldn't do it. I told her no. You were innocent. You should not be harmed for my sin."

I think she may have tried to anyway, thought Coraza, though she did not speak it aloud.

"The whole matter preyed upon me so that my work suffered," Salamago went on. "My wits were departing me. So, I left the world. I abandoned Filipo…poor Filipo. I hope good fortune finds him. He was like a son to me. I came back to this place to make my last creation. I feared for my Hades-bound soul, Coraza. So I infused my soul in a sword, to cheat death, to cheat the Madre. And yet…I wanted to make some good of myself. So I arranged for this sword to be sent to you, even if you chose only to sell it for the money."

"I would never have sold it," Coraza said.

Salamago nodded. "You are a good girl, Coraza. You deserved better family. I do not know whether I should ask you for forgiveness. How could you when we compounded sin with neglect? But I still ask your understanding, Coraza. I never meant to be cruel or to harm you. I had wished that you would forget me and be happy. But fate has not allowed that."

"You say you were Molochista," Coraza said. "Tell me, why do the Molochistas sacrifice their children?"

"Because children are the most precious thing and therefore a worthy gift to a god."

Coraza could not hold back the anger welling up within. "If you believe children are so precious," she growled, "why did you abandon me?"

Salamago looked away. "As with anything precious, children come with a high cost. Sometimes, for some, that price is too great to pay." When he gazed at her once more, his eyes held a blend of regret mixed with a chilliness that frightened her. Her father was clearly more concerned with the state of his soul than with the state of her heart. Yet, for good and ill, she sensed their similarity. He was strong and stubborn, flawed but persevering, as she was. And there was caring in his eyes, his words, even if it was not the sort she most dearly wished.

"Well, it is not fair that you chose my fate before I was even born."

"No, it was not. But that happens in this world often. Princes and princesses must walk the path of a royal personage. Humbler children take on the family trade. Now you face the task you were created for. Perhaps the Madre laughs at our hubris by allowing our plans to come to fruition, demanding your sacrifice like any hungry god. Is it not said, 'beware what you wish for, for your wish may be granted?' "

"I just wish...I just wish..."

"That we had been an ordinary family? I understand. Looking back, I wish I had not been born as I was. But surely you must see that was simply not to be? Know, this Coraza. I do wish I had taken more care of you. I am astonished and delighted and, I confess, a little frightened at what you have become. After all we have done, you are not a monster. You are a thinking, feeling being, however extraordinary. I am very proud of you."

Coraza's heart twisted inside. Those were the very words she had longed to hear, needed to hear. But the weight of her father's confession made them sour, like a delicious fruit that had begun to rot. "Thank you. I...wish I had known you better," was all she could say in return.

A hearty grin appeared on Salamago's face. "After all you have heard, I would think you would not! Anyway, I have one last request. I want to make some good of my life. Let me help you destroy the Great Tzinn. I know some things. Sere things, that may be useful. Carry me in your hand as you attack. Use me as your weapon, and I will give you what guidance I can. Will you do this, Coraza?"

Knowing she would need any help she would get, Coraza said, "Of course." Her heart swelled just a little to think, for just a short while, she would be together with her father on the task. For a moment, it banished the emptiness she felt at the reunion, so rushed and pressured by events.

Salamago smiled. "You are the finest of all my creations, Coraza. If we succeed, then I will have done at least one good thing. It may not be enough to redeem me, but at least I will know it was done. Now, let us get you back aboard that train."

Coraza gasped again as a curtain of burning fire swept over her. Then it was gone, and she teetered just inside the door to the private car on El Dragón.

The porter squeezed her arm with white-gloved hands. "Señorita, are you all right?"

Coraza felt Sorrow on her back, humming from the absorbed power of the warding. She raised her chin and nodded. "Yes, I will be fine. Just a momentary spell of dizziness, that's all."

The porter guided her to a plush leather seat as the other porter strapped down the wheelchairs of the ancient wizards of the Protectorado. Still disoriented, Coraza put her arm on the sill of the window beside her and looked back over her shoulder. Dr. Raimundo still watched the train from the platform. A shrill whistle blew as the Captain shouted the last call for boarding. The doors shut, and the car lurched as El Dragón pulled forward. As the train began to roll away from the station, a man in a green visor ran out of the station office frantically waving a white piece of paper. Dr. Raimundo intercepted the man, apparently to ask what was wrong. The man in the visor gesticulated wildly at the train, red-faced and upset. Dr. Raimundo looked back at the train once, with a gaze measured and grave. Then he turned back to the man and patted his shoulder reassuringly, guiding him back to the station office as if nothing were the matter.

Coraza turned around to face forward again, her back and neck sore. She wondered what the urgent message might have been and whom it might have been for. *I suppose I will never know*, Coraza mused. She tried to sit back, but the sword between her shoulder blades made it uncomfortable. Knowing her father was in some way in the sword did not help.

Sorrow is a burden, she thought, and that was true in so, so many ways.

Filipo paced up and down to throw off nervous energy as the afternoon wore on by the Rio Colorado. More men were coming to the field of battle as word spread of the Great Tzinn's arrival. Small groups of native warriors came out of the hills: Mojave warriors in leather loincloths and blue geometric tattoos on their faces, bearing clubs carved from mesquite; Apache bowmen dressed in deerskin leggings, tunics and caps; Diegueño shamans in black and white calico; even a band of Paiute horsemen down from the north, bearing longbows of cedar. The native groups regarded each other warily but were willing to cooperate in a desperate common cause. Agente Palabo set the Diegueño to work at once, creating a warding line along the west bank of the river.

Even a couple of Yanqui riflemen, their long-barreled firearms hanging on their saddles, showed up accompanying the Apache. Even though such weapons might be outlawed in Califia, the vigileros welcomed the riflemen and found positions upland with good brush for cover that would be advantageous to their skill.

Filipo stared across the river as the enemy also began to organize their ranks, lining up near the river. As Agente Aciles strode up beside him, Filipo said, "The Molochistas don't appear to be so many. Perhaps no more than four hundred."

Aciles snorted. "Cortez took all of Mexico with only four hundred men. Pizarro conquered the Inca with only one hundred and seventy. And he didn't have a tzinn. Strategy and luck matter more than numbers, son. These men who have joined us, they are brave, and their skills will be useful. But in my heart, I feel the thing that will decide this battle will not come from military might."

"A spell you mean, then?" Filipo said. "From magic?"

Aciles shook his head and blinked up at the sky. "We need a miracle." He walked on, toward the river and Agente Palabo.

At the thought of miracles, Filipo looked around for Friar Juan-Pablo. The old man was bustling at work with a group of his acolytes. The young monks were creating piles of fist-sized stones, and Filipo noticed the leather slings swinging from their rope belts. Filipo walked over to them, hoping the ancient friar had words of encouragement.

The Padre looked up as Filipo approached, and he held his arms out to indicate the work of the missionarios. "My boys are going to be outliers!" he said proudly. "Alexander harried the Persians at Gaugamela with them, to great effect."

"Everyone's giving me history lessons now," said Filipo.

"As well they should, for, Madre willing, today shall make history. And history shows the Madre favors the well prepared."

Filipo noticed a small crate and looked inside. Six earthenware spheres stoppered with cork and marked with the trisect circle lay within.

"A cart arrived from Los Mesanjeros with a few holy water bombs. And we found a couple more in our stores," young Miguelito said. "But I heard they didn't work on the tzinn."

Filipo shrugged. "Maybe we used them wrong. It's good that you brought these anyway. Perhaps we'll find a use for them."

"Señor," Miguelito began, tentatively, "do you think...do you think we have a chance?"

Filipo looked down, seeing fear naked and open in the younger boy's face. "What are you saying?" Filipo replied. "Of course, we have a chance! Is the Madre not with us? She would surely not let evil overrun her blessed Califia. And look, Agente Palabo is creating a wall of magic nothing could get through. And look at all these archers and warriors who have come to join us. Would they be here if they thought it was hopeless?" He put his hand on the boy's shoulder. "We will survive this. We will chase them all away like that tzinn last night, yes? Listen, those Molochistas had me tied to a post, at the mercy of that big black serpent just hours ago. See these cuts? That tzinn tried to chop me up and eat me and you know what? I broke their Molochista magic, and I got away, and I spit in its face when it tried to chase us across the river! They're not so powerful. We'll be fine. You wait and see."

"Thank you, señor," said the boy softly. His eyes shone a little, taking heart from Filipo's words.

Filipo patted the acolyte's shoulder and turned away quickly, sick with the lies he'd had to tell. He walked over to the Padre and asked softly, "Why are there no soldiers here? Surely there must be an outpost within a day's ride."

The Padre paused and looked around to see that no one else was close by. Softly he answered, "The porter from Mesanjeros brought strange news. Something bad has happened in the city. The Governadora is rumored to be in jail. There was some rioting in the streets. He wasn't clear on the details. But it seems no soldiers will be available to come to our aid. I'm afraid we are on our own."

"Oh. I see." Filipo turned and studied the Molochista army across the river. The Madre had seen fit to let him cheat death twice already, once after the fight with the soldiers at the inn, the second in the camp of the Molochistas. He doubted he would succeed a third time.

Blessed Madre, if this is the day I die, then give me the strength to make it a day the enemy shall never forget.

Coraza stared out of the window of the train as the afternoon wore on. She had recognized the place where she and Dr. Raimundo had jumped off...had it only been days before? Now, past the Santa Ana foothills, she was in unknown territory, a new existence. The landscape the train rushed through became dryer and emptier. Now and then, Coraza glimpsed a lonely ranch or a group of native dwellings, but mostly she saw scrub and grassy desert. She had tried to engage the three wizards of the Protectorado in conversation, but the old ones were unresponsive, slumped in their wheelchairs, perhaps conserving energy. Even Doña Vincenza would do little more than wave her limp hand in response to Coraza's inquiries.

By the time the sun was low on the western horizon behind them, the land beyond the train tracks was barren and blasted. Iron stained buttes, the hearts of ancient dead volcanoes, stood amid a flat wasteland. Coraza pressed her face against the glass, amazed at how beautiful it was. With a guilty glance at the resting sorcerers, she unlatched and slid up the window.

She raised her mantilla and let the dry, warm air blow across her face. She felt strangely at home.

This must be where the tzinn live, she thought. The emptiness was soothing, inviting. She felt as though her spirit could expand forever in the land.

The clack of the latch of the car's door behind her startled Coraza. The Captain walked in, accompanied by two white-gloved stewards. One of the stewards presented Coraza with a glass of lemon water with a precious chunk of ice floating in it. With an indulgent smile, the steward lowered her window again to just an inch open.

"The air here is dry, yes, señorita? So dry it will shrivel you if you endure it too long. We cannot have that happen to a pretty girl like you, can we?"

Coraza smiled politely and sipped at the lemonade, but it seemed all wrong, incongruous in this land of the tzinn, and felt odd on her tongue.

The other steward was solicitously checking each of the wizards, finding them no more responsive than Coraza had. The Captain stood in the center of the gently bobbing and rocking car, keeping his balance as ably as a sailor on the deck of a ship. "Señor, señoras and señorita, we will be crossing the Rio Colorado in about fifteen minutes and entering into Arizona Territory. Madre willing, we should be arriving in La Phoenicia in only a few more hours. Dinner will be served in one hour. If there is anything you need for your comfort, you need only ask one of our stewards, and we will do our very best to fulfill your request. Is there anything you would like to ask of me? No? Very well, then. I will return at dinner to look after your continued comfort." He bowed and motioned to the stewards, and they swept out into the car ahead.

Pleased that they were gone, Coraza raised the window again. She could smell the river, though she could not put a name to that smell—a dankness in the air that grew as they approached. She wrinkled her nose. Ah, well, El Dragón would be past it soon enough. Coraza closed her eyes and leaned her head against the window frame, letting the train car rock her like a cradle.

A bright flash forced her eyes open. The window beside her, all the windows in the car, shattered as a low roar smote her ears like a hammer. Iron groaned, and the front of the car raised upward, the red blaze of flames glowing through the forward door window.

Ai, mi, no! thought Coraza. *Are the Molochistas attacking the train? We are not ready!*

Coraza flew forward from her chair, suspended in space, her mouth opening to an O as she lost sense of balance. She heard faint screams in the distance. *What is happening? What should I do?* She gazed down at the ancient wizards strapped in their wheelchairs. Doña Vincenza seemed to be murmuring something, her hands fluttering in weak gestures.

Coraza fell to the floor as her train car bumped hard against the roof of the car ahead. Then the world went sideways as the train car twisted and fell to the right. Coraza was weightless for one, two, three moments as the train car plummeted to the river below. The side of the car hit the surface of the river, and Coraza slammed down hard onto the side of Doña Vicenza's chair.

"Great-grandmother! Great-grandmother!" Coraza gasped, ignoring the pain in her side as she grasped the Doña's shoulders. There was a bit of blood on Doña Vincenza's right temple, but her green eyes were open and focused.

"Coraza! It is time. You must change," rasped the old sorceress.

"No! No!" Coraza said. "Too soon!" Water was boiling up through the broken windows as the train car sank into the river. The cold water soaked into Coraza's long skirts. Coraza struggled at the straps holding Doña Vincenza in her chair, but they would not unbuckle. Doña Vincenza weakly slapped at Coraza's hands as the water crept up closer and closer to the old woman's face.

"Leave me!" she commanded. "Change and remember the word Lucita taught you. Go!"

"We're too far away from the tzinn! And I need you!"

"This was meant to be, Coraza! I have seen it! Go!" and then the green, murky water closed over her cheeks, her chin, her mouth.

Coraza tugged at the old woman's shoulders, trying to bring her head above water. But her hands slipped ,and the rushing river water bore her up as it filled the train car. Doña Vincenza's eyes glowed brightly green beneath the surface for a moment, and then faded.

"Great-grandmother!" Coraza screamed. Bursting with anger, fear and despair, Coraza drew Sorrow from the scabbard on her back with shaking hands. As the water pressed her against the top of the car, Coraza raised the sword out through the window and screamed, "Zhoguroch!" as the water rose up to her neck. Her skin itched and burned from the water as the Change came upon her. She let her emotions overwhelm her, a scream of her soul, and she Changed—

A moment later, Coraza hovered over the fallen train car, suspended in air, her dress hanging in black tatters. The smell of burnt cloth and flesh filled her nostrils. Lightning flashed from the sky. Coraza raised Sorrow, and a blinding bolt struck the tip of the blade. The sword blazed with light, like a sliver of the sun. Warmth like liquid fire flowed from the sword into Coraza through her arm, and suddenly she was *aware*. Her consciousness seared into the stone of her tzinn body, not to fade away like before.

Spirits drifted up like smoke from the car below. They still held the vague form of Doña Vincenza and the other two wizards of the Protectorado. They reached out to Coraza, and Coraza drank them in, letting the ghosts of the heroes of the Great Revolt fill her with their magical energy, their knowledge, their fortitude. Enormous black clouds roiled across the sky, north to south, bringing premature night. She looked down and saw the water of the Rio Colorado diverted, spilling down a side canyon, as the jammed debris from the bridge and the train blocked its flow. Her awareness expanded to hear the windblown grains of sand across a nearby mountainside, to feel the eddies of the hot wind around her. And from a sense she had no name for, she knew where the Great Tzinn of the Molochistas was. But Coraza, herself, was now a Great Tzinn, and the time had come to claim the land as hers.

Holding Sorrow out before her, Coraza flew on the wind, over the bed of the Rio Colorado, thunder booming at her back.

"The river's going down!"

The cry from a scout sent a ripple through the hodge-podge forces gathered by the Rio Colorado. Filipo stood, letting the pumice stone he had used to sharpen his sword fall from his lap. He had made the sword with his own hand back in Salamago's forge, and though it was no more than a serviceable Espada, Filipo was pleased enough to die with it in his hand. He gripped the hilt hard and clenched his jaw to hide his gnawing fear.

The wind rose with an unexpected chill to it. The sun had set behind the barren mountains to the west, casting long, dark, fingerlike shadows across the forces gathered to face the Great Tzinn. Dark, unnatural clouds were swiftly gathering to the north. Filipo wondered if the Molochistas had summoned them to bring the darkness of night on even faster.

Agente Palabo waved his arm. The Diegueño shamans chanted and shook gourd and shell rattles to evoke the magic of the ward-line they had built along the riverbank. Friar Juan-Pablo began a loud prayer to the Madre. The Apache archers arrayed themselves behind what little scrub and bush there was for cover and nocked arrows to their bowstrings. The Mojave club men eagerly massed near the river, swinging their weapons and whooping with eerie howls. The Paiute steadied their nervous mustang ponies. The two Yanqui riflemen raised their guns and squinted for careful aim.

Across the river, the Molochista forces had moved closer to the eastern bank. The array of men in front, a line of perhaps thirty, all carried oval leather shields on their left arm and balanced atlatl spears on their left shoulders. Above them, the Great Tzinn Itzlicoatl circled lazily like a tame black eel in a fishbowl.

The enemy line parted in the middle, and a cylindrical object, like a hay bale but taller than a man, was pushed to the river's edge. It appeared to be made of wood and woven fiber, and protrusions jutted out at regular intervals along the edges. *Some sort of war engine?* Filipo wondered. *Is it meant to roll over and flatten us?* He trotted down to Agente Aciles at the river's edge.

"Agente, what is that?"

"I don't know, but I expect we will find out soon enough. The water is lowering fast."

Indeed, rocks that had lain entirely below the surface were now halfway visible, glistening in the setting sunlight.

Aciles's bushy gray brows scowled northward. "The evil they had planned is done. We can only hope it was just the trestle bridge and not the train itself that went down."

Filipo's throat tightened as he thought about the innocent lives lost and the guilt of not being able to stop it.

The boiling black clouds now covered half the sky, rolling southward, soon to blot out the sun. "They've set something in motion," Aciles murmured, "something bigger than we expected. If this tzinn was a mere feint and there is a greater creature in the Molochistas' quiver, then our stand will be a brave gesture and nothing more. One way or another, this battle will be decided quickly."

Filipo looked back at the forces arrayed on their side of the river. Agente Palabo and Friar Juan-Pablo were going from group to group, more like emissaries than generals. With such disparate troops, one could only suggest courses of action and hope they would cohere into a useful strategy.

Filipo tried to keep despair from gnawing a hole in his stomach. "May I see your spyglass?"

"Certainly." Aciles handed him the brass tube.

Filipo focused on the Molochista line. He still could not tell what the fiber and wood contraption was, although he could now see colorful yarn woven along the edges and what might be painted symbols. The spyglass's peculiar quality caused him to observe that the Molochistas themselves were watching the clouds in the sky with some disquiet. "They seem a little anxious," Filipo said, as he handed the spyglass back to Aciles. "I don't think they intended these atmospherics."

"Wouldn't be the first time wizards summoned more than they could handle," Aciles grumbled. "That's something at any rate. You feel ready to fight?"

"To the death."

"Good. Let's hope it doesn't come to that."

"Where would I best serve?"

"Given your fortitude, perhaps with the Mojave, since they are of like mind." Aciles pointed with his chin to the cluster of loin-clothed clubmen a few yards to the north. More softly, he added, "May the Madre go with you, son."

"And with you, Agente." Filipo looked for Agente Palabo, but the other vigilero was deep in discussion with the leader of the Apache bowmen.

Filipo walked upriver to the group of Mojave. The young men were grinning, hopping from foot to foot, eager for the fight. One of the taller of them, with shoulder length black hair and many indigo tattoos on his face, stepped forward. "What do you want?" the Mojave asked in halting Spanish.

Filipo gave him a short bow. "May I have the honor of fighting alongside your warriors?"

The Mojave leader looked him over a moment, then nodded. "Stand over there. Stay—"

The sky went dark as the black clouds closed over the sun. Conch shell trumpets blared in the Molochista line, and their warriors began to march forward to the very edge of the riverbank.

"It has begun," said the Mojave leader. He raised his club and swung it around over his head by a leather strap, leading his men in an eerie answering roar of defiance.

Excitement flowed through Filipo's blood, and every scent in the air, from the sage brush to the damp moss left behind by the thinning river, seemed clear and sweet. The chill wind brought goosebumps to his skin. He drew his sword and gripped the hilt tight.

The Molochistas walked their enormous wood contraption to the very edge of the riverbank and lowered it down into the bed itself. Several men shoved hard on it and it rolled, or rather unrolled across the river, becoming a low bridge that easily cleared the foot-deep water.

Of course, thought Filipo. *They probably carried it in small, lightweight parts, only putting it together once they needed it. That's why we didn't see their preparation.*

A knot of Molochista wizards, shields raised like a leather wall, began to shuffle forward, chanting, onto the wood and rattan bridge. The Great Tzinn Itzlicoatl followed over their heads waving like a giant black pennant of war.

Immediately, a flight of flaming arrows arced from the Apache forces. But the few that landed on the bridge and the Molochistas' shields quickly sputtered out.

The bridge is warded, Filipo realized. *Just like the tracks of El Dragón.*

A group of five Mojave, unable to contain their bloodlust any longer, charged into the now-shallow river to attack the Molochistas on the bridge. But their footing was treacherous on the slimy river rocks and a flight of atlatl spears from the line of Molochista warriors on the bank took them down.

The Paiute, with wailing cries, urged their mounts forward. As they thundered toward the bridge, the Great Tzinn turned its leonine head and roared at them. All the horses reared, screaming in fear, throwing their riders. The horses turned and fled, eyes rolling, trampling some of the Paiute warriors beneath their hooves. Filipo watched in horror and dismay, glad that his horse Tulio had been taken back to the mission. *Although, if we cannot stop the tzinn, it will hardly have mattered,* he thought.

"Lampi!" yelled both Agente Palabo and Agente Aciles. They each threw a fireball out over the river. Each magical sphere of flame exploded in a harmless cascade of cinders as it reached the side of the bridge. The column of Molochistas beneath the tzinn didn't miss a step.

Crack! Crack! The Yanqui riflemen fired their guns, and the two wizards at the front of the Molochista column went down. Filipo and the Mojave cheered, but their joy was short-lived. The Molochistas on the bridge rushed forward while the marksmen were reloading.

A roar across the river caught Filipo's attention, and a group of perhaps twenty Aztecan mace fighters charged down the riverbank toward him and the Mojave.

The battle is joined at last, thought Filipo as he raised his sword. The Mojave fiercely rushed into the river to meet the Aztecans, but Filipo waited up on the bank, where the footing was better. In moments, one of the Aztecans broke free of the defending Mojaves and ran up the bank at Filipo.

Filipo had never fought an opponent with a shield and had certainly never tried his sword skill against someone wielding a club edged with embedded obsidian blades. He ducked and dodged the heavy mace, but his sword could not cut through the shield. It was only by luck that Filipo slipped low enough that he could slash below the shield, cutting the Aztecan's hamstring. With a cry, the warrior fell to the side, and Filipo finished him with a stab to the chest. He fought the nausea rising in his gorge, for he had never killed a man before. But now he had to bury such feelings and charge on. He had no time to rest as another warrior came at him, one more skilled with the shield, forcing Filipo to futilely beat at the hard leather with his blade, never getting through.

Filipo swung hard to the side, and the sword blade became stuck in the wood frame of the shield. The warrior flung his shield sideways, pulling the sword out of Filipo's hand. With a fierce grin, the Aztecan warrior brought down his mace on Filipo's left shoulder. The pain and force were tremendous, knocking Filipo to his knees. Before he could scramble aside, the club came down again to the side of his head with a blinding flash of pain. Filipo lay flat on the ground awaiting the killing blow.

"Amo!" came a cry from the bridge. "Ayamo! Ye cahua!"

The warrior scowled at the Molochistas, then grunted in surprise and disgust. He kicked Filipo's side once, hard, and strode off in search of new opponents.

Curled up in pain on the ground, blood streaming over his left eye, Filipo was amazed. *They let me live. Why?* Then he saw the glowing eyes of the Great Tzinn, staring at him with raw hunger. *Ah. They wish me to be a living sacrifice. They wish to feed my heart, freshly torn from my chest, still beating, to their monstrous godling.* Again, Filipo wished he could somehow become poisonous, so that his sacrifice might bring the destruction of Itzlicoatl.

"Shuora!" the vigilero Agentes shouted, and the wardline along the western riverbank erupted into a wall of purple flame.

The column of Molochistas stopped at the westernmost edge of the bridge. They drew from behind their shields short spears tipped with long, pale crystals. Filipo realized they were not spears but very large wands.

"Tlazah!" the Molochistas intoned, and flashes of light flared from the spear-wands toward the warding wall.

The sorcerous barrier erupted in an enormous explosion of heat and light. Even on the ground, Filipo was pushed back, rolled over and over by the force of the blast. Screams of agony filled the air. Something hit the ground beside Filipo that smelled like charred meat. He propped himself up on his right elbow. It was Agente Aciles, his right side blasted away, his eyes open but already empty and soulless. Filipo's heart clenched in sorrow.

Someone crawled toward Filipo, grunting in pain. The man's hair was singed black and his left arm was a bloodied mass pressed against his chest. "Aciles? Filipo?" the man moaned.

"Marzo?" Filipo didn't think his heart could ache any worse. "Marzo, here. Let me help you."

"No," Agente Palabo groaned. "Leave me. We must...keep fighting. The tzinn must be stopped. Go..." He collapsed, exhausted.

"Marzo!"

"You are a vigilero now," Palabo grunted through a grimace of pain. "Your duty...is to protect Califia. Go. That...is an order."

"Yes, Agente." Finding the strength from somewhere within, Filipo stood, his legs shaking. He gazed out over the battleground.

Things were going very badly now. The Molochistas were running off the bridge onto the western bank. The Apache sent another flight of arrows, mostly to be caught on the leather shields. The Yanqui riflemen fired again, taking another wizard down. Then a Molochista aimed his crystal spear at the tree in which one of the riflemen perched and set it ablaze with a fireblast. The rifleman fell out of the tree screaming.

I don't have much time, Filipo thought. Fighting to will away the pain in his side, shoulder, and head, he staggered toward the place where the Padre and the missionarios had been stationed. "Miguelito! Miguelito!"

"Here, señor!"

Filipo stumbled toward the voice until hands grabbed him. "Miguelito—"

"You are hurt, señor," said the boy acolyte. "Let me tend your wounds."

"No time for that! Where is the holy water?"

"Over here, señor. In the box, just where they were before."

Filipo fell to his knees beside the crate. He reached in and pulled out one of the terracotta flasks. "Forgive me, Madre," he murmured. Then he yanked the stopper out and poured the cool water into his open mouth.

"Señor! What are you doing? That is blasphemy!"

Filipo swallowed the hallowed water down. "Get the padre," he rasped as he grabbed another flask and unstoppered it. The water tasted sweet as it trickled down his tongue.

"Padre, Padre! Señor del Utherio has gone mad! He is drinking the holy water!"

"My son, I beg you, stop what you are doing!" cried Friar Juan-Pablo as he ran up beside Filipo. "You are wasting our last weapon!"

"I am our last weapon!" Filipo cried. He unstoppered another flask and poured the contents over his wounds on his head and shoulder. "The tzinn wants my blood, so my blood it shall have." Turning to kneel before the friar, Filipo said, "Bless me, Padre."

Understanding at last what Filipo intended, the old friar placed his trembling hands gently on Filipo's head. "In the name of the Madre, may you be blessed, my son. May She make you the instrument of Her justice."

"Thank you, Padre. May I have a sword? Any will do."

"Here, take mine. It's a Salamago, actually, so it would be fitting, though not one of his more impressive works."

"Is it?" Filipo asked as he took the hilt of the long, slim blade in his hands. "Does it have a name?"

"It is called Endurance, my son."

"May it live up to its name, then," said Filipo. While he still had the courage and the strength, he stood. Half blind from matted blood over his left eye, he tried to see the Great Tzinn on the battlefield.

So, here is where it ends. Madre, may my life be of worth in my death. His gaze locked on the glowing golden eyes of Itzlicoatl, and he ran toward it.

Slashing Endurance left and right, screaming like a madman, Filipo charged at the tzinn. To his surprise, the Molochistas who tried to block his way fell aside quickly, distracted by something in the sky. Filipo spared a quick glance upward and thought he saw an angel fly across the heavens, bearing a flaming sword. Filipo took it as a sign.

"Here I am!" he shouted at the Great Tzinn. "My blood is yours! Come and get it!"

Itzlicoatl lowered its enormous jaguar head and opened its jaws.

"For the Madre! For Califia!" cried Filipo, and he leaped into the monster's gaping maw.

On the wind of the supernatural storm, Coraza flew over the raging battle below. The spirits of the fallen drifted upward like faint wisps of smoke, but Coraza did not attempt to claim them. Gouts of purple and green fire, spells hurled by the Molochistas, arced across the Rio Colorado. By their light, Coraza saw the darker-than-shadow form of the Great Tzinn.

She sensed other tzinn stirring at the disturbance of their landscape, their territoriality, as the horrible army commander had put it. *I must call to them. We must fight together.*

Coraza drew upon the power she had absorbed from the Protectadoras and sent out a pulse of magic across the sky. *To me, to me! You who defend your dry lands! An intruder has come! One not like us. Who means to destroy us. To me!*

She felt their spirits boil out of the earth. Tzinn wolves and antelope. Lost miners and explorers. Tzinn whose shape was like nothing natural, yet their spirits still burned with a hunger for life they did not possess. Even, there below, Coraza heard the familiar wail of La Llorona herself, Queen of the Tzinn, come to join the battle. Though the chill of the tzinn form filled Coraza, a tiny shred of warmth bloomed in her heart that her demon mother had come to her call. Coraza held the blazing blade of Sorrow aloft and pointed toward the Great Tzinn. Focusing all her will, she blasted her thoughts down to the massing throng of ravening sprits. *There! There is our enemy! Destroy it!*

The growls and shrieks of the tzinn horde rolled like thunderous music through Coraza, over the land to the Molochista wizards guiding their horrific monster. Like a roiling wave of boiling sand, her tzinn flowed toward the Molochistas. The enemy sorcerers turned to behold what was approaching. Coraza felt their fear, and she laughed.

The Molochistas turned to create a wall of sorcery to hold off the mass of Califian tzinn, but this took their attention and energy away from their charge, and Coraza could tell the magic that sustained it and their control of it was weakened. As Coraza drew ever nearer, Molochista wizards threw ensnaring spells up toward her. With a swipe of the sword, Coraza easily parried or dissolved the spells; they were like buzzing bees to her. Someone ran at the Great Tzinn, and the creature's great mouth gobbled him up like a bear catching a fish.

At once, Coraza sensed something wrong with the Great Tzinn. It began to writhe and spin, no longer in the control of the Molochistas, its own faint will broken and distracted by pain within.

Her father's voice filled her mind, and a warm humming animated the sword in her hand. "Now is the time!" An image of him flew alongside her, the way he had seemed in her vision, alive and vital. "Let me assist your hand, Coraza, so that my endeavors may have worth, and your destiny may be achieved. This will be the last act my spirit can do in this world. Please permit me to make it a worthy one."

Coraza nodded to him. She felt an ache inside. If she had been in a form that could shed tears, she would have wept. The hand of her father's image covered hers and felt warm, even though it was an illusion. Though she never had his companionship while he lived, at least now, in this dire moment, they could be together, his guidance and her spirit working as one to deliver their unique gift to Califia. It was not what a child would want, but for Coraza it was enough to soothe her heart.

They flew over the Great Tzinn, which rolled to and fro as if in agony. "You must be close as you can," her father said, "so our blow may strike deep."

Coraza arrowed down through the sky and landed to sit astride the Great Tzinn, just behind its huge feline head. The tzinn bellowed and twisted, trying to throw her off like a horse trying to lose its rider. Coraza dug in with her feet and knees, deep amid the tzinn's obsidian feathers. Her skin was now as living stone so the blade-like feathers could only scrape, not cut her. The tzinn shrieked and twisted, a noxious vapor issuing from its mouth. Maddened by some inner torment, the creature was drifting ever closer to the trickle of water that remained between the Colorado's banks. The obsidian feathers were like armor for the creature, but there was at least one place it was as vulnerable as any animal. Coraza raised the sword Sorrow, leaned forward, and drove it into the Great Tzinn's right eye.

With a scream like the cries of a thousand souls in hell, the Great Tzinn stiffened and shuddered. Sorrow blazed so brightly that even Coraza had to squint her eyes nearly shut. She felt her own power being drained through her arms, out of her body. Sere sorcery symbols flowed down the blade, etched in blood-red and black. Salamgo's spirit shouted, "Maquixtizquich!" The sword Sorrow released all the energy it had gathered, all at once.

The silent, eerie explosion filled the valley with light. Coraza felt the body of the Great Tzinn come apart beneath her. Black twisted forms, the life force of the myriad sacrifices the Molochistas had offered to the Great Tzinn, peeled away, keening softly.

The person who had been the Great Tzinn's last intended meal was revealed to be Filipo. His eyes were closed, his mouth taut, grimacing, his body contorted in pain. Coraza stared in horror, hope, and despair. She stretched her hand out to him, but the blast of the sorcerous explosion pushed her up and away, and Filipo fell, far out of reach.

Coraza sighed, feeling drained, weak, and insubstantial as a feather. She closed her eyes and let the storm wind blow her where it would, drifting like a fallen leaf on the desert air.

Chapter Twenty-three

Filipo stared up at the grand Palace of the Governor, its upper balconies lit with gaily-colored lanterns. In the distance, a lively mariachi song drifted on the night air. "For the last time, Marzo, I'd rather not have come here."

"And refuse the honors our new Governor would give you? Don't be so ungrateful, Filipo." With a wave of his right arm, Agente Palabo waved away the coachman of the carriage that had just brought them. Palabo's left arm, still withered from his wounds at the Battle of the Rio Colorado, was hidden under his black and red serape.

Filipo shifted his shoulders beneath his elegant black silk jacket. Everything was too tight: his fine pointed boots, his trousers, his frilly shirt, his ribbon tie. His back hadn't been quite right since he had fallen out of the tzinn onto the rocks in the river below. His right leg, bitten by the creature's jaws, had healed, as had his myriad cuts, in the five months since the attack. But he still did not feel comfortable in his own skin.

Don Malaguez had easily obtained the king's appointment as new governor of Califia. Worse yet, Filipo had learned that Coraza had been on El Dragón when the train had been blown up over the Rio Colorado, and she had not been found among the survivors. His spirits had not recovered from the news.

"Why not?" grumbled Filipo, "The offer of a land grant and the rank of hidalgo is just a bribe."

"Of course, it is," said Palabo. "One you would be wise to accept. You are a hero of Califia now, admired by many. It is only natural that Don Malaguez would seek to have your support."

Filipo winced. "Have you grown so cynical, Marzo? I was to become a vigilero such as yourself, was I not?"

"And who is to say you still cannot?"

"But, a hidalgo with land holdings to manage—"

"Might be the perfect cover for a spy for the Protectorado, yes? I have no illusions, Filipo, that this new regime will be fair and just. We must keep a watchful eye on our new Governor. And with the old Protectadoras now dead, there are few of us left to do so. Accept his bribe. Let him think he has bought you. If you would continue to serve Califia and the cause of justice, become an hidalgo so that we will have eyes and ears in the halls of power."

"But is that...honorable?"

"Ask yourself, what would be the right thing to do?" Palabo clasped Filipo's shoulder. "Now if you will excuse me..." He turned away.

"Where are you going? Filipo asked, slightly alarmed.

"I shall use a different entrance, for my own reasons, and it is better that you seem independent of my influence. Don't worry. You'll be fine." With that, Agente Palabo vanished amid the small crowd gathered beside the tall iron gates of the Governor's Palacio.

Not helping his nerves, this group of people had become aware of his standing there and gazed on Filipo with curiosity and admiration. One of them, a woman in a store-made but elegant green dress pulled away from her male companion and, a little shyly, approached Filipo. "Señor del Utherio, I am so pleased to see you again alive and well."

"Señ...ora?" Filipo asked, uncertain of her marital status. "Forgive me, have we met?"

"Of course, you would not recognize me since we last saw each other. I am the one who was known as Sister Phoebe, and we encountered each other in Don Malaguez's hacienda. Not in the best of circumstances."

"No, it was not," Filipo agreed, remembering the holy sister's dire attempt to retake Coraza.

"But I have since left the holy order, and I am now simply Ana Delmara. I could not remain after...after being forced to..." She looked down, unable to finish.

"I understand. Would it be rude of me to say I'm glad? Coraza spoke well of you and how you defended her. You were a good influence on her."

"I am grateful that she thought so."

"And that horrible Mater, what of her? Still running the orphanage?"

"Oh, no. The Protectoradas, before all the fighting started, did a strange thing. They said they were promoting her for her efforts, but she was sent to the Cathedral, where she is now in charge of preserving their ledgers and records. I am certain she is not happy."

"More good news, then. I wish I could tell..." Filipo trailed off.

"Yes. As we are speaking of Coraza...is anything more known about her fate? I heard she was in the battle."

Filipo shook his head, the reminder of her bringing another pang of sorrow. "No. She has not been found."

"I am so sorry." The former Sister Phoebe lightly touched his arm, then took her hand away.

To change the subject as quickly as possible, Filipo asked, "So what brings you to...all this?" He indicated the palace.

She looked back at the young man whose side she had left. "The man who invited me is taking a secretarial position in the new government. He used to make deliveries to the orphanage and would indicate that he had... an interest in me. I accepted his invitation to determine if I also had an interest in him."

"Well. Good luck to you both."

"Thank you. Now perhaps you ought to go inside. Many are looking forward to meeting the Hero of the Battle of Rio Colorado."

Filipo grimaced at the title that he did not feel was deserved and walked through the tall iron gates. Immediately, a butler appeared and ushered him into the great hall of the Governor's Palace. Filipo winced at the bright lights and the sight of so many in fine dress. His name was announced and met with thunderous cheers and applause by the men and ladies present. Filipo waved and nodded bashfully. He was guided upstairs to the dining hall where a long table at which many dignitaries were seated filled the room. Don Malaguez himself, his mustache waxed and gleaming, was the first to stand, applauding. The Doña Malaguez stood beside him, beaming at Filipo with her large brown eyes. On the other side of the new Governor stood Dr. Saturnin Raimundo, looking insufferably smug.

Filipo was glad he was seated well across the table from the sorcerer so that he would not feel tempted to do violence to the new Minister of the Interior of Califia.

The table was laden with roast beef, venison, fish, and boar. Silver platters overflowed with grapes and olives, oranges and apples. But Filipo found he had stomach for very little food. The Dons and Doñas seated beside him gently pestered him with questions.

"What was this great tzinn like?"

"Was it horribly frightening?"

"You must be so awfully brave! What sort of wounds did you suffer?"

"Was it a lengthy battle? Describe the fight to us, won't you? Tell us every detail!"

"Did you get any souvenirs off that beast? I heard it had magical feathers."

Filipo replied as little as possible, which only seemed to impress them more.

"How humble he is! How modest! Not boastful like so many men are."

And Palabo wants me to spend the rest of my life among these people? he thought.

At last, Don Malaguez stood, clinking his crystal glass with a spoon. "Señores y señoras, if I may have your attention a moment. Certainly, this is a night for celebration. Not the least of which is that our beloved Colonia of Alta Califia is once again guided by sensible government."

This was greeted with many shouts of "Verdad!" and "Olé!" Filipo held his tongue and smiled with a rictus grin.

After a few moments of unabashed basking, Don Malaguez patted the air with his hands to quiet the sycophantic aristocrats. "But, of course, this could not have been possible were it not for the extraordinary courage of one young man whose single sacrificial act saved us from the villainy of the dreaded Molochistas of Nuevo Azteca. Gentlemen and Ladies, I present to you, the Hero of the Battle of the Rio Colorado, Señor Filipo del Utherio!"

Again, there was much cheering and applause. Filipo stared down at his china plate, blushing uncomfortably.

"Some here may not be aware," Governador Malaguez went on, "that I knew Señor del Utherio from when he was just a boy, serving his apprenticeship in the great Salamago's forge. I like to think that I have served to the young señor as an example of how one behaves as a man of courage and proud blood."

Filipo gripped his seat tight to keep from breaking something. *The man is shameless!*

"Therefore, it is with great pleasure that I announce that I have received approval from His Majesty King Ferdinand IV to award Señor del Utherio the rank of hidalgo accompanied by two grants of land. One of these shall be acreage that contained the forge of his former master, which, you will be pleased to hear, is adjacent to my very own hacienda. The other will be one hundred hectares alongside the Rio Colorado where the fateful battle that saved our colony occurred. Henceforth, the young señor shall be known as Don Filipo del Utherio del Colorado."

Again, came a resounding round of cheers and applause through which Filipo seethed. *The land on which Salamago's old forge stood should have been Coraza's, had she lived. And the land on the banks of the Colorado,* Filipo thought, *belonged to the Mojave natives. How convenient for the Governador to give away land he has no right to.*

There came cries of "Speech! Speech!"

Slowly Filipo stood, and the room silenced. Filipo looked around, noting the hungry faces, among them a few Russians, Yanquis, even Chinese. *Yes, Marzo was right. Califia needs a watchdog against this pack of coyotes.*

"Honored Governor, gentlemen and ladies. I am only a simple blacksmith, born in a family of fishermen. I am a man of few words. Therefore, unworthy as I am, I wish to thank Don Malaguez for his efforts on my behalf, and I thank His Majesty for granting this lowly fighter for Califia a reward he had never thought to achieve." Filipo raised his hand to still the beginnings of another round of cheers. "In addition," he said, in a louder voice, "I will continue to look to Don Malaguez in future, in hopes that I may see good examples of wisdom, justice, and gentlemanly behavior." He raised his glass to the Governor with a meaningful nod.

Although cheers broke out again in earnest, Don Malaguez locked his gaze with Filipo's, his eyes narrowing just a little. "We thank the young Señor for accepting our gifts so...graciously. And we are glad he will continue to look to us, for it is clear, young as he is, that he has much to learn. Now—" Governador Malaguez clapped his hands together. "Let us bring on the dessert and brandy and afterwards, the dancing!"

Long minutes later, Filipo made his way out to a balcony. He leaned on the iron railing, sorely tempted to vomit over the side. *What have I done? Should I have rejected the honors? Will I, in time, become as corrupted by wealth as the noblemen at that table?*

"Ah, there you are!" cried Doña Malaguez, as she bustled out onto the balcony behind him. "People were wondering where you had disappeared to."

"Forgive me, señora," said Filipo, straightening up to turn and face her with a curt bow. "I...merely needed some air."

"Yes, such change we are all undergoing, it can cause the head to spin." She fluttered her face with her lace fan, her large, dark eyes shining. "But we are so proud of you and all you have done, Filipo."

"The señora is too kind."

"Listen," she leaned closer. "Perhaps I can make your evening a bit more pleasant, hmm? There is a young lady down in the gardens who is most anxious to speak with you." She patted his arm like a doting aunt.

"What?" Filipo blinked a moment, and then he understood.

Now that I have noble rank and land, every mother, aunt, and duenna with an eye toward society will be pressing girls upon me for marriage.

"If you please, señora, I am not yet ready for the...privilege of courtship."

"Oh, hush hush, I will not hear you say no. Meet with this one at least. As a favor to me. You will not be sorry."

Filipo sighed. The Doña Malaguez was the one person he liked amid the noble cabal, and he wanted to keep her good will. *Besides, I suppose I had better get used to it if I am to continue playing this role.*

"Very well, señora. As a favor to you."

"Wonderful! Follow me. We'll go this way so no one will be watching." She led him down a side staircase that curved directly down from the balcony to the gardens. Smiling, almost giddy as a girl, she guided Filipo to a tall hedge next to a small, dim side garden. "Here he is!" she called out to someone behind the hedge. Patting Filipo's arm a last time, she said, "Have a most pleasant evening, señor!" She hurried away back up the stairs, her silk petticoats rustling.

Filipo watched her go, feeling vaguely abandoned to fate. He heard footsteps rounding the hedge and a clearing of the throat in front of him. Filipo turned and nearly jumped out of his skin.

The woman before him had a long, dour face, and from the gray at the temples of her long wavy hair, she could only by an excess of politeness be called "young." She wore many necklaces of bulky, strange beads, and many copper bracelets jangled on her arms.

"Señor..ita?" Filipo said.

She looked him over with a long, judgmental gaze. "Well. Could have been worse, I suppose."

"I beg your pardon?"

"You're not what I expected, from the glowing stories I'd heard."

"Perhaps there has been some mistake," Filipo said, hopefully.

"Are you Filipo del Utherio?"

"I am," Filipo admitted, hopes dashed.

"Well, then. Follow me." She turned on her heel and strode into the garden behind the hedge.

Reluctantly, Filipo followed, wondering how he could politely excuse himself from the situation, or prove himself entirely unsuitable quickly, or perhaps just allow himself to be utterly rude and run away. It was quite dark in the side garden, just a little moonlight and distant lantern light. Perhaps he could hide.

"All right, then," said the woman, her face turned away. "You may speak with him, but don't take too long. And no taking advantage, señor, or you will sorely regret it. My curses can bring down the strongest of men."

"Eh?" Now Filipo was greatly tempted to bolt, until he saw the lovely girl, face pale in the moonlight, approaching him. "Coraza," he whispered, his heart glowing like a blacksmith's forge.

As she neared him, her heart filled with muted longing, Coraza wondered if she'd done the right thing. "Filipo," she said softly.

"But this is wonderful!" Filipo said, grasping her upper arms to pull her closer. "I thought you were dead!"

"I am amazed that I survived also," said Coraza.

"You were on the train when it blew up, I heard."

Coraza nodded. "I was also at the battlefield."

"The angel with the flaming sword...that was you?" He placed his so warm hand against her cheek. "Ai, your skin is cold."

Coraza turned her face away. "It is the night air. I have been waiting out here a while for you. Yes, I carried Sorrow to the Great Tzinn, and together, my father's spirit and I, we killed it."

"So Salamago proved himself at the last. A pity no one else will ever know or understand. You both saved me, saved us all. You are the true hero of the Rio Colorado."

Coraza shrugged, feeling uncomfortable. "I...did what I was meant to do."

"What of the sword Sorrow?"

"Gone. Destroyed."

"Perhaps just as well. And...Salamago himself?"

Coraza sighed. "I cannot know for certain, but I believe he is destroyed also. My father gave up his soul to dispel the Great Tzinn."

Filipo nodded. "I knew he was a good man at heart, and that the slanders against him were baseless."

Coraza decided it was better not to tell Filipo what Salamago had revealed to her about her parentage and birth. "So it would seem."

"But what happened to you after? Why didn't you send me word you were alive?"

"I was lost in the desert for...many days. Some people found me and helped me get back to the city."

"Come, we should go to the Governor and his guests and tell them about your part in the battle."

Coraza shook her head and stepped away. "No! It doesn't matter."

"Yes it does! Don Malaguez has given me Salamago's land that is rightfully yours. Should be yours. If he tries to fight the claim, well, then... we could be married and—"

Coraza whipped around and placed gloved fingers on Filipo's lips. "Shhh...no, Filipo, that can never be." She ached for having to disappoint him so, but matters had become very clear to her in her return to Mesanjeros. She wanted to share some sort of future with him. After all, who knew her better? But it could not be the life of hidalgo and wife.

Filipo paused. "That was what Doña Vincenza said. She said you were meant for other things. But you won the battle for Califia. You have discharged your duty. Why can we not be together?"

"You are to be hidalgo. You will be a man of society, a public man. All you do, everyone you have in your life, will be scrutinized, judged, gossiped about. Especially the woman you marry. I would only do your reputation harm...because of what I am."

"No one needs to know you are a...a...whatever you are."

"You don't understand," Coraza protested. "They will search for record of me at the Cathedral, and the holy sisters there know. They put it in my trisigil long ago." She placed her hand over her chest where the symbol lay.

"If they kept your secret this long, surely they could be convinced to keep it longer."

Coraza shook her head. "A nobleman's life isn't private, don't you see? One has servants watching all the time. You can't hide everything."

"What are you afraid they might see? Ah...you think they might see you...change?"

"Not exactly. Because of the sorcery I did for the battle, I will never change again. But I am still far from a normal girl."

"No matter, I will go reject the honors and land."

"No!" Coraza insisted. "You deserve the honors you have been given. And I want you to have my father's land and forge. You will take the best care of it."

"But what of you?"

"I have been given a place. Dr. Raimundo has arranged a small rancho out in the desert for me and my duenna, Serena, whom you have just met. He wants me to be...a sort of secret weapon, to protect Califia when needed. Serena is a very accomplished bruja and she has much to teach me. But my existence must remain secret."

"Is that what you want, Coraza?"

"I...have wanted many things in my life. To know where I came from, who I am. I now know these things. But most of all, since knowing Sister Phoebe, I have wanted to be a protector. It is truly what I was made to be. Now I have that chance. I will be a Protectadora of Alta Califia. Just...a somewhat strange and secret one. It feels good. My life has purpose and worth, and I am ready to learn so much more."

"That...is good, I guess." Filipo looked at his shoes. "Do you...do you care for me, Coraza?"

Coraza blinked and grasped his hand with her gloved ones. "More than anything! You are the dearest person to me, the only man in my heart."

His smile was both pleased and sad. "But still you say there is no hope for us. That...will be hard for me. You are the most amazing girl I have known, and none will compare to you."

Despite everything she had said, Coraza did not want to give him up. "Yes...I...I don't know," Coraza said. "Sometimes people can make their secret lives merge for a time." She looked up at the balcony above, where Doña Malaguez was guiding Agente Palabo by the arm, ostensibly giving him a tour of the Palacio. Their eyes, however, were only on each other.

Filipo turned to follow Coraza's gaze. "Ah. I see. A love in the shadows. Sweeter for the fleeting moments together."

"Perhaps. Yes. We can try. And if it cannot be, at least we will have tried. If...that is all right with you." She desperately hoped it would be all right with him.

"If that is all I may wish for, then it is my dearest wish as well." He leaned forward and lightly kissed her lips. "Ai, your lips are cold as well."

"You know," said Coraza, looking back up at Palabo and the Dona, trying to distract Filipo's attention in hopes he would not ask questions about her changes just yet. "I wonder if things will be easier or more difficult for them, now that she's the wife of the Governor."

"Hmm. I suppose we must wait and see," Filipo replied.

"And...I wish I could have said good bye to Sister Phoebe one last time."

"Do you?" said Filipo. "She's here, you know. Sister Phoebe, only she's not called that anymore. Can I at least tell her you are alive? It would please her to know."

Coraza smiled, her feelings both sad and happy. "Yes, but I don't want her to see me as I am. Let her remember me as I was."

"All right." Filipo sighed and looked up at the stars. "So. Our lives shall move on like two ships on a foggy sea. Well. Since we are together in this moment, what shall we do with the time we have now?"

Coraza looked around at the dimly lit garden with its sparkling fountain, night-blooming flowers and cheerily chirping crickets. There was one dream left from the orphanage, which now seemed so long ago. "If you will indulge me, there is one thing I would like."

Filipo's gaze returned to her with a little more hope in his eyes. "Anything, querida. You need only ask."

"For now," said Coraza, "I would be pleased to dance like an eislada, in this pretty garden, with the handsome man in front of me."

"In that case," Filipo said with a bow, "Señorita, may I have this dance?"

Coraza put her gloved hand in his and let him slip his arm around her waist. He guided her around the garden, not the most graceful of dancers. It didn't matter. Coraza waltzed on air. Because a tzinn's feet never need to touch the ground.

The End

Kara Dalkey is the author of sixteen published novels and more than twenty short stories of fantasy and speculative fiction. She was born in Southern California and studied Anthropology at the University of California at Los Angeles. She always knew the creative arts were her destiny and she has been an artist and musician before becoming a writer and author through membership in the Scribblies writers group in Minneapolis. Most of her work is historical fantasy, and she is best known for her books Little Sister and Heavenward Path, set in Heian era Japan, as well as The Water Trilogy set in Arthurian Britain. A Sword Named Sorrow, although an alternate history, is drawn from the rich historical heritage of the state of her birth.

Ms. Dalkey currently lives in the beautiful Puget Sound region near Seattle.

WWW.EERIERIVERPUBLISHING.COM/SWORDNAMESORROW

More from Eerie River

We want to take a moment and thank you for purchasing this copy of **A Sword Named Sorrow,** by Eerie River Publishing. We hoped you enjoyed this historical fantasy storie and the characters within it. Please consider taking a few moments and reviewing this story on Amazon, Goodreads or wherever you obtained your copy. Reviews and recommendations are the cornerstone of small press publishing.

Without you, there is no us.

Eerie River Publishing, is a small independant publishing house that is devoted to releasing quality dark fiction books and anthologies.

To stay up to date with all our new releases and upcoming giveaways, follow us on Facebook, Twitter, Instagram and YouTube. Sign up for our monthly newsletter and receive a free ebook Darkness Reclaimed, as our thank you gift.

https://mailchi.mp/71e45b6d5880/welcomebook

Interested in becoming a Patreon member?
Patreon membership gives you exclusive sneak peeks at upcoming books, early chapter releases, covers art as well as free ebooks and discounts on paperbacks.

https://www.patreon.com/EerieRiverPub.

The Banished have returned, and they will have their revenge.
In Solitude's Shadow by David Green

https://www.eerieriverpublishing.com/empire-of-ruin